Readers love
BRU BAKER

D1608213

Island House

"I had a really good time with this book. There was a good level of angst and drama. It was sexy, romantic and fun, with some sad and achy. A very good read."

—Gay List Book Reviews

"I adored this story. Ms. Baker knows how to spin a tale that I'll enjoy and I can't wait to read more from her."

—The Blog of Sid

"This book had me captivated from the beginning. I really enjoyed Bru Baker's storytelling style. The writing is intelligent and funny, the pace is great, the characters are well-developed…overall just a good, solid read."

—Mrs. Condit & Friends Read Books

Campfire Confessions

"Some of the scenes in the book are laugh out loud enjoyable…. this novella will leave readers with a happy smile.

—The Romance Reviews

"This short by Bru Baker is a cute one and goes after the friends to lovers theme in a little different way."

—Hearts on Fire

"This was a cute story. Lots of humor in it. I loved it. The characters are funny, sexy, compassionate, and not a couple till Mitchell tells him what he wants.

MM Good Book Reviews

By BRU BAKER

The Buyout
Campfire Confessions
Diving In
Dr. Feelgood (DSP Anthology)
Traditions from the Heart

DROPPING ANCHOR SERIES
Island House
Finding Home

Published by DREAMSPINNER PRESS
http://www.dreamspinnerpress.com

FINDING HOME

BRU BAKER

Dreamspinner Press

Published by
Dreamspinner Press
5032 Capital Circle SW
Suite 2, PMB# 279
Tallahassee, FL 32305-7886
USA
http://www.dreamspinnerpress.com/

Finding Home
© 2014 Bru Baker.

Cover Art
© 2014 L.C. Chase.
http://www.lcchase.com
Cover content is for illustrative purposes only and any person depicted on the cover is a model.

ISBN: 978-1-63216-003-4
Digital ISBN: 978-1-63216-004-1

Printed in the United States of America
First Edition
June 2014

Shannon, Betsy, and Jenn: Thanks for looking at Ian and seeing beyond his pretty playboy veneer. He really bloomed under your encouragement and cheerleading!

And as always, thanks to my husband for being supportive and wrangling the kids when my deadlines loom.

ONE

"THANKS, EVAN."

Ian's pulse was still racing from his climax, and he shifted to his side to watch the guy he'd just fucked pull on clothes that had been strewn about the room in their rush to get to the bed.

"It's Ian, actually," he said, bizarrely bothered by the fact the man didn't know that. It was incredibly hypocritical of him. Ian had been inside him minutes earlier and didn't know his name, either. At least this guy had tried to remember Ian's. Ian wasn't even sure he'd *asked* for his. Names were an unimportant part of Ian Mackay's pickup routine.

"Sure," the guy said easily. He sat on the edge of the bed, his back curving as he bent to put on his shoes. Ian wanted to roll toward him and pull him back in for another round, but he wasn't sure that would be welcome.

"Are you on the island much longer? I could show you some of the nightlife. There aren't many bars here on Tortola, but the one we were at is far from the best one." Ian winced at the earnestness in his voice. What was he doing? He never tried to hook up with a tourist more than once. Usually, he was ushering his conquest out of his bedroom as quickly as possible; what was wrong with him? He didn't know anything about this guy other than the fact that he had sensitive nipples and liked to be taken from behind. Or maybe he didn't and he'd just asked for that position because this was a one-off. It would make sense. Ian favored the position himself because it was less personal.

1

"Uh, no. Sorry. I crew for a regatta team. We're heading out in the morning," the guy said. He'd finished with his shoes and was standing now, everything about his posture screaming discomfort. "Actually, the guys are probably looking for me. We were supposed to meet up for drinks."

At the dive where he had picked him up about forty minutes earlier, Ian surmised. He forced an easy smile and waved lazily, not bothering to get up. The sheets had pooled around his hips, and he saw a brief flare of interest from the other man. Ian knew exactly how sexy he looked in that position; he'd perfected his lazy allure years earlier. It was a carefully crafted pose that screamed casual sex, and he used it to telegraph his intention that he wasn't the type of guy who'd ask for a phone number or any sort of contact after someone left his bed. Now, apparently, he was trying to use it to lure someone back *into* bed, and the moment he realized it, Ian straightened and cleared his throat.

"Do you need directions to get back?" he asked briskly.

The man visibly relaxed. He'd obviously just been looking for a quick vacation fuck, something Ian was usually very happy to supply. There were definite bonuses to living on an island swarming with tourists, and that was one he exploited ruthlessly.

"No, it's just a few blocks." The guy fiddled with his collar and finally looked up. "Thanks again for a good time, Ian."

"It was my pleasure," Ian drawled. He quirked an eyebrow at the man, who got the message after a drawn-out pause.

"Keegan," the guy supplied, clearly amused.

Huh. Ian would have guessed something more like Jason or Jack. Back on solid ground, Ian grinned and nodded. "Keegan."

There was a finality in his tone that had Keegan moving toward the bedroom door. Ian's house was small, and from the open door, he saw Keegan let himself out the sliding glass doors that led to the beach. He didn't look back.

Ian slumped against the headboard, his sweaty skin sticking uncomfortably the moment he touched it. The sleek white leather had been chic in his air-conditioned LA apartment, but it didn't work as well in the tropical heat. He'd considered retrofitting the house with central AC, but it wasn't necessary most of the year. Tortola was fairly temperate, as most Caribbean islands were. The wide plantation shutters were open, letting in a breeze from the beach, and when it got too warm, the large-bladed fans in every room did an adequate job of cooling things off. He'd been meaning to replace his furniture with pieces more suited to island life, but he hadn't gotten around to it in the four years he'd lived there.

God. Had he really just tried to ask a one-night stand out on a date? Hell, Keegan hadn't even been a one-night stand. That implied a lot more time spent together than a ten-minute pickup and a twenty-minute fuck. Was there a word for a quick afternoon fuck? Jesus. Ian rubbed a hand over his face, shrugging off his mortification. Maybe it was time for a change of scenery. He was going a bit stir crazy on the island; that must be it. It was nothing a vacation couldn't fix. He grinned as he threw the sheet aside and stood, uncaring of his nudity as he strode into the living room to grab his laptop. The locals knew well enough to avert their eyes whenever they walked by Ian's house, since more often than not he was lounging around naked. It had garnered him more than one interested tourist, though.

He grabbed some ice water as he waited for his laptop to boot. The cool glass felt good against his sweaty skin when he pressed it against his cheek. Maybe he'd go somewhere cold. Though he hated bundling up in sweaters and jackets. They hid his best asset, his body. Ian knew he had a nice smile and great hair, but his body was the reason he never had a problem finding someone to warm his bed. So, no cold-weather getaway.

He scrolled through the site aimlessly, looking for something that inspired him. Usually, he enjoyed finding vacation spots, but none of his customary excitement was present at the moment. He definitely needed to do something to pull himself out of his funk.

He bypassed a banner ad for Mexico with a flick of the mouse. Cancún and Cozumel were fun, but not the kind of scene he was looking for. Mexico tended to attract a younger crowd. It had been a good time when he was in his twenties, but Ian wasn't interested in partying with a bunch of college students who thought Señor Frog was the height of amusement.

Vegas was a possibility, he thought as he scrolled past offers for the Venetian. After a moment's consideration, he kept going down the site. Ian enjoyed gambling and all the opportunities for unapologetic debauchery in Las Vegas, but he didn't think the itch he was feeling could be satisfied by bright lights and raunchy sex alone. He was feeling uncomfortable in his own skin, which usually happened when he'd gone too long without some sort of physically taxing outdoor activity. Besides, if he ended up in Vegas, he'd catch hell from Niall for not coming up to Seattle to see him.

Niall's partner, Ethan, was a dedicated outdoor sports enthusiast and had a bunch of great toys, so maybe a visit to Seattle was in order. He'd been to see Niall several times since Niall left Tortola to move in with Ethan almost a year ago, and he always enjoyed himself. Niall had surrounded himself with an eclectic group of friends there, and Ian liked all of them.

He was tempted to call Niall and take him up on the open offer to visit. There were great clubs and bars in Seattle to keep him occupied at night, and the chance to go rock climbing and rowing with Ethan was a big tick in the plus column. Ian had always preferred rowing to sailing because it was so much more physical. He loved the way a good hard row made his muscles scream. Just thinking about it made the itchiness simmering under his skin flare, and suddenly he was desperate to get out in a scull. Seattle would be good for that, too.

But there were definite drawbacks to Seattle. Now that Niall was in a relationship with Ethan, he seemed to be succumbing to whatever horrible matchmaker disease infected people in monogamous relationships. Ian's last trip to Seattle had been a bore, featuring a string of blind dates Niall had surreptitiously arranged for him. Niall and Ethan's group of friends also gossiped like hens and were too observant for their own good, and Ian had no doubt it wouldn't take long for them to suss out his malaise and descend on him like locusts.

So not Seattle. Maybe Boston? It was August so it was plenty warm there, and his mother would love a visit from him. She'd be busy with the academic term starting at Boston University, where she was a mathematics professor. He could cruise for pickups during the day and be back at her place to have dinner with her and his stepfather before going out to the bars in the evening. She and Paul had come to see him in Tortola for Christmas during her winter break since they knew there was little to no chance of getting Ian to brave snow and ice in Boston, but it would be nice to see them before that.

His mother, Elisabete, had been born and raised there, and she always teased him that his Scottish blood should have inured him to the cold, since it was only a little warmer than Boston on average. Then again, it wasn't like Ian came from sturdy Scottish farming stock—his father, Alban, was a banker in the same bank Ian's grandfather had managed until his death. The Mackays were decidedly unathletic and partial to indoor activities. If anything, Ian had inherited his athleticism and spirit of outdoor adventure from his mother, along with the Morais family traits of olive skin and hazel eyes. The Mackay genes hadn't given him much aside from his curls—his dark sandy hair color came from a ridiculously expensive stylist at one of the posh resorts on the island. He'd started lightening his normally dark brown locks with sunkissed highlights and a lighter overall color because it furthered his image as a beach bum. Dark hair made him look too serious. It was a pain in the ass to maintain, though. Lately he'd been thinking about going back to his natural color, even if it did make him more likely to be mistaken as Spanish or Greek.

Neither was correct. His grandparents had settled in Boston when they'd emigrated from Portugal a few years before his mother was born. There was a huge Portuguese community there, and Ian had always loved visiting his grandparents as a kid and being among people who looked like him. He stuck out a fair bit in Edinburgh, and he'd always been self-conscious as a child. He and his mother had moved to Boston when Ian was fifteen, but he still stuck out because of his obvious Scottish accent.

Now, though, Ian loved the momentary confusion when he first spoke with someone who was sizing him up. No one expected the Scottish accent. He'd gotten the side-eye from more than one bouncer when he hit the bars around New Haven while an undergrad at Yale since, to most Americans, the name Ian Mackay generally conjured images of red hair and pasty skin. If you ignored the fact that his middle name was Mateus, that was. Not that most people knew it was a Portuguese name. Often people assumed he was Spanish before he spoke.

Most people's idea of a stereotypical Scot didn't actually exist. Even though he'd been born there and lived in Edinburgh until he was fifteen, Ian didn't own a kilt, and he'd never had haggis. If his father's family had a tartan, Ian had certainly never seen it. He also found Fair Isle sweaters to be both scratchy and unflattering on his broad shoulders. His grandmother had dutifully sent him care packages full of them until she'd died six years ago. The hefty inheritance had allowed him to quit his job and move to Tortola to live a life of leisure.

Ian blew out a breath and refocused on the laptop. Going to Boston was probably a bad idea. His mother didn't approve of Ian's playboy lifestyle, so staying there while he was trying to rack up some meaningless sex would only spark arguments. He'd see them at Christmas at any rate.

The travel site had an ad for St. Lucia on the front page, and Ian glanced up at the picturesque view out his front window and wrinkled his nose. No islands. But beaches were good. Ian looked great in a pair of board shorts, and he knew it. Mainland beach vacation it was.

He scanned the colorful photos until his eyes stopped on one that had been taken in a busy club. Miami. Ian took another drink of his water and scratched at his stubble, absently making a mental note to shave before he headed to the bar after dinner. Scruff was useful when going out for an afternoon hookup because it gave him a friendly beach bum look. Nighttime was for clean shaves and designer clothes, even if they were mostly wasted in the small bars the island had to offer.

Miami had potential. He'd been there once before, and all he remembered from his weekend was a lot of drinking, dancing, and some very hot hookups. It might be just what he needed.

TWO

LOUD MUSIC spilled from the club, following Ian into the street when he ducked outside for a breath of fresh air. Not that the hot and humid air in Miami was particularly refreshing. Still, it was an improvement over the wall-to-wall crowd inside, with its overwhelming mix of cologne, sweat, and alcohol. Unfortunately, quite a few other people had the same idea, and Ian had to wander about half a block from the club before he could stake out a spot. He leaned against the smooth exterior of the art deco grocery store—and really, wasn't that taking the South Beach theme a little far?—his stiff posture sending the message loud and clear that he wanted to be left alone. He breathed in car exhaust and smoke from a huddle of men who were debating something animatedly a few feet away. It made part of him yearn for a brisk Scottish morning, which was disturbing.

Scotland hadn't been his home for nearly two decades, so when he found himself tweaked by homesickness for a place he'd hated, he knew something was seriously wrong. It was what had driven him to Miami. Ian had thought he just needed to scratch an itch that only a bigger city could, with gourmet restaurants, serious shopping, and clubs like the one he'd just left. Apparently, he'd been wrong.

Ian had come to SCORE tonight to do exactly what the club name implied, but he hadn't found anyone amid the throbbing music and flashing lights who had interested him. That was a sad commentary. Ian wasn't picky about who he invited into his bed, and the club offered more than enough delectable morsels for him to choose from. He'd already turned down an offer from several twinks and a proposition for a threesome with an adventurous husband and wife whom he'd have literally jumped on a few months earlier.

He sighed, scuffing the bottom of his Ferragamo loafer against the rough sidewalk. He'd made a conscious effort not to overdress for the club, paring down his normal going-out attire to a pair of form-fitting dark-washed jeans and a skintight lavender T-shirt that showed off the pectorals and biceps he slaved over in his home gym. Even his daily workouts weren't as enjoyable as they used to be. At some point, maintaining his body had become monotonous and mindless work. Just one more thing that had changed lately.

It was late in Miami, but the three-hour time difference meant it was still an acceptable time to call the West Coast. Ian had his phone out of his pocket and had dialed before he'd really processed his sudden desire to hear a friendly voice.

"This had better not be a late-night booty call, Mack."

Confused, Ian held the phone away from his ear to look at the display. He'd definitely called Niall, but Ethan had been the one to answer. He tried to ignore the warmth in his chest at Ethan's greeting. He hadn't had a friend who'd insisted on calling him by an obnoxious nickname since college. It was comforting. "You know I don't have that kind of patience, Bettencourt. I prefer my booty calls to be in the same state."

"So you're in the US, then? Vegas again? Tahoe?"

"Miami. Where's Niall?"

Ethan snorted at the brush-off. "In the shower, but I figured if you were calling, there might be some sort of emergency. You don't usually dial him up to exchange knitting patterns."

Ian laughed and leaned against the building, most of the tension flowing out of his posture. This was the kind of easy relaxation he'd been looking for when he'd gone out clubbing tonight. "We're more into macramé."

"Macramé," Ethan repeated with a snicker. "Yeah. So what's going on, Mack? You need bail money or something?"

Ian grinned. "That happened once."

"That happened twice," Ethan countered in a severe tone that Ian knew was Ethan's version of teasing.

"Twice in the same trip. It counts as once. The first time was just a warning and didn't involve bail. You didn't have to pony up any money until the second one." Two public intoxication pickups in one trip—Ian had loved his time in Reno. In fact, he was still banned from two of the casinos. Good memories.

"Semantics," Ethan said flippantly. His voice took on its more serious tone, one that Ian knew he used in boardrooms and press interviews. It never boded well to get that tone from him. "Seriously Mack, are you all right? Niall's been worried."

"Niall worries like an old woman," Ian answered, but his heart wasn't in the snark. The silence stretched on until he broke under the strain of the quiet. "I'm fine. Maybe. Mostly."

"Maybe mostly fine," Ethan said slowly. "Not the best endorsement, Mack. Something happen in Miami?"

Ian snorted. The problem was that *nothing* had happened in Miami. He'd come for a few quick, meaningless fucks, and aside from a blow job in the back of a club the night before, a few hours after his flight had gotten in, Ian hadn't felt the slightest twinge of interest in anyone. Even the blow job had been mostly a way to calm his racing mind after his flight so he could get some sleep. There had been nothing sexy about it, and he hadn't even reciprocated. The guy he'd taken with him to the shadowy corner hadn't minded; he'd seemed to enjoy himself immensely, if the vigor he pulled himself off with as he'd swallowed Ian had been any indicator. Getting off had been functional, like brushing his teeth before bed.

Maybe he *should* take up macramé. Obviously he needed a new hobby, if casual sex was off the table. What the hell was wrong with him lately?

"Nah," he said, realizing he'd left Ethan hanging for too long. Ian rubbed his eyes tiredly. "I'm going back to my hotel to catch some sleep. Maybe I'm coming down with something."

If only. Was there some sort of flu that manifested in sexual boredom and general malaise?

"Where are you staying?"

Ian rolled his eyes. He knew all about Ethan and his propensity toward saving people. If he told Ethan where he was staying, he and Niall would be there by sunup. Ethan using his private plane to chase after Niall over a year ago when Niall had freaked out and left him had been romantic; the two of them rushing to Ian's rescue because he was feeling a little down would be absurd.

"I thought I made it clear this wasn't a booty call," he said, forcing his voice to be light and teasing. "Though I might be willing to make an exception to my in-state booty call rule for the two of you. Do you have a thing for accents, Ethan? Trying to get two expat Europeans in your bed at the same time?"

It wasn't playing fair, but Ian didn't care. Niall had told him Ethan thought the two of them had been dating on Tortola. It had sparked some sort of jealous fit, which frankly, Ian would have loved to have seen. Ethan was usually completely in control of himself; seeing him unravel a bit could be fun.

"You're an American citizen, Mack."

Ian wasn't going to question how Ethan knew that. Ian didn't think even Niall had known. "One expat European and one nonresident American, then."

Ethan laughed. "So here's what's going to happen. You're going to text me your hotel info. To my phone, not Niall's. And then you're going to get your bag packed, get a good night's sleep, and check the front desk in the morning because Susannah is going to overnight you a ticket to Seattle."

"I don't rate Joe?" Usually when Niall demanded a visit, he had Ethan's secretary Susannah and his pilot Joe handle the arrangements. Niall seemed to be settling in to living in the lap of luxury rather well, in Ian's opinion.

"Joe's already round-tripping to Newark in a few weeks, so I don't think he'd appreciate another cross-country-and-back haul. Niall was planning to call you next week to see if you'd come out to Seattle anyway, so this is kind of kismet, right?"

"Flying to Newark to bring back Niall's family, I assume? Do I need to be planning a bachelor party for you two?" The comment was flippant, but Ian was half-serious. He'd been expecting to get a call like this one for a few months. It was obvious that Niall and Ethan were going to get married sooner rather than later, especially since it would help Niall get the green card he needed to stay in the States.

"I'm terrified of the kind of bachelor party you'd throw together on such short notice, Mackay," Ethan said, but his voice was warm. "And yes. We're not having a big ceremony, but Niall wanted you to be there. We figured you'd be more likely to come if you didn't have much advance warning."

That was fair, but it did sting a little. Ian was loud about his disdain for the sacrament of marriage, but that didn't mean he wasn't happy for Niall and Ethan. "So you were going to, what, call me and tell me to be on a plane to Seattle twenty-four hours before the ceremony?"

"We were going to give you a week's notice. We're not that mean. And Mrs. Jim had strict instructions not to let it slip before Niall told you."

That explained why Niall's old neighbor on Tortola had been avoiding him. Mrs. Jim was usually chatty to the point of being annoying, but she hadn't checked in with him in weeks.

"Mack, I'm sorry."

Ian could hear the guilt in Ethan's voice, so he gave him an easy out. "Be honest. You just didn't want to give me the opportunity to plan that bachelor party. You can't find quality escorts for private parties without at least a week's notice."

"There's that, too," Ethan said with a quiet chuckle. Ian could hear someone talking in the background. Niall must be out of the shower.

"Don't get pouty," Niall said when he took the phone. "I wanted to tell you as soon as Ethan and I decided on a date, but you're allergic to planning anything more than a week or two in advance."

"Just how long have you had yourself a fiancé, Niall?"

Niall was quiet for a beat, and Ian imagined him biting his lip endearingly the way he did when he was uncomfortable. "Four months?"

Ian couldn't believe Niall had kept his engagement from him that long. They talked almost daily by e-mail and texts, and Niall usually called him at least a few times a month to chat. Never once had he even hinted at the wedding.

"I'm surprised Bettencourt held out a whole eight months after you moved in to pop the question," he said, because as much as he liked to yank Niall's chain, he knew Niall and his propensity to feel guilty over ridiculous things would make him fixate on whether or not he'd hurt Ian's feelings by keeping the secret.

"He didn't. He asked me the day I moved in, and I said no," Niall said haughtily, and Ian figured he was probably fixing Ethan with a chastising look.

"Good on you," Ian said once he'd stopped laughing.

"Ethan tells me you're joining us early, though. So you can help me with the final preparations," Niall said, and all of Ian's mirth fled.

"I'm not picking out a garter or lending you something blue," he said, prompting Niall to make a disgusted noise.

"It's something borrowed *and* something blue, you heathen. And a garter would clash horribly with my tux."

"So this is a formal affair? I didn't bring my tux to Miami." Ian kept talking as he stepped into the street to hail a cab. There was no use going back to SCORE or any of the other clubs in South Beach. Knowing Ethan, he'd have his secretary book the earliest westbound flight she could find to punish Ian. He'd go back to the hotel and sleep instead.

"Why didn't you tell me you were going to Miami?"

"Why didn't you tell me you were getting married?" Ian asked smugly.

Niall made a sound that was close to a harrumph, and Ian grinned. A cab stopped, and he slid into the blissfully air-conditioned backseat and gave the cabbie the name of his hotel.

"It's not formal," Niall said after a moment. "No tuxes."

"Oh God," Ian said, wrinkling his nose as a thought struck him. "Tell me you're not getting married on the beach. Promise me, Niall. As one of your best friends, I can't let you live that kind of cliché."

There was the sound of a tussle and then Ethan's voice came through the phone. "What did you say to him, Mack? He's actually speechless."

Ian closed his eyes and sank back against the tattered leather seat with a sigh of resignation. "You're getting married on the beach, aren't you?"

"Yes, why?"

Ian groaned. "No, no, no. I won't stand for it."

"You won't stand for me marrying Niall?" Ethan's voice rose, and Ian could just picture his outraged face.

"No, you can marry him. But I won't stand for you two embarrassing yourselves like that. Jesus. Getting married on the beach? Were you planning on doing it barefoot with linen suits on? Could you be any cornier?"

Ethan must have repeated his words to Niall, because Ian heard Niall shout "I'm not some maiden who needs permission to marry, Ian Mackay!"

"Does that mean I won't be walking him down the rose-petal-strewn aisle? I'm crushed," Ian drawled.

"You're an asshole, Mack," Ethan said fondly.

"Don't I know it. Listen, e-mail me the details for your impending nuptials. Hopefully, you haven't done anything irreversible yet. I'm guessing Clare's the one who's been planning this? Because a wedding on the beach doesn't sound like Susannah's style, and I *know* Niall hasn't been planning this by himself. I also know you don't care where you marry him, so you've probably stayed out of it."

"You can be terrifyingly observant when you want to be. Has anyone ever told you that?" There was clear admiration in Ethan's voice, and Ian laughed.

"I've been told, yes."

He'd been a hedge fund trader before his large inheritance had given him the opportunity to be a man of leisure, and he'd been known for his attention to detail and almost prescient ability to track stocks. There wasn't any big secret to it. Ian knew he was good at reading people and tracking patterns.

He hadn't had much opportunity to hone those particular skills in a while, but he cared about Niall and made a point of paying extra attention to him. A lot of his charm when he was on the pull was down to his ability to read his potential conquests and figure out what approach worked best on them.

Ian had only met Niall's flighty but loyal friend Clare a handful of times, but she exuded schoolgirl romantic vibes. He'd made a move on her the first time they'd met because for all her ditzy New Age act, Clare was hot. Her brother Frank was even hotter, but he'd been obviously taken. Clare had rebuffed him gently, and Niall's laughter at the epic pickup fail still haunted Ian from time to time.

"Susannah just e-mailed me your itinerary. Your flight leaves at noon," Ethan said.

"That was quick work for the ever-efficient Susannah. She deserves a raise."

"I'm not giving her a raise just because she booked you a flight that left after 9:00 a.m.," Ethan said drily.

"Well, maybe I'll send her some sort of token. That kind of loyalty deserves a reward." Ian liked Susannah. She was no-nonsense and all business, but she was also wickedly funny and happily married, which made her a good candidate to pair up with when Niall and Ethan dragged him out for blind dates under the guise of going for drinks. She was his antiwingman.

"Stop bribing my employees," Ethan said with a mock growl. "And when did you get to Joe? He just texted to tell me to tell you he'd talk to you tomorrow about bachelor party plans."

"Shouldn't the question be how did Joe know you were on the phone with me?" Ian asked. The cab drew to a stop under his hotel's awning, and he slipped the driver two twenties and waved away the change as he got out. The doorman hurried forward to usher him inside, and Ian nodded at him as he held the door.

"He and Susannah gossip like you wouldn't believe."

"I actually have no problem believing that," Ian said. They'd shared plenty of gossip about Ethan with him when he'd taken them out for drinks when he'd helped Niall move. He punched the elevator button and stepped back as the numbers started declining. "I'm getting in the elevator now. I'll see you tomorrow. Tell the blushing bride he's a dick for not telling me."

"Ian says he's really happy for us, babe," Ethan said, not bothering to muffle the phone as he spoke to Niall.

"Lies," Ian muttered, but he couldn't stop a chuckle from rumbling out. "Fine. I'm happy for you, and I hope you have a happy marriage and two point seven kids and a pony. I'm going now."

He ended the call before Ethan could respond, a grin spreading across his face as he imagined Ethan's outraged look when he realized Ian had hung up on him. Ian loved getting the last word in with Ethan, mostly because it rarely happened.

The elevator dinged, and Ian stepped aside to let a couple shuffle off. They were wrapped around each other like limpets, and it made something in him gag. As happy as he was for Niall and Ethan, he couldn't see attaching himself to one person for the rest of his life. Codependence wasn't a good look on him.

By the time he'd ridden up to his room, his phone had chirped with an incoming text. Unsurprisingly, it was from Ethan.

Niall says don't skimp on the pony. He wants a Shetland. Only the best for our imaginary 2.7 children.

Ian laughed all the way down the corridor.

THREE

THINGS WERE much more dire than Ian had imagined. Clare had been given free rein, and there were kitschy touches all over Niall's wedding plans. She'd even planned a picnic lunch on the beach after the ceremony, which was absolutely untenable. There wasn't even going to be a wedding cake.

There were fewer than twenty people on the guest list, which had come as a surprise to Ian. Ethan was a well-connected businessman, and Ian had figured he'd have a high profile wedding that served as a thinly veiled excuse for networking with his clients. He should have known better. Ethan was also intensely private, as was Niall.

Still, he wasn't going to let them get married on the beach, even if the witnesses were only going to be their closest friends and family. Ian spent most of his flight to the West Coast going over the plans Clare and Niall had e-mailed him. If not for the open bar in first class, he wasn't sure he'd have made it.

Ian started making calls as soon as the plane touched down in Seattle. By the time Joe picked him up at baggage claim, he'd arranged for a caterer and florist. A cake would be hard to wrangle on such short notice, but he hadn't inherited the Morais charm for nothing. His uncles were notoriously glib-tongued; he'd learned from the best. Ian was sure he could charm Ethan's housekeeper into making something for the wedding. He didn't know Hortensia well, but she was always mothering Ethan and Niall whenever he saw her. She was probably beside herself at the thought of toasting the happy couple with Clare's homemade kombucha.

"You look pretty self-satisfied," Susannah said drily as she took Ian's satchel. Ian let her have it since it freed him to grab his luggage when it went by on the carousel. "Let me guess. A quickie in the first class bathroom? Flight attendant or passenger?"

Ian batted Susannah's hand away when she moved to take the handle of the bag Ian had just liberated from the belt. "Neither."

Susannah's eyebrows rose. "Better not have been a pilot. The FAA has really cracked down on rules about them leaving the cabin. I've had to file some of that paperwork for Joe, and trust me, there's a lot of fine print." She squinted at Ian for a moment. "Air marshal?"

"Jesus. Is it so hard to believe I made it through a six-hour flight without getting off?"

"Yes." Susannah fixed him with a judgmental stare, and Ian rolled his eyes.

"I spent the last forty-eight hours in Miami. Maybe I'm taking it easy."

Susannah started to lead him across the terminal after Ian indicated he had all his luggage. He hadn't packed much, since he'd only planned to spend three nights in Miami. He was going to have to raid Ethan's closet until he could fill out his wardrobe. The wedding was in a little more than a month, and Ian wasn't going to spend the entire time in his clubbing clothes. He did have a pair of leather pants in his suitcase he planned to wear around Clare to torment her, though. He might have backed off trying to get her into bed, but that didn't mean he had to stop trying to get a rise out of her. It was ridiculously easy to bait her into an outraged argument.

"You know, Ethan warned me something was off. Are you doing okay, Ian? Really?" She stopped at the curb, and a moment later a Lincoln Town Car pulled up with Joe at the wheel.

"I'm fine," Ian said shortly, annoyed at the implication that just because he'd kept his dick in his pants for a six-hour commercial flight something was *wrong* with him. "Why are you even here?"

"Full-service travel planning is part of my job," she said as she climbed into the front seat, leaving Ian to ease into the back alone like he was being chauffeured. Which, he supposed, he technically was. But he knew Ethan usually rode up front when Joe drove him. Though having Susannah with them threw a wrench in that. Either way, it was awkward. Joe and Susannah worked for Ethan, sure, but Ian counted them as friends.

"Bullshit," Joe said as he slid behind the wheel. "Niall said you were having an early midlife crisis, and Susie wanted to see it for herself." He checked his mirrors and merged into traffic, finding Ian's gaze in the rearview mirror as soon as he was done. "I thought a midlife crisis involved *more* sex, not less. Frankly, I'm disappointed, Ian."

Ian's face hurt with the force of his grin. He really needed to visit Seattle more often. "Missed you guys, too."

"Call me Susie again and regret it. Don't forget who actually cuts the checks Ethan writes," Susannah said with a fierce glare in Joe's direction. Ian's smile widened when she craned her head around to point at him in the backseat. "Niall has three guys lined up for you, and Clare knows some woman she swears is perfect for you because you two, and I quote, 'resonate on the same frequency.' Be afraid, Ian. Be very afraid."

"Ah, well. That's why it pays to be in good with the person who makes all of Niall and Ethan's reservations, doesn't it? You can give me advance warning so I know when dinner out with them is just dinner or when it's a blind date I have to figure out how to get out of."

"I don't think he's quite forgiven you for setting that alarm on your phone to go off during dinner and then loudly excusing yourself to take your herpes meds," she answered with a grin.

"It was inspired, wasn't it?" Ian said proudly.

"It was something. The guy was one of the big donors for Even Keel. I don't think either of them was amused."

"I made it up to him," Ian said with a shrug. And he had. He didn't think the donor had pulled his support for Niall's charity endeavor, but just in case, Ian had wired him a hefty donation of his own. Not that Niall necessarily needed the help; Ethan was more than willing to fund any shortfalls at the sailing school. If he could convince stubborn Niall to take the money, that was.

"Just so you know, Niall put you on the schedule as an instructor this week. He had me rush your background check through so you wouldn't have any excuse not to do it."

Ian raised an eyebrow at her. "Don't you need my signature for that?"

Susannah turned around fully, a predatory gleam in her eye. "Yes. And?"

Ian whistled. "Felony forgery looks good on you."

"Damn straight," she said as she settled back into her seat. "He says it's because you'll be at loose ends with nothing to do, but I think it's really because he misses you and wants to spend as much time with you as he can."

"Try that again."

"Okay, he's worried about you and thinks the laughter of small children can cure your evil, blackened soul," she joked.

"Plus he's nervous as hell about the wedding," Joe added.

"They're perfect for each other. Why is he nervous?" Ian asked, scooting up as much as his seat belt would allow. He rested his elbows on his thighs so he could support his head with steepled hands as he pushed himself forward so he could see them.

"He hasn't really said, but I think it has something to do with Nolan," Joe said, looking over his shoulder to briefly meet Ian's eyes.

And that made a lot of sense, Ian realized. He hadn't known Nolan, but Ian knew he and Niall had practically been an old married couple when Nolan was killed. Knowing Niall, he was sure Niall felt guilty about marrying Ethan when he hadn't taken that step with Nolan. Niall had mostly gotten over his guilt about moving on, but this was taking his relationship with Ethan to a point where it would surpass what he'd had with Nolan. That had to be hard.

"Fine, I'll help teach Tiny Tim to sail. You don't need to pull out the big guns," Ian said breezily. He slid back in his seat, ending the serious moment with a kick to the back of Susannah's seat.

"Please say that to Niall. Please. But wait until we're there to see his face when he hears you refer to his students like that," Susannah said with glee.

IAN MET Niall when he'd been looking for a home on Tortola. Ian had booked appointments with three different agencies on the island, but the moment he'd walked into Niall's cluttered office, he'd known Niall was the real estate agent for him. He'd been instantly attracted to him, not that it had gone anywhere. They'd bonded despite Ian's constant attempts to worm his way into Niall's bed. At first he'd thought it was simply a matter of professionalism, so Ian had backed off until after Niall helped him secure his tidy little beachfront cottage.

He'd asked Niall back to the unfurnished place for an afternoon quickie after the paperwork was signed, and Niall had turned him down flat. Usually, Ian walked away from a challenge, since he was only looking for a bit of fun. Sure, the hunt was part of that, but that only applied to conquests who were already interested.

Niall not succumbing to his charms despite obviously being gay and at least a little attracted to him, which Niall had admitted readily, had made him intriguing. So Ian had pursued him and ended up forming an odd friendship with him that included a lot of harmless flirting on his part and exasperated sighs from Niall.

They'd become friends of a sort, and Niall had opened up about what brought him to the island. Ian had found himself sharing his own story, which wasn't something he often did—half the time he didn't bother to ask the name of whoever he was chatting up at a bar or on the beach, so telling them all his dark secrets wasn't in the realm of possibilities. He preferred to project an image of aimless trust funder because it was what people who were visiting an island wanted in a casual hookup.

Ironically, he and Niall had only become closer once Niall moved to Seattle. Niall and Ethan visited the island frequently to check on Niall's boat, the *Orion*, and stay in the little bungalow Niall kept there, and Ian visited them as well.

Ian had stayed in with Niall and Ethan the night before, opting to catch up with them and enjoy a meal cooked by Hortensia instead of hitting the clubs. He'd be there for more than a week, after all. There was plenty of time to go out and have fun. Plus not going out had given him the benefit of being able to conspire with Hortensia and get her to agree to bake a wedding cake for Niall and Ethan. She'd been ecstatic, which confirmed Ian's suspicion that she and Clare had probably been butting heads over the wedding plans. He'd already called Clare and arranged to meet her for lunch tomorrow; it was going to take every bit of his inestimable charm to smooth things over with her when she realized he'd completely rearranged her plans.

He and Niall didn't share a lot of common interests, but sailing was definitely one of them. He knew Niall had a dim view of Ian's abilities in that respect, which made it a surprise he'd insisted Ian help him teach kids how to sail at Even Keel, the afterschool program Niall and Ethan had started in Seattle.

"So am I here as a student or a teacher?" Ian asked as Niall gave the catamaran a thorough inspection twenty minutes before the kids were due to show up. They'd already been through the two smaller sloops tied up on either side of it.

"A bit of both," Niall answered as he hopped from the boat's deck to the dock. "You can sit in with us while I go over our lesson for today, and then you can do some one-on-one mentoring when we come on board."

Ian stepped back so he could take the entire boat in. "You going out today?"

"Not this time. School started this week, so I only have them for an hour. We did a sailing camp in July, but from August through May we only sail on Saturday mornings."

Ian had spent a good half an hour examining all the photos that covered the walls of Even Keel's office. It was a warehouse space located at the same pier the boat was docked at, which had to be pricey. From the expressions on the kids' faces in all the pictures, though, Ian knew it was worth every penny Niall's investors had sunk into it.

"I'm first mate this weekend, I assume?" Ian drawled, but he knew Niall wouldn't believe his bored tone for a moment. Niall had picked up on Ian's excitement at being involved at Even Keel the moment they'd started talking about him coming down to the pier to help out for the week.

"That's Josh's spot. You can be helmsman on a sloop," Niall said with a grin, obviously proud of the teenager Ethan thought of as an honorary son.

"Ouch," Ian answered, holding a hand over his heart like he'd been dealt a mortal injury. It wasn't surprising Niall didn't trust him to take Ethan's catamaran out. The sloop was actually a lot better choice for him; he'd never been at the helm of a two-hulled vessel before, and Ian didn't think being out at sea with a boat full of rowdy kids was probably the best time for him to learn, either.

"I'm taking the other one. Josh earned his ASA sailing certification last month, and I think he's been itching to take over as helmsman. He does a great job with the kids. I was thinking of having him take the cat out with the older kids this weekend."

"While you and I schlep sticky-fingered youngsters around in the sloops?"

"Exactly," Niall said with a challenging look. "If you think you can handle it. I have a really promising six-year-old in mind who can do it if you're not up for it."

Ian flashed his teeth at Niall menacingly. "Oh, I can handle anything you throw at me, Niall."

"And here I thought the flirting would stop when I got married," Niall said sarcastically. He double-checked the moorings on all three boats and headed up the dock to the building on the pier.

"You're not married yet," Ian pointed out. He glanced at his watch, surprised to find the kids were due to start arriving soon. Time flew when you were doing menial chores with your best friend, apparently. His lips quirked as he laughed at himself. Between dinner the night before and trailing around after Niall today, Ian had been having more fun in Seattle than he'd had in his alcohol-soaked club tour in Miami. It was beyond bizarre.

Niall didn't bother turning around, but he held his left hand up and wiggled his fingers. The sun glinted off the white gold band he wore on his ring finger. Ian had pried the story of their engagement out of them the night before. Ethan had proposed on the catamaran at sunset, which was so romantic and predictably *them*, it made up for the utter triteness of it. It was also why Ian's plans for their wedding were so much better than Clare's. Then again, he'd had the benefit of knowing Niall for longer than she had. If he was feeling magnanimous when Niall chose his plans over hers, Ian would be sure to remind her of that.

"What group do you have today?" Ian asked when they'd traded the sun-bright pier for the much dimmer warehouse interior. Niall had done a fair job with the place. Huge oceanic maps and sailing diagrams covered the walls, but he hadn't done anything to try to disguise that the place was actually on the pier. The soaring ceilings and rough concrete floor were practical; Ian knew Niall dry-docked the sloops in the warehouse when necessary. Ian suspected that the floors also made for easy cleanup after a small army of children traipsed through.

"The youngest," Niall said. He was already pulling props out of the storage closet for the sailing lesson. It looked like it would be about knots, if the numerous lengths of rope in Niall's arms were any indication.

Even Keel served at-risk kids from age six up to eighteen, providing sailing lessons, counseling, and excursions onto Puget Sound on the weekends for free. Once a week Niall also gave private lessons, and the proceeds from those helped supplement the donations that funded the school. Niall worked with a network of social workers and schools to find kids who could benefit from the one-on-one attention at Even Keel, and the afterschool lessons helped keep a lot of kids out of trouble.

For all that Ian teased Niall about being the Mary Poppins of sailing, he was a big supporter of Even Keel's mission. He'd been involved in something similar after he and his mother moved from Edinburgh to Boston, though it had been rowing, not sailing. His parents' divorce—hell, his parents' *marriage*—had been hard on him. Add the stress and uncertainty of moving to a new country where he didn't know anyone who wasn't related to him, and fifteen-year-old Ian had been a ticking time bomb. He'd been lucky enough to cop community service instead of jail time when he'd been caught taking a stolen car out for a joyride.

He'd also been forced into an afterschool program as part of his probation. All the community rec centers had been full, so his exasperated mother had enrolled him in a program that taught kids how to row. Learning how to channel his anger, frustration, and boredom into physical activity had been an eye-opener for Ian. Rowing had probably been a lifesaver for him.

He'd helped pay for Yale by teaching at the program over his summers and giving private rowing lessons to students while he was on campus.

Even with his enthusiasm for the project, though, Ian had to suppress a shudder at the news they'd have twenty kids ages six to eight roaming around the warehouse in a few minutes. He could joke with teenagers, but he had no idea how to talk to anyone under thirteen.

It must have shown on his face because Niall took pity on him. "You don't have to join in. Josh and Ethan are coming by to help with the practical part of the lesson. I'll go over some of the common knots we use in sailing and then Josh, Ethan, and I will let them practice. We usually take them out to the docked sloops for the last twenty minutes and let them climb around and get used to being on a sailboat."

Ian relaxed marginally. That didn't sound so bad. He was more than willing to help out with the sailing and probably even mentoring the older teens when they came by for their lessons, but the very idea of tiny humans being entrusted to him was terrifying.

"They'll be your sloop crew on Saturday, so you'd probably better at least introduce yourself," Niall said a beat later with what Ian interpreted as a wolfish grin. He'd obviously been baiting Ian into feeling comfortable before going in for the kill.

"You're seriously going to stick me on a boat with a bunch of toddlers?"

Niall laughed. "They're hardly toddlers. We have one six-year-old signed up and the rest are seven or eight. You won't have the whole twenty, anyway. We split up into groups of six and they're each assigned to certain Saturdays."

That was something, at least. Ian doubted even a large sloop could hold twenty kids. And even if it could, he didn't think *he* could manage it without being tempted to jump overboard.

He was about to reply when the bell on the warehouse door chimed. A flood of voices followed, most of them screaming at the top of their lungs for Niall.

"Is that normal?" Ian asked, alarmed.

"Completely," Niall answered. He made his way out into the main room and was immediately mobbed with children. It was utter pandemonium. The kids who weren't clamoring for Niall's attention were climbing on tables and running at full tilt through the cavernous building. The noise level after only a minute was enough to make Ian wish for earplugs.

Niall looked over his shoulder at Ian, his grin bigger than ever. He raised his fingers to his mouth and whistled. The sudden quiet was almost as deafening as the noise had been.

"Muster at midship," Niall called out, and suddenly twenty small bodies were hustling toward the middle of the warehouse. One of the older kids manned a pile of carpet squares Ian hadn't noticed before, handing one out to each child as he or she passed by. The kids laid them in neat rows on the concrete and sat on them, all eyes on Niall, awaiting their next instruction.

It was incredible. Ian had to resist the urge to clap. He'd never seen Niall with kids before, other than Niall's niece Camille, and she'd certainly never snapped to attention for him when he talked to her like the kids in front of them had.

"We have a friend of mine with us this week. Everyone say hello to Ian. He's going to work with us today while we learn some basic knots. Raise your hand if you're scheduled to go out for a sail this weekend."

Six hands shot up, and Ian studied the kids with trepidation. These were apparently his charges. "Nyah, Yusef, Leo, Cameron, Jilly, and Sam, you'll be with Ian. Everyone else will split between me and Josh for their practical lesson."

The smallest boy's hand remained in the air after everyone had lowered theirs, and Niall nodded toward him. "Leo?"

"Is he ASA certified? What crafts does he have experience with?" The boy pointed at Ian, his chin jutted in clear challenge. Ian liked him already.

Niall spread his hands in Ian's direction in invitation. Ian stepped to the front of the group. "I'm a part-time instructor for a sailing school that administers ASA tests, so yes, I'm certified." That was a bit of a half-truth, but Ian wasn't going to split hairs with a six-year-old. He didn't actually teach any of the certification-track classes; Ian preferred to take the day-trippers out for sailing boot camp, which was basically a thinly veiled excuse for him to flirt with the clients while he took them for a sail around the island. He was certified, though. That was the relevant thing.

"Have you sailed a sloop before?" The kid wasn't backing down. It was impressive.

"Yes, though I work with most of my students on a Sunfish. I usually only teach one student at a time, so the smaller boat makes more sense."

"I've been out with him, Leo. Ian's a good captain," Niall said. Ian almost snorted in response, recalling the time he'd taken Niall out on *Romeo's Rowboat* near twilight on Tortola. Niall had spent the entire time white-knuckled and critical of Ian's sailing expertise. Of course, that could have had more to do with the fact that Ian had been more focused on seducing Niall than sailing. It had been the night Ian had realized Niall was far more valuable as a friend than as a potential notch on his bedpost, and they'd been close ever since.

"I can have the ASA fax over my certification notice if that helps put your mind at ease," Ian offered, amused. It was probably a good idea for Niall to have a copy anyway.

That seemed to appease the little boy. He relaxed onto his carpet square but kept his eye on Ian like he was still sizing him up. "Okay, then," he said.

Ian couldn't help himself; he laughed at his obvious ploy to get the last word. Maybe working with these kids wouldn't be terrible. They really were just tiny adults.

FOUR

"SO YOU'RE going to be Ethan's best man, Josh?" Ian pushed his beer toward the kid, letting him have a sip before reclaiming it. They were planning a bachelor party together, after all. He could let Josh have *some* fun.

Ian laughed at the face Josh made when Josh took a taste of the dark lager. He didn't know Josh well, but Ethan was always bragging about him whenever they talked. They'd met when Ethan was assigned to be his mentor when Josh was eight. Ten years later, they were as close as father and son. Ethan had a college fund set aside for Josh, and Ian knew Ethan helped Josh's mother with bills when she couldn't make ends meet.

"I guess," Josh said, clearly uncomfortable. He took a drink of the Coke on the table in front of him. "I told him it really should be Aaron. I mean, he's Ethan's brother, you know? But Ethan said he wanted me."

The words were tinged with pride, and Ian nudged Josh's knee under the diner table. "You're special to him, Josh."

"I know," Josh said, looking down. "But I'm not in high school anymore. The program ended in May. He doesn't have to hang out with me anymore."

Ian drank his beer to give himself a moment. He wasn't really equipped for this type of conversation, but it was obvious Josh was upset and needed someone to talk to. Ethan was his go-to person, but Josh couldn't exactly go to him with this. Niall had gotten close to Josh over the last year, but Ian didn't figure Josh could talk to him about it, either. And it wasn't like Josh was awash in male role models. That left Ian and maybe Joe, though Ian could see how that would be awkward, since Joe worked for Ethan.

He cleared his throat. "He hangs out with you because he loves you, Josh. Ethan isn't going to walk away from you just because his tenure as your mentor is over."

"He'll start with a new kid, and he won't have time for me. It's stupid. I'm an adult now. I don't need a mentor anyway."

Josh shredded the paper wrapper from his straw. He seemed to be full of nervous energy. Ian knew how that felt, to be eighteen and without a real father figure. His uncles had been wonderful, but there was no substitute for having a father to talk to you about stepping up and being a man. Ethan was that person for Josh, and Josh thought he was losing him.

"I haven't heard Ethan say anything about that, but even if he does take on a new kid, you're always going to be in his life, Josh. He loves you like a son. You're never going to get rid of him."

Josh visibly brightened. "You think?"

"I'm sure," Ian said drily. "Just yesterday he was telling me about your university course load, and Niall won't shut up about how proud he is that you're working with him at Even Keel and you got your ASA certification. Looks like you've got two honorary dads now."

Josh grinned and looked up at Ian for the first time since they'd slid into the diner booth ten minutes earlier. "And an honorary uncle?"

"Uncle Ian does have a certain ring to it, doesn't it?" he replied. "Too bad you're too old to take to the park and use to pick up chicks."

"Or dudes," Josh put in. "Niall told me I'm supposed to watch out for you at the bachelor party. He thinks you're going to hook up and disappear on them."

"I would never," Ian said with mock affront. He snorted at Josh's look of disbelief. "Okay, I would. But I'd come *back*."

"Well, now you've got a wingman to make sure that doesn't happen," Josh said with a grin. He reached to take another swig of Ian's beer, but Ian yanked it out of the way.

"Too bad for you I'm not in the market for a wingman," Ian said.

This time when Josh gave Ian's beer a longing look, Ian let him have another small sip. Josh's face screwed up into the same puckered dislike as he swallowed it, so Ian figured it was probably all right on the whole for him to be letting the kid try it. "That's gross. Besides, I thought you wanted me to help you pick up people in the park. That's what a wingman does, right?"

Ian laughed. "I didn't want you as a wingman, I wanted you as *bait*. But you're a little old for that, so I guess wingman-in-training will have to do."

Ian tipped the beer glass toward Josh again and had to fight to suppress a smile when Josh vehemently shook his head to decline the offer. Niall could thank him later for putting Josh off beer before the kid had a chance to start swilling the glorified water most of the on-campus parties would be serving. Niall wasn't a huge Guinness fan, but he'd have a pint with Ian from time to time. The dark, bitter beer was an acquired taste.

The waitress stopped by the table to see if they were ready to order, and her overtly interested gaze lingered on Josh as he thanked her. Ian shook his head as Josh remained oblivious to her attentions.

"Lesson one, learn to figure out when someone is flirting with you," he said when she'd walked away.

Josh looked around, completely confused. "What? Who?"

Ian rolled his eyes and inclined his head toward the bar, where the waitress was picking up another order of drinks. "She was putting out all kinds of vibes, but you weren't picking any of them up."

Josh made a face. "It's her job to be nice to people."

"It's her job to smile and bring people the food they order. It's not her job to fix your collar where it's tucked under or ask if you go to school around here," he said, giving Josh's now-perfect collar a significant look.

"Huh," Josh said, a faint blush coloring his cheeks. He slid his gaze over to the waitress, who was now chatting with a coworker at the server station. She noticed him looking and winked, and Josh's eyes widened before he looked away.

"You're hopeless." The words were too amused to be harsh, and Josh smiled in response.

"Good thing you've taken me on as wingman-in-training, then."

Ian snorted. "I suppose." He studied the menu he'd kept after they'd ordered. "When she comes back, order a side salad."

"Is that some sort of dating code? Salad means I want your number?"

Ian fixed him with an incredulous look. "No, it means Niall was worried you weren't eating anything that remotely resembled a vegetable in the college dorms, and he made me promise I'd feed you something healthy. Even if you don't eat it, I can tell him I made you get one."

"So I have to order it, but I don't have to eat it? I'm beginning to doubt that you're a good role model, Uncle Ian."

"I never claimed to be one," Ian answered flippantly. "And on the topic of leading you to a bad end, let's talk about the bachelor party. What are you thinking? Strippers? Pub crawl? Thai massage parlor?"

Josh made a face. "Ethan said he wants to go camping, but Niall refused. I think Niall wants to go to some fancy microbrewery."

Ian picked up a fork and mimed stabbing himself. "Boring."

"Yeah, well, you know them. They *are* boring."

Josh flicked a glance toward Ian when the waitress interrupted with their food. Plates laden with french fries and burgers ate up most of the table space a moment later. Ian nodded encouragingly, though he wasn't sure if Josh was looking for a sign to chat up the waitress or confirmation that Ian had been serious about the salad. Both were a go, so Ian sat back and watched with interest instead of digging into the burger he'd been so eager to get.

"So, uh," Josh started, and Ian wanted to laugh at the flush that was spreading up his neck. He was obviously flustered, but it seemed to be working for the waitress. She leaned in closer. "Can I get a side salad?"

"It's for my benefit," Ian said glibly when the waitress frowned. "Josh is having a little too much fun with the college experience. I've told him beer isn't a substitute for vegetables, but I don't think the lesson has sunk in. He really needs a keeper. At this point, I'm worried about scurvy."

The waitress beamed at him, and Josh shot Ian a confused look. God, he was setting the kid up perfectly, but Josh wasn't taking the hint.

"If you're worried about scurvy, I'd recommend the lemon vinaigrette. Lots of vitamin C," she said.

"That would ease my mind greatly," Ian said. He tipped forward and lowered his voice to a conspiratorial whisper. "If only getting a keeper was as easy. You don't attend the University of Washington by any chance, do you?"

The waitress giggled. "No, but I don't live far from campus." She looked at Josh and hesitated a moment before pulling out her order pad and scrawling something on it. She ripped it off and pushed it across the table at Josh. "I'm Georgia. Call me before you head out to another party. We can grab a bite to eat first, and your dad won't have to worry about you so much."

Josh nodded and looked at it before he slipped the paper into his pocket with a smile. "Thanks, Georgia."

"My pleasure. I'll be back with your salad in a minute."

The moment her back was turned he pumped a fist in the air and pulled the paper out of his pocket, holding it up for Ian to see. "She gave me her number!"

"I saw," Ian said, not bothering to try to hide his amusement.

"I'm pretty smooth," Josh said, preening.

"*That* I didn't see. But we'll work on it."

"I have a date!"

"You have the phone number of a girl who might be willing to go on a date with you. It's not the same thing." Ian patted Josh's shoulder when Josh deflated a little. "But yes, well done."

Josh huffed out a breath but was still smiling ear to ear as he picked up his hamburger. "I'm still not saying yes to strippers."

"I don't technically need your permission, you know," Ian answered. He dug into his meal, relishing the taste of the juicy burger. The food in Miami had been too refined for his taste, and there wasn't any place on Tortola that served good bar food. The burger was perfect.

"I'm the best man. I'm pretty sure you do," Josh pointed out. Ian liked the confident authority in his voice. If only he could get Josh to talk to women that way instead of turning into a bumbling fool when confronted with a pretty face.

"Well, I'm vetoing camping," Ian said with a mock shudder.

"Niall already did. How about a progressive dinner?"

"Unless the progressive part of the evening is the amount of nudity at each venue, how about no?"

"HAVE A good bachelor party planning session?" Niall asked, ignoring Ian's graphic hand gesture in favor of turning the chicken on the grill.

"You know you're just damning the kid to debauchery instead of saving yourselves embarrassment, right? We might not be able go to a strip club with him in tow, but that doesn't mean the night won't involve something morally dubious somehow."

"Josh is an upstanding young man who would never help you plan something like that," Ethan said as he came through the patio door with a beer for Ian.

Ian took it and tipped it at him in thanks. "Speaking of Josh, you should talk to him about where he fits in, Bettencourt. Kid's freaking out you're going to forget about him and move on."

Ethan's brow crinkled. "What are you talking about?"

"He's worried that now he's gone off to college, you'll get a new kid to mentor and he'll never see you again," Ian said. He shrugged off the incredulous look Ethan shot him.

"That's ridiculous. Josh knows how much he means to us. He's a member of this family," Ethan answered.

"You think he knows, but have you ever actually said that to him?" Ian raised an eyebrow at Ethan, who looked distinctly uncomfortable and shook his head.

"Not outright, I guess," he said.

"No matter. I told him he was basically your surrogate son and he'd never be rid of you." Ian gave Ethan a hearty slap to the back. "Congratulations, it's a boy."

Ian glanced over at Niall, who was choking back laughter at the grill. "What are *you* laughing about, stepdad?"

That seemed to sober Niall up, and the look he exchanged with Ethan was so private and intimate, Ian wished he could unsee it. Ian wasn't sure how to handle Niall looking fond and parental. Hell, he wasn't sure why he knew what that look *was*.

He clapped his hands together, shattering the moment. "I'm going. It looks like you two have dinner plans, and I ate with Josh earlier." He sent a pointed look at Niall before Niall could interrupt. "And yes. He ordered a salad. I've done my due diligence. Kindly carry out all future attempts to parent your bundle of joy on your own."

"You're welcome to have a glass of wine and sit with us while we eat. We can all go out later," Niall offered.

"You'd cramp my style," Ian said wryly.

"In fact, we were talking about meeting up with some people Ethan rock-climbs with," Niall continued, ignoring Ian entirely.

"And with that incredibly unsubtle segue into yet another blind date, I'm out," Ian said. He waggled his fingers at Niall. "Let tonight's victim down easily, will you? Tell him I had to wash my hair or something."

IAN WAS completely serious when he'd told Niall he was heading out to a club—maybe Pony or The Lobby Bar, which were two of his Seattle favorites—but when the taxi picked him up, he'd found himself asking the driver to take him to a quiet neighborhood bar instead. Ian didn't know the area well, so he'd simply asked the man to take him to his favorite place.

Surprisingly, instead of using it as an opportunity to drive Ian all the way across town and run up the meter, the cabbie had driven about ten minutes into town and stopped in front of a nondescript place with wrought iron tables outside and cafe curtains in the window. Ian would have assumed The Weathered Mast was a diner if not for the glowing neon sign in the window that said bar.

"There's not a lot of action, but the selection on tap is good and there's live music after ten," the cab driver told Ian.

It was the polar opposite of the raucous club he'd intended to visit, but Ian figured it was as good a place as any to spend his evening. He'd have a few beers and give Niall and Ethan a chance to leave the house and then call a cab to take him back to their place. After all, he was piloting a boat with a hoard of small children in the morning; it would be irresponsible of him to go clubbing, wouldn't it?

The excuse was thin even to his ears, but Ian went with it. It was easier to blame his newfound solemnity on that than admit having a quiet drink and then getting to bed before sunrise actually sounded like a rip-roaring good Friday night to him at the moment. He wondered if he should go to The Lobby Bar anyway and try to jolly himself out of this funk. Fake it 'til you make it, or however that went.

"You going in, buddy? I can take you somewhere else if this doesn't look good."

Ian hadn't realized how long he'd been deliberating. "No, this place seems fine," he said. He scooted forward and handed the cab driver the fee flashing on the meter plus a generous tip. "I'll probably be done here in an hour or so. If you're in the area, stop back by, okay?"

"Sure thing."

Ian climbed out and tapped on the door when he closed it. The cab driver nodded in response and idled at the curb for a moment like he expected Ian to change his mind and jump back in. Ian looked down at his tight T-shirt and equally tight jeans. It was probably a fair assessment, since he certainly didn't match the bar's clientele. The people gathered around the tables outside looked like they'd stopped by after work. He was the only one there without a collar on his shirt.

Ian waved at the cabbie and walked into the bar. This crowd was different from the young professionals outside; most of the people at the scarred bar top looked like retirees, and the few people at tables were dressed casually. Ian still stood out, but more for the tightness and cut of his clothes than because they were jeans and a T-shirt.

No one spared him a glance when he found an empty barstool and took a seat, though, so Ian settled in comfortably.

"You meeting someone?" the bartender asked as he slid a napkin across the bar.

"I am now. I'm Ian. Are you busy later?" Ian countered with a flirty smile. The bartender was a little younger than him and hot as hell. Ian doubted the guy was gay, but it was worth a shot, if only to keep himself in practice during his unfortunate self-imposed dry spell.

The bartender laughed incredulously. "Does that ever actually work?"

"You'd be surprised," Ian answered honestly. He leaned back on his stool and dropped his predatory leer.

"I'd be absolutely astounded if it worked once," the guy said with a shake of his head. "What can I get you? Besides my number. Don't even ask," he said, cutting Ian off neatly when Ian opened his mouth to take advantage of the opening.

"Well done. That was nicely played. It was almost a perfect brush-off, but you did give me an opening to regale you with tales of my conquests. If you really want to steer flirts away, don't ask questions." Ian gave the bartender a genuine grin when the man shrugged, conceding the point. "What local lagers do you have on tap?"

IAN WAS enjoying himself immensely. He'd gone outside with another twenty-dollar tip for the cabbie when the man returned an hour ago to pick him up, not wanting to waste the guy's time but not ready to leave yet, either.

The crowd had changed over the last two hours. The retirees and casual dinner crowd had filtered out, and the hipsters who'd been outside had migrated in. Ian no longer looked out of place in his dressed-down couture, though his lack of visible tattoos or glasses did seem to mark him as something of a novelty. He'd already had two offers for a more intimate nightcap on what he was pretty sure was the merit of his Scottish accent alone.

The bartender's name was Luke, Ian had learned after he'd proven he wasn't moving from the bar after his third round. He was taking up valuable real estate, since the new crowd seemed to want to stand around it in a giant, fashionably-dressed herd, but Luke didn't seem to mind. Ian was helping him fend off drunk admirers.

He'd gotten Luke's name as a reward for turning away a particularly persistent woman who'd reached across the bar to pull Luke toward her by the tails of the ridiculous tie that was part of his uniform. Ian had stopped her neatly by curling an arm around her shoulders and easing her back. Ian had seen enough situations like that in clubs and bars to know she was a drink or two away from turning volatile, so he'd abandoned his prized barstool and gently guided her through the now-crowded space until they'd found the friends she'd come with.

When he'd returned to the bar, Ian had expected to find his seat taken. He'd been pleasantly surprised to find a bottle sitting in front of it and the bartender's dish towel covering the seat.

"On the house," the man had told Ian gruffly when he'd tossed the towel back across the bar and slipped onto the stool. "My name's Luke."

"I appreciate it, Luke," Ian said, tipping the bottle toward Luke congenially before taking a sip. It had a leering cartoon frog on it that wasn't entirely without charm. "Not that I don't appreciate the gesture or the variety, but this isn't the kind I was drinking earlier."

"It's a pale ale from Hop. It's a microbrewery in town. Not a well-known one, but my buddy runs it, and I help him bottle when he has new brews."

"So you made this?" Ian took another sip, rolling the beer around his tongue like he was some sort of connoisseur evaluating a fine wine. "You're a man of many talents, Luke. It's good."

"I didn't brew it, I just hauled the kegs," Luke said with a sharp smile.

The comment drew Ian's attention to Luke's forearms, which were bared in deference to the heat in the crowded bar. It had been comfortable earlier, but with so many people packed into the space to hear the band, it was edging toward outright hot. The bar uniforms seemed to be a crisp white button-down shirt with a fitted black dress vest and tie, and Ian had already noticed several of the waitstaff with rolled up sleeves. It looked better on Luke, he had to say. Luke's arms were corded with noticeable muscle, which surprised Ian. With the sleeves of his uniform down, Luke looked trim and fit, but nothing suggested that sort of strength. It was intriguing, to say the least.

"You must be pretty good at that job," Ian murmured, and he saw the moment Luke realized he was flirting again. Luke stiffened, and he took a step back. Ian frowned.

"Doesn't take much to be good at hauling heavy things," Luke said dismissively. Ian would have retorted, but a new throng of people pushed their way to the forefront of the crowd, all of them clamoring for drinks. "Enjoy the beer," he told Ian as he turned away to help them.

"Well, damn," Ian murmured at the clear dismissal as Luke pulled a beer for a customer. The shirt and vest were fitted enough that Ian could easily follow the lines of Luke's shoulders and back as he worked the tap.

He was formulating a plan to get back in Luke's good graces when his phone buzzed in his pocket. It was too loud in the bar to even attempt to answer it, so he declined the call and immediately texted Niall back to see if it had been important.

Ethan is talking about renting a Breathalyzer for tomorrow morning before letting you out on the boat.

Ian laughed as he thumbed a response. *Not drunk, just enjoying the local scenery.*

The response came almost immediately. *You're missing out, then. Best view of the bay is right here in our living room.*

It had taken Niall a few awkward months before he'd been comfortable calling Ethan's place "ours," so the casual mention of it in the text made Ian smile. He held the phone up and covertly snapped a photo of Luke from behind. His ass looked fabulous and pert in the uniform-issue black trousers he was wearing, and the way the tidy little vest hugged his waist made Ian's mouth water. The lighting wasn't the best, but the photo was clear enough to show Niall what had caught Ian's attention. *Can't beat that*, he texted with the photo.

He'd finished his beer by the time Niall texted back a few minutes later. The delay was enough to make Ian worry he'd offended him.

Did you hook up with him?

It was an unusually candid question coming from Niall. He was all for matchmaking, but he usually steered away from actual details, especially of Ian's bar conquests.

Not for lack of trying, he texted back.

You can try again tomorrow. Come back. Ethan is going to be pissed if he has to take the kids out tomorrow. I told him he could sleep in.

Ian sighed and slid his wallet out of his pocket. It was just after eleven, much earlier than he usually packed it in during a night out on the town. Of course, he'd planned to be back at Niall and Ethan's over an hour ago, though Niall didn't know that.

He slapped more than enough to cover his tab—including the beer that had been Luke's treat—and a nice tip down on the bar, putting the beer bottle over it to hold it down. Usually he'd pay a tab with his card, but he had a feeling Luke wasn't going to be coming over with a check any time soon. He was still mixing drinks and pulling beers for the ever-growing mass of people clustered at the end of the bar.

Besides, Niall was right. He knew where Luke worked, so he was at an advantage. He'd slip away now and come back tomorrow. Luke had been in a bit of a snit over Ian's blatant leering at him, and giving him time to cool off before pursuing a more subtle flirtation would be a good game plan.

Calling a cab now, he texted Niall. He stood and put his wallet in his pocket before shooting an oblivious Luke one more glance and melting into the crowd. He'd pick his outfit a little more judiciously tomorrow night, Ian decided. He wouldn't stoop as low as the fake hipster glasses he saw on a lot of the crowd, but he could dress up a bit and give Luke something to drool over. Ian knew how to dress to maximum advantage, and he had all afternoon tomorrow to outfit himself accordingly. Maybe he could take Josh with him and get the kid something suaver than the ratty jeans and sweatshirts he seemed to favor. If he was going to be an honorary uncle, he was going to do it up right, and besides, if Josh was going to be his wingman at the bachelor party, he'd have to look the part.

FIVE

"ARE YOU kidding me?" Ian asked, holding the neon yellow life jacket Niall had thrust at him as far from his body as he could manage.

He didn't have a hangover. That wasn't the reason he was so damn tired, no matter how many winks and nudges Josh had given him over breakfast. Ian hadn't slept well, but he'd been sober as a stone by the time his cab had dropped him at Niall and Ethan's a little before midnight. He'd been exhausted but unable to drift off, alternating thinking about the next morning's boating outing and going over his conversations with Luke with a fine-toothed comb to try to suss out any weaknesses Luke might have. Ian wasn't going back in that bar without a plan, and he wasn't going to stop until he had Luke under him. He loved the chase, but Ian had never been so exhilarated by a challenge before. It would be one thing if Luke hadn't been interested, but the attraction between them had been undeniable. Ian had given him ample opportunity to stop the flirting banter between them, and Luke hadn't taken a single one of them. Ian wasn't sure if Luke's hot and cold reactions to him were part of the way Luke flirted, or if there was some other reason, but he was determined to find out. It had been preferable to think about that than to worry over taking the Even Keel out in the morning, though that had been the main reason sleep had eluded him.

"You have to wear it. Don't be an ass about it," Niall said as he pulled a similar life jacket on over his head. Down by the catamaran, Josh already had his on. They all had Even Keel's logo stretched across the back, and there was a rolling storage bin with a dozen more in smaller sizes sitting on the dock between the two sloops.

39

"I concede to the necessity of wearing a life jacket. It's this particular one that I object to," Ian answered. "These are ridiculous."

"They're highly visible, which makes it easy to spot where the kids are on the boat. I'm not going to make the kids wear something I'm not willing to wear myself, especially the older ones. So everyone's is the same." Niall rolled his eyes when Ian wrinkled his nose in disgust. "Look, I've never had one go overboard, thank God, but they'd be very visible in the water, too."

"I don't doubt that," Ian said. He bared his teeth at Niall when Niall stared pointedly at the life jacket in Ian's hands, reluctantly slipping into it. "Happy?"

"Deliriously," Niall deadpanned.

"Looking good, Uncle Ian!" Josh yelled from the catamaran's deck.

"Uncle Ian?" Niall questioned, lips twitching.

"It has a nice ring," Ian said with a shrug. He knew Josh was just messing around, but Ian kind of liked the moniker. He didn't have any siblings, so it wasn't like he'd have a nephew of his own someday. He could get behind adopting Josh, especially since Josh was already an adult. It gained him a nephew without any of the downsides, like diapers or babysitting.

Niall gave him a sidelong look Ian couldn't interpret. "Does it?" he said carefully, like he was mentally sizing Ian up.

Ian was saved from further questioning by the arrival of the first group of kids. The small boy who'd called out Ian's credentials was among them, and he instantly attached himself to Niall's leg in a fierce hug.

"Can I go with you?" he asked, and Ian frowned at the way the kid, who'd seemed confident and self-assured the day before, sounded so hesitant and needy.

"You're with Ian today, bud," Niall answered. He disentangled himself from the tight hug and dropped down to a squat so he could look the kid in the eye. "Everything okay today, Leo?"

This was the part of working with Even Keel that had kept Ian up last night. Niall had given him a brief rundown of all the kids who'd be on his boat, and Ian had read through the files before bed. The program might have started out as a lark, an extension of Niall teaching Josh and some of his friends from the mentoring program about water safety and the basics of sailing and how to care for the boats, but it had grown quickly. Word had spread, and before Niall knew it, he'd had twenty kids showing up on the dock just about every day after school. It had taken some finagling to set up the nonprofit, which Ian had helped with so Even Keel could get the proper insurance and start raising money to support the endeavor. It was obvious to Ian that Niall hated the paperwork, but that helping the kids was the most fun Niall had ever had. He got to spend his days on the water, working with kids and building their self-confidence and responsibility by teaching them one of his favorite things in the world, sailing. It was a perfect job for him, though Ian had been surprised at how easily Niall had taken to working with the younger ones.

Niall and his staff of volunteers were also mentors for the kids. They provided a safe space for the Even Keel students and assistance if they needed it, whether it was help learning multiplication tables or just an adult to listen when they talked about problems at home.

From the way Leo was crowding Niall, Ian had an uncomfortable suspicion things were not all right with the young boy. He didn't have any visible marks on him, but Ian knew that didn't mean anything. There were a lot of ways to hurt a child other than physically.

Before he could second-guess himself, Ian dropped into a crouch beside Niall. The two of them blocked Leo from the rest of the dock, and the boy seemed to relax a bit.

"Did someone hurt you, Leo?" Niall asked softly. He looked over Leo's shoulder to Ian, who knew his face probably mirrored the concern he saw on Niall's.

"No," the boy said without hesitation. Something eased in Ian's chest; Leo didn't sound like someone who was hiding something. "I almost didn't get to come today because she's here, but then she was still asleep so my uncle brought me anyway."

Niall blew out a breath, and from the look on his face, Ian knew whoever this mysterious "she" was, it was someone Leo had confided in him about before.

"You can switch your weekend any time your mom's in town, Leo. You know that," he said in the same calm, quiet voice. Ian could see Niall's frustration, even though he hid it from Leo well. The wrinkles on

Niall's forehead and the way his smile didn't light his eyes as it normally did said a lot about what he thought of Leo's mother.

"But I don't *want* to," Leo said, his hands flexing into fists at his side. "I don't want her here, I don't. And we never know when she's coming or when she's leaving, and she's always sick and *mean*. And she smells bad sometimes."

Ian's lips curved up in the ghost of a smile at Leo's outburst. The kid seemed fierce; he liked that. He tried to remember if Leo's file had listed anything about his mother, but he couldn't place it. Several of the kids he'd have out on the sloop today lived with guardians other than their parents, mostly because of incarcerations. His heart clenched a little at the thought of a kid as young as Leo not having a parent in his life.

"I'll talk to your uncle at pickup, okay? Maybe he knows how long she's staying this time. Is she at your apartment, or is she staying with your grandma?"

Leo's expression was stony. "I was at Grandma's last night, and she was supposed to be there, but she didn't come home 'til breakfast."

Niall glanced at Ian and then looked at Leo, nodding. "That's right. Your uncle works late on the weekends, doesn't he?"

"Just Friday nights," Leo said. He rubbed his eyes, and Ian looked away, trying to give the boy a little privacy to pull himself back together. "Saturdays are supposed to be family night, but she's here and it's gonna mess everything up."

"I'll talk to him," Niall said again, this time squeezing Leo's shoulder. "How about you show Ian around the boat? He hasn't done his safety check yet, so you can show him what he needs to do."

Leo's chin jutted out fiercely. "His name is Mack."

Ian chuckled. Ethan had come by Even Keel in time to help Ian and his motley crew practice knots on the day Ian had met Leo, and it seemed that Ethan had taken Leo under his wing. They were definitely closer than Ethan seemed to be with the other kids in their group, though Ethan didn't fight Leo's battles for him when the older kids good-naturedly teased him. He'd conspiratorially whispered with Leo toward the end, loud enough that Ian could overhear them but quiet enough the other kids couldn't. Ethan had told Leo that Ian allowed his friends to call him Mack, which was ridiculous because *no one* other than Ethan called him that, but Leo seemed to blossom when Ian casually told him to call him that as the kids were leaving for the day.

"That it is," Niall said. He stood, and Ian followed suit. They both watched as Leo ran down the dock toward the larger sloop that was farthest out. "Walk on the dock!" Niall yelled after him. "And get a life jacket!"

Leo slowed a tiny bit and detoured over to the bin to dig out a yellow life jacket in his size. He waved it over his head at Niall and then pulled it on before he hopped onto the sloop's deck and disappeared behind the sail.

"Maybe you need to call Ethan after all," Ian said. He rubbed the back of his neck, uncomfortable. "I don't know what to say to these kids about sailing, let alone whatever things they're dealing with at home, Niall."

"Did I say anything to him? Did I offer him any grand, life-changing advice?" Niall asked, an eyebrow raised in challenge. Ian shook his head. "No, I did not. I just listened, and I promised him I'd say something to his uncle later. And that's what I'll do. It's not rocket science, Ian. We're here to listen and give them something fun and constructive to do. If a child tells you something that concerns you or sets off alarm bells, tell Marcia. It's what she's on staff to do."

Ian hadn't met Even Keel's resident child psychologist yet, but he knew he would some time that week. Niall had explained earlier she wasn't on-site for the Saturday sails, but she came by for office hours three afternoons a week when the kids were there. Dr. Marcia Green was the only Even Keel employee who was actually paid. Niall didn't take a salary, and Ethan and Josh were volunteers, as were the handful of other ASA-certified instructors who helped out.

Ian was fairly sure Niall was paying Marcia, not dipping into the fund Ian had set up for the charity's overhead. He'd helped Niall invest the money that had come from selling Niall's real estate firm on Tortola to start an endowment for Even Keel, and Ethan had kicked in and bought the two sloops they used, as well as letting Niall use his catamaran for the older kids' lessons.

The fees he charged his advanced sailing students paid the rent on the pier warehouse, but Ian didn't think there was enough left over between that and the endowment annuity to pay Marcia's salary. That had to mean that Niall or Ethan was footing the bill, and Ian knew how stubborn Niall was about money. If he had to guess, he'd say the funding was coming from Niall's pocket despite the fact that Ethan's ran much deeper.

"I suppose I can do that," Ian admitted. Another small knot of children were making their way down the dock, huddled together and talking excitedly. He recognized a few of them as kids who'd raised their hands when Niall had called out children for Ian's boat.

"Jilly and Nyah, find Leo," Niall said as the group drew nearer. "The rest of you help Josh on the catamaran." He pulled a kid who looked to be about fourteen aside, waiting to talk to him until everyone else had left. "Jacob, you know you're not on the schedule this weekend. Is something up?"

The teen cast a nervous look toward Ian, who took that as his cue to leave. He was already in over his head, and he had a feeling whatever the fidgety boy had to tell Niall would definitely be out of his area of expertise. "I'm going to see what's going on before Leo leads my crew in a mutiny and they decide to set sail on their own," he said, leaving Niall to his conversation.

He'd always respected the hell out of what Niall was doing at Even Keel, but he had a whole new perspective on it now. Ian squared his shoulders, adjusting the ridiculous life jacket he'd just about managed to forget he had on, and set off after his charges. With any luck they wouldn't have any problems that weren't sailing related.

IAN UNDERSTOOD bad home situations. He was the byproduct of what probably would have been a one-night stand between Elisabete Morais and Alban Mackay if his mother hadn't unexpectedly gotten pregnant with him. She'd been a student at St. Andrews at the time, while his father had been a bank clerk looking for a bit of fun with the town coeds. Somehow she'd managed to finish, and after she'd graduated, they'd moved to Edinburgh. To say they'd been incompatible would have been a gross understatement, and quite a few of Ian's childhood memories were of the two of them ruining dinners and the rare family outings by screaming at each other. While his father hadn't been physically abusive, he'd rarely been sober. He also blamed Ian for their problems and had never been quiet about that fact. Ian's tough skin when it came to angry jilted lovers had been earned through years of being the focus of his father's insults and denigrations. There weren't many names someone could call him that he hadn't already heard from his father, and somehow being called bastard by someone who wasn't blood-related just didn't have the same sting.

Ian was fifteen when they'd finally divorced, and he'd been nothing but relieved. He and his mother had left Scotland and returned to her hometown, Boston, and even though the move hadn't been easy on him, it had been preferable to staying near his father.

So when Leo dragged his feet after their sailing lesson and tried to find excuses to stay on the sloop, Ian understood. He knew all about finding reasons to avoid going home; he'd played just about every sport available to him in primary and secondary school, not because he'd necessarily enjoyed them—though he had—but because it kept him out of the powder keg of a house.

"What about this one?"

The other kids had already been picked up, and Niall had been by once already to tell Leo his uncle was waiting for him in the parking lot. It was clear Leo didn't want to go home. He was currently going through all the knots listed on the laminated poster Ian had used to help them visualize the square knot they'd practiced earlier.

He looked over Leo's shoulder. "It's an anchor hitch."

Tying the sloop off at the dock had been the last part of the lesson. Everyone had taken a turn, and Leo had struggled. Ian wasn't sure if he was actually having a hard time tying the hitch or if it was just another stall technique like their current game of twenty questions.

"Like when you anchor at sea?"

"That's one time you'd use it. It's designed to stay tight even if the rope gets a strong tug, like when an anchor settles." Ian knew he should be hurrying Leo along, but he couldn't bring himself to do it. He felt for the kid. He'd lightened up a lot while they'd had the sloop out, but as soon as Ian had started guiding them back to the pier, Leo's mood had soured considerably. Ian hadn't prodded him about it, but Leo had dropped a few comments that made it clear he didn't want to go home because his mother would be there.

Ian looked up and saw Niall standing on the dock, watching them quietly. "Okay?" he mouthed when he saw he had Ian's attention.

45

Ian nodded. "How about you take this with you today, Leo? Niall can grab you some rope from the office, and you can work on your knots this weekend. If you can master the anchor hitch, I'll let you help me teach it to the group on Wednesday."

Having something to do while his parents were fighting had been a godsend for Ian. He'd retreated to his room with puzzle books and video games when things had gotten bad, and he figured the knots would keep Leo busy and distracted during his mom's visit.

Leo's face lit up. "Yeah!"

"Let's go then, bud. I'm sure your uncle is ready. You can show him what you've been working on," he said.

Niall was beaming at him when he and Leo stepped onto the dock.

"Shut up," he muttered under his breath before Niall could comment on the exchange.

"I will not," Niall said, his tone dripping with mock affront. "You're a natural, Ian. You should move here and do this every day."

Ian snorted out a laugh. "Right."

"Really, though, you were great today. Cameron told me how the lesson went, and just now? You got Leo to smile and willingly go home, even though he doesn't want to. You gave him something that made him feel special and important. That's huge, Ian."

Ian cringed at the earnestness in Niall's voice. "I gave him a project. It's hardly a cure for cancer," he said dismissively, hoping Niall would drop it.

Niall did seem to get the picture, because he backpedaled quickly. "Plus you won me twenty bucks, so all in all, it's a good day."

"How did I win you money, exactly?"

"Ethan said you'd give up before the lesson even started. I told him you'd stick it out. I win," Niall said with a gleeful smile.

"You two bet on whether or not I'd have a mental breakdown?" Ian's lips twitched; he'd have put his money on the same bet as Ethan, frankly.

"I think the language was more 'run screaming' than 'mental breakdown,' but yeah," Niall answered unapologetically.

Leo was waiting for them at the door to the warehouse, and Niall opened it and ushered both of them inside.

"Can I really help you teach on Wednesday?" Leo asked a bit shyly.

"Sure, if you can get the knot down," Ian said with a shrug.

"Cameron will freak! He says because I'm in first grade and he's in third that he's smarter than me, but he's not. He didn't even know which part of the boat was the bow today."

Ian couldn't help but privately concur that Cameron wasn't the brightest of the bunch, but he wasn't about to smack-talk an eight-year-old. He was an ass, but he had *some* standards. Ian kept his smile hidden as best he could. "Just do your best. You can show me Wednesday before lessons start."

Niall materialized next to them with a length of nylon rope that was long enough for Leo to practice with but not long enough for him to get himself too tangled in.

"I'll walk you out, kiddo. I've already talked to your uncle about family night. He says your mom wasn't at your grandma's when he dropped by earlier, so you guys are going to have your normal dinner and movie without her," Niall said.

Leo's smile grew even brighter as he followed Niall out, which only made the ache in the pit of Ian's stomach grow. He didn't think Leo's mom was abusive; there hadn't been any indication of that, at least. Niall clearly wasn't worried about that, and he knew the situation much better than Ian. Leo's obvious distrust and dislike for his mother hit a little too close to home for Ian.

His father had never been abusive either, but he'd been hell to live with. As an adult, Ian understood his father was an alcoholic, but as a child he'd only known his dad couldn't be counted on for anything. He'd learned to deal with his father's unpredictable mood swings and broken promises early on, and he could see the same thing in Leo. At least Leo had his uncle; Ian hoped he was half as stable and loving as Ian's mother. She'd made his childhood mostly bearable, and it looked like Leo's uncle was doing his best for the boy as well.

Even though he'd been born in Scotland, Ian was a US citizen. He'd had a US passport since he was an infant, which had been possible because his mother was an American citizen. He'd never given it much thought, since he and his mother had visited Boston often to see his grandparents and uncles, but she admitted later she'd made sure he was an American citizen to give them an escape route in case his father's drinking escalated from maudlin to violent. It never had, thank God, but being a US citizen had made their move to Boston when he was a teenager much easier.

Ian had briefly returned to Scotland for his grandmother's funeral five years ago, but aside from that he hadn't been on Scottish soil since he had emigrated. His relationship with his father was nonexistent, and his grandmother had been fond of traveling and had come to see him in the States often when she'd been alive.

The pier parking lot was mostly empty by the time he and Niall finished up with the boats and locked the warehouse to go back to Niall and Ethan's for the day. Ian had half expected to see Leo sitting on the curb resolutely refusing to get into his uncle's car, but it looked like Niall's talk with the two of them had smoothed out Leo's mood.

"So, lunch?" he asked Niall as they climbed into Niall's Jeep. It was almost exactly like the one Niall kept on Tortola—a housewarming gift from Ethan because Niall had fretted about leaving the Jeep he loved so much.

Ian went over and drove it once a month or so, and Niall's neighbor, Mrs. Jim, kept an eye on it and Niall's cottage the rest of the time. Ian had expected Niall to sell the house when he'd moved, but he and Ethan had kept it as a vacation home. It was nothing like the sprawling mansions Niall had shown Ethan when Ethan had been in the market for his own island house, but it suited the two of them. They usually stayed there or on Niall's yacht when they came out.

That hadn't been entrusted to Ian's care, not that he blamed Niall for it. Though he was certified and knew his way around boats, he didn't do much with the larger crafts. Ethan had given Niall a berth at the ritzy marina on Tortola as a Christmas gift their first year together, and that's where the *Orion* sat most of the year. With Niall's visits to Tortola becoming less and less frequent, Ian figured it was only a matter of time before he relocated the yacht to Seattle.

"I told Clare we'd pick her up and do some wedding planning," Niall said as he shifted into gear.

"She's going to kill me," Ian said with a snicker.

"That's why we're letting her choose the restaurant," Niall said, grinning when Ian groaned in response. Letting Clare choose where they ate would mean something vegetarian, or worse, vegan.

"Can we stop for something on the way? You know she's not going to let us eat anywhere with actual food," Ian pleaded.

"The last time I did that, she smelled the french fries the second she got in the car. I ended up on a three-day juice cleanse," Niall said with a shudder that told Ian he wasn't exaggerating.

"I did a juice cleanse once," he offered.

"A two-day bender where all you did was drink pineapple juice with rum is not a juice cleanse," Niall retorted.

"Lost six pounds," Ian continued, ignoring the interruption.

"Probably more from dehydration from all the sex than because of the juice," Niall said drily.

Ian considered it, then nodded. College spring break weeks were a guaranteed good time on Tortola.

"BUT HOW is that different from the ceremony on the beach I was planning?" Clare asked, more curious than bitter, which surprised Ian. He'd been expecting her to get territorial and hate all of his ideas, but she'd taken the news that Niall was letting Ian take over wedding planning with nothing but grace. Then again, it was Clare. Not much knocked her off her Zen. Not even Susannah, who was sitting in the corner of the booth and resolutely refusing to eat anything at all. She'd made it clear from the beginning she was just there to snoop on wedding plans, not eat. Ian was a little jealous that he hadn't thought to make a stand like that; Clare's disapproving moue would have been preferable to the crap masquerading as food on his plate.

Ian had just laid out the revised plans for Niall and Ethan's wedding over tofu tacos that Clare had raved about. He was unimpressed, and from the way Niall was surreptitiously scraping his tofu into a little cave he'd made with his pico de gallo, it looked like he wasn't enjoying it either.

"It's completely different," Ian answered. "The beach is overdone and trite. But getting married on Ethan's catamaran? That's inspired, and it's reflective of who they are. Sailing is important to them."

He'd arranged it with Ethan already, and Josh was excited that part of his duties as best man would be to sail the wedding party out and anchor in the bay. The catamaran could easily hold the small group, and it was a much more appropriate setting for Niall and Ethan's ceremony.

Niall hadn't heard the plans before Ian had unveiled them at lunch. He'd smiled ear to ear and seemed genuinely pleased, which was what Ian had been hoping for. Ethan had reacted much the same when he'd pitched the idea to him. If the two of them had been sold on the beach wedding, Ian supposed he could have left it alone, but Ethan had agreed exchanging vows on the catamaran was much more them.

Clare was fighting a grin, and Ian felt the tips of his ears flush under her scrutiny. "Ian Mackay, you're a closet romantic. I love it."

"I am not!" he denied vehemently.

"You are! Don't be embarrassed, it's adorable. Niall told me about your mystery man from last night. Are you going to be seeing him again?"

Susannah made an interested noise, and Ian cringed. He focused on Clare instead of Susannah, who had scooted forward and started paying more attention at the topic change.

"I haven't 'seen' him at all, Clare. He was just someone convenient to flirt with." Ian knew no one at the table believed the lie.

"Oh my God, he's *embarrassed*," Susannah crowed. Ian glared at her, momentarily forgetting his resolve not to make eye contact with her. She was relentless when she sensed weakness, and he was sure that's what she'd read in his eyes.

Ian felt the flush spread from his ears to the back of his neck. "I don't know what you're talking about."

Niall snickered. "Come off it, Ian. I've never seen you so into someone, and you didn't even get anywhere! I can't think of a time you've said more than a few words about anyone you've slept with, yet you texted me a picture of him last night."

"I texted you a picture of his ass! His ass, Niall. It's a thing of beauty, yes, but I'm not doodling his name in my notebooks or planning a double wedding."

Niall seemed to pick up on Ian's defensiveness because he backed off. "Fine. I'm just saying, he seems different."

Ian had to admit Niall was right, though he refused to do it publicly. Privately, he very much agreed that Luke was different. It spooked Ian a bit. It wasn't just that he'd invested a lot of flirting in Luke and wanted to see it through; he actually wanted to know more about Luke. Hell, he wanted to know his last name. Ian couldn't remember the last time he'd asked someone he was interested in for their last name. Half the time he didn't even ask for their first.

"I will point out that I have not seen a picture of this fabulousness. I'd be happy to issue a final ruling if you'd like. Niall's biased. He only has eyes for Ethan's ass," Susannah said. Clare gaped at her, scandalized.

"Susannah! This man is a human being. While I'm glad Ian's finally found someone he's really interested in, that doesn't mean we should be a party to objectifying the poor man. We don't need to see his ass," Clare said firmly.

"I don't think I've ever heard you say ass before," Ian said. He nodded appreciatively and handed over his phone so she could see the picture. "I like it. You sound feisty when you're vulgar."

Clare *tsk*ed at him. "The word 'ass' is not vulgar. I'll never understand why we as a society insist on assigning negative connotations to the correct terminology for our bodies. Do you know that most girls don't know the difference between their vagina and vulva? It's disgusting, the way we—"

"Can we *not* talk about that while we're eating?" Niall interrupted. He was looking a little green, but Ian couldn't tell if it was the talk about vaginas or the tofu.

"But talking about Ian objectifying a man because of his ass is acceptable table conversation? Better look out, your double standards are showing, Niall," Clare said tartly.

"Dial it back, Ms. Steinem. I think it's more vaginas in general Niall wants to steer clear of. While he doesn't think less of you or me for having them, they're not something he has any interest in," Susannah said drily.

Clare narrowed her eyes and glared at her for the feminist dig, but she sat back and stopped tearing into Niall. Niall, for his part, looked torn between being relieved and apologetic. Clare took one look at him and gave up her sulk, her lips twitching into the perky smile that was almost always on her face.

"Why don't we talk about this man's other attributes, like his personality and wit? He must have something special to have Ian this tied up in knots over him," she said.

Niall had shoved his phone across the table to Susannah some time during Clare's diatribe, and she was currently looking at the picture Ian had texted him.

"I don't know. It's a very nice ass. Full points. Five out of five, would look again," she said smugly.

Ian choked on his water hard enough that Niall had to clap him on the back to help him clear his lungs. "You waited until I'd taken a drink on purpose," he accused when he'd recovered enough to breathe and talk.

Susannah didn't look repentant in the least. "Maybe," she said with a shrug. "But it is a nice one. I approve. Go get 'em, tiger."

Ian rolled his eyes. He hadn't told Niall he planned to go back to see if Luke was working again tonight, and now he definitely wouldn't be divulging that bit of information. He'd never live it down. It was almost enough to dissuade him from going. Almost, but not quite. Susannah was right—it was a spectacular ass.

"Not to sound conceited, but can we talk more about my wedding? As interesting as this is, I'd like more details about everything Ian has changed," Niall put in. He squirmed in his seat a bit, looking uncomfortable at the topic. Ian had texted him the picture just to put that expression on Niall's face, but he'd been oddly enthusiastic about the bartender last night when he'd talked to Ian after Ian had gotten back. Ian wondered if Clare's presence was giving Niall a crisis of conscience. Still, he took the lifeline.

"I'm having a caterer set up a reception in the warehouse after the ceremony. Hortensia's baking a cake," he said. He met Clare's eye, cutting her off before she could protest. "And no, I didn't have Ethan tell her to do it. I asked if she'd like to, and she jumped at the chance. She was feeling left out of all the planning. Besides, Ethan loves her buttercream frosting."

Niall twitched at the mention of frosting, and Ian decided to be generous and not comment. If he pissed Niall off, they probably wouldn't stop for real food on the way home, and Ian was starving. Besides, if Niall had told Ian the story of exactly how he'd found out Ethan loved his housekeeper's frosting, he'd probably told Clare as well. From the way she blushed rosily, he was probably right. Niall wasn't the type to talk out of turn, but he was also a pretty lightweight drinker. Stories flowed easily during drunken nights out; it made for some interesting conversations.

"What am I missing here?" Susannah asked.

"Nothing," Clare said quickly. "If it really means that much to Hortensia, then I'm on board."

Her jaw was still set stubbornly, but Ian was safe from her ire for the moment, though that wouldn't last long when she found out the menu for the evening included beef.

"Niall has an appointment with the florist Monday morning. If you're free, you could join him," Ian said by way of a peace offering.

"What? Me? It's *your* florist. You go!" Niall spluttered.

"It's the florist I found for your wedding. You need to go. There has to be at least one decision you make yourself, Niall. Besides, Ethan is picking the catering menu, so it's your turn."

"Ethan agreed to pick the catering menu? My Ethan? Meeting with a caterer?" His surprise was clear. "Or do you mean to say you asked Ethan to do it and he said he'd send Susannah? Because that I believe."

Susannah snorted. "Ethan doesn't randomly volunteer me to do his bidding. I said I'd go. I mean, it involves food. I'm in."

At the mention of food, Ian gave up all pretense of picking at the meal in front of him and pushed the still-full plate away. He motioned for the waitress to take it and politely declined a refill on the wheatberry soda he hadn't finished. He'd needed something to wash away the horrible tofu taste and the soda had served that purpose, but it wasn't what he would call good.

"Besides, he's involved. I'm having the caterer bring samples by Tuesday, and I already blocked out the time on his schedule as a lunch meeting," Susannah said.

Ian grinned. He doubted Ethan had any idea he'd be sampling food and choosing the wedding menu for his Tuesday lunch meeting. Susannah was devious. It's why they were friends, though he preferred she aim her skills at others instead of him. "That leaves the flowers for you, Niall. The florist already has the venue information, so I'm guessing he's just going to want to ask you some questions about your preferences for flower type and colors," he said.

"I don't have a preference for flower type or color," Niall said flatly.

"So point to something random. Or let Clare choose. Just keep the appointment," Ian said impatiently.

"Why don't you do it?" Clare asked. She edged forward in her seat and stole a bite of quinoa off Niall's plate, since apparently her own helping of the stuff hadn't been enough. Ian didn't know how she managed to make it look like she actually enjoyed it. Saying that his had tasted like cardboard would be insulting to cardboard.

"Because I have a flight back to Tortola Monday morning, and I won't be back 'til a few days before the wedding. Joe said I could fly back with him and Mrs. Jim."

"What? No! I thought you were going to be staying through," Niall protested.

"Niall, it's four weeks away. I'm not staying here without any of my things and be underfoot for you and Ethan for a month. It's fine. Everything's set in motion for the wedding, and I'll leave Clare and Susannah with all the info so they can tie up any loose ends. I'll be back a few days before you walk down the aisle, just like you originally intended."

He hadn't mentioned his plans to anyone other than Joe. Being in Seattle and hanging out with Niall and Ethan had settled his restlessness, but Ian didn't want to be settled. He wanted to have some meaningless sex to clear his head and get rid of all these notions of wanting a life like theirs.

"I'm not worried about the wedding plans, I'm worried about *you*," Niall blurted.

"I'm worried about me too," Ian said playfully. "I'm worried my dick is going to fall off if it doesn't get some action soon."

Clare stifled a giggle with her hand. "What?" She said when Niall shot her a look. "It might. I mean, he didn't hook up with the bartender last night, right? So it's been at least twenty-four hours. That's a long time for Ian."

It had been more like a week, but Ian wasn't going to dig himself a deeper hole by admitting that. Christ, he hadn't gone this long without sex since the time his stepfather had a heart attack and he'd been holed up in the hospital with his mother for four days straight. Even then, he'd managed a hand job in the staff locker room after it was clear Paul was going to make a full recovery.

"You don't have to come down to Even Keel if it bothers you," Niall said, but Ian waved away his concern.

"It's not that. You guys have your life here, and I have a life waiting for me on the island. I'll be back for the wedding."

"You don't have a life on Tortola," Niall snapped. "You have a string of one-night stands and a few part-time jobs that keep you busy, but it's not a life. Damn it, Ian, when are you going to grow up? I thought maybe this latest funk was you figuring out you're wasting your life doing nothing, but maybe I gave you too much credit."

Niall's raised voice had drawn attention from other diners. His eyes widened after the words escaped, and Ian felt a warm wave of affection at Niall's slightly horrified expression. He obviously hadn't meant to say that, and the fact that he was concerned enough to say it out loud was nice. The sentiment wasn't, of course, but it was hardly the first time someone had called him out on his lifestyle. His mother's attacks weren't nearly as circumspect as Niall's.

"I'm sorry," Niall said immediately. "Just, like I said. I'm worried about you. And I swear to God, Ian, if I thought you were happy catting around the island like that, I'd leave you be. But you're not."

"I moved to the island to do exactly what I'm doing," Ian reminded him.

"Yeah, four years ago. And when you bought that house, you were that guy. You were ridiculous, Ian. But you're a different person now. Everybody changes and grows. You just aren't giving yourself the chance to do it."

"I don't want my old life, Niall. That guy was an asshole. And yeah, I'm one, too. But he was a really unhappy asshole. I don't want the eighty-hour work weeks or the thousand-dollar suits."

Ian had gone into investment banking because it was the best revenge he could think of against his father. His dad railed against "the corporate machine" in banking because he'd never been able to work all the way up the ranks. Ian saw his success in doing just that in the financial world as the best "fuck you" he could give to his old man.

He'd pushed himself harder and worked longer because of it, not because he enjoyed what he did, but because he wanted to prove he was better than his father. He'd hated his job and hated living in Los Angeles, but it hadn't mattered because he was successful.

It was stupid, and he regretted it now. When he'd gotten his inheritance after his grandmother had passed, Ian had donated a fairly large chunk of it to charity. The rest he'd invested, and he was still living off those dividends. He didn't technically need to work at all, but he couldn't just sit around and do absolutely nothing. That had worked for the first six months he'd been on Tortola, but after that he'd started to go insane. So he had part-time jobs doing trivial work, like being a sailing instructor at the marina and a scuba diving tour guide.

And yes, Niall was right. It was all pretty meaningless. But Ian wasn't ready to give it up yet. He hadn't intended for Tortola to be anything other than an extended vacation. His plan had been to buy a house and spend a few months sleeping around and relaxing, and then he'd figure out what he wanted to do with the rest of his life. But those months had turned into years, and now he was thirty-six and still had no idea what he wanted to be when he grew up. Going back to school didn't interest him at all, and neither did picking up where he'd left off in his career.

"I'm not saying you have to go back into banking, Ian. God, why would you? But you need to find something real to do."

"Like move to Seattle and open a sailing school?" Ian teased, trying to lighten the mood. Their fellow patrons had returned to their meals when Niall had lowered his voice, but people were still peeking at their table from time to time.

"Market's glutted," Niall muttered.

"But you could move here anyway," Clare put in with a sunny smile. "I bet Ethan would give you a job."

Ian snorted. "Yeah, I'd be so suited to it, too."

He expected Susannah and Niall to laugh as well, but they didn't. "You could be, you know. It's not all computer stuff there," Niall said.

Susannah nodded, a serious expression on her face. "We have a sales and marketing division I bet you'd take to, or there's the finance division. I know you said you don't want to work for a bank again, but it's not exactly the same, is it?"

"I don't know anything about corporate finance management or sales and marketing," Ian said, exasperation creeping into his voice. "I'd do better working for Niall as a sailing instructor."

"I'd be happy to have you," Niall said with a challenging smile.

"Yeah, but your fund manager would kill you for taking on another paid employee," Ian answered.

"He's a pushover. I know how to work his buttons," Niall said confidently. "Right now he's thinking about relocating."

And God, did Niall ever know how to push Ian's buttons. A few minutes ago he'd been anxious to get back to Tortola to resume his life. Now that the idea of moving to Seattle had taken up space in his mind, it pulsed like a beacon. God, Niall was a meddling brat.

"He *is* a pushover," Ian agreed. "Hell, he doesn't even take a fee out of your account for managing it for you." Niall had offered to pay him, of course, but Ian had declined. "And right now he's thinking about steak and a beer." He gave Niall's full plate a significant look.

"I'm going to pretend I didn't hear that," Clare said with a disapproving frown. "I'll go with Niall to the florist, Ian. If Susannah and Ethan are taking care of the caterer, is there anything else that will need to be done?"

"Hortensia's going to have a big cook-out or something at the house the night before, but she's arranging all that. Susannah's in charge of invitations for that and handling the wedding RSVPs," Ian said. He leveled a pointed look at Niall, who squirmed.

"Listen, you were always invited. I just wasn't going to send it to you until a week before. I didn't know you'd go all *Queer Eye* on me and replan the whole wedding. I thought you'd try to talk me out of it."

Ian snorted. "I can't exactly *Queer Eye* you if you're not straight, Niall," he said with a laugh. "And I don't have a problem with you marrying Ethan. I'm sure you feel like it's the right thing to do, and I'm happy for you. Am I going to rush out and get married? No. But do I think you shouldn't because I happen to think the institution of marriage is ridiculous? No."

SIX

IAN'S PARENTS' messy divorce (and even messier marriage) had put him off the idea of the institution itself. His mother had remarried his freshman year of college and was happy with her new husband, but Ian thought that was probably an anomaly. How could someone be happy tying themselves to one person for the rest of their lives? Ian rarely slept with the same person twice, and he'd had a grand total of three actual relationships in his thirty-six years. Two of those had been in college, and the third had only lasted as long as it did because his partner had traveled frequently for work so they were rarely in the same city.

Still, he had to admit Niall and Ethan were very happy. They'd been living together for less than a year, but they were already settled into a routine like an old married couple. And while Ian had always thought of that as a bad thing, it worked for them. There was something cozy and comforting about watching them move around each other in the kitchen making coffee in the morning before Niall was really awake, or listening to the two of them bicker about Niall parking his Jeep in the driveway and blocking Ethan's car in the garage.

When Ian found himself smiling at Niall bitching about Ethan leaving his socks on the bedroom floor for the housekeeper to pick up instead of putting them in the hamper, Ian knew it was time to go home.

He'd fled Seattle for his own mental well-being. The heart-to-heart Niall had pulled out of him had soothed most of Niall's worries, and he and Ethan had let Ian go without further argument. It had been a relief, because if Niall had pushed much harder, Ian probably would have stayed.

Just like he was now considering leaving Tortola mostly because of Niall's earnest suggestion that Ian join him in relocating to Seattle. Despite Ian's ostentatious lifestyle, he didn't have enough money stockpiled to live anywhere in the world without working. Tortola was fine. It wasn't terribly expensive to live on the island, and he'd already paid for his house with the lump sum he'd gotten from selling his condo when he left the States. The part-time jobs paid for drinks and dinners, leaving the bulk of Ian's investments to accrue more dividends for him to reinvest.

Moving to Seattle would be a different story. Housing was a lot more expensive there, as was living in general. The weather was a factor as well—it was going to take some adjustment to get used to overcast skies and chilly rain being the norm. Lacking the sun-soaked beach and other distractions to fill his days, he'd be bored out of his mind without a full-time job.

To be honest, he was starting to miss working. Sailing lessons and scuba tours were fun, but they were more of a way to hook up with people than actual work. He got to flirt and be outside, which he loved, and very few of his customers ever turned him down when he ramped up the charm. Ian had perfected roguish allure, and it worked well on the island with tourists who were looking for a wild night or illicit afternoon romp. The scene in Seattle was totally different. To its credit, it was more laid-back than LA; he wouldn't be thinking about moving otherwise. He'd hated his time in Los Angeles, though he'd loved the flash of his lifestyle.

But moving to Seattle…. Ian was a little worried at how easily he'd accepted the idea as something to think about. Six months ago he'd have laughed at Niall. Then again, six months ago he wouldn't have spent his last night in Seattle sitting at a bar waiting for a glimpse of a bartender he hadn't even gotten to first base with.

Luke hadn't been working. Ian had swallowed his pride and asked one of the servers he recognized from the first night, and she'd told him Luke rarely worked any night other than Friday. The bar just wasn't as much fun without Luke to harass, so Ian had finished his drink and gone back to Niall and Ethan's. It had somehow turned into Susannah and her husband, Trevor, coming over for drinks, which had morphed into Clare showing up with her brother, Frank, and his partner, Warner, to play Trivial Pursuit.

Ian had lost. Badly.

It had also been the most fun he'd had in months. They'd played teams, and since Clare and Ian were the only unmatched people, they'd been thrown together. No one could beat Warner and Frank, though Niall and Ethan had given them a run for their money. Halfway through the game, Clare and Ian had bowed out, preferring to drink and heckle the others to getting their asses handed to them on the game board.

If Ian lived in Seattle, he could have that every weekend. He knew Niall and Ethan had the group over a few times a month for silly things like movie nights and games or cookouts. How would it feel to be there with a significant other of his own to play Trivial Pursuit with? Ian couldn't even imagine.

He shrugged off the introspection that was becoming a lot more common these days. He'd hoped coming back to the island and getting into his normal routine might change things, but it hadn't. If anything, the last week at home had given him more time to think. At least in Seattle his days were full of volunteering at Even Keel and running around with Niall and Clare. He'd gone out a few times since he'd been back, but Ian hadn't even made a token effort to hook up with anyone. Even the owner of his favorite dive bar had noticed and asked if he was all right. It was quickly becoming a major issue.

Luckily, he was again on the schedule at work. His part-time jobs had always been something he looked forward to, and now that was even truer. Ian was in dire need of a distraction, and the scuba excursion he was due to lead in an hour was a perfect one. If he didn't hightail it over to the shop, he was going to be late. His gear was stored in the same supply room the other diving instructors and tour guides used, and he was sure that after a two-week absence, his things would be strewn all to hell. Most of the others were part-timers like him, and a good number of them were only in it for the hookups and free dive time. That didn't lead to a very organized roster, and no one took much care following any kind of system in the supply room. Everyone was certified on safe diving practices and their excursions were always carefully planned and monitored, but everything else was a complete mess.

He wasn't surprised to find his wet suit missing. It was no small miracle that everything else was tucked into his locker. He didn't exactly want to lead a group of German tourists on a reef dive in just his swim trunks, though, so Ian began the arduous task of sorting through the piles of equipment to find his suit or another that would work.

"Arlen borrowed your kit. He didn't realize you were on today. We haven't seen you in a while, man. Figured maybe you found some epic parties in Miami and decided to stay." Craig was the closest thing the dive shop had to a manager. He was the only one of them, aside from the owner, who worked full-time. Ian had let him know about his vacation, but he was a little surprised Craig remembered where he'd been.

"The club scene's pretty unreal there," Ian agreed noncommittally. He wasn't usually circumspect about his conquests, so it wasn't a surprise when Craig pushed him for details. If there had been any to give, Ian would have shared them gladly, but he didn't want to admit he'd come up dry.

"One word, Craig. Swingers," Ian said with a wink. It wasn't a complete lie. He *had* been propositioned by a couple at SCORE in Miami. He just hadn't taken them up on it, but Craig didn't need to know that.

Craig wolf-whistled. "Only you, Ian. I don't know how you do it. You're a hoss, man."

Ian gave Craig his best leer. "It's a real hardship," he joked. Luckily the ding of the shop bell saved him. His German tourists had apparently arrived.

"Later I'll buy you a beer and you can give me all the details. I'll get them started on gear. Just grab a suit from the rental pile. I'll make sure Arlen gets your stuff back in your locker today."

Ian caught the set of keys Craig tossed to him and disappeared into the tiny back room where they stored the rental gear. He helped himself to a wet suit and left the door open since Craig would need in there to get the tourists sorted out.

IT HAD been nice to be back in the water. Ian always enjoyed leading dives, even when they were made up of barely qualified tourists. Usually, Ian was busy returning the rental equipment and signing the customers out when he came back from a dive, but Craig was still in the storage room, so Ian left the grunt work to him and ducked into one of the curtained changing rooms to get out of the too-small wet suit that had bothered him for the whole dive.

He had one leg out of the suit when the curtain was opened and then closed again. "I've never done anything like this," someone said, and that was all the warning Ian got before a warm hand tickled his naked ribs.

"What the hell?" he yelped. The surprise had him stumbling, and before he could right himself, Ian lost his balance and fell against the gorgeous blond from the tour. The two of them tumbled to the floor, with Ian coming to rest on top of the other man.

Ian pushed up off of him and scrambled to his feet. "What do you think you're doing?" he snapped at the wide-eyed tourist. They'd flirted a bit on the boat, but Ian hadn't expressed an interest in anything more.

"The other tour guide said you liked to have sex in here," the man said. He looked terrified. Ian didn't blame him; he could only imagine how furious he looked at the moment. Apparently, he needed to channel that toward Craig instead.

"He was wrong. Get out," Ian said coldly. The man stood and backed through the curtain with his hands raised.

Ian stripped out of the wet suit as quickly as he could, forgoing drying off in favor of pulling a shirt on with his trunks. He stormed into the shop barefoot.

"What the fuck, Craig? Are you fucking whoring me out now?"

The few remaining tourists lingering in the shop fled at Ian's angry words, and Ian's pulse jumped at the way Craig shrugged in response.

"Chill, man. He's your type. I figured when you disappeared you wanted me to send him your way. No harm, no foul."

"No harm? Craig, someone I don't know came in and put his hands on me without my permission. That's the definition of harm."

"Why are you so angry? Jesus. It's not like he'd be the first dude you hooked up with in the changing room."

Craig looked honestly bewildered, and that took some of the righteousness out of Ian's rage. When the tourist had said Craig sent him back, Ian really had thought Craig was expecting him to sleep with the guy as part of the tour. And yes, it had happened before, but only when Ian was the one doing the asking. He wasn't available for Craig or anyone else to pimp out, regardless of whether or not the person was his type.

"Because I didn't ask him to come, Craig. Look—forget it. Just don't do it again."

Ian's muscles were quivering from a combination of the exertion of a rough dive after weeks out of the water and the adrenaline crash as he calmed down from his unwelcome surprise. He wanted a shower and his bed, and arguing with Craig was keeping him from it.

He waved off Craig's apologies as he cleared his things from his locker. He wouldn't have another shift until after Niall's wedding, and he didn't see the point in keeping equipment there for the other dive instructors and guides to rifle through.

"Have Arlen stick my suit in my locker. I'll call you when I'm back from Seattle to get on the schedule," Ian said shortly when he passed Craig on his way out.

"Look, man—"

There was real concern in Craig's features, but Ian shook his head. "I'm pissed and I'm tired. Let's just not. I'll see you when I get back."

The drive to his house seemed to take twice as long as it normally did. Ian didn't know if it was because he was still so angry or because he usually didn't make the drive in wet clothes. Either way, he was uncomfortable. By the time he finally let himself into his house, he was shivering and completely miserable.

Ian made a beeline for his bedroom, shucking his damp swim trunks and T-shirt as he went. Instead of starting the shower, though, he found himself pulling on a comfy pair of fleece pajama pants and backtracking to the living room, where he'd dropped his duffel, so he could dig for his phone.

He didn't even let Niall say hello, launching into the conversation the moment Niall picked up. "I know you're mad at me for leaving, but can I come early?"

"What happened?"

Ian realized how desperate he must have sounded and immediately backpedaled. "Nothing. I just thought I'd swing over this weekend instead and spend a few weeks. I can text Joe my flight info when I book it, but if he's not free, I'll just catch a cab."

"You were dying to get home a few days ago. So what changed?"

"I missed your sunny smile?" Ian tried for nonchalant, but he knew he'd failed when Niall's sigh came over the line.

"You're going to fly out this weekend? Text me and Joe. One of us will be there. I'm not sure what Ethan's schedule is. He has a meeting in Utah at some point this week. He and Joe might be there when you get in. I'm not sure what day he's going. Come whenever you can, and someone will be there to get you."

Ian blew out a breath he hadn't realized he'd been holding. He hadn't expected Niall to say no, but he was surprised to get Niall's acquiescence so easily.

"It'll probably be Friday. You know the puddle jumper off the island leaves at the crack, so I'll probably be there midafternoon. I'll get you the details when I book it," he said. Ian paused, unwilling to wrap up the conversation because Niall's voice was a comfort. He wasn't sure if he was shaken up by the tourist's unwanted advances—though he'd stopped them easily enough—or because the advances had been unwanted in the first place. Craig hadn't been wrong; the blond German was exactly Ian's type.

"You don't sound like yourself, Ian. Are you sure everything's okay?" Niall's voice dropped to the soothing pitch he used with kids at Even Keel. It shouldn't have been comforting to know Niall was trying to gentle him, but it was.

"I had a run-in with someone who was a little handsy," Ian said, brushing off the concern. "Actually, it was probably just karmic payback for all the times I snuck one in on you."

Knowing how startling and wrong it felt to have someone touch him without his permission made Ian feel a bit sick about the times he'd done the same to Niall. He'd thought he was being flirtatious, and he'd always stopped when Niall said no, but Ian was beginning to realize he'd been a real asshole to Niall at the start of their friendship.

"Ian, no," Niall said firmly. "You were an annoying shit some of the time, but you never did anything that made me uncomfortable. Are you all right? Should I have Mrs. Jim check on you?"

Ian laughed. "No, I'm fine. He took me by surprise, and I ended up knocking us both over, which took the wind out of his sails, so to speak. I think mostly it's my pride that's bruised."

"Did he give you any trouble?"

"No. I think I scared the shit out of him, actually." Ian grinned at the memory of how shell-shocked the tourist had looked when he'd yelled at him. Now that he was home safe and sound and in dry clothes, Ian could take a more objective look at the situation. It had been an honest—though stupid—mistake on Craig's part to send in the guy, but the man had backed off as soon as Ian told him to. No harm, no foul, as Craig had said. Ian also knew how lucky he was the guy *had* taken no for an answer. The knowledge that just a few weeks ago he wouldn't have stopped the guy was enough to make him want to reevaluate his lifestyle. How many unsafe situations had he been in and hadn't fully realized it?

"I'm going to want to hear more about that," Niall said, but Ian could hear the smile in his voice. "He must have been a puppy dog if you were able to scare him."

"I am a big, muscular, manly specimen," Ian protested. He held the phone between ear and shoulder and set about making a pot of coffee to finish warming up. Getting into dry clothes and talking to Niall had done wonders for his adrenaline crash, but he was still chilly. A hot shower would probably be better, but the last thing Ian wanted at the moment was to be wet again. It was counterintuitive, since he knew it would make him feel warmer in the long run, but Ian always loathed getting wet when he was already cold.

"You are a complete pacifist who would probably hurt himself more by throwing a punch than his assailant," Niall said with a laugh.

Ian might be fighting fit, but he'd never been a fighter. That much was true. He exercised religiously and kept himself in great shape, but he'd never had any interest in learning how to throw a punch or any desire to hit someone.

"You're hardly running a fight club yourself," he deadpanned.

"If I was, you'd never know. First rule of—"

Ian cut him off before Niall could make a complete fool of himself. "Whatever."

"You sound better," Niall said.

Ian considered shrugging it off, but he knew Niall was being sincere. He didn't always have to be the lighthearted clown with him. "I feel better. Thanks."

"I'm always here if you need to talk," Niall said seriously. "Have you thought about how long you'll be here? Ethan and I aren't taking a honeymoon because he's got a beta release for a new product line next month. You're welcome to stay with us after the wedding. We'll probably spend a few weeks in Tortola as a belated honeymoon around Christmas."

Ian had been planning to come home after the wedding, but the house was suddenly the last place he wanted to be. Looking around, it occurred to him he'd never really moved in. Most of his things were still in storage in Los Angeles. He'd brought some of his furniture and other things, but the bulk of it had stayed behind. It was like he'd been on a four-year vacation, and he was just now realizing he was ready to go home.

"I don't have any solid plans. I'll be staying for a bit, I guess," he said.

SEVEN

IAN HADN'T been planning to hit the town as soon as he touched down in Seattle, but he also hadn't expected to get a text from Niall with profuse apologies and the number for the local cab company while he was standing at baggage claim waiting to be picked up.

Clare's brother apparently had appendicitis, and Niall had driven her to Portland so she could be there when he came out of surgery. Ian liked Frank; not only was he every bit as attractive as Clare, he also ate meat and had a wicked sense of humor. Too bad he also liked Frank's husband, Warner. They were another couple that seemed perfect for each other, just like Niall and Ethan.

Pass along my well-wishes, he texted back.

Will do. Almost to Portland now. Warner says Frank's surgery is going well. Ethan is in Salt Lake 'til tomorrow, but the gatehouse has a key for you.

Ian wasn't in the mood to lurk around Niall and Ethan's house alone, but he also didn't feel like calling up Susannah or Joe to go out. Not that either was probably around. Joe probably would have flown Ethan to Utah, and Susannah often went along when the trips were short. Odds were good both of them were in Salt Lake City with Ethan.

The baggage belt beeped and lurched to life, and Ian staked out a spot to watch for his luggage. He'd brought two huge suitcases this time. Ian wasn't sure what he was going to do, but he wanted to be prepared for a longer stay. Niall had made a few off-hand comments about Ian starting a job search in Seattle, but the longer he'd thought about it, the more merit the idea had.

Susannah sending him a list of short-lease apartments the day before hadn't been a coincidence. Ian had a niggling suspicion that when he finally talked to her or Niall, they'd have a list of openings for him to apply for, and that was assuming Susannah hadn't just worked her scary mojo and applied for them on his behalf. She was very determined when she wanted to be, and he knew she fully supported Niall's campaign to have Ian move to Seattle.

He pretended to be annoyed with them when they started in on him, but truth be told it was nice to be wanted.

Ian lugged both suitcases off the conveyor belt as they went by, hitching his laptop bag higher on his shoulder before negotiating the suitcases into a position that allowed him to roll them both. Everything was precariously balanced, but he didn't have far to go. He'd never had to use the airport's taxi stand before, but he knew it was just outside the doors.

He allowed himself to drift a bit during the ride into the city, rousing enough to hand his passport to the security guard at the imposing gate that guarded the entrance to Ethan and Niall's neighborhood.

It had taken Niall a few months to adjust to living in such splendor, and Ian still got a kick out of thinking about Niall living in a sprawling house that could easily fit six of the tiny bungalow he owned in Tortola. Ian's house on the island wasn't much bigger; he was certain any apartment he rented in Seattle would likely be larger than the seafront cottage he lived in now.

Of course, it wouldn't have the benefit of the beach as an extended living room, so that was a consideration. The cottage didn't feel small because it was light and airy, with windows and walls that opened onto the beach to blend the indoor and outdoor spaces. Any apartment or townhouse he found would have to be larger to make up for lacking that.

Ian sighed and rested his head against the leather seat as the cab wended its way through the landscaped streets toward the house. He told himself he hadn't made a decision either way about moving, but when he was tired and his thoughts got away from him, they almost always seemed to be about returning to some semblance of a normal life, and doing it in Seattle. Apparently his psyche agreed with Niall that it was time to grow up and buckle down in the real world.

A whistle broke him from his reverie. "Nice place," the cab driver said as he pulled up in the circular drive.

"It's not mine, but I'll pass along your compliment," he said.

The large house was dark upstairs, but someone had left on the foyer lights inside for him. The porch was brightly lit and welcoming, but Ian found himself suddenly desperate to be somewhere else. Somewhere with a cacophony of sounds and lights and things to focus on that didn't involve his apparent existential pre-midlife crisis.

"Can you wait just a minute?" he asked the driver as he pulled the suitcases up the front step. "I'm just dropping these off. Let me get them inside and I'll be right back."

He was sure the cab driver thought he was insane, since he'd already paid the man. Ian shrugged off the thought; he honestly didn't care what the driver thought of him as long as he waited.

He wasn't dressed for a night out at the clubs, but he did know of a place where he wouldn't stick out in his jeans and button-down shirt. He was just in time to hit the tail end of the dinner rush, and his grumbling stomach was glad for it. It wouldn't have been the first time he'd drunk his meal, but if he was turning over a new, responsible leaf, Ian figured food was probably in order before he got himself liquored up.

He left the suitcases and his laptop bag in the foyer and locked up the house, pocketing the key on its ridiculous Seattle Space Needle key chain he was certain Niall had gotten just to mess with him. The outline of it was clear through his tight jeans, and he could see Niall snickering in his mind. The spare key had been on a plain ring a week ago.

He ducked into the waiting cab, feeling oddly energized at the thought of going out as he gave the driver the address. He'd been expecting a night in with Niall, but The Weathered Mast was quickly starting to feel like a second home. Maybe he'd look for an apartment within walking distance of it. He liked the idea of having a neighborhood pub. When he found himself a job, he'd probably fit in well with the hipster jackasses who clustered outside. Ian shuddered a bit at the thought. The downside to moving to Seattle would be rejoining the workforce. He'd been out of the competitive corporate banking business for four years, and he knew he wouldn't be starting on the same rung he'd left on the corporate ladder. It was a depressing thought.

It honestly hadn't occurred to Ian it was Friday night until he walked in and spotted Luke at the bar. Ian couldn't stop a huge smile from overtaking him, even though he knew he must look like an idiot. Or a stalker. An idiot stalker? That was him, Ian Mackay.

"Back again?" Luke asked as Ian took a seat. "I figured when I didn't see you last week, you'd found a new stool to grace."

Ian preened. "You missed me."

Luke raised an eyebrow and continued to dry the glass in his hand. Ian watched as his long fingers moved the towel over the surface efficiently; it was mesmerizing. "I didn't say that."

"You didn't need to. You noticed I wasn't here. That means you noticed I *was* here the week before. So you missed me."

Luke laughed and shook his head. "I don't usually hear logic like that before someone's fourth or fifth drink. Were you pregaming it somewhere up the road?"

"Nah," Ian said, waving a waitress over. He took the menu she held out to him and nodded his thanks. "I just got off a plane, actually. I'm tired, starving, and ridiculously sober."

"Well, we can solve two of those things," Luke said. He leaned in, and Ian could smell the tang of soap on his skin. He liked that Luke wasn't wearing cologne; it made him different from most of the men Ian slept with. It seemed right that Luke wouldn't drown his natural scent in perfume. "I'd go for the poutine. Have Chrissy bring it to you with duck on it."

Ian tried not to huff in disappointment when Luke moved out of his personal space. He'd liked having him so close. A quick scan of the menu showed him that poutine was some sort of dish with french fries, cheese, and gravy. It sounded disgusting and was absolutely what he was in the mood for. Grease would chase away his exhaustion nicely.

"The menu says it comes with bacon, not duck," he said, not looking up. It was pretty upscale for bar food, though it hit the right quotient of fried and salty. It was definitely trendy enough to be the reason the hipster professionals flocked there for happy hour, though the smattering of traditional favorites like burgers and fish and chips were there to assuage the old-timers who were sitting at the bar with him.

"Yes, but if you know the cook, he'll top it with some of the shredded duck from the pancakes they serve with hoisin. That's not very good, but the duck is great," Luke said.

Ian closed the menu and put it on the bar. Luke had finished drying the glasses and moved on to tidying up. "But I don't know the cook. I only know the gorgeous bartender."

Luke laughed. "Eh, the bartender's in good with the cook. I think you'll be okay."

"You would use your standing with the cook to garner me a favor?" Ian held a hand over his heart. "I had no idea we were so far along in our relationship, Luke. Why, in Victorian England, a man vouching for another for the sake of shredded duck was practically an engagement."

"Don't fetch your dowry from Mr. Bennet until after you've tried it, but I think you'll find it's worthy," Luke teased.

Ian's heart sped up at the easy banter between them. The last time he'd seen Luke, he hadn't been anywhere near this laid-back. Tonight's flirting was far removed from the slightly standoffish way Luke had conducted himself a few weeks earlier.

"Does that make me Elizabeth in this scenario?"

Luke smirked and shook his head. "Lydia."

"Ouch. Anyway, my dowry is impressive. I think you'd like it," Ian retorted, but he was well aware his smile was genuine, not the suggestive leer he usually employed when delivering pickup lines. Tonight wasn't about trying to get into Luke's pants, though he definitely wouldn't turn down the opportunity. He wasn't going to ruin things by going full steam ahead, though. He was enjoying the relaxed back-and-forth too much. It was the same cozy feeling he got from snarking with Niall. Besides, he was enjoying getting to know this side of Luke. He wouldn't have figured him for an Austen fan.

Luke gave him an unreadable look and shrugged lightly. "I'm sure I would. I doubt anyone who's been offered your dowry has turned it down. Too bad I'm not in the market for one at the moment."

Yeah, he definitely needed to introduce Luke to Niall. They could bond over their mutual immunity to Ian's not insignificant charms. Then again, having the two of them together wouldn't do Ian's ego any favors, so setting them up was probably a bad idea, no matter how epic their bromance potential was.

The waitress chose that moment to reappear, giving Ian an excuse to manfully ignore Luke's brush-off as he ordered his meal. She didn't bat an eyelash at his request to add the shredded duck to his poutine, which sent an irrational pang of jealousy through Ian. Was this part of Luke's routine? From the surly way he'd treated Ian and everyone else the last time Ian had been in, he hadn't pegged Luke as the type of bartender who flirted and charmed for the sake of tips, but maybe he was wrong. He didn't like the idea of Luke conspiratorially sharing his off-menu ordering tips with anyone else.

"Want a beer with that?" Luke asked, completely oblivious to Ian's ridiculous inner debate.

"How about a cider? Anything you have on tap is fine." He wasn't interested in getting drunk, and Ethan wasn't there to judge his choice. He liked to take the piss when Ian ordered anything lighter than a lager.

Luke stood in front of the taps for a moment before choosing one and pulling the cider carefully. Ian liked watching the process; Luke had perfected leaving enough room in the pint glass for the foamy head without slopping it over the side like most bartenders did. He appreciated that Luke didn't rush it, even when he was several customers deep in orders like he had been the last time Ian was in.

"It's the crispest one we have on tap. Should go well with the duck. You want something a little dry and tart to cut the richness of the duck and the cheese," he said as he put it in front Ian.

"Let me guess, you moonlight as a sommelier or sous chef when you're not at The Weathered Mast then?" Ian asked. The good-natured dig was a subtle way to try to get Luke to open up and tell him what he did outside of bartending. Ian didn't want to show his hand and let Luke know he'd come looking for him the night after they'd met, so he couldn't easily bring up the fact that one of Luke's coworkers had let it slip Luke only worked on Friday nights. Ian was okay with being persistent, but admitting to stalking Luke's schedule was too creepy even for him.

Luke chuckled softly. "Nope. I'm just your run-of-the-mill bartender."

There wasn't anything run-of-the-mill about Luke, but for once Ian didn't have a glib retort at the ready. He took a sip of his cider instead, swallowing slowly to let the flavor burst over his tongue. Luke might not be a sommelier, but he knew his drinks. Ian had enjoyed the beer Luke recommended before, and he was more than happy with his cider choice.

"You're a little tenser than last time I saw you. Or is sober Ian just more tightly wound?"

Ian could have used any number of lines about how much tighter he could be wound in bed, but he surprised himself by answering honestly instead of shrugging off Luke's concern. "Too many long flights lately. My back's a little jacked up."

"I might be able to help with that," Luke said, and Ian perked up. That sounded like an invitation. He'd used the line plenty of times himself.

Luke pulled his wallet out and retrieved a card. Ian took it, disappointed when a glance showed it didn't have Luke's contact information on it. Unless Luke lived at The Mind Body Connection, which he doubted.

"It's a yoga studio," Luke said, and Ian's hopes of a night of hot, back-stretching sex evaporated.

"And yoga's going to help me how?"

"It's great for flexibility," Luke said. He grabbed the card and scribbled his name along with a date and ridiculously early time on the backside before sliding it across the bar. "This one's a Hatha class. It's one of the less intense yoga practices, so you're less likely to aggravate your back even more during it. It's really just an hour of deep stretching. Give them the card at the front desk, and they'll get you to the right place."

Ian pocketed the card. "Will you be there?"

"I never miss a Wednesday," Luke answered with a grin.

"Consider it a date."

Luke studied him for a moment but didn't get to answer before he was hailed loudly from the other end of the bar.

Ian watched Luke help a group of overexcited girls who were celebrating someone's twenty-first birthday. Luke made a grand show of mixing some bright pink drink for them, pouring it into martini glasses with a flourish that had Ian shaking his head. He held his breath for a moment when the birthday girl grabbed Luke's hand and batted her obviously fake eyelashes at him. Luke responded by reaching into his pocket and pulling out a card to press on her, and Ian's heart sank.

Luke smiled at them and served the rest of their drinks. They seemed disappointed when he didn't stick around, but the tightness in Ian's chest didn't ease as Luke returned to his end of the bar.

"That yoga class is getting pretty full," he said, aiming for nonchalant but sounding more hurt than he'd intended. Damn.

Luke looked confused for a moment, but when he followed Ian's glare down the bar to the group of girls, he laughed.

Ian wanted to be offended, but he really couldn't blame Luke. How many times had he hit on someone while out with someone else? Too often to count. And it wasn't like he was on a date with Luke. He was a customer in the bar, and Luke was the one pouring the drinks. Ian had no right to expect anything from him.

Luke rolled his eyes and pulled another card out of his pocket to slap on the bar in front of Ian. It was for a cab company. "The bar's owners have a deal with the company. They give free rides for twenty-first birthdays. I'm told it's pretty good for business; those girls will remember that ride and call that cab company again when they're out next time."

Ian bit back a grin. Instead of feeling foolish, he felt elated. "So they're not coming to yoga."

"They're not coming to yoga," Luke said patiently.

"Because yoga is a date." Ian knew he was pushing it but couldn't help himself. He blamed it on the irrational jealousy—it wasn't a feeling he was familiar with, nor was it one he wanted to get acquainted with intimately.

Luke gave him a long-suffering sigh, but he nodded. "Yoga is a date. Kind of. If yoga goes well, we can talk about a date."

Well, that settled that. Ian wasn't interested in yoga in the slightest, but he was definitely interested in Luke. It looked like Ian was going to get in touch with his inner Zen. Clare and Niall would have an absolute field day with Ian taking a yoga class as a date. Hell, Niall would be insufferable just from the act of Ian going on a date alone. He didn't date. He was not the type of guy who went on dates.

Except apparently he was—at a yoga studio, no less. He didn't even know Luke's last name, and Luke was already completely upsetting the balance of Ian's life. It was kind of exciting.

IAN DELIBERATELY didn't visit The Weathered Mast again before his yoga date. He'd been tempted to go in and see Luke during his lunch shifts, but he'd resisted. He was too curious to see if Luke would actually show up at the yoga studio, and he didn't want to scare him off. So he'd bummed around Niall and Ethan's and bothered them and spent a few afternoons at Even Keel helping out. Ian found it a lot less intimidating than it had been at first, probably because he'd gotten to know quite a few of the kids and could tell them off by name when they acted like little terrors. It made a difference.

He also hadn't told Niall about running into Luke at the bar Friday night or the date they'd planned. Part of him didn't want to listen to Niall gloat, but another, more tender, part of him was afraid the date would go badly, and he didn't want it to be something Niall poked at. So he'd kept mum about the whole thing and snuck his yoga mat into the guest room when Niall had been holed up in the library with Ethan.

Ian arrived at The Mind Body Connection early because he had no idea what he was walking into. He'd set three alarms to make sure he didn't miss the 7:00 a.m. class, and he'd almost talked himself out of going half a dozen times on the trip over. He wasn't a morning person.

He'd never taken a yoga class before, though the clerk at the sporting goods store where he'd gotten his mat and a pair of bike shorts to wear under his loose running shorts had given him some idea what to expect.

Niall had laughed himself silly when he'd walked in on Ian trying on the bike shorts, which just solidified Ian's resolve to find a place of his own to lease. Susannah's list had a few places that did fully furnished, month-to-month contracts. It was a step up from a hotel, and he'd probably be happier there than in Niall and Ethan's guest room.

The yoga studio wasn't anything like Ian had pictured. The name Mind Body Connection conjured things like hemp curtains and other hippie accessories, but the place was actually quite modern in design. The wide-planked floor provided the only warm color in the entryway; the rest of it was cool tones and metal. Frosted glass doors opened off it like spokes, and Ian was surprised to see that one of the doors was labeled "gym." Apparently Mind Body Connection offered more than just yoga. He'd have to look into a temporary membership if the yoga went well. He could run outside, but he'd been relegated to sneaking into Ethan's company gym with Niall to fit in weight workouts. It would be nice to have a place of his own to go.

"Namaste," a woman at the front counter greeted him when he made his way toward her. "How can I help?"

"I was told there was a class at seven," he said, waving his yoga mat vaguely. "Hatha or something, he said?"

Ian felt ridiculous, but the woman clearly understood what he was referencing. She picked up a binder and flipped a few pages in. "Have you taken classes with us before?"

Ian shook his head. "I'm new in town." He remembered Luke's instruction to hand the card over, fumbling for it in his gym bag. He'd had no idea if yoga studios had locker rooms or showers or how sweaty he could expect to get in a class, so he'd come prepared. He'd felt silly lugging it and the mat down the street, but he was glad he had it now. Maybe he could get a real workout in at the gym after the yoga class.

The woman's eyebrows shot up when she flipped the card over. "Interesting," she said, giving Ian a thorough once-over. She jotted something down in the binder and attached the card to it with a clip. "The men's locker room is to the left," she said, nodding at the frosted glass door that was clearly marked Men.

"The locker room has entrances to the yoga studio and the gym, so you can go right to class from there." She handed him what he assumed was a locker key. "We have a policy of no bags in the studios or on the gym floor, so please use one of the guest lockers that are located against the back wall of the locker room."

"Do I need to pay in advance?"

A smile ghosted across her lips. "No, it's taken care of. If you enjoy the class, we can get you set up with a membership when you return your key, but today is on the house. Please feel free to check out the gym or the spa area after your class if you're able."

"If I'm able? This is a beginner level class, isn't it?" he asked, alarmed.

Her smile grew. "The Hatha class isn't overly challenging, no." Before he could question her further, the door opened and a stream of people entered. "It's one of our more popular classes, so I'd suggest hurrying in to stake out a spot near the front so you get the best view of the instructor."

Ian wasn't sure if the clerk was being cryptic or if she was just odd, so he cut his losses, thanked her for the key and the free class, and made his way into the locker room. It was every bit as modern and stark as the lobby, with black marble floors and banks of birch lockers lining the walls. He could see showers around the corner and what looked like a steam room off to the side.

The key was labeled with a number, so he found his guest locker easily enough. He made quick work of stowing his things so he could get to the studio. There weren't many other men in the locker room at the moment, but Ian didn't know if that was due to most of the class being women or if he was late.

The instructor wasn't there yet when he entered the room that had been marked with the class name, but the clerk had been right—it was ten 'til seven and already the wooden floor was crowded with mats. Ian found a spot near the front and unrolled his mat, grimacing at the plastic smell. He felt out of place in his running shorts and ratty T-shirt, but Luke had laughed and shaken his head when Ian asked if he needed to invest in a pair of yoga pants. There were a good dozen people in the studio, and of the three guys, only Ian wasn't clad in black Lycra.

The two other guys stretched and chatted with the women around them. They seemed at ease, and no one had given him a second look, even though he wasn't in the standard apparel. They were also a lot more flexible than him, and while that was intriguing on several levels, it was also concerning. Ian blew out a breath and sat on his mat, resigning himself to an hour of embarrassment. Luke had said he'd be here, which was the only thing that kept Ian from rolling up his mat and fleeing to the gym.

IAN WAS about to wave and point to the space next to him when Luke breezed past and dropped his mat on the small raised platform at the front of the room.

"Sorry I'm late. Traffic," he said as he peeled off his hoodie, revealing a mouthwatering strip of stomach when the sleeveless shirt he had on underneath it rode up at the stretch. When he toed off his shoes,

Ian's pulse ratcheted up. He'd never considered himself a foot man, but for some reason seeing the light sprinkling of hair on Luke's tanned feet was titillating. It felt illicit, even though there was nothing inappropriate about the way Luke was dressed. "We'll get going in just a second. For now, center yourselves on your mats and start to reach inward. Make the commitment to be present on your mat for the next hour, forgetting the hassle of the journey to get here, the pile of work waiting for you, the bills on the table at home. Tune out everything outside this room."

Ian usually had a hard time quieting his mind, but he had a feeling it wasn't going to be a problem for the next sixty minutes. He hadn't even considered Luke might be the *teacher* for the class. He'd been excited enough at the prospect of meeting up with him outside the bar; this was a whole new level. He was going to be allowed to stare at Luke unapologetically for the next hour. Suddenly the smile the desk clerk had given him and his free admission for the day made sense. From the initial look of surprise on her face, Ian figured Luke didn't invite people often. That had to be a mark in his favor.

He folded himself into the cross-legged pose he saw everyone else adopt, but instead of closing his eyes like the rest of them, he continued to watch Luke as he gingerly made his way through the maze of mats and pulled a key off a stretchy orange bracelet wrapped around his wrist. He used it to open a door Ian hadn't noticed before, since it was paneled in mirrors like the rest of the wall. It revealed a small closet that Luke disappeared into for a moment before reappearing with a large metal rolling bin.

"Some of the stretches we'll be employing today will be more beneficial if you use a strap or a block for them. Remember we're all at different stages in our practices. Our bodies are different, and some of us will need more support in certain poses than others. There is no stigma against using these aids. Please put your hand up if you'd like one, and I'll drop one beside you."

Ian was floored by the authoritative but soothing way Luke spoke to the class. He'd never have guessed that Luke, who seemed uncomfortable talking to people behind the bar and was about as far from chatty as it was possible to be, could be so relaxed while teaching a class. It was undeniable that Luke was absolutely in his element. Ian sneaked a look around and saw that most of the class had their hands raised for one of the aids Luke was passing out. He put his up as well.

"Keep your eyes closed and start your three-part breath. Breathe in deeply. Envision the air filling your chest, and then bring it down into your abdomen. Feel your ribs expand as you hold the air in and then slowly breathe out. Keep your mouths closed; we're breathing through our noses only. Feel the heat of it in the back of your throat and envision that heat filling your body, traveling with the oxygen as it feeds your limbs. We're going to be working those muscles today, so get them energized with this breath."

Luke crouched next to Ian's mat to place a foam block and a cotton strap next to him. He lowered his voice, pitching it just for Ian. "Close your eyes. You don't need to watch what everyone else is doing; just let my voice guide you."

Ian followed the directions, surprised when a moment later he felt a warm hand between his shoulders. "Pull up through your abdomen and straighten your posture. I want a strong back here."

Ian straightened, pulling in a breath as Luke moved his hand around to the center of his chest. "Try to push my hand out with your breath."

Ian breathed in, no small feat with as breathless as the contact was making him. He felt like some sort of giddy schoolboy with a crush. It was a nice tickle in his stomach that radiated out, different from his usual full-on lustful attraction but no less pleasant.

Luke's hand traveled incrementally lower, his fingertips brushing against Ian's navel. Ian had to fight not to gasp at the unexpected touch. "Relax," Luke said soothingly, which did nothing to calm Ian's racing pulse. He wondered if Luke's teaching voice was the same as his bedroom voice; it was low and measured enough to be extremely sexy. "Keep drawing your breath in after you've filled your lungs. Move my fingers with your breath."

Ian's lungs were burning, but he obeyed, focusing on following Luke's instructions. When he felt like he might burst, Luke tapped his stomach lightly and removed his hand. "Now blow out that breath slowly through your nose. Good."

Even with his eyes closed, Ian knew when Luke stood and moved on, the loss of the heat of his body noticeable. When he spoke again to the class, it sounded like he was back at the front of the classroom.

"Finish your breath and then open your eyes and join us as we start our practice," Luke said.

Everyone was facing ahead, eyes trained on Luke. More than a few of them looked like they were appreciating Luke's low-slung sweatpants and tight sleeveless tank every bit as much as Ian was. He suddenly understood why the front desk clerk had snickered when she'd told him the morning class filled up quickly. It was obvious Ian wasn't the only one who was enjoying the eye candy.

"We all come to our mats today with different goals and needs. If yoga is your spiritual refresher, please feel free to set an intention for today's practice, whether it's to center yourself for the day, heal an area that needs mending, or anything else you wish." Luke met Ian's eyes, a bit of challenge in his expression. "Not everyone feels spiritually connected in yoga, and that's fine, too. Use this time to check in with your body and see what needs your focus. Maybe your back is strained from long hours of travel. Maybe your neck is tense from stresses at work. Take inventory and acknowledge anywhere that needs extra attention. We're not here this morning to push ourselves. Quite the opposite. We're here to energize and refuel with the help of our asanas—that's what we call our poses, for those of you who are new," he added, quirking a small smile at Ian. "If at any point during an asana anything hurts, please pull back to a rest pose. Remember that every person's practice is different, and every practice is different. Don't judge yourself based on what your neighbor is doing or even what you could do last class. We are fully present on our mats and doing what feels good for us today in this moment."

Ian wondered how much of the warning was something Luke did at the start of every class and how much was aimed at him. He was highly competitive, a trait he was sure hadn't escaped Luke in their aggressive flirtation.

"We're going to start today with something simple. Please roll forward onto your hands and knees. Keep them shoulder-width apart and try to ground yourself evenly through each point of contact with the mat," Luke said.

Ian tried to roll forward gracefully the way the rest of the class did, but he didn't have enough momentum to pull himself out of his seated pose. He swore he saw Luke's lips twitch at his failed attempt, but when he looked over to meet his gaze full-on, Luke was already looking away and moving on. Ian set his jaw tightly and tried again, almost crowing in triumph when he ended up on all fours.

"Take inventory for a moment. Are your elbows in? Do your toes feel better tucked against the mat or flat? Does it feel like your weight is evenly distributed between each limb?"

Luke dropped onto the bare wood floor next to Ian. His back formed a perfectly straight line as he squared his shoulders.

"Now that we've gotten comfortable in neutral spine, let's take that first big stretch of the day. Arch up into cat, really focusing on rounding those shoulders. Tuck your chin down against your chest to deepen the stretch through your neck, and then let's hold it instead of flowing back."

Ian felt ridiculous, but he kept his eyes trained on Luke's form and tried his best to emulate it. At first he couldn't focus on much more than how silly he must look—God, even Luke looked like an idiot, and the man was built like a dream—but after a moment he gave himself over to the stretch. His muscles protested, especially through the back of his neck and upper shoulders, where he tended to keep all his tension.

"All right, good. Now let's flow down into cow. Bow your back and raise your head, eyes to the ceiling. Send your shoulder blades back, like you're trying to make them touch. Open up your chest and feel the stretch radiate through your deltoids and pectorals."

Ian was sure his flow wasn't a quarter as graceful as Luke's, but he followed his directions. It felt almost as good, but when he risked another glance at Luke, he couldn't help but tense up. Luke was holding the position along with the rest of the class, but he looked like sex on wheels. His loose sweatpants had ridden down enough to expose the dip of his hips, and the way the position thrust his ass into the air was almost obscene.

Luke caught him looking and raised a questioning eyebrow, but Ian just winked and went back to looking at the ceiling. Hopefully they wouldn't do too many other poses that made Luke look so incredibly fuckable, otherwise Ian was screwed. Or quite the opposite, he realized. He'd watched Luke systematically shoot down every person who'd approached him at the bar, including Ian. Yet he'd invited Ian to the studio to take a yoga class with him, and he had obviously taken a special interest in Ian since he was monitoring him so closely. Ian was acutely aware he had been given a special opportunity to see the real Luke, and he didn't want to mess it up. If he hit on Luke during the class, he'd be written off as just another lecher from the bar. Ian didn't want that, so he marshaled himself and tried his best to ignore the fact that seeing Luke in the cow pose made him want to bend him over the nearest flat surface and fuck him senseless.

"Come back to neutral spine, and then sink into *balasana*, or child's pose. Try to get your belly flat against your thighs and stretch those arms out as far as they will reach."

Ian sneaked another look around and tried his best to emulate what the others were doing. It was awkward and uncomfortable, but everything had been so far.

"This is a rest pose, but that doesn't mean it isn't also a working pose. Feel your shoulder blades separate and stretch. Feel your lower back and thighs stretch. Press into the pose until you can let more air into your lungs as your torso lengthens."

A hand rested between Ian's shoulder blades. "Reach forward and get as much of your arms on the mat as you can without lifting your hips," Luke said softly. He held pressure on Ian's back as Ian moved his arms forward. "Feel the stretch here?" Luke skimmed his palm until it came to a rest midway down Ian's back. Ian fought the urge to shiver, both from the contact and the surprisingly good stretch once he'd followed Luke's instructions.

"Yeah," Ian managed.

Luke leaned in so he could whisper in Ian's ear. "You sound a little breathless. Pose too much?"

He choked on a laugh. "No. Not the pose."

Ian couldn't see Luke's expression since his head was burrowed against the mat, but he was willing to bet it was smug. "Good," Luke murmured before he stood.

"Now that we're warmed up, let's get started," he told the class.

Ian was pretty sure he was going to die.

HE MADE it through, but only just. Ian was grateful it was a sixty-minute class instead of the ninety-minute offerings he'd seen on the schedule taped to the inside of the locker room door. Thirty more minutes of contorting himself into ridiculous poses while listening to Luke's smoky-sweet voice probably would have done him in.

He'd struggled most with *shavasna,* which was supposed to be nothing but relaxation. Luke had the class lay on their backs with towels over their eyes and instructed them to let all of the tension bleed out of their bodies and allow their minds to wander. The music had softened, and all Ian had to focus on was the sound of Luke's voice guiding them through a short period of meditation. It had been anything but relaxing. Luckily, they'd all been told to keep their eyes closed until they'd come up to a seated pose to end the class. Otherwise everyone would have been treated to the sight of exactly how relaxed part of Ian *wasn't* in Luke's presence.

He'd lingered in the seated pose as everyone else had packed up their mats and left. Not only had it given Ian's erection a chance to fade, it had also provided the opportunity to finally get Luke alone.

"So the whole 'men don't wear yoga pants' thing," Ian said, breaking the ice after the last student had left.

Luke laughed. "Maybe don't was the wrong word," he said with a shrug. The sleeveless T-shirt he was wearing accentuated the way his biceps moved and flexed as he rolled up his own mat. "Shouldn't would have been better."

"The view wasn't too bad from where I was," Ian joked, which earned him a stern look from Luke.

"You could hurt yourself if you're more focused on what's going on with other people than your own practice," he scolded. Ian hoped he wasn't imagining the slightly jealous tint to the words. "Relying on watching others as a baseline is also the way to pick up bad habits."

Ian stood and moved around the room with him, helping Luke pick up discarded straps and blocks to marshal back into the bin. "Nah, I think this guy knew what he was doing. He really made the pants work for him, too."

Luke stopped rolling the bin of blocks and pursed his lips. "Marshall and Gary are both much further along in their practice than you, but that doesn't mean you should try to emulate them. Marshall has a habit of taking his pigeon too low without support, and Gary's stance is always wrong in balance poses. You'd be better off just watching me."

Ian grinned. "I was."

Understanding bloomed over Luke's face, along with what Ian thought was a slight blush. He gave himself a mental fist-pump. Luke was well armed against flirting at the bar, but he seemed vulnerable to sneak-attack compliments at the gym. Ian filed that away as important information.

"These aren't yoga pants," Luke said as he wheeled the bin into the small closet.

"Whatever they are, they definitely work on you," Ian said with an exaggerated leer.

The plain sweatpants were nowhere near as immodest as the yoga pants the other guys in the class had been wearing, but they fit Luke like a glove and were threadbare enough to dip tantalizingly low on his hips. They were more suited to a lazy Saturday in bed with breakfast and a newspaper than teaching a yoga class. Not that Ian had shared many lazy Saturday mornings in bed with his lovers, not even the three he'd had relationships with. But he'd seen enough romantic comedies to know a good outfit for it, and the sweatpants were pretty similar to a pair he'd seen on Ethan last week when he and Niall were having coffee in the breakfast nook and doing the *New York Times* crossword puzzle together.

"You're impossible," Luke said with a shake of his head. It was said fondly, though, so Ian wasn't worried he'd crossed a line. After all, Luke had technically made the first move by inviting him to his yoga class, right? Ian was definitely counting that as a sign of interest.

"I'm just making an observation," Ian said. He held his hands up innocently, but he didn't disguise his interest as his gaze traveled from Luke's hips back up to his face.

"I'd ask if you hit on all your yoga teachers, but I don't think you've had any but me."

"Ouch. Was it that obvious?"

"The flirting or the novice status?" Luke joked easily. He motioned Ian toward the door and flicked the lights off as they exited.

"I'd worry about you if it was the flirting. I've made my interest pretty obvious from the get-go," Ian said as he followed Luke to the locker rooms. The hallway wasn't quite broad enough for the two of them to walk shoulder-to-shoulder, so he couldn't see Luke's expression. His snort of laughter made it fairly clear he was amused, though. Ian counted it as a win. He liked loose, relaxed yoga teacher Luke even better than not-in-a-snit bartender Luke. They were both *miles* better than his first encounter with him, and even that version of Luke had been intriguing. He was a bit of a mystery, and Ian liked that.

Luke held the locker room door open for him and Ian passed through, admiring the way the motion made Luke's biceps bulge. The T-shirt had obviously been a well-worn favorite before Luke cut the sleeves off. It was ripped at the collar and riddled with small holes. It gaped and allowed Ian a glimpse at Luke's chest, which was every bit as defined as his arms. Ian doubted Luke maintained that kind of muscle mass through yoga alone.

He hoped Luke's locker was near his so he could confirm that the rest of him was as nicely built. Hell, if Luke's locker wasn't close to his, he'd just choose a random one and pretend he'd lost his key. Ian had been curious about Luke's body ever since he'd gotten a look at his forearms the first night they'd met; now that he knew what his arms and chest looked like, there was no power on earth that could prevent him from trying to get Luke out of the rest of his clothes.

"You did great for a first-timer. And next time you'll do even better since the poses will be more familiar," Luke said, and Ian felt a zing of victory surge through him.

"Next time? You're assuming a lot here," Ian teased.

Luke surprised him by taking a step closer and caging him against the nearest lockers. He wasn't near enough to touch him, but Ian could feel his breath against his cheek when Luke spoke. "I don't really think I am," Luke said in a low voice that went straight to Ian's groin.

Luke gave him a heated look and then pushed off the lockers. Ian wanted to grab him and pull him back, but even though Luke had been flirting openly with him, he had yet to touch Ian. He'd never pursued someone who sent such mixed signals as Luke did. It was both maddening and exciting. Ian was determined to let Luke set the parameters for their flirting, so he squared his shoulders and followed Luke deeper into the locker room, gripping his yoga mat to keep him from reaching out.

"No, you're not," Ian said when Luke stopped at the bank of lockers closest to the showers.

Luke flipped the band of his sweatpants down, exposing even more of his hipbones and a tantalizing glimpse of ridged muscle. Ian's mouth watered as Luke tugged the pants out so he could unclip the locker key he'd secured there. Ian had found it curious that the keys came with a safety pin attached, but now it was clear why. And God bless whoever was responsible for the idea, he thought fervently.

"Not really," Luke answered. He stuffed his hoodie and bag into the locker and dug out a pair of battered sneakers and some socks. "A lot of people flirt with bartenders. It's kind of expected they'll flirt back, so it's easy. And then you've got your contingent who think bartenders are easy lays and come in looking for a one-night stand."

Ian felt the tips of his ears burn when Luke swung his gaze to him at that, but Luke's lips were curved into a sly smile. Ian might have been looking for a one-night stand when he'd walked into The Weathered Mast and started chatting Luke up, but he'd abandoned all thought of that by the end of the night. No one-night stand would be worth the amount of pursuit Ian was putting into this. If Luke ended up in his bed, he'd be keeping him there for more than one round.

"I was surprised you came back after I shot you down the first night, so you got points for persistence. I had fun talking to you, even though I was in pretty poor spirits that night. I was kind of disappointed when you didn't come back for a week or two."

"Ha! I knew it. You missed me."

"I did." Luke sat on the bench and laced his sneakers. "And I never in a million years thought you'd show up at the yoga studio. I had you pegged wrong, and that was my mistake. So if you want to take another class, I'd love to have you here. And if you want to join me across the hall, I can show you around the gym, and maybe we can work out together and go for coffee afterward to get to know each other outside the bartender-customer context."

Ian knew he was grinning like an idiot, but he couldn't stop himself. There was no question now. Luke had definitely just asked him out. Forget the fact that Ian hadn't had an actual date in years, let alone one as safe as a coffeehouse. He was ecstatic. And also very sore from his inaugural yoga class.

"I'll take you up on the tour and the coffee for sure, but we'll have to see on the workout. You've already handed my ass to me once today."

Luke squinted and sized him up. "You can take it."

"You'd be amazed at what I can take," Ian retorted without missing a beat.

Luke laughed. "And this is why it took me three meetings to ask you out, Ian. God. That was terrible. I'm actually reconsidering our coffee date right now."

Ian quirked an eyebrow at him. "I tend to grow on people."

"I see. I may need a character reference before we progress past the coffee."

Ian smiled sweetly and followed Luke into the main gym. He couldn't remember having this much fun in forever. It was definitely worth a bit of muscle soreness.

EIGHT

IAN TRIED to ignore the persistent knocking on his door, but after a solid thirty seconds of pounding, he conceded defeat. "It's open!" he called.

The knocking didn't stop, and Ian buried his head in his pillow, growling his displeasure. When it became clear that whoever was outside his door didn't intend to come in on their own, he finally rolled out of bed and padded over to open it. He wasn't surprised in the slightest to see Niall standing there with two steaming mugs of coffee.

"Morning, sunshine," Niall said, not waiting for an invitation before sidestepping Ian and walking into the room.

"You could have just come in," Ian snapped as he followed Niall over to the small bay window.

"I could have, but then you'd still be in bed," Niall answered agreeably. He settled onto a cushion in the window seat and held out Ian's coffee. Ian took a sip. It was perfect, which meant Hortensia had to have made it. It must be later than he realized if she was already here for the day.

"And what if there's a reason I was in bed? I could be sick." Ian knew he was whining, but he didn't care. He was sore as hell from stacking a yoga class and a full workout. And he hadn't even had a chance to go out with Luke afterward. Luke had been called away for something. He'd offered Ian a rain check on the coffee and they'd exchanged numbers, but it had been disappointing. Ian had gone to a yoga class for the man, for God's sake! Muscles he didn't even know he had hurt. Ian rolled his shoulders, trying to dispel the tightness between his shoulder blades. It didn't work.

"You were up and out of the house early yesterday morning, so I didn't want to risk missing you today," Niall said with a frown.

"I joined a gym."

"Did you now?" Niall asked. His gaze traveled to the corner, where Ian had left his yoga mat. Damn it.

"I thought I'd try something new," Ian said lightly. He shrugged but immediately regretted it; his entire back was one big ache.

"And how did that go?" Niall looked like he was holding back a snicker, so Ian kicked him from his perch on the end of the bed.

"It went fine. Why is everyone so surprised that yoga could be a thing I do?"

"Everyone? Who else knew you were going to class?"

Ian looked down at his coffee, but he could feel Niall's interested gaze on him.

"The bartender from the other night. He invited me, kind of as a date. Turns out he's the instructor," Ian said.

Niall sat forward, his eyes sparkling. "Kind of a date, eh? Do you have any more kind of dates planned?"

Ian couldn't help but laugh. "No, but he said he's interested in getting coffee or whatever else people do on dates. He gave me his number, and I *kept it*, Niall. I'm in so far over my head."

IAN MADE up his mind not to call Luke. He'd never been one for games—at least, not games like that. Pretending to be interested and getting a number he never called, *that* was the type of game Ian played. This should-I-call-or-not crap was completely new territory for him. Ian had hoped going out for a bit with Niall might take his mind off it, but it hadn't worked.

He knew it was ridiculous, but Ian swore his phone weighed more with Luke's number in it. It was the only explanation for him constantly being aware of it in his pocket and for checking it four times in the last half hour. He thought he'd gotten away with it, but on the fifth time, Niall grabbed it before Ian could stick it back in his pocket.

"Did you just discover a new porn Tumblr or what?" Niall asked. Luckily the screen was locked, so when Niall thumbed over it to wake it up he didn't see Luke's contact information. He'd been debating whether or not he should be the one to text, though he'd managed to convince himself not to so far.

"Look at you, knowing what Tumblr is," Ian said snarkily as he yanked his phone out of Niall's clutches. "Living with a tech mogul has done wonders for you."

"Ha ha," Niall said, sticking his tongue out before settling into a pout. "I want to know what has you chained to your phone."

"A two-year contract with Digicel. Just re-upped too. Roaming here is a bitch."

Niall groaned and let his head fall into his hands. "You're such an asshole."

"I'm glad my efforts don't go unnoticed," Ian replied glibly. He felt his phone vibrate and wondered if he could check it without drawing Niall's attention. He doubted it. Damn.

If the phone had felt like a dead weight before, it was an absolute anchor now. It vibrated a second time and he nearly jumped out of his skin.

"Get me a refill if the waitress comes by, will you?" he said as he edged his chair back. It clanked into the wall behind them, and he flinched this time.

"Seriously, what?" Niall said flatly.

"Seriously, get me a refill," Ian said.

"You're going to check your phone, aren't you?"

Ian couldn't help it; he blushed at Niall's accusation. It was like he had no control over himself anymore—the clumsiness, the blushing. Jesus.

"You are!" Niall crowed, drawing looks from several other patrons. He grinned and winced, lowering his voice. "You are! I've never seen you like this. Is it the bartender?"

Ian knew when he was outmatched. If he didn't admit it, Niall would blow things out of proportion and make an even bigger deal of it than he already was. "Yes."

"Are you setting up another, what did you call it? Kind of date?" Ian's cheeks flamed hotter.

"I don't know. Someone's keeping me from checking the text."

Niall sat back and opened his hands wide in invitation. "By all means."

Ian huffed in displeasure but sat down. There was no use in keeping up the ruse of going to the restroom now. He unlocked the phone and couldn't hold back a small grin when he saw that Luke had indeed texted him—twice.

Want to work out today? Going for a treadmill run @4pm before my Ashtanga class.

Ian had no idea what Ashtanga was, but it evoked images of Luke in those hip-hugging sweats.

The second text made Ian's grin turn into a smile.

Could meet for coffee first? My treat, since I ditched you yesterday.

"Good news, I take it?" Niall drawled, and Ian flipped him off with one hand while answering the text with his other.

You're the fitness expert. Shouldn't we be drinking wheatgrass or something before a workout?

He looked up at Niall. "He wants me to have coffee with him and then go work out. I'm not convinced this isn't some sort of hard sell on a gym membership," he said drily.

Niall snorted. "This from the man who once flirted his way into convincing a tourist to sign up for a dive tour even though the guy wasn't scuba certified?"

"Why the hell was he in a dive shop if he wasn't certified?" Ian was not taking the blame for that one. "And I refunded his money when we got back to shore."

"And blew him."

"And blew him," Ian admitted. The guy had been hot. There was no shame in it.

His phone vibrated again, and Ian didn't even make any pretense about checking it immediately. Screw Niall.

You can have wheatgrass if you want, but I'm having something with enough caffeine to keep me upright.

Ian laughed out loud, and Niall leaned across the table, not hiding his interest in the slightest. Ian rolled his eyes but showed him the phone so he could read the texts.

"I like him," Niall said with an approving nod.

"Well then, I'll alert the media."

"*You* like him. We *should* alert the media," Niall retorted, and Ian kicked him under the table. "What? It's true. This is a newsworthy event. Ian Mackay is texting someone other than me or his mother. When was the last time you actually gave your real number to someone?"

Ian shrugged, uncomfortable with Niall's scrutiny, teasing as it was. Niall knew him well enough to know what he was doing with Luke was a big deal. And he also knew that Niall was trying to jolly him out of his panic about it, but it wasn't working.

"Hey now," Niall said, hooking his foot around Ian's under the table and tugging to get his attention. "Just go get coffee. He's not asking you for a major commitment, Ian. Just coffee and a workout. We used to do that all the time."

"Yeah, but I didn't want to lure you into the locker room and fuck you in the showers," Ian said bluntly.

"Uh, yes, you did," Niall answered, and Ian tried to hold a frown but failed miserably.

"Fine, but I knew there was no chance of you letting that happen."

"Now that's true," Niall said agreeably.

Ian kicked him again for good measure. At the time he'd been amused by the challenge of trying to get into Niall's pants, but he was glad it had never worked. Niall was his best friend; Ian didn't know where he'd be without him, and wasn't that a maudlin thought? Following Niall halfway across the world like an abandoned puppy was bad enough. He didn't need to have a Hallmark moment over it. Niall knew how much he meant to Ian. It wasn't something that needed to be said.

Ian's phone vibrated again, and he felt a zing of excitement as he opened the text. Teasing back and forth with Luke was almost like foreplay, but less pleasure-focused. He was surprised to find he was enjoying it.

Carl at the gym cafe confirms he can make you a wheatgrass latte. Tempted to order you one just to force it down your throat.

Ian swallowed a laugh, his thumbs flying over the keyboard to answer before he'd even thought things through.

You wouldn't have to force anything down my throat. Open invitation. Any time, any place.

Niall snickered as he read the exchange over Ian's shoulder, and Ian startled a bit when he realized he'd been so focused on texting he hadn't noticed Niall get up and walk around behind his chair.

"I thought you didn't want to scare him off?"

"I hardly think offering him a blow job will scare him," Ian said lightly, but he did feel a sense of relief when his phone vibrated again. Luke obviously was the kind of guy who took things slowly, and Ian had no frame of reference for that. Literally none. The three long-term relationships he'd been in had started up just as fast and furious as his normal one-nighters. They'd just found a reason to hang around after. Ian didn't know how to do slow.

I'll keep that in mind. Stashed my bag and heading to the coffee shop a few blocks over after I sort out a scheduling thing with the boss. Joining me?

Ian opened his mouth to make his excuses, but Niall was already paying the bill. Another thing he hadn't seen arrive. Damn. Was dating usually this distracting? How did people manage?

"Drop me home and you can take my car to the gym," Niall said after he finished signing the credit card slip.

"Who says I'm going?" he answered nonchalantly, even as he brought up a new text and informed Luke he'd be there in twenty minutes, tops.

I'll order so we have time before we hit the gym. What do you want?

"Tell him to get you a Caffé Misto," Niall said, not fooled at all by Ian's dissembling. "It's like half espresso, half milk, but it sounds manlier than a latte. And then you can discreetly add all the sugar you like."

"I don't take sugar in my coffee."

Niall huffed loudly. "Right. We have no secrets, you and I. Think what you like, but who do you think told Hortensia how to make your coffee? Me."

After some of the drunken late-night phone calls from Niall when he and Ethan hit a few rough patches after they'd moved in together, Ian wished they *did* have secrets from each other. He had no problem talking about sex, but some of the things he knew about Niall and Ethan, inside and outside the bedroom, weren't things he had any right to know.

"I don't care if he knows I like lattes," Ian said petulantly, but he texted the coffee order Niall had given him anyway. He'd never heard of it, but it sounded much better than the plain black coffee he'd resigned himself to ordering.

"Ian, we've been friends, what, almost five years? And until right now when I forced you to admit it, you wouldn't even tell *me* you take cream and sugar in your coffee. I don't even know how many bad cups of coffee you suffered through at my house before I realized you winced every time you took a sip."

"What's the big deal? So I don't want anyone to know I have a sweet tooth."

"The big deal is that you make people pry details out of you. I've never seen you open up to anyone easily, other than maybe Susannah, but that's more a reflection of the fact that no one says no to Susannah than any personal growth on your part." Niall waited until Ian had buckled his seat belt before pulling out into traffic with a lurch. "If you're going to try dating, you need to go all the way with it."

"Believe me, I'd love to," Ian said drily.

"Not what I mean," Niall said, but he sounded more fond than annoyed. Or maybe Ian's filter for reading that sort of thing was broken, because a second later Niall reached over and smacked him hard on the chest. "You have to put yourself out there. If you actually want to date this guy, you have to let him get to know you. The real you," Niall said with emphasis.

"The real me is an asshole too," Ian said ruefully.

"Yeah, but he's an asshole who takes sugar in his coffee and cares about his friends enough to drop everything to help them plan their wedding."

Ian dropped his head against the window as he watched buildings go by. "It's more than just that. I'm happy for you and Ethan and I want to help you, but I need to be here as much for me as for you. The real me was getting tired of the clubs."

It was a big confession, and Ian was so, so grateful when Niall didn't make a huge deal of it. He figured it had probably been obvious to Niall. Hell, Niall had probably figured it out before Ian had. He was wily like that.

"So don't hide putting the sugar in your coffee and see what happens," Niall said.

"He's a health nut. He's going to be disgusted."

"And then you two are going to the gym and you'll burn it off. It's two spoonfuls, Ian, not a truckload. He'll deal."

Ian was pretty sure they were talking about a lot more than sugar at this point, but he hoped Niall's advice held in other arenas, too.

"So TELL me about Asha-whatever," Ian said, working hard not to sound like he was panting as he ran alongside Luke.

Ian was in good shape and ran outside most days, but he couldn't match Luke's long-legged stride. He'd tried, but after the first mile he'd conceded defeat and bumped his speed down to a more manageable pace. Luke hadn't made any sign he'd noticed what speed Ian was running at in the first place, but Ian couldn't help but feel chagrined by not being able to sprint as fast as Luke.

"Ashtanga," Luke said easily, and Ian silently cursed him for barely being out of breath three miles into their workout. He had no idea how far Luke intended to go, but Ian was going to stick with him or fall off the treadmill trying. "It's a faster-paced class than the Hatha session you took."

That didn't sound bad. If Ian hadn't been so hyperaware of Luke during the class, he was sure he'd have gotten bored. The poses had been a bit difficult, but they'd eased into all of them and there had been plenty of time to figure them out.

"Sounds good."

Luke looked over and grinned as he sang: "Baby, I don't think you're ready for... my Ashtanga."

Ian choked. "Did you seriously just—" He couldn't finish his sentence. Luke was adorable when he was flirty. And now he was singing

Destiny's Child while running. "I can handle your bootylicious Ashtanga jelly, I promise."

He fought off a smile when Luke laughed. "You're not ready for my Ashtanga class. It's advanced. You did great in the Hatha, and if that wasn't a good fit, you could try Yin or Vinyasa."

"Do you teach either of those?"

"Nope," Luke said. He winked. Ian couldn't understand how Luke could do that without falling. He could barely run in a straight line on the treadmill even while looking forward. He kept finding himself nearly off the treads as his feet wandered. "But I could take one of the classes with you if you want."

Ian's mouth went dry at the thought of having Luke on a mat next to him during a class. It had been hot enough seeing him slip into poses in between walking around the room to adjust people or offer advice; an hour of watching Luke bend and flex would probably kill him. He'd definitely like to test the theory.

"We could probably arrange that," he said with a grin.

"I'll take a look at the schedule and text you what works for me. I think Christine has a Vinyasa class one of the mornings I don't teach."

"You and your morning classes," Ian said. He had a stitch from trying to regulate his breathing while talking and running at the same time, and he pressed a hand to his side to try to ease it.

"I work in the afternoons, and I have evening obligations," Luke said lightly. "That leaves early mornings."

"Don't try to pretend you're all Zen with the sunrise or something. I saw you suck back a venti Caffè Americano like it was manna earlier."

"Manna is food, so technically I think the word you were looking for was ambrosia," Luke said matter-of-factly.

"Oh my God, you're one of those," Ian said in mock horror.

"What, a literate coffee drinker?"

Ian grabbed the towel he'd draped over the arm of the treadmill and mopped at his face and neck. He was sweating like a pig and Luke was rosy-cheeked with a light sheen that made his skin glow. And now he had to go and be all sarcastic and intelligent. It was ridiculous. Luke was ridiculous. "A pedantic scholar," Ian retorted.

Luke's stride faltered, but he recovered easily. If Ian hadn't been watching him closely he wouldn't have noticed anything was amiss.

"I'm not."

"Pedantic? I beg to disagree, Mr. You-Can't-Drink-Manna."

"A scholar," Luke said, and Ian picked up the tension in his voice even with the rhythmic interference of their feet hitting the treadmills and the buzz of the machines and voices around them. "I just like to read things."

"Like I said, a scholar," Ian teased.

"A scholar is someone who is well educated in a certain subject. I don't have expertise in anything other than pulling a nice head on a beer and helping people master Downward Dog," Luke said. Something in the strain of his voice told Ian to drop it, so uncharacteristically, he did.

"Would you like to master my Downward Dog?" he asked instead, though the joke came off more suggestive than he'd intended since he was breathing hard from the run.

Luke accepted the drastic change of topic with an amused chuckle. "I don't see you as the type to ever heel to anyone."

"I'm versatile," Ian purred, and he mentally celebrated when Luke faltered again. He actually tripped this time, which Ian would have felt guilty about if he wasn't so pleased with himself over finally managing to surprise Luke with his innuendo.

"Are you now?"

Ian didn't think he was imagining the interest in Luke's voice. At least, he hoped he wasn't. He'd been enjoying flirting with Luke and spending time with him, but if he didn't get some action soon, Ian was going to explode. Maybe literally. He'd never been so sexually frustrated in his life.

"We could go back to your place and I could demonstrate," Ian said, and for a moment he thought the line had worked. Luke slowed his pace on the treadmill and brought it down to a walk, and Ian quickly followed suit.

"Not a chance," Luke said easily. He tapped the stop button on the treadmill and hopped off. "I've got to go get ready for class. Want to help or do you want to keep running? I don't want to hijack your workout."

Ian would have laughed if the cramp in his side had let him breathe enough for that. He'd run four miles already, and at a faster pace than he was used to. Honestly, he'd probably been done a mile ago, but he'd carried on for the sake of machismo. Working out with Luke was going to either be very good for Ian's fitness level or very bad for his ego.

"It's cool," he said casually, though he saw the way Luke's lips twitched up at Ian's eagerness to stop the treadmill and step off. "Lay on, Macduff."

Luke rested a hand against Ian's lower back. It should have been disgusting because he was dripping with sweat, but it didn't seem to bother Luke, and Ian was so starved for contact with him he couldn't be bothered to care. "I shouldn't be surprised that the Scot can accurately quote *Macbeth*."

"It's one of the most misquoted of the Bard's lines," Ian offered. He only knew that because people seemed to think it was hilarious to use the quote on him, and he found it equally hilarious to point out their mistake when they quoted it as "lead on" instead.

"It's not my favorite drama, but I bet with your accent, it sounds amazing when you read it," Luke said. It wasn't the first time someone had used that line on Ian, but when Ian looked over to call him on it, Luke looked completely earnest.

"I'd be happy to oblige," Ian answered, quirking his eyebrows so the innuendo was clear.

"You're incorrigible," Luke sighed, but he was smiling. "And I was serious."

So was I, Ian thought, but he kept mum as Luke opened a door marked Employees Only and guided him through it. A second later Ian's back was against a row of shelves and Luke's mouth was on his. The kiss was so unexpected Ian stumbled, but Luke's hand was still on his lower back. He steadied Ian by pulling him closer, deepening the kiss at the same time.

Ian was entirely unprepared for Luke to be the instigator of any sort of intimacy. He'd figured he'd have to coax and cajole his way into their first kiss, but this was much better. It only took him a moment before he relaxed into Luke's embrace, letting his weight rest on the shelves behind him and wrapping his arms around Luke for balance.

Way too soon for Ian's taste, Luke broke the kiss. He rested his forehead against Ian's for a moment before shrugging lightly out of Ian's arms and taking a step back to put some space between them.

"Don't think I'm complaining, because I am definitely not, but what prompted that?" Ian fought the temptation to tackle Luke and start the kiss again when Luke blushed.

"You quoted Shakespeare correctly," he said with a shrug.

"Really?"

Luke laughed. "No. I wanted to do that at the coffee shop, but I'm not big on public displays. This was the first convenient dark corner I could herd you into." He studied Ian for a moment before shrugging lightly. "But the Shakespeare certainly didn't hurt."

"I'll keep that in mind," Ian said drily.

"And now I really do need to get to class. Should I text you about that Vinyasa class?"

The question in Luke's words was clear. The ball was in Ian's court. After that kiss, Ian was definitely interested in sticking it out for the rest of the game. "I'm sure I'll be free. Not much on my schedule these days."

The storage room was dimly lit, but he could still make out Luke's blinding grin.

NINE

IAN'S INVESTMENT accounts were enough to comfortably support him for the time being, but he was starting to get a bit twitchy with no income coming in, enough to sit down and take a serious look at his finances. He was more hands-on with his accounts than most clients, but Ian still worked with an investment manager to handle the day-to-day practicalities. He'd had the firm send over updates so he could see where he stood and what he could liquidate if he made the move to Seattle, and he was in the process of making a risk analysis spreadsheet to look at his options.

Or at least he had been before Susannah and Clare had invaded his cozy spot in Ethan and Niall's breakfast nook.

"So give it to me straight, Scarlett. Are you going to have to start wearing the curtains?" Susannah asked, unapologetically paging through the reports Ian had spread out over the table.

"Susannah!" Clare pulled the sheaf of paper out of Susannah's hands and tucked it under Ian's elbow. "You need to respect peoples' boundaries."

"Ian doesn't have any boundaries," Susannah answered.

Since she was right, Ian let Susannah take over his laptop without protest. Clare squeaked a bit again, but Ian waved off her concern. "It's fine, Clare."

Ian could pinpoint the exact moment Susannah realized what the spreadsheet was because she let out a very undignified squeal that cut off a second after it started when she realized what she'd done.

"You've been holding out on us," she accused. At Clare's questioning look, Susannah leveled a well-manicured finger at Ian. "He's moving here."

"You're—"

Ian cut Clare's excited words off. "I'm *thinking* of moving here. What part of risk analysis is unclear? I know you recognize the formulas. Otherwise what do you do all day for Ethan?"

"Secretaries don't need to be able to read risk reports," Susannah sniffed as she paged through the spreadsheet. Ian had quite a few factors entered, comparing things like estimated income, housing costs, transportation, insurance, food—everything he could put a number value on to help him compare Tortola versus Seattle.

"Right," he drawled, unimpressed. Susannah hadn't been a secretary possibly ever, though her official title was administrative assistant. She was in charge of scheduling pretty much every aspect of Ethan's life, and she served as his gatekeeper, but even Ian knew she was no secretary. He'd worked with her a few times when Niall had needed help setting up Even Keel, and she was smart and business savvy. Anywhere else, she'd probably be a vice president. And if he didn't miss his guess, that's what she was in all but name at Ethan's company. Her designer clothes and fancy car hinted at more than an administrative assistant's salary, and Ian was sure she deserved every penny.

"You've underestimated salary in the area." Without asking, she replaced the value in the cell and moved on, tweaking numbers here and there. "Most places are going to charge you for parking, so I added that into the housing figure."

"You're making a pro and con list for moving here?" Clare leaned forward, apparently brave now that she saw Susannah wasn't getting rebuked for her nosiness.

"No," Ian and Susannah answered at the same time.

"He's doing a risk analysis for moving. Looking at things like possible income over time, housing trends, the opportunity cost of staying in Tortola versus moving here," Susannah continued. "By assigning values to things, he can plug it into a formula to show him where his best chance of future success is."

Clare leaned back, a horrified look on her face. "That's a pretty bloodless way to do it. What about the joy of living someplace? The interpersonal relationships? The cultural opportunities?"

Ian wrinkled his nose. "It's impossible to measure intangible things like that."

"Exactly!" Clare scoffed. "I can't believe you'd base a huge life decision off numbers instead of your gut."

"My gut?"

Clare held a hand against her navel and dragged it upward until her fist was sitting under her sternum. "Here. When you think about moving to Seattle, what does it feel like here?"

Ian exchanged a baffled look with Susannah. "Uh," he stalled, unsure of what Clare wanted from him.

"There's no passion in a spreadsheet, Ian. Where's your passion?"

Susannah was the first to snicker, and a moment later she and Ian succumbed to gales of laughter. Clare watched them with a tight twist to her lips but didn't say anything.

"Ian's passion is his dick, and his dick is leading him to Seattle," Susannah said inelegantly when they'd finally calmed.

Clare threw up her hands in frustration. "Honestly, the two of you—"

"I don't have one," Ian interrupted, and they paused and looked at him. "I don't. It used to be my career, but that swallowed me whole. And then it was just doing whatever felt right, living on the beach and having a bunch of meaningless sex. And now I don't know. I think I might find it here, though, which is why I'm thinking about moving."

Clare's face crumpled a bit like she was about to burst into tears or say something supportive, which Ian absolutely could not handle. Susannah was scowling at her, so he doubted she wanted to deal with an emotional Clare either. They needed help. Where the hell were Niall and Ethan? If Susannah was there, Ethan had to be home for the day. She never left the office before he did.

"Did you two come by for a reason? Not that I don't love sitting here and justifying my raison d'être with you, but I feel like we could be doing something more productive and worthwhile. Something that involves alcohol."

"They were supposed to entertain you while I changed for dinner. We have reservations at nine," Ethan said from the kitchen doorway. He was still wearing most of the suit, though Ian bet it had started the day considerably less rumpled. Ethan hadn't made it upstairs to change yet, even though he must have been home for a good twenty minutes if he'd come in with Susannah.

Ian checked his watch. "It's ten 'til. Do we need to get going?"

Niall appeared, red-cheeked and almost as mussed as Ethan. "Yeah, we'll only be a little late if we leave now."

Susannah clucked her tongue at them and made a show of shaking her head as she clacked her way across the hardwood floor in a pair of truly terrifying stilettos. "We'll be on time because I made the reservation for nine twenty."

Ethan took a step back, but Susannah grabbed him by the elbow. "That doesn't mean you have time to change," she said with a raised eyebrow. He stood still while she smoothed down his hair and finished unknotting his tie so she could pull it free. He'd already lost the suit coat somewhere along the way. "That'll do," she said after she'd fixed his collar. "I'm not letting you two out of my sight, or we really will be late."

Clare looked from Ethan to Niall, then blushed. "Did they...?" her whispered question trailed off, but from the slight widening of her eyes, Ian was pretty sure he was correctly interpreting it.

"Probably."

She coughed and flushed a little darker. Ian curled an arm around her shoulders and pulled her across the kitchen. "Clare and I are riding with Susannah."

"What? No. I haven't seen Clare in days. She's riding with us," Niall protested.

"You'll see her at the restaurant. She's already traumatized by Ethan's sex hair. Think of the damage you'll do when you can't keep your hands off each other on the drive there."

IAN NEARLY fumbled his phone overboard when Josh came up behind him and slapped him on the back as he was preparing the boat for the usual Saturday sail.

"If Niall catches you, he's going to take it away," Josh warned.

Ian didn't look up from the web page he was looking at. "He's not even on the boat."

"He doesn't need to be. He'll have a bunch of spies to report back to him in a few minutes," Josh said. "He was so pissed when he took mine, I didn't get it back for two days. Ethan had to beg him. Not that I want to know what that entailed."

Ian snickered. "While I'm sure it was a true hardship for Ethan to take one for the team on behalf of your mobile phone, I'm not dumb enough to be on it while we have kids on the boat. I'm assuming you were?"

He looked up in time to see Josh flip him off. "That's what I thought. Hey, come here. Have you ever been to this place?"

Josh was still scowling, but he came to look over Ian's shoulder anyway. "The Garage? Yeah. Why?"

Ian had met up with Luke for two more workouts over the last week, including the Vinyasa yoga class Luke had recommended. It had gone about as well as Ian had predicted; he'd nearly face-planted several times because he'd been watching Luke's ass instead of the instructor. Still, the not-dates had gone well enough Luke had suggested they get together and do something more traditional than the gym or grabbing coffee together. He'd claimed the gym and coffee dates had been his idea, so it was Ian's turn to plan something. And then he'd suggested bowling. Seriously.

"Date," Ian said with a shrug. "He wants to go bowling. I've never been, so I have no idea what constitutes a good bowling place. Does this one look okay?"

Josh laughed. "First of all, it's an alley. Bowling *alley*. I refuse to believe you didn't know that. You're just too pretentious to admit it. And secondly, yeah. That's a pretty cool place. Plus there are pool tables if you get tired of bowling. I'd get a reservation if I was you, though. It fills up fast on the weekend."

They weren't going on the weekend because Luke worked Friday nights and wouldn't agree to a date on a Saturday or Sunday. He was pretty close-lipped about why, but Ian figured Luke probably worked at the brewery or another of his seemingly endless string of part-time jobs. Luke was always reticent to talk about his jobs aside from yoga, which he would gladly babble on about for hours if Ian asked the right questions.

Their second coffee date had been little more than Luke going on and on about the different styles of yoga and his favorite poses in each of them, and Ian had been all but riveted even though he had no actual interest in yoga. Watching Luke talk about something so animatedly had made it well worth it. He lit up when he talked about yoga or literature, which made Ian eager to guide conversations in those directions whenever he could.

"How about on a Monday afternoon? Luke wanted me to find a place that was open around three."

Josh raised an eyebrow at him. It was a look borrowed directly from Niall; he was clearly a horrible influence. "You're going on a daytime date? That's serious."

"That is not serious. That is the opposite of serious. It's unserious or—" Ian was flustered at the accusation, and Josh wasn't even trying to hide the fact that he was laughing at him. "—screw you, I know it's not a word. But it's not serious. It's a convenience thing. He works a lot."

The excuse sounded weak even to his ears. Ian was no expert on dating, but even he knew seeing Luke almost daily for the last two weeks was bordering on serious, even if the two of them were only just now going on an actual date.

"Whatever helps you sleep at night, Uncle Ian," Josh teased. He caught sight of a group of kids on the dock and whistled at them sharply, raising a hand to wave. "To answer your questions, yes, The Garage is a good place for a bowling date. No, I wouldn't go through the bother of making reservations that early on a weekday. And now you'd really better put the phone away, because Niall's right behind them, and he's going to have your ass if he sees it."

Ian stuffed his phone into his pocket and hurried over to help the kids climb on board. No matter what Josh thought, Ian did take the kids' safety seriously. He was hypervigilant while they were on board, making sure everyone was safe and accounted for. Besides, having his phone out in the presence of five kids on a boat was just asking for trouble. The odds of keeping it from going overboard would not be in his favor.

He did a quick headcount, biting back a smile when he saw he had Leo again for the day. Niall switched up the groups frequently, but Ian almost always had Leo. He was pretty entertaining for a six-year-old, and his smart mouth kept the older kids in line better than Ian could manage.

Though Ian was getting better at talking to his charges and keeping order, he couldn't cut through their drama as easily as Leo could. It didn't win Leo any friends aside from Ian, but Leo didn't seem to care. At the moment he was engaged in a quickly escalating argument with a bigger boy, and Ian figured he'd better intervene before it progressed.

He clapped his hands together, marginally surprised when the fight and other chatter stopped and five attentive faces plus Josh's smirking one turned toward him. "What do we have to do before we can head out, sailors?"

Ian was a bit surprised when Leo's hand didn't shoot up. His sailing knowledge was excellent, and he was always quick to volunteer. Ian's gaze lingered on Leo, who looked sullen and more withdrawn than a fight with a fellow student would usually cause.

It wasn't the time to call him out on it, though. They had to get things squared away first, and Ian had had enough experience over the last few weeks to know any conversations with kids about nonsailing things needed to be private, anyway. So he forged ahead. "Nyah?"

"Check the sails and the rigging," she said, and Ian nodded and pointed over his shoulder. She took off with Josh, giggling at being chosen.

"Next?" Leo's hand stayed down. The boy he'd been fighting was shifting around and not making eye contact, a sure sign that while he wanted to participate, he didn't want to seem uncool by raising his hand. Ian called on him anyway. "Jason?"

"Check the radio?" Jason asked tentatively.

"Perfect." Ian beamed at him, and Jason straightened out of his slouch, a small smile on his lips. "Go ahead. Do you remember where it is?"

Jason bobbed his head and took off for the captain's chair to toggle the radio switches and test it.

Two of the remaining kids had their hands up, but Leo had stuffed his in his pockets and was studying the deck, his face pinched into a frown. Ian called on him even though he wasn't volunteering. "Leo, what else?"

Without looking up, Leo answered: "Check everyone's safety gear."

Ian nodded. "Good. We'll do that right before we pull anchor. You can be in charge of roll call. Karen?"

"Check the radar, which we already did with Niall. It's clear."

"Excellent. Greg."

Greg's brow furrowed, but a moment later, he grinned. "Look at the tide schedule."

"It's over by the radio."

He loped off to join Josh and Jason at the controls, leaving Ian with Leo and Karen. "Karen, were you listening when Niall explained what course we're plotting today?"

Niall gave the kids a mini lecture on navigation on Saturday mornings before turning them out to the boats. Karen was an Even Keel veteran. She was only seven or eight, but she'd been one of Niall's first students. It was probably time for her to take on more responsibilities and move up to more advanced lessons.

"I was," she said and squealed in delight when Ian pulled a laminated chart out of his back pocket and unfolded it, handing it to her.

"Go see Josh, and get the boys to help you plot our bearings," he said. The megawatt smile she gave him before flouncing over to the captain's chair was staggering. Even though he had no idea what he was doing most of the time, Ian was enjoying working with these kids.

That left him alone with Leo, who was still looking down at the deck. "Something bothering you, bud?"

Ian had made a concerted effort to learn all the kids' names and use them, but Leo absolutely preened when the instructors called him by a nickname, so Ian had started calling him bud or buddy instead of by his name. Even now in his sulk, Leo perked up a bit at the term.

"My mom's in town again."

Ian had read up on Leo after the first time this happened, and he was surprised she was back again so soon. Her visits didn't fit any particular pattern, but it was almost always a month or more between times Leo talked about her being there.

"Is she staying with you and your uncle?"

Leo kicked at the deck with his shoe but still didn't make eye contact. "No. My grandma. But she says she's staying this time. She's going to ruin everything."

Ian swallowed thickly. He was so out of his depth here, but he knew this was a discussion Leo needed to have, and the only one there to do it was Ian. God, he wished Niall wasn't out on the water. He was so much better at this. Even Josh might be a step up from Ian, but Leo didn't seem to open up to him as much as he did with Ian or Niall.

"How does her being here ruin things, Leo? Aren't you excited to see your mom more?" It was dangerous territory he was steering them into, and Ian knew it. The file didn't have a ton of information, but it had made it clear primary custody had been granted to Leo's uncle because his mother was an admitted drug addict who'd abandoned him when he was an infant. Volunteers didn't get details. Ian didn't know where Leo lived, or his uncle's or mother's names, for instance, but the file had enough in it to give Ian an idea of what Leo's home life was like and highlight any issues he might need help dealing with.

"I wish she'd go away and never come back," Leo said fiercely. When he finally looked up at Ian, Ian saw his eyes sparkled with unshed tears and his jaw was tightly clenched.

"Aw, bud." Ian took a breath, trying to figure out where to take things from here. "Do you want to help me do the final safety check and cast off, or do you want to talk some more?"

Leo tilted his head up, and Ian could practically see him shuttering his emotions. He still looked upset, but Leo was no longer near tears. "I want to go sailing."

"Okay, then. We'll need to talk to Niall when we get back, though. It might be good for your uncle and your mom to come in and talk to Dr. Green."

"We have."

"Well, I think it might be good to do it again, especially if things are changing. But we'll worry about that later. Let's go check the life jackets and get going."

"Aye aye, captain!" Leo shouted and saluted him, and Ian's heart broke a little at the mask he saw slip into place. All of the kids wore them from time to time—they wouldn't be at Even Keel if they didn't have a rough home life, after all. But he hated seeing Leo pretending everything was all right.

IAN SPENT Monday morning in an interview for a bank job he resolutely did not want but had felt obligated to show up for since a friend of his in the industry had arranged the contact. It was patently obvious from the get-go he'd be a horrible fit, but the guy he met was cool, and they spent a good two hours exchanging banking and investment horror stories and passing industry gossip back and forth.

Alec tucked his phone number into Ian's suit pocket when they parted ways, and Ian gave him an apologetic smile and told him he was seeing someone. It felt curiously exhilarating to say that, which gave Ian a lot to think about. Not that he and Luke had talked about dating exclusively. They hadn't come close to that topic. But Ian definitely got the feeling Luke was a one-man kind of guy, and Ian was having too much fun doing whatever this was with him to jeopardize it for the sake of a quick hookup, which is what he was pretty sure Alec was offering.

Niall told him it showed real personal growth, and Ian pretended to be offended but was secretly pleased. The two of them were picking out Ian's outfit for his date with Luke, though Niall was being less than helpful.

"You know it doesn't matter what shoes you wear, right? You're going to have to exchange them for rentals when you get there."

Ian looked up from the closet floor where he'd been examining his Ferragamos, wondering if they needed to be shined. "What?"

"Your shoes. You can't wear them at the bowling alley. You'll be renting special shoes. Have you really never been bowling?"

He honestly never had. "Renting shoes?" He didn't bother to try to disguise the horror in his voice. Who in the world would willingly put rented shoes on their feet?

Niall slid off his perch on the bed and sandwiched Ian's face between his palms. "You're so adorable."

Ian shook him off and scrambled to his feet. "You're joking about the shoes, right?"

NIALL HADN'T been joking. Ian arrived at The Garage a few minutes early, so he went in to grab a lane since Josh had warned him it filled up fast, even on weekday afternoons. Sure enough, there were rows upon rows of shoes behind the counter.

Forewarned was forearmed, so Ian had come with an extra pair of socks in his pocket that he could throw away after wearing the shoes. He'd also passed on the Ferragamos, since there was no way in hell he was leaving a pair of $500 shoes in a bowling alley cubby. By the time Luke arrived, Ian had his rental shoes on and a lime green ball picked out and ready to go at their lane. He'd been watching the people around him bowling, and it didn't look that different from boccie, just with a bigger ball and the gutter.

"You look focused. You're not secretly an internationally ranked bowler or something, are you? Am I about to have my ass handed to me?"

Ian smiled enigmatically. He was pretty sure his inexperience would show the moment he threw the ball, but he may as well let Luke wonder for now.

"Though if you were some sort of secret bowling savant you'd probably have your own shoes," Luke said, drawing a pair of stylish suede shoes out of the bag he was carrying. They looked nothing like the scuffed neon monstrosities Ian was wearing.

"You set me up, didn't you?" Ian asked, resigned.

"This isn't my usual spot, but I've been known to indulge in a few frames from time to time." Luke gave him a smug smile as he sat on the booth's fake leather seat across from Ian.

"In that case, you should probably be made aware of the fact that I have never bowled before." Ian looked down at his feet. "Also, I'm wearing two pairs of socks."

Luke laughed, delighted. "That seems like a wise course of action." He finished lacing his shoes and reached into his bag again, drawing out a bowling ball this time. "How about I go first? You can watch me this frame, and then when it's your turn I can help you if you want."

Any plan that involved watching Luke's ass in the pair of sinfully form-fitting jeans he was wearing was one Ian could happily agree to. "Be my guest."

Luke sauntered up to the desk and set up the game, chatting about how the frames were scored and giving Ian tips. It was adorable; he obviously took bowling very seriously.

"So you know the basic premise now, right?" Luke waited until Ian nodded before taking his ball out of the return and holding it aloft. "There are darts on the floor to help you line up your shot. Use them as a guide and just let it go."

It looked a lot more complicated than that, from the way Luke ran up to the end of the lane and raised the ball behind him. He let it go with fluid ease, kneeling slightly so one leg was bent under the other, and Ian held his breath as he watched the ball spin flawlessly down the polished wood until it cracked against the pins at the end. They scattered in every direction, all of them ending up on their sides.

"That's a strike," Luke said, grinning. He hopped down off the slightly raised platform and grabbed Ian's hands, pulling him up. "Think you can do it?"

"If I say no, will you help position me?" Ian batted his eyelashes dramatically, drawing a laugh from Luke.

"Do you actually not know how to bowl or is this just another one of your attempts to get my hands on you?"

"Does it matter?"

Luke handed Ian the lime green ball. "Nope, not a bit."

"Well, then let's save my pride and say it's just a lure to get you to touch me."

Ian stepped up to the mouth of the lane and Luke cozied up behind him to get him into position. "Your instinct is going to be to try to get that ball down the exact center of the lane, but the ball is going to naturally curve, so you need to take advantage of that and aim a bit off center."

He ran his hand up Ian's raised arm, and Ian shivered at the contact. "So the motion is like this," Luke continued, guiding Ian's arm slowly until the ball was out in front of them. "You want to bring it down in a smooth motion."

He trailed his hand along Ian's side and briefly skated it over his hip before he stepped back. Ian found it hard to concentrate on throwing the ball with the phantom warmth of Luke's palm lingering on his ass, but he mimicked Luke's odd step-hop and brought his arm up, remembering to release his fingers just in time.

It rolled straight into the gutter and slowly made its way toward the pins until it disappeared at the end. Luke, the bastard, was bent over laughing when Ian turned around. He stopped when he saw the scowl on Ian's face. "Everyone gutters on their first try. You'll get the hang of it,"

Luke said. When Ian's ball popped out of the return, he held it out to him like a peace offering. When Ian took it, Luke surged forward and pressed a quick kiss on his lips. "Consolation."

Instead of leaving it at that, Ian leaned in and kissed him again, this one longer and a little deeper. "Motivation," he said with a shrug when Luke raised a brow at him.

Ian's next attempt didn't go any better. Neither did the next three. By the fourth frame, Luke had two strikes and a spare, and Ian had a small crowd of onlookers who hooted and whistled whenever he threw the ball. At least he'd kept it in their own lane this time; he hadn't been so lucky with the second shot in their third frame; the ball had sailed right past their lane and into the one next to them. Sadly, it hadn't knocked any pins down there, either.

"You have a fan club," Luke said when Ian slumped into the seat next to him after yet another pair of gutter balls that had been roundly cheered. "They like you."

"It's schadenfreude," Ian said with a pout. "They like how much I suck at it, not me."

"Ian," Luke said, shaking his head. "It's a bachelorette party. Trust me, they probably don't have any clue what the score is. It's four o'clock, and they're drunk off their asses and catcalling the hottest guy in here."

That got a snort of amusement out of Ian. "You think I'm hot?"

"Like burning," Luke said flatly. He snorted when Ian stuck his tongue out at him. "Of course I do. You're ridiculously attractive. And funny, and a little sweet when you're not being a dick. And you're also really, really bad at bowling."

Ian tilted his head, considering Luke's words. "That's fair."

"Like how you agreed to go bowling with me even though you'd never tried it before and it meant rented shoes," Luke said. He kicked at the shoes, and Ian's lips twitched up into a smile.

"In the spirit of full disclosure, I didn't know about the shoes until right before," he admitted.

Luke chuckled. "But you still came."

"I did."

Luke leaned over and kissed Ian gently. "I'm enjoying our date."

"The date sucks, but I'm enjoying you," Ian said, and even though it sounded like a total line, he meant it.

"I almost canceled on you," Luke admitted, and Ian tried not to find the bashful way he looked down when he said it cute. "I had all kinds of family drama this weekend and this week isn't stacking up to be much better. But I'm glad I came."

They hadn't discussed their families much, so Ian didn't know what to say to that. He grabbed Luke's ball out of the return and thrust it at him instead. "Go rub my nose in my failure some more," he said, smacking Luke on the ass when he took the ball.

The resulting cacophony of shouts and whistles from the nearby group of women was startling. Luke turned around and shot him a look over his shoulder that Ian had no trouble reading: it was smugness. Ian was surprised when Luke ambled back to the booth and leaned down to give him a thorough kiss, which only amplified the catcalls from their audience.

"Just wanted to make sure they knew who you were here with," Luke said with a wink before he sauntered back to the lane.

"I don't think that deterred them in the slightest," Ian said when Luke came back. He'd had his first gutter ball of the afternoon, and Ian hoped it was because he'd been distracted by the kiss. "If anything, it gave them ideas. The tall one has been talking about taking us *both* home."

Luke laughed. "I'm not into sharing."

Ian coughed. "Ever?"

"Is that a problem?" Luke tilted his head quizzically.

"Probably not," Ian answered honestly. He enjoyed threesomes, but they weren't a deal breaker. Though he didn't want to rule anything out, especially since he and Luke hadn't had sex yet.

"Probably not," Luke echoed, his lips quirked into a grin. "Good to know where I stand," he joked.

"Oh, we can stand, sit—hell, we can swim, for all I care. I'm not picky and you're very flexible. It's a good match. I see a variety of sexual positions in our future."

Luke brought a hand up to cover his face as he laughed. "I'm not quite sure what to do with you."

"Like I said, I'm not picky," Ian teased. "A fact I'm willing to demonstrate at your command."

"On that note, I have to get to work," Luke said, and Ian slumped onto the bench in exaggerated defeat. "You knew I had to go early. Plus, even if I didn't, I'm not going to sleep with you yet."

Ian perked up. "Yet?"

Luke looked like he was already regretting tacking that onto his statement. "We'll see."

"You can't take it back! You're thinking about having sex with me," Ian crowed a bit too loudly. The bachelorette party cheered.

"At this moment I can definitely say I am not," Luke said, rolling his eyes when the women booed.

"Don't worry, I'm working on it," Ian shouted in their direction.

TEN

AFTER THE third time Ian walked in on Niall and Ethan in a compromising position around the house, he resolved to find a place of his own. Since he didn't know where he'd be working—or even if he'd be able to find a job and stay for sure or not—he targeted fully-furnished places that offered month-to-month rents. The risk analysis he and Susannah had done came down firmly in favor of moving to Seattle, though Ian wouldn't rule out Susannah stacking the deck to achieve her desired result. It was okay, though, because the result had pleased Ian; it was clearly his desired result as well.

Things were finally starting to move a little faster with Luke, but Luke resolutely refused to invite Ian back to his place. As much fun as making out with Luke was—and it was, Ian hadn't enjoyed something as simple as kissing this much in a long time—Ian was more than ready to move things along. Luke had alluded to having a roommate who didn't allow him to have men over, but he'd cut off Ian's rant before he'd been able to get up a good head of steam. The only thing Luke would say was that it was a complicated situation, but he swore up and down he wasn't married or living with a significant other, which were the two main reasons Ian could think of that would explain Luke's reticence about having him over.

He was more than willing to have Luke come to Niall and Ethan's, but Luke was gun-shy about that as well. So that, paired with Luke's weird work schedules, meant they hadn't had a chance to move past some very heated make-out sessions. They'd spent the last two weeks hanging out at the gym and going for coffee and the occasional lunch when Luke could spare the time between jobs. And Ian had visited Luke enough times at

The Weathered Mast that a few of the waitresses had written his name on the barstool he usually used.

Plus Hortensia had started giving him searching looks over breakfast, and Ian had enough practice reading his mother's judgmental looks to know what those meant.

It was time for him to find a place of his own.

He thought he'd been subtle about it, he did. Ian knew Niall would be offended if he moved into a hotel room, but he was hopeful finding a semipermanent place might make Niall happy. Both Niall and Ethan had been extremely vocal about their insistence that Ian stay with them until he found a job. Ian appreciated their hospitality, but he wasn't accustomed to living with anyone, and being in their pockets was just too much.

When Susannah texted him a list of addresses, Ian didn't question it. She'd seen his spreadsheet, after all, so she knew his budget and God knew her preternatural ability to read people had probably given her everything she needed to know about his preferences, too.

He googled the first one, not shocked to find it was an upscale apartment complex not far from Niall and Ethan's. He rolled his eyes and dialed Susannah as he looked up the other two.

"I'd go with the second one on the list if I was you," she said without preamble when she picked up. "The first one has a dog park, which means putting up with shedding mutts in the elevator, and the third one has a playground, which means an abundance of kids. The second one is a solid choice. It has a pool."

"Frankly, I'm surprised you haven't already forged my signature on a lease," he said with a snort. A quick perusal of the websites left him with the same impression as Susannah's—the second one seemed the way to go. The building was a converted factory, and the apartments were loft-style. There were a lot of clean lines and a minimalist design, plus the pool had a deck that would be prime real estate for watching his dogless, childless, and probably ridiculously hipster and attractive neighbors read *War and Peace* on Adirondack chairs and frolic in the state-of-the-art saltwater pool.

"They want first and last month's rent. I don't care for you enough to pony that up," she said drily. "I have a lease ready to go. It's a three-month term with the option to buy. Most of the units in the building are owner occupied. It's past time for you to be out on your own, baby bird."

She could be frustrating as hell at times, but no one could ever doubt Susannah's efficiency, Ian marveled. She apparently took his silence for approval, because she barreled on without waiting for him to speak. "It's not furnished, but that shouldn't be a deal breaker. I have the number for a place that rents furniture short-term, or you could just suck it up and admit you're going to stay, and either have your furniture shipped from Tortola or buy new. I'd recommend buying. Freight shipping from the island is going to be horrible."

Ian knew that all too well. He'd left most of his furniture in storage in Los Angeles when he'd moved to the Caribbean, but he'd taken a few large pieces, like his bed. It would undoubtedly have been cheaper just to buy new, but he'd been attached to the bedroom suite.

"Do I at least get to go see the place in person, or am I just supposed to send you a cashier's check?" He'd already made up his mind this was the place for him, sight unseen. If it's what Susannah recommended, it would be what he chose. He didn't want to inflate her ego any more than it already was and admit that, though.

"The real estate agent is expecting you at two today. Bring the check with you. I'll text you the amount."

"And they're okay with renting to someone who doesn't have a job? I thought that was a pretty standard requirement with rental companies."

"You'll be leasing directly from someone who works here."

"And you just happened to hear about it and know someone who was looking. How convenient," Ian teased. He had no doubt Susannah had engineered the sudden availability. "What poor schmuck did you oust from his apartment?"

Susannah scoffed. "One, it's a condo. Two, Brett just closed on a house in Bellevue, and he moved out three weeks ago. I happened to hear his place was about to go on the market, and I persuaded him to rent it to you for three months instead. It's a win for both of you. The market is soft right now; odds are he'll be able to bilk whoever buys it in a few months—probably you, by the way, because it's gorgeous and exactly your style—out of more money for it."

"You're kind of an evil genius. Has anyone ever told you that?" Ian didn't try to keep the admiration out of his voice. Hell, he was tempted to buy the place outright just on her recommendation. Renting for a few months was more sensible, though, and Ian knew it. He could probably swing buying the loft, but he'd have to liquidate a lot of investments he'd rather hang on to, so renting it would be.

"Are you going to be there when I show up at two?"

"Of course I am. You're taking me to lunch after you sign the paperwork," she said.

"You mean you're actually going to let me sign the lease instead of just forging my signature? That's uncharacteristic."

"Your attitude sucks," she sniffed.

"So does yours."

Susannah laughed. "See you at two."

HE SHOULD have known Niall was up to something the moment he suggested going out, but Ian wasn't exactly at the top of his game after spending all day stuffing envelopes and calling donors about Even Keel's fundraising gala.

"Joe and Ethan are going to a Marlin's game, so I figured you, me, and Clare could go out for dinner and cocktails," Niall said.

Niall's idea of a good night with friends usually involved pizza, beer, and his living room, so that was Ian's first clue he was up to something. The second came forty minutes later when Niall pulled into a parking lot that looked extremely familiar.

"The Weathered Mast. Really?" Ian asked, too amused to fight it. It was Friday night, after all, and that meant there was a good chance Luke was working. Ian had planned to see him again after Niall and Ethan inevitably wandered off to do a crossword puzzle together, or whatever couples did after they got married, so it wasn't a big deal.

"You seemed quite taken with the scenery last time you visited," Niall said innocently, though Clare snorting with laughter gave the game away. Niall glared at her. "Subtle."

She shrugged. "Like he didn't know what you were up to the moment you stopped the car."

"*He* is right here, and yes, he did. He also thinks speaking in the third person is creepy and requests that we get out of the car and get a drink to end the awkwardness," Ian said.

"Because going into a bar where you took a picture of the bartender's ass the last time you were here isn't going to be awkward at all," Niall snarked back. He unfastened his seat belt and got out of the Jeep, though, so Ian counted it as a win.

"The last time I was here, I had an iced tea and a chat with a lovely waitress whose ass, while delectable, was not something I cataloged for posterity," Ian said with a prim sniff. He hopped out and held Clare's door open. He took her hand and helped her stand even as she started laughing.

"Posterity," she chuckled, and Ian winked at her. He ignored Niall, even though he'd seen him rolling his eyes. Clare grinned at him and then slung an arm around Niall. "Posterity. Posterior. It's funny."

"I got it, I just didn't want to encourage him," Niall said. His lips were quirking up at the corners in a fight not to laugh; as much as he liked to pretend that Ian's puns were painful, Niall enjoyed them. Or maybe he didn't; either way, they got a reaction out of him, so Ian made a point of going for the worst possible pun whenever possible.

"Don't lie. You love me and my puns," Ian teased.

"I tolerate your puns because I love you," Niall corrected.

"Whatever," Ian said breezily. He held the door open for Clare and Niall, letting them walk in first. He took advantage of being last to lag in the doorway, his gaze skimming the bar area until he found the man he was looking for. Luke was in the same uniform as the last time Ian had seen him, but he looked flustered and a bit too disheveled for the early hour.

"Do they serve food at the bar or should we get a table?" Clare asked.

It wasn't terribly crowded yet; it wasn't even eight o'clock, and from previous experience, Ian knew it would probably stay fairly empty for another hour or so. Plenty of time for them to enjoy a leisurely dinner in one of the booths and then move to the bar so he could flirt with Luke.

"Let's get a table," he suggested. He didn't know if Luke had seen them come in or not, but he was careful not to look over at him again.

Niall's eagle eyes never missed anything, Ian knew, and from the way he elbowed Ian in the ribs as they hailed a waitress and followed her to an empty booth, that included Ian's feigned disinterest.

"Is that your bartender?" Clare asked after the waitress left. She made no attempt to hide her scrutiny.

"Yes. Would you like to take out a billboard? Maybe invest in a neon sign? There's a reason I usually don't bring you two along when I go out on the pull," he said lowly.

"That is such a lie. He's lying," Niall told Clare conversationally. He didn't look up from his menu. "He used to drag me out on Tortola to help him scour the bars for fresh meat."

Ian rolled his eyes. "I never needed your help."

"That is also a lie," Niall said. He put the menu down with a thump and pointed an accusatory finger at Ian. "How about the time I saved you from getting your ass handed to you by that woman's husband?"

"To be fair, he wasn't her husband. Nor was she wearing a ring."

"He was her fiancé, and they were getting married the next day! And she did have a ring. A very large, very sparkly engagement ring you couldn't have missed if you were standing on the moon," Niall said sourly.

"Like I said, he wasn't her husband. And an engagement ring is *not* a wedding band. Totally different," Ian said. It was easy to be flippant about it now, but it had been heart-stoppingly terrifying when the woman's fiancé was hauling him out of the bar by the scruff of his neck and looking murderous.

Niall had saved him by following them out and then rounding on Ian like a jealous boyfriend, screaming at him and calling him every name in the book. He'd caused such a scene the fiancé had left Ian in Niall's capable, vengeful hands, apparently appeased by Niall's browbeating as much as he would have been by the physical beating Ian was sure he would have received if Niall hadn't intervened.

"Does Ethan know half of Tortola heard you shrieking about my inability to keep my cheating cock in my pants, by the way? You were in pretty rare form that night. It was Oscar worthy."

"Ethan knows my interest in your cock is nonexistent. And yes, I told him about that."

"How does something like that even come up?" Clare leaned forward curiously, her eyes alight. "It's not like you and Ethan sit around and talk about Ian's exploits, right?"

"Everyone's interested in my sexploits, darling, didn't you know?" Ian drawled, laughing when Niall picked up his discarded menu and bopped him over the head with it like he was chastising a disobedient dog. "Two for two, Niall," Ian crowed, unrepentant. "You smiled at that one, you did. You know you love my puns."

"I'm not even going to acknowledge that." He ignored Ian and turned to Clare, who was giggling uncontrollably now. "Funnily enough, it came up while we were bailing Ian out of another ridiculous situation. Literally. As in, going to Tahoe to *bail him out of jail*. Ethan asked me if that was the sort of thing I had to do for Ian often, and I told him about all the times I had to save Ian from a thrashing on Tortola."

Clare sized Ian up. "I never pegged you as a criminal. Interesting."

"Criminally handsome," he answered, preening.

"Criminally stupid, you mean," Niall said with a huff. "Drunk and disorderly with a lewd conduct charge tossed in for good measure."

"Who knew it was illegal to have sex in a bathroom? Nevada has some strange laws."

"It's illegal to have an electromagnetic wave generator here in Seattle," a new voice said.

Ian's head whipped up, and he couldn't contain his smile when he saw Luke standing at the edge of their booth with a tray of beers.

"Is it, now?" he asked, turning toward the end of the table so he was facing Luke. He heard Clare titter behind him but didn't care.

"Yup. I'm not sure what it is and I don't know what I'd do with one, but knowing I can't own it makes me kind of want one anyway," Luke said with a wink. He handed Ian a bottle with a familiar-looking label and put two more on the table for Niall and Clare. It was from the microbrewery Luke worked at, but a different flavor than last time.

"New batch?" Ian asked as he tilted the bottle so he could read the label.

"Pumpkin ale. 'Tis the season," Luke said with a grin. "Or at least, it will be the season soon. 'Tis almost the season?" Luke tilted his head in consideration. He looked so serious Ian couldn't help but laugh. Luke shrugged. "Anyway, these are from our test batch. We're trying to get some feedback before we bottle the rest."

"Our test batch, eh? Still maintain you're just a bottler?" Ian teased.

It was hard to tell in the dimly lit bar, but Ian was pretty sure Luke blushed. "I may or may not be more involved than I let on when we first met," he said, and Ian laughed. There was a lot that Luke played close to his chest. Even after several more dates and their now-usual gym trips, Ian knew he was only starting to scrape the surface with Luke. "This one's my concoction. I'll bring you David's next. It's a lot hoppier and has apples and cloves. You're definitely going to like the pumpkin better."

"Are we, now?" Ian asked, amused.

"Well, you will. Niall might like the other one. He likes his beer on the bitter side." He turned his megawatt smile on Clare, the one Ian recognized from sitting at the bar when Luke harmlessly flirted with women. "I'm Luke. I don't think we've met."

Luke knew Niall? What the hell? Before Ian could latch on to that, though, Clare started babbling.

"I don't like beer. It's full of corn syrup and GMO corn. Not that I think *your* beer would contain GMOs. I mean, if it does, that's your choice, obviously. The non-GMO grains are more expensive and a lot of small breweries can't afford them. I'm sure your beer is great. I mean, you look like a nice man, and you obviously know Ian and Niall, and they're good judges of character. Well, Niall is, sometimes Ian—" Ian stepped on Clare's foot, not hard but with enough pressure to make sure she didn't vibrate out of her skin. "My name is Clare."

Luke brought a fist up to his mouth and coughed, but Ian could tell he was hiding a smile. "Nice to meet you, Clare. And you're right, a lot of beers do use GMO grains. At Hop, we try to use locally sourced ingredients whenever possible, and our preference is for non-GMO products. The pumpkin ale has none in it, and I don't think David's does, either. I can bring you something else from the bar, though. What are you drinking?"

It was Clare's turn to flush with embarrassment, and Niall snickered as he answered for her. "Clare said she wanted margaritas tonight. With a mix that is certainly full of high fructose corn syrup and tequila that is not locally made nor ethically harvested."

Luke didn't bother trying to hide his laugh this time. "We make our own margarita mix here, so you're safe on that account. No high fructose corn syrup," he said, eyes twinkling. "I'll send Julie over with one in a minute. I need to get back."

Ian didn't let up on Clare's foot until Luke was a safe distance away. "Seriously, Clare?" he drawled.

"Shut up," she said without looking at him. She was staring at Niall with something that bordered on glee. "You know Ian's hot bartender. He greeted you by name," Clare gushed. "This is totally fate at work. We all think we live in our own bubble, but really the universe pushes and pulls us whichever way it wants. I feel very good about this, Ian. It's like meeting the bartender was woven into your soul's tapestry." She turned to Ian, clutching his arm. "He uses non-GMO grains in his beers. If you don't date him, I'm finding someone else to set him up with. We can't let that one get away."

Ian spared a moment to give her a sour look before ripping into Niall. He liked Clare, he did. But sometimes her New Age hippie crap was too much, especially when he was already in the middle of a crisis.

"You recognized his ass when I texted you, didn't you?" Ian accused. He felt unaccountably stung. Why had Niall let him go on and on about Luke if he'd known him all along? And more importantly, why hadn't Niall said something earlier or offered to set the two of them up? Had he not thought Ian was good enough for Luke? They obviously knew each other more than just in passing, from the way Luke had spoken to him.

God, was that jealousy he was feeling? Ian was horrified. He was *jealous*? Of Niall? It was ridiculous.

Niall was looking distinctly uncomfortable, which under other circumstances Ian would enjoy being the cause of. Right now it just intensified the feeling of something he'd label betrayal if he didn't know better. Ian had no frame of reference for these feelings, and he didn't like it.

"One, yes, I know Luke. He has a *name*," Niall said, looking at Clare in distaste. He turned to Ian, and his expression softened, which made Ian wonder what he must look like. Was his shock and hurt showing on his face? He certainly hoped not. "And two, I didn't say anything because you seemed genuinely excited about him. I didn't want to get involved and have you pull back and claim I was meddling."

That made a lot of sense, Ian realized. The surest way to make him run the other direction would have been for Niall to set them up on a date. Niall was craftier than he gave him credit for. Ian was a little proud.

"But after I went back and saw him again, you didn't stop me from going on and on about him," Ian whined. "And you could have warned me he was a yoga instructor. I was completely blindsided! That was just cruel."

Niall laughed and held up his hands placatingly. "That one isn't on me. I didn't know he teaches yoga. I only knew he works here and at Hop."

"And don't think I didn't notice how you dodged the original question. How *do* you know him? This doesn't seem like the kind of place you and Ethan would regularly haunt."

Niall's gaze flashed down to the table and back up again, and Ian thought he looked nervous and distinctly guilty. "That I can't tell you."

Ian was sure his eyebrows were practically in his hairline. "What?"

"I can't say." Niall met his gaze, his eyes serious. "Don't push on this, Ian. I'd tell you if I could, but I can't. You'll find out soon enough, I'm sure."

Well, that sounded ominous. Niall had been in Seattle less than a year and didn't have a huge circle of friends. How would he know Luke? "Can I ask Ethan?"

Niall's lips twitched. "You can certainly ask, but he's not going to tell you either." He leaned forward conspiratorially. "You could do the unthinkable and just ask *Luke*, you know."

Ian huffed out a laugh. He actually hadn't thought of that. It was the simple answer, and it gave him an excuse to talk to Luke. A win-win, though he was apprehensive after how secretive Niall was making it.

"Fine, I will. We're going out for a scull tomorrow morning before lunch shift. I'll ask him then."

"Scull?" Clare asked, confused.

"Rowing," Niall answered before Ian could. "Our Ian is a world-class rower. He was on Yale's heavyweight crew team."

Ian laughed, deciding to let Niall steer the conversation away from how he and Luke knew each other. He'd find out soon enough, after all. That didn't mean he was going to let Niall get away with his cloak and dagger routine unscathed. "You say that like you know what it means."

"I do!" Niall said, his eyes crinkling at the corners as his smile returned. Ian grinned back.

"You can't tell a rudder from a rigger." He gestured in Niall's direction and leaned toward Clare. "I took him out once on Tortola. It should have been an easy row, half an hour tops. We were out for nearly an hour and a half because Niall couldn't get a decent catch with his oar to save his life. Literally. If our lives had depended on a quick getaway, we'd have died out there."

"I had a horrible teacher," Niall muttered, and Clare snorted.

"Excuse you, you had a fabulous teacher. I still don't understand how you failed to grasp concepts ten-year-old kids took to with ease in my classes."

"You used to give rowing lessons? Maybe you should add those at Even Keel, Niall," Clare said.

"I would in a heartbeat if I could get Ian to commit to staying."

Ian waved the comment off. "Don't try to butter me up. I'm mad at you."

"You're going to feel really stupid for being mad at me when you find out why I'm not telling you," Niall answered calmly, not taking the bait.

Ian resorted to sticking his tongue out at Niall, which of course was when Luke rejoined them. He huffed at Ian's display of immaturity but slid into the booth next to him anyway.

"I was on the early shift today, so I'm out, but I wanted to stop and say good-bye." He pressed a kiss against the side of Ian's mouth. It was frustratingly chaste, but the fact that he'd done it in front of Niall had Ian's stomach turning over with butterflies.

"Join us?"

"Can't," Luke said with an apologetic smile. "I had to barter half my soul to get my shift traded tonight because I have somewhere to be, but I didn't want to duck out without telling you."

"We're still on for tomorrow, right?" Ian tried to sound casual, but from the way Niall snickered, he was sure he'd failed. Damn it.

"Wouldn't miss it," Luke said cheerfully. "I'll meet you at the boat rental place at ten. Should I bring a lunch?"

Ian was planning to bring a picnic for the two of them, but he was damned if he'd admit that in front of Niall. "Nope, no need."

Luke pulled out his phone to check the time. "Gotta go." He gave Niall a quick wave. "Niall, nice to see you. Don't let Ian get you in any trouble tonight." He bobbed his head at Clare. "Nice to meet you."

"The pleasure was all mine," Clare said. She looked so smug, Ian figured she'd be purring if she were a cat. "I have a feeling we'll be meeting again. I've never seen Ian so smitten."

Smitten. He was going to kill her.

Luke laughed. "I don't think smitten would be a good look on Ian."

"Oh, it definitely is," Clare answered. She jumped when Ian kicked her under the table.

"I hate you both," Ian sulked when Luke disappeared.

Clare looked at him thoughtfully. "You should consider a kava kava supplement for your mood swings, Ian. I think it could do you a world of good."

"Or maybe I should consider getting new friends. That would probably do more good," Ian snapped. God, what was he doing? Did he really seem smitten over Luke? Ian wasn't even sure what that meant. Maybe he should cancel on Luke before things got out of hand.

"Stop," Niall said, and Ian looked up at his stern tone. "You're sitting there second-guessing yourself. I know you," he continued when Ian opened his mouth to protest. "Look, it's not like you've got the market cornered on emotional baggage. Remember what you told me when I was so torn up about my feelings for Ethan?"

Ian shook his head. "It's different."

And it was. Ian worrying about getting invested in a relationship with Luke couldn't be compared to Niall feeling guilty about falling for Ethan. Ian was aware enough to know he was a self-centered prick. His hesitation was about not getting hurt. It was nothing like Niall's struggle to get past the loss of his partner, Nolan. Ian remembered the first time Niall had told him about Ethan. It had been impossible for Ian to really understand, since he'd never been in love with anyone other than himself.

"Of course it's different," Niall said "But that doesn't mean the same advice doesn't apply. You told me to give myself permission to feel whatever I was feeling. You have no idea how much that helped me. So I'll tell you the same thing. It's okay to be scared you're falling for him."

"I'm not falling for him," Ian protested.

Niall scowled. "Semantics. That you *could* fall for him, then."

Ian sighed. He didn't flinch when Clare laid a hand over his on the table and patted it soothingly, like some sort of maiden aunt.

"Just enjoy the time you spend together," Niall said. "Whatever happens, happens."

IAN DIDN'T have any idea what to pack for a picnic, so he did what any self-respecting man would do: he lounged casually in the doorway to the kitchen where Hortensia was cleaning up after breakfast and gave her his most charming smile.

Ian had spent more than a few mornings hanging out in the sunny kitchen while Hortensia banged and clanked around. He knew she hadn't liked him much during his first few visits, but they'd actually had some good conversations and gotten to know each other since he'd come to stay with Niall and Ethan. It probably helped that he hadn't shown up at breakfast lately still buzzed from the night before, like he had on previous trips. She'd been genuinely happy to help him plan Niall and Ethan's wedding, and things had been a lot easier and more casual between them because of it. It wasn't totally out of the realm of possibility he'd drop by just to see her, but he could tell she wasn't buying it from the distinctly unimpressed expression on her face.

"Niall told me about your date. He was very impressed you were making lunch for your gentleman. He said it was a sign of how serious you were about him, and you'd turned over a new leaf." She raised an eyebrow at him. "I'm making chicken sandwiches for you. You're lucky. I have a few slices of that chocolate cake you like so much left."

Ian grinned sheepishly and ran a hand over the back of his neck. He'd been planning to beg her to help him, but he should have known Niall would have gossiped all about his date to her already.

"I don't suppose you know Luke, do you?" It was a long shot, but if Niall knew him, it was possible Hortensia did too.

"I do not. Though Niall showed me the picture you took of him." She pursed her lips and shook her head. "You need to be more respectful."

He sincerely hoped his mother never met Hortensia because they were eerily similar. Together, they'd be a force of nature. If they teamed up on him, he'd probably be married with a picket fence and a Labrador retriever in no time.

"It was a joke," he muttered, chastised.

"You need better jokes," she said sternly but ushered him into the kitchen anyway. He couldn't be in that much trouble if she was letting him have his customary spot at the breakfast bar. He'd been banned from the kitchen for a lot less than a distasteful photo.

Everything Hortensia made was excellent, but it looked like she was really outdoing herself for the picnic spread. Chicken sandwiches sounded simple, but they actually seemed to be some sort of complicated wrap. There was also a bowl of her homemade potato salad and a container half-full of sliced strawberries. She picked up her knife and used it to wave Ian over toward the coffee maker before she resumed slicing.

"Get yourself some coffee and talk to me about this man. Niall said he has you tied up in knots. I like him already."

Ian wrinkled his nose at the description. "I am not tied up over him. Nor am I smitten, which is what Clare said last night. To Luke's face." Ian shook his head and brought his coffee back over to the breakfast bar so he could slide onto a stool and watch her assemble lunch.

Hortensia clucked her tongue sympathetically. "Clare is a wonderful woman, but she's lacking in social graces," she conceded.

"Clare is crazy as a loon and completely unfit for polite company," Ian groused. He dropped his frown when Hortensia put a bottle of creamer next to his cup. Ian always took his coffee black in social situations, but thanks to Niall, Hortensia knew his dirty secret: he actually preferred to douse it with the kind of disgusting french vanilla creamer that was by no definition actually cream. The first five ingredients were chemicals Ian couldn't even pronounce, and they were delicious.

"Everyone feels that way about their family," Hortensia said matter-of-factly.

"So she's family now?"

Hortensia put her knife down and gave him another serious look that was so maternal, it made Ian squirm. "You like to pretend you don't need anyone, but you do. And you have people who care about you, Ian Mackay. Including Clare."

Ian didn't know when he'd managed to become so thoroughly adopted by Niall's friends, but it had definitely happened. He'd never been the sort to have many close friends, so it was an adjustment. The learning curve was steep, but Ian was slowly getting the hang of having people he could, say, drop in on to ask to make lunch for him and a date.

"She's still crazy."

"Of course she is. It's all the supplements," Hortensia said with a rare grin.

No one Clare cared about was spared the horror of her custom herbal concoctions. Niall had given in long ago and dutifully downed the array of vitamins and herbal remedies Clare gave him, but Ian wasn't a convert. That didn't stop her from bringing him foul-smelling smoothies and bottles of unmarked capsules, but nothing was going to convince him to take medical advice from someone as batty as Clare, Ph.D. or no.

"What did she give you?"

"A ginko supplement to prevent senility. Senility! I'm sixty-four!"

Ian laughed. Only Clare would be ballsy enough to present Hortensia with something like that.

"And you don't look a day over twenty-nine," he said smoothly.

She sent him a dark look. "I already told you I'd pack some of the cake in your basket. You don't need to try to charm me."

"Try? Does that mean it isn't working?"

"Your brand of charm didn't work on me when we first met, and it doesn't work now," she said tartly.

"Maybe you should be taking that ginko after all. I am inherently charming. This may be the first sign of decline," he said dramatically.

She swatted him on the arm with the lid of the plastic container she had just filled with strawberries. "Watch it." She secured the lid and tucked the container into a wicker picnic basket sitting on the center island behind her. "Now tell me about your date. The only thing I know about him is that Niall approves."

"Well, if Niall approves, I'd better just go out and get the wedding bands now," Ian said sarcastically.

She leveled a flat look at him as she assembled the sandwiches and wrapped them in parchment paper.

Ian sighed. "He's around my age, I'd say. Probably younger but I wouldn't think by much. He's a bartender at The Weathered Mast about a mile from here, and he teaches yoga. He also works at a brewery sometimes, so I'd say he's a little flighty, not ready to commit to a career."

"Like you," she put in.

"Yes, like me. He's a little taller than me but a lot more built." Hortensia quirked an eyebrow at him like she knew what it cost Ian to admit that. He was pretty vain, but he had to give credit where credit was due. Ian worked hard to keep his body in shape, but Luke worked harder. Some of the strength and balance poses Ian had seen him do were mind-boggling.

"And he's funny and smart. He doesn't watch television but devours all sorts of books. I think I've seen him with six or seven different ones in the two weeks we've been dating."

"Clare's right. You're smitten," Hortensia said.

Ian felt his cheeks heat. "I don't even know what that means. I'm not the type of guy who gets smitten."

She gave the picnic basket she'd just packed for him a significant look. "You're not the type to make a romantic lunch and go for a date in a park, either."

"I didn't make the lunch," he said petulantly.

She gave him a censorious look, and he caved. God, she was almost worse than his mother. "Thank you for making me a lunch to take, Hortensia. I do appreciate it."

She smiled and handed him the basket when he slipped off the stool and came around the counter to give her a kiss on the cheek.

"Just bring the basket back and put it in the hallway closet. And you can tell me all about the date the next time we have coffee," she said slyly. "And I won't tell Niall you didn't make it yourself. He was on cloud nine about it this morning."

Ian could just imagine. Niall had been insufferable before he'd found out Ian's plans for today; now that he had proof Ian was turning into some sort of Nicholas Sparks protagonist, he was never going to shut up.

"I'm not going to feed him strawberries on a riverbank," Ian muttered as he took the basket.

"I should hope not. I packed forks," Hortensia said with motherly disapproval.

"I just—never mind," Ian said, shaking his head. He knew he wasn't some sort of closet romantic, and that was good enough. Let Niall think whatever he wanted. He kissed her cheek again. "Thanks for this. I need to get out to Green Lake to get the boat from the rental place."

Hortensia walked him out, and Ian slid the basket in the trunk of Ethan's Lexus CT. He hadn't decided if Seattle was the type of city he needed a car in. Ian had leased one when he'd lived in Los Angeles and bought one to drive around Tortola, but that was because public transportation wasn't great in either place. Here in Seattle it seemed to be a viable option, though he didn't really want to mess around with a huge picnic basket on a bus.

Luke was already at the boat rental building when Ian wandered up. He looked adorable standing there with his back up against the rough-hewn fence that cordoned off the boats from the walkway, his head ducked as he read a battered paperback.

The enormity of this being an official date suddenly weighed heavily on Ian. He'd actually planned a date, something romantic and involved, not just spur-of-the-moment drinks or an invitation to take a stroll on the beach as a thinly veiled screen for casual sex, which was much more his speed. It was a lot more than agreeing to meet up at the gym or spending an afternoon bowling. This was a date, with intent. He was wooing Luke.

For a moment, Ian was tempted to go back to Ethan's car. What was he doing? He wasn't the type of guy who packed picnic lunches. Hell, he wasn't the type of guy who had meals with his "dates" at all.

Before he could talk himself into turning away, Luke looked up and spotted him. His smile was incandescent as he straightened from his slouch and tucked the paperback into his back pocket, and Ian's doubts fled. He still had no idea what he was doing with Luke, but his worries about being in over his head were gone. That, in and of itself, should be worrying, but Ian pushed those thoughts aside and resolved to take Niall's advice and enjoy the day. It was a picnic, not a marriage proposal.

"Ready to get out on the water?" Ian asked, and was surprised he didn't have to fake enthusiasm. Maybe Clare was right about the kava kava. His moods were all over the place lately.

"I think so. I'm ready to give it a shot at least," Luke said with a grin. He surprised Ian by reaching out and twining their fingers together for a tight squeeze in greeting. Ian stepped closer when Luke let go, hoping for a kiss, but Luke was already turning toward the rental building. "I've been out in a canoe before, but I'm sure this is different. I expect you to give me the primer."

Ian trotted forward and grabbed the door before Luke could, holding it open for him with an exaggerated bow. Luke laughed and shook his head. "Gallant."

"Always," Ian said with an answering grin. Flirting was easy and familiar, and Ian felt like he was back on even ground. As long as they kept things light, Ian was in his element. He guided Luke to the counter with a hand against his lower back, pleased when Luke didn't shy away. Ian had never been with anyone who was less inclined to casual touches than Luke, though he'd never waited this long to sleep with someone either, so apparently he was in for a whole string of firsts with Luke.

The scull Ian had reserved was already at the dock, and they were both quiet while Ian arranged Luke in it to his satisfaction and pushed off. The first few strokes felt like cutting through molasses until Ian's muscle memory kicked in. He relaxed into position with a contented sigh. He'd missed this.

"All right. First things first: you said you've canoed?"

"A few times. It's not like I'm an expert," Luke said as he flailed in the water with his oar.

"Yeah, that's pretty obvious, actually," Ian teased. He yelled when Luke flicked the paddle toward him, dowsing him with cold water. "Okay, I deserved that. But it's good you don't know what you're doing. Fewer bad habits for me to correct."

They settled into an easy banter as Ian instructed him on the proper way to hold the oar and guided Luke through the strokes. After a few minutes of splashing around to get his bearings, they were making decent progress across the lake.

"This is a lot harder than it looks," Luke said when they finally hit their stride. It wasn't a race pace by any means, but Ian loved the burn in his arms and the pull in his back as they cut through the water.

"Everyone seems to think rowing isn't an athletic endeavor, but it's actually the hardest sport I've ever done. It works your entire body. You'll be feeling this tomorrow for sure."

Luke snorted. "I feel this might be payback for your first yoga class."

"Damn straight it is," Ian answered. He'd barely been able to walk the day after that.

"It'll get easier the more you do it," Luke said. "Yoga, I mean. That is, if you're planning to come to more of my classes."

The tone was teasing, but Ian could read between the lines and see the statement for what it was. Luke was feeling him out to see if Ian was interested in seeing him more seriously.

"I liked the Vinyasa class we took. Think I'm ready for your Ashtanga yet?"

Luke hummed a few bars of "Bootylicious" under his breath before shaking his head. "Not yet."

Ian took it as the challenge it was meant. "We'll see."

Luke laughed. "Will we, now?"

"I'll tell you what. If you can lift your arms over your head without wincing tomorrow morning, I'll keep taking the Vinyasa class until you deem me ready for yours."

"Deal," Luke said without hesitation. He picked up speed, and Ian wondered if he'd just been played. Luke was wearing a long-sleeved T-shirt, but Ian had gotten a glimpse of his shoulders and biceps in the yoga class. He noticed Ian watching and gave him a sharp smile. "Rowing machine. Best full-body workout in the gym."

"Well, shit."

"This is definitely harder, though," Luke conceded. "Tell me where you learned to row."

Ian shook his head good-naturedly. "I should have known. You don't get arms like yours in Downward Dog."

"If you feel Downward Dog in your arms you're doing it wrong," Luke said with a pointed look. "So, rowing? Where'd you learn?"

Ian shrugged, which wasn't easy while maintaining his strokes. "I started when I was a teenager in Boston, then I did the whole collegiate rowing thing through undergrad at Yale."

Luke whistled appreciatively. "You went to Yale?"

"You sound so surprised. I was at Yale for undergrad and graduate school," Ian said drily. He was used to it. Most people were shocked when they found out he had an MBA from an Ivy League school. Ian couldn't say he blamed them. He wasn't exactly the poster boy for overachieving the way most of his classmates were. Or at least, he wasn't anymore. He'd been on that track before he left everything for Tortola.

"I'm not surprised, I just—" Luke's tone was apologetic, but he stopped talking when he saw that Ian was laughing. "Okay, fine. Yes. I'm surprised. And impressed. I didn't go to college. It must have been a great experience."

The unvarnished longing in Luke's voice sobered Ian much more effectively than the splash of cold water that accompanied it when Luke tipped his oar at him again.

"It was. That's not to say it was all rowing meets and keggers, but I had a good time," Ian said. He was more than a little shocked that Luke hadn't gone to college. He was unusually well read and articulate, though Ian knew that didn't necessarily mean anything. Hell, he *had* gone to college and he hadn't read a few of the books he'd seen Luke carting around. That meant nothing. "Do you wish you had? Gone to college, I mean. Not that you couldn't go now if you wanted."

"Ian, I work three jobs, and I have—" Luke faltered, like he was swallowing his words. When he started again, there was a false brightness to his tone. "It would have been nice to go, but it wasn't in the cards for me. I wouldn't rule it out eventually, but I have no idea what I'd study. It seems like a waste of money if I don't have a plan."

Ian was sure that wasn't what Luke had been about to say, but he left it. It was clearly a touchy subject. "So you have no idea what you want to be when you grow up either, huh? I've been looking for a job, but I can't narrow down what I want to do."

Luke laughed, as Ian had hoped he would. "So the job search isn't going well, I take it?"

Ian had been looking in earnest the last week, but he hadn't found anything that excited him. He was lucky he had a financial cushion that made it possible for him to live well while he decided what he wanted to do, and suddenly he felt guilty for how thoughtless he'd been when talking about financial matters with Luke. He'd known things must be tight for

Luke—no one worked as many jobs as Luke did just for fun—but he hadn't thought about how callous and privileged he probably came across.

"It's going," Ian hedged. "It's been awhile since I looked at what the options were in my field."

"Which is something with money, I know. You probably gave me details, but I'm afraid I tuned them out." Ian stole a glance at Luke and saw that he looked as chagrined as he sounded.

"Most people do. Money isn't something anyone other than us financial types likes to talk about. I'm not sure what I want to do, at any rate. Probably something managing money, but I'm open to other things."

"Careful, or you'll end up like me. Jack of all trades, master of none." Luke's tone was light, but Ian could hear the self-deprecation in it.

"Not everyone can multitask like you, I'm afraid. I'd go crazy with your schedule."

Luke laughed. "Who says I haven't?"

"Good point. You are, after all, out on a date with me," Ian said, giving Luke an exaggerated leer.

"And I'm even enjoying it. A sure sign of psychosis," Luke answered.

It probably was. Ian wasn't a nice guy, and Luke most definitely was. Ian wasn't sure what Luke saw in him, but he supposed that didn't matter as long as Luke was having a good time. Maybe dating wasn't as scary as Ian had been making it out to be.

AS IDYLLIC as sculling around the lake with Luke was, they were on a timeline. Luke had to work at two, which meant they needed to move things along. Ian had been having such a good time, he was reluctant to bring the boat in and start their picnic, but he didn't want Luke to have to go into work without eating first.

"I'm having a hard time imagining you owning a picnic basket," Luke said when Ian put it down in front of him on the grassy patch they'd staked out.

"It's borrowed."

"I'm curious to see what you made. I've been obsessing about it since last night," Luke admitted. "I just can't see you in the kitchen, no matter how hard I try."

Ian felt a thrill steal through him at Luke's confession, even if it wasn't some sort of wild sexual fantasy, which Ian would have preferred.

"I was definitely present in the kitchen during its preparation," he said, keeping a straight face.

"Present but not actively involved?"

Ian's composure broke, and he laughed. "You'll thank me for it. I'm every bit as horrible in the kitchen as you probably imagined."

"So Niall made it?"

"His housekeeper. Niall's just as culinarily inept as I am." Ian set out their food, keeping his tone casual. "Speaking of Niall, he wouldn't tell me how he knows you."

Ian wouldn't have noticed the way Luke's posture relaxed unless he'd been looking for it.

"Niall's a good guy," Luke said cryptically. He toyed with the strawberries on his plate, flattening them with the tines of his fork.

"And so are you, and Niall said when you were ready to tell me how you two know each other, you would, so you can stop murdering the poor fruit now."

Luke looked down at his plate as if he was surprised to see anything on it. He dropped the fork against the porcelain with a clink but didn't say anything.

"I don't know him all that well. He's more of an acquaintance," Luke said stiffly.

Ian hoped he hadn't ruined the date by bringing up the apparently taboo subject. Luke's evasiveness only heightened his curiosity, but he was sure Niall would have told him if the reason for the secrecy was something bad. What that would be, he wasn't sure. After all, Niall had bailed him out of jail and sent care packages full of condoms, both of which were things he hoped Niall wouldn't mention to Luke if Luke asked him the same question about how he knew Ian.

They ate in silence, and afterward Ian rose to his knees and started piling things back in the picnic hamper. He didn't want to end their date on a sour note, so he let the dozens of questions he had about Luke and Niall go.

"Think we have time for another quick tour of the lake before you have to go?"

"I'm not sure that 'quick' and 'you' belong together when you're talking about me in a boat," Luke said.

He offered Ian an easy smile, and Ian figured he was forgiven for pushing him earlier. "Maybe it's my teaching. I took Niall out last year, and he was worse than you."

Luke stacked their plates and gathered up the cutlery and other odds and ends. "I don't think my inability to distinguish right from left can be pinned on you."

Luke's coordination out on the water had been pretty abysmal. "But you do just fine in your yoga classes."

"That's because I'm the one calling the instructions in class."

"So you need to be in charge? I guess you're more coxswain than sculler."

Luke pursed his lips in amusement.

"The coxswain is the person who mans the rudder and steers us on a scull. They're the most important person on the boat because they call the shots. They're in charge of setting the tempo and pace for the rowers and keeping the boat moving in the right direction."

Luke tilted his head as he considered it. "So you're calling me bossy?"

"What is it with you and the implied name-calling today? No, I'm not calling you bossy. Or well, I guess I am. But bossy's not the right word. Authoritative, maybe?"

Ian was used to being the aggressor in his relationships, and he was certainly filling that role so far between him and Luke. But there was no denying that, for all his aggressiveness and initiative, Ian was ceding control of their interactions to Luke. The weight of that was lost on Luke since Luke didn't know him very well, but it was very clear to Ian.

"Fair enough," Luke said agreeably. God, he *was* bossy, even if he didn't realize it. Ian kind of liked it. How messed up was that? "So, another tour around the lake and then some cake?"

"Aye aye, captain."

ELEVEN

IAN HAD never looked for a job before. Internships had fallen into his lap in college, and he'd had several prominent money management firms bidding for him before he'd formally graduated. When he'd moved to Tortola, he'd just mentioned casually to friends that he was thinking about picking up some work and offers had come in from the dive shop and boating school.

He'd never thought about how lucky he'd been. A week into his searching, Ian was beginning to realize finding a job was a full-time job in and of itself. He'd dusted off his resume, and Clare had helped him creatively frame his time on the island so it didn't look like he'd just taken a four-year vacation from his life, but that had been the easy part.

There were plenty of positions he was qualified to do, but none of them sounded remotely interesting. Ian's background in investment banking gave him a solid foundation to branch out into other types of finance, but he hadn't found a single listing that didn't sound like he'd be selling his soul.

He'd fit in well with the corporate investment banking world, but he'd hate every moment of it. Ian knew his personality was well suited to such a cutthroat business. He was observant and had very little compunction about being manipulative to get what he wanted. He was good at it, but that didn't mean it was something he necessarily enjoyed.

"Well, what would you do if you weren't dependent on the money and could do anything you wanted?" Niall asked over coffee the second week of Ian's job search. Even though he'd moved out two days ago, Niall's kitchen was still Ian's go-to place for comfort.

"Live on an island and lead scuba tours?"

Ian batted away the piece of toast Niall threw at him, but a glare from Hortensia had him scrambling out of his chair to pick it up off the floor. "Mature," he said to Niall as he tossed the toast back on his plate.

"Short of going back to Tortola—which I know you don't want to do so it totally doesn't count, you sarcastic ass—what would you be doing? Would it be something in finance at all? You could always go back to school, you know."

Ian shuddered. He'd enjoyed college, but he had no desire to repeat it. He couldn't imagine term papers and group projects at his age. Besides, there wasn't anything he was interested in other than investments and banking. He just hated the atmosphere of the financial industry. "I guess I'd do what I'm doing for Even Keel, but get paid for it."

Niall perked up, which made Ian slump in his seat. "No, I'm not going to work for Even Keel full-time," he said before Niall could speak. "One, you can't afford me. And two, we'd kill each other within a week if we worked together."

He could tell from the gleam in Niall's eyes that he wasn't put off by that in the least. "You're right, I can't afford you. I can't afford *myself* right now. We're barely making ends meet. Let's brainstorm."

Ian thunked his head on the table and instantly regretted it. It was covered in crumbs from their toast fight, and they were sharp.

Niall took Ian's laptop away from him and started scrolling through the e-mails from the headhunter Ian was working with. So far she'd turned up a lot of jobs someone with Ian's background would be perfect for, but nothing that really caught his interest.

"Mutual fund manager."

Ian didn't bother raising his head. "Pass."

"Director of the accounts payable department at a major midsize corporation."

"Double pass."

"Zookeeper," Niall offered, and Ian flipped him off without looking. "No? But shoveling shit is such a big part of the financial industry, I figured you'd fit right in."

"Screw you."

"Okay, how about this. Vice president of charitable contributions. Candidate must have an MBA and at least five years of experience in corporate investment finance and be comfortable managing a small staff."

Ian looked up. He'd specifically asked the headhunter to keep an eye out for nonprofit fund management jobs, but she'd laughed and told him those never come through her office. They were almost always filled internally. "Which nonprofit?"

"It's a corporate job. The administrator will be responsible for managing the company's charitable endowment and allocating the funds to charities that apply for support." Niall had closed the laptop and was looking over Ian's shoulder. Ian turned and saw Ethan leaning against the breakfast bar.

"Susannah brought me an interesting proposal last week. She audited our accounting department and found it was spending more time dealing with charitable contributions than had been allocated in Cloud Technologies' budget. Apparently, diverting those responsibilities into a new department dedicated to that will save me quite a bit of money in the long run," Ethan said. "Know any out-of-work former hedge fund managers who have big hearts and a soft spot for charitable work, Mack?"

Ian scowled. "Oh, fuck you. You don't need to create a position for me. I'll find a goddamn job eventually. Jesus."

Ethan threw back his head and laughed. "Yeah, Susannah was right. You'll fit in perfectly with the management team. Look, whether or not you take the job, Cloud Technologies will be hiring someone to head up the new department."

Ian wanted to be outraged, but he also didn't want spite to be the reason he passed up the best opportunity he'd had since moving to Seattle. A corporate position where he could manage funds but also oversee charitable contributions did sound like the perfect job. Even though he'd told Niall in no uncertain terms that he didn't want to work for Ethan, he had no problems with the company or working under Ethan. He just didn't have any interest in the type of work Cloud Technologies did. Helping invest and direct the charitable endowment Ethan had set up for the company when it had hit it big, though, was a different story. All he had to do was swallow his pride and let Ethan do this favor for him.

His pride wasn't worth much, anyway. "Do you have a short list?"

"Are you saying you're interested? Because if so, then yes. A very short list," Ethan answered, all trace of his teasing smirk gone. No matter what, he was a good businessman. Ethan wasn't the type to hire based on sentimentality. "We've been talking about making this move for a while. Susannah's audit was the kick start we needed to prove it was fiscally the right decision. I've had a number of people contact me with recommendations, and honestly none of them are nearly as qualified as you. I'd hire you in a heartbeat if you wanted the job."

Ian was a fan of facts and figures. He liked to see hard data and have all the information before he made any major decisions. The last time he'd leaped before he looked, he'd landed in Tortola. But this felt right. Right job, right time, right place. "Just one sec," he said, pulling his phone out. He shot off a text to Susannah, who must have known they were having this conversation right now because she answered in less than a minute.

Yes or no? he texted.

Yes.

She was even more analytical and pragmatic than he was; if Susannah was on board, so was he.

"Yeah. Let's do it," he told Ethan, and a moment later Niall was whooping and draped over his back.

IAN KNEW it made him an asshole, but he was starting to get seriously frustrated with his lack of progress with Luke. They'd been on several more official dates, but Luke never let things progress past a few heated kisses. He also still resolutely refused to let Ian come back to his place, which was frankly becoming alarming. Ian's imagination was running away with reasons why Luke wouldn't want him in his apartment.

Ian planned to turn the tables that night. He'd officially moved out of Niall and Ethan's place a few days ago, and the loft was all set up. All he had to do was get Luke to agree to come by, and then maybe the two of them could finally put an end to the sexual tension that was practically tangible between them.

Ian had spent the evening on his customary barstool keeping Luke company on an uncharacteristically slow Friday shift. It had given them plenty of time to chat, and Ian had been dropping ridiculous pickup lines all evening, getting sillier and sillier as the night went on. Luke had been into it for a while, but as soon as Ian asked him to come over after his shift, the mood changed and Luke suddenly became somber.

"We need to talk."

Those weren't the words Ian had been hoping to hear.

"This isn't something I have personal experience with, but Hollywood would have me believe that nothing good ever starts with that phrase, especially after I've just asked you to come back to my place. Which, FYI, was definitely code for 'to have sex,'" Ian said drily.

Luke snapped his bar towel at him, catching Ian on the shoulder. "Don't be an ass. And I know why you were inviting me over. You're not subtle." He gave Ian a stern look before walking away to pull a beer for a customer who'd tipped his empty pint in his direction. "And for once I'm not shooting you down flat. I know you'll find this hard to believe, but I would like to have sex with you at some point. There are things we need to talk about first."

"My safe word has always been jasmine. There was a brief period where I had to rethink that because I was spending a lot of time in strip clubs, and I don't know if you know this, but about a decade ago, Jasmine was a pretty common stripper nom de guerre, as it were, but—"

"Goddamn it, just stop. Not everything is a joke, Ian. I need to have a fucking conversation with you. Can you be serious for one minute?"

Ian's throat went dry at the anger in Luke's voice. He'd seen him annoyed and irritated before, but never angry. He'd wondered if anything could completely throw Luke off his stride; it looked like he'd finally found something.

"I can," he answered, dropping his flirty voice. He picked his phone up off the bar and shot off a text. Luke put a hand to his breast pocket when his phone buzzed in response. "My new address. Should I look for you after your shift?"

Ian pulled out his wallet and left enough money to cover his drinks and a nice tip on the bar. Luke usually comped him at least a few, but Ian was feeling petty, and he knew the move and the dismissal it implied would hurt Luke.

"Ian—"

Ian waved off the apology he knew was coming. The earnest expression on Luke's face bordered on painful. Ian wanted to wallow in his hurt feelings for a bit without seeing Luke's side of things. "You wanted to see me serious? This is me being serious, Luke. I'll see you in a few hours. Text me if you decide not to come by."

Ian felt guilty by the time he reached the doors, but he pushed through them and out into the chilly air without looking back. This was why he avoided relationships. He didn't want to worry about how his actions affected another person. He didn't want someone else to have the ability to upset him with a few careless words. He'd spent his childhood and adolescence under a constant stream of verbal abuse from his father, and even Luke's relatively gentle rebuke had feelings Ian would rather never remember resurfacing. He hadn't realized he was still so sensitive, but Ian supposed that was probably because he'd never let himself get emotionally invested with any of his lovers before. The list of people who could hurt Ian Mackay was notably small, though apparently it had grown by one at some point, unnoticed by Ian.

Damn it.

He shoved his hands into his pockets and trudged down the street. It was late enough the streets were mostly empty. Usually Ian either drove or took a cab, but his new loft was a lot closer to The Weathered Mast than Niall and Ethan's. Besides, the cool night air felt good against his overheated skin. The walk would do him good.

He'd calmed down completely by the time Luke got there. He looked exhausted, and Ian felt a twinge of guilt at making Luke's late night even later by insisting he come over after work if he wanted to talk. Then again, he wasn't going to make it easier on Luke if Luke wanted to break up with him. Hell, Ian hadn't realized they were dating exclusively until Luke had uttered those words that people the world over seemed to dread.

"Let's get this over with," Ian said with a resigned sigh as he let Luke into the loft.

"Be still my heart," Luke said sarcastically. "Your greetings never fail to make me feel cherished."

"You said you wanted to talk. You're here. Talk." Ian closed the door and leaned against the frame.

Luke frowned, but after a moment his expression cleared. "Oh, no. I'm not breaking up with you. I actually meant we have to talk."

Relief coursed through Ian. "You could have said that."

"I did!"

"You said it with your Serious Adult Voice," Ian accused.

"I don't have a serious adult voice," Luke groused. "And stop getting me off topic. I need to tell you something, and it's a big deal, all right? Stop joking around for once and let me talk."

Ian mimed zipping his lips and held his hands out placatingly, motioning Luke to continue. Luke sighed but complied.

"I've had a really good time with you. I don't usually let myself do things like go to the movies in the middle of the day or have a picnic just because. I go to work, I come home, I read, I go to work again. But you've changed that. In a good way," he added quickly when Ian opened his mouth to protest. Ian pressed his lips together and nodded.

"You asked me how I knew Niall last week, and I really appreciate that you didn't push me to answer you. It reassured me a lot about who you are that you didn't press or automatically assume the worst," Luke said. He took a breath and held it for a moment before continuing. "I know Niall from Even Keel."

He looked at Ian, but Ian didn't know what kind of reaction Luke was looking for. Given Luke's general cluelessness about sailing, he'd dismissed Even Keel as a possibility, but it wasn't shocking. Niall didn't know many people in Seattle outside his and Ethan's circle of friends and the people he'd met through the sailing club. There were an impressive number of people on Even Keel's volunteer roster, even though the majority could only give a few hours a month, if that, and most of them were not on the sailing side of things. There were plenty of things Even Keel needed done to stay afloat, so to speak, that had nothing to do with sailing.

"It's—there isn't an easy way to tell you this. Especially since I know I should have said something weeks ago when we had our first date. But we were having so much fun and I didn't want to ruin it."

Luke paused to take a breath before meeting Ian's eye again. "I don't have a roommate. We never go back to my place because there's someone there I didn't want you to meet, until now."

Ian was still baffled, and Luke sighed. "You want to know how I met Niall? I met him at orientation, just like all the other parents. My kid goes to Even Keel," Luke said bluntly, and Ian's stomach dropped. "You going to say jasmine?"

Despite his shock, Ian couldn't help but smile. "Not safe wording, no."

Luke's smile was so genuine, it made Ian's throat ache. "Really? Because this is a lot."

"I've never been with someone who had a kid. It's a shock. But it's not too much, not right now at least. I'll let you know if that changes."

"You haven't met him yet. He can be a handful," Luke said ruefully. Ian had imagined all sorts of things, but a kid had never been one of them.

"A handful, huh?"

"Yes," Luke said with a snort. His expression turned serious before he spoke again. "I didn't want to sleep with you until you knew about him, and I was afraid if I had you alone in a place it was socially acceptable to jump you, we'd never talk."

"And look at us now, two grown adults who both know you have a kid, here all by our lonesome in the privacy of my new place," Ian all but crooned.

The corners of Luke's eyes crinkled as he laughed. "I bet you say that to all the guys you bring back here."

Ian knew he was using sex as a distraction from Luke's very startling confession, but the tension in the room was unbearable. They were both in desperate need of a laugh or an orgasm, and Ian wasn't above trying to introduce some levity into the situation to get both. Luke having a kid didn't change things so drastically Ian didn't still want this with him, whatever "this" was.

"I do, actually," Ian answered, pulling Luke farther into the room. The rental furniture had been delivered yesterday, and Ian wanted to see if the couch was as comfortable as it looked. He sat and tugged Luke down next to him, their hands still joined. "Is it working?"

Luke studied him, a hesitant look on his face. "Are you sure? I just—if you aren't interested in dating me, I'd understand. But I don't want to have sex with you if you're going to walk away."

Ian should have been used to such bald honesty from Luke, but having Luke lay his cards out like that still took him by surprise. "I'm not the kind of guy who makes promises, but I'm not walking away right now," Ian said. It was the best he could do. Who knew what tomorrow or next week would bring? He had nothing to judge this against. For all Ian knew, he'd lose interest as soon as they started having regular sex. Or maybe Luke would be the one to call things off.

"Then yes, it's working." Luke squeezed Ian's fingers and ran his hands up to Ian's elbows so he could pull him over. Ian went willingly, letting Luke maneuver him however he liked. A moment later, his torso was awkwardly draped over Luke's lap, but the discomfort only lasted a second because all thought fled as soon as Luke brought their mouths together.

It was nothing like the furtive, stolen kisses and brief make-out sessions they'd had over the last few weeks. While it had been thrilling to kiss Luke senseless up against a wall where anyone could come by, it was even better to have the freedom to lean into the kiss and let his hands wander without fear of who would see them.

Luke seemed to agree, because he was already scrabbling at the hem of Ian's shirt, rucking it up enough to expose a strip of skin at his waistband. His palms were almost impossibly hot when he slid his hands inside and traced Ian's sides before grabbing hold so he could pull him closer.

Ian rolled, managing to get Luke horizontal with him without either one of them ending up on the floor. There was barely enough space for the two of them, but Ian rectified that by straddling Luke when he had him flat on his back underneath him. Luke let out a breathless moan when Ian's crotch brushed against his, which had Ian's already racing heart skipping almost painfully in his chest. God, he wanted this.

Luke was still in his bartending uniform, and Ian struggled a bit with the tiny buttons on the vest. Luke batted his hands away and got it open, and Ian started on the shirt underneath it, brushing his thumbs over Luke's tanned skin as he exposed it button by button. Luke's breath hitched every time. It was an addictive sound.

Ian didn't bother pulling Luke's shirt off all the way. Once he had it unbuttoned and the vest out of the way, he nosed at the hair just above the waistband of Luke's black dress pants. It was soft and tickled against Ian's lips when he kissed the warm skin there. Luke didn't protest when Ian sat back and unbuckled his pants, so Ian snaked his hand inside and brushed his palm down the hard length of Luke's boxer-covered cock.

"Fuck," Ian cursed under his breath when Luke bucked into the light touch, his thigh curving up and rubbing against Ian's erection.

Luke trailed a hand up Ian's back and tangled his fingers in Ian's hair, using it to urge him to resume the kiss Ian had abandoned in favor of getting Luke's shirt unbuttoned. The position tweaked his shoulder and wasn't at all comfortable, but Ian didn't care. He slipped his hand out of Luke's pants and fumbled with his own until they were pushed down around the tops of his thighs. He canted his hips enough to align himself with Luke, pulling Luke's cock out of his pants and lining them up. Ian stretched his fingers around the two of them, trembling with the effort of holding himself up with only the soft cushion underneath them as leverage.

Luke groaned against his lips and shifted until he could bring a hand up to join Ian's, his long fingers doing a better job of encasing both their cocks. The added friction made Ian's toes curl. He swallowed a gasp when Luke's palm grazed over the head of his dick on the next upstroke. A few moments later, Luke tensed underneath him before coming with a loud intake of breath. Ian eased back a fraction after Luke's hand stilled, and he jacked himself roughly, his lips still meshed with Luke's, until he came hard all over Luke's stomach.

Ian slumped to the side, careful not to let all his weight rest on Luke as he relaxed. The silence between them felt easy and amicable, which wasn't something Ian was used to experiencing after sex.

"I've got to be up in a few hours," Luke said apologetically after a few minutes. Ian shifted over and let Luke roll off the couch. He didn't bother hiding his laugh when Luke tripped over the coffee table and nearly fell, a contrast to his usual grace.

"Sex-stupid after something that tame? We may have to keep you in a padded room after the first time you actually fuck me or you'll break something," Ian teased.

Luke stopped buttoning his shirt and gave Ian a shy smile. "I thought you were versatile."

Ian snickered. "Fine, after I fuck you."

Luke finished with his shirt but shrugged the vest off instead of buttoning it. "Maybe." He hesitated, looking like he wasn't sure what to do next. "Will you have lunch with us?"

Ian sat up and ran a hand through his hair. "Yeah. Yes."

Luke beamed. "Is next weekend okay? I'd say this weekend, but we've got a family thing."

Part of Ian wanted to get the meeting over with quickly, like pulling off a Band-Aid, but the larger part of him was relieved to have a week's reprieve. "That's fine. Niall's wedding is Saturday, but I could do Sunday."

Luke nodded. "Sunday it is."

TWELVE

IF IAN was honest, he'd admit he'd spent the week after Luke's confession avoiding Luke and quietly freaking out. Ian knew it must seem to Luke like he was hiding after Luke's confession and their shared orgasms on his couch, but that was only partly true. It had just been a busy week, between last-minute wedding errands and Niall and Ethan's bachelor party, which had legitimately been the reason Ian had missed his first Friday night at The Weathered Mast since his return from Tortola.

He was trying hard not to let his issues bleed through today, though, since it was Niall's wedding day, and Niall needed him. Ian hadn't even gotten the chance to work up a good buzz the night before at the bachelor party because Niall had been a neurotic mess, and God only knew how much Ian could have used a night of drunken debauchery. He was bound and determined to get wasted and have a good time at the reception as soon as his best man duties were dispatched.

Ian and Luke had texted back and forth a few times to check in and make plans for Sunday, which Ian was dreading. Luke didn't want to get more involved with Ian until Ian met his kid. Ian was still a little pissed Luke had kept something so vitally important from him for so long, but he could grudgingly understand Luke's reasoning. He wasn't a parent, but even Ian understood that you didn't introduce your booty call to your kid. Luke had to be sure Ian was going to stick around before he brought him into his kid's life. When he'd told Niall about Luke's bombshell, Niall hadn't been surprised by the revelation at all, so Ian figured that meant he knew Luke fairly well. If Niall hadn't already been a basket case about the upcoming wedding, Ian probably would have given him the silent treatment over not divulging that secret. Niall didn't need one more thing to make him more anxious, so Ian was being the bigger person and not pouting the way he wanted to. It was a banner day. Personal growth all around.

"You can always divorce him if you change your mind later," Ian said as Niall paced back and forth. They were sequestered in Niall's office at Even Keel, waiting for the signal from Josh it was time to board the boat and sail out for the ceremony. Niall was a ridiculous traditionalist; he'd insisted he and Ethan get ready in different rooms and not see each other before they were ready to set sail.

"You're a jackass," Niall snapped, but some color seeped back into his cheeks, and he stopped pacing. Ian called it a win.

"I'm a realist," Ian answered unapologetically. It wasn't like Niall didn't know his views on marriage. Ian wasn't going to pretend to be a closet sap to put Niall's mind at ease.

A sharp rap on the door interrupted them, and a moment later it opened and Ethan peeked around the edge. "You upsetting my husband, Mack?"

"Not your husband yet," Niall said faintly, and Ian noticed he looked pale and nervous again.

"Oh, for Christ's sake. You already live with him and spend all your bloody time together. A marriage certificate might make it legal, but you two have been married in all but name since you moved here." Ian might not believe in marriage, but after being around Niall and Ethan twenty-four/seven for weeks, even a pragmatist like him couldn't deny they were in love.

Niall brightened a bit, settling down enough to apparently remember he hadn't wanted Ethan to see him yet. "You're not supposed to be here," he said, pointing at Ethan.

"I know. But I have something for you," Ethan said. He slipped into the room and closed the door behind him. Ian heard Niall's breath catch when he reached out to take the shiny dog tags Ethan held out to him. Ian had seen a pair like them before. Niall had kept them on the *Orion* in a framed box. He knew those belonged to Niall's deceased partner Nolan, though he and Niall had never talked about it. The boat was still docked in Tortola, but Niall had brought the box with him to Seattle.

Niall reached up and let the metal necklace pool in his palm as Ethan released the chain, bringing the tag closer so he could inspect it. When

Niall had come back from the States after starting his relationship with Ethan, he'd told Ian all about their connection through Nolan. It had been after that conversation that Ian had noticed Nolan's framed tags on the boat. In fact, Ian had been the one to unscrew the case from the wall and pack it away for Niall's move.

Ian knew Ethan had served in Afghanistan with Nolan, and he wondered if Ethan was giving Niall his dog tags from his years in the service so he could hang them together. It seemed like an odd thing to do before they got married, but apparently Nolan had meant a lot to Ethan. And who was Ian to judge prewedding customs? This was the first wedding he'd ever attended sober; usually he had a bridesmaid or three (or, on one memorable occasion, the best man *and* the maid of honor) on his arm and a flask on his hip as a means to get through.

"Oh my God," Niall said quietly. He sounded so shattered Ian instinctively stepped forward to see what was wrong. Niall handed him the dog tag wordlessly, and Ian peered at it curiously. The back was inscribed with Nolan's name and dates of birth and death. Ian flipped it over and saw the front had been engraved with what looked like some sort of constellation.

"Orion," Niall murmured as Ian handed it back to him. "It was something Nolan and I did to feel closer to each other when he was deployed. Orion was visible from Afghanistan and England, so we could always find it in the sky and think of each other."

Ian hadn't realized the constellation had any significance to Niall, though he had wondered why he'd named his boat after it. It made perfect sense now.

"He's a part of you," Ethan said quietly. Niall turned around, facing Ethan, and Ethan pressed a chaste kiss to his lips.

Ian felt like he was intruding on a very private moment, but Niall shot a hand out to grab his suit coat when he moved aside to edge his way out the door. Niall didn't look at him, but it was clear he wanted him to stay, so Ian shuffled back two steps and didn't move again, even when Niall let go of his sleeve.

"When did you have this made?" Niall's comment was directed toward Ethan and his voice was thick with emotion.

"When you flew back to Tortola to shut up the house and get ready to dry-dock the *Orion* to move here. I spent a lot of time missing you and thinking about you being the love of both my life and Nolan's life and Nolan being gone. And the more I thought about Nolan, the more I realized he'd be laughing his ass off at us for running away from each other." Ethan kissed him again, lingering a bit longer this time before pulling away and burying his head against the column of Niall's throat.

Niall hummed softly but let Ethan pull the dog tag out of his hands and slip it over Niall's head. Niall's eyes teared up when Ethan pressed a kiss to the tag before tucking it under Niall's shirt so the cold metal could rest against his heart.

"All right. Now that Nolan's here with us, we can get married," Ethan announced.

Ian had to fight not to roll his eyes. He couldn't think of any bigger romantics than the two of them, and it made him a little nauseated. But they seemed genuinely happy, just like his mother and Paul. It wasn't enough to make Ian rethink his stance on marriage being the source of all evil, but it was enough for him to wonder if there was something there he just didn't see. He wasn't ready to profess his undying love for Luke, but for the first time in his life, Ian was at least open to the possibility of a real relationship. It was a scary precipice to stand on, especially now that he knew Luke had a kid.

THE CEREMONY went flawlessly, with the exception of Niall's niece tripping on her way down the aisle and throwing her bridesmaid's bouquet overboard as she'd flailed for balance. She hadn't fallen, but she'd been horrified. Niall had given her a hug and a kiss on the cheek and the crowd had laughed and clapped. It had been a great way to break the tension at the start of the ceremony. Before that Niall had been stiff and anxious, but after Camille's comedic relief, he'd relaxed completely.

They were almost back to the harbor when Niall stepped up beside him. "Remember when I said you'd find out how I know Luke? Get ready."

Ian frowned. "Get ready? What are you talking about? You're the blushing bridegroom here. I'm just an accessory."

The kids from Even Keel were going to line the pier and throw confetti as Niall and Ethan got off the boat and walked to the reception at the warehouse. He'd toyed with the idea of keeping it a surprise, but Clare had been insistent that Niall would want to know in advance. Ian had to admit she was right. Niall didn't particularly like surprises, and if Niall didn't react well to the kids being there, it would hurt a lot of feelings. Luckily, Niall had taken the news with enthusiasm. He seemed apprehensive about it now, though, which made no sense to Ian. The hard part was over. Niall and Ethan had gotten through their vows and signed their marriage certificate. Niall definitely had his pensive face on, but what was left to be worried about?

Niall motioned with his chin to the dock. They were almost at the berth, and he could see quite a line of Even Keel students waiting for him. He hadn't known how many to expect; it was an odd request, but the kids had seemed excited to be part of Niall's wedding, especially when they'd found out they'd be throwing things at him. Ian had sent a note home a week ago inviting the kids and their guardians to greet Niall and Ethan when they returned to shore and stay for cake afterward. That detail had given the caterer fits because apparently serving the cake before the dinner just wasn't done. Ian had been just as insistent that it would be done, or he'd be finding a different caterer, but from the way the woman had huffed at him when he'd checked in with her before the ceremony, she was still of the opinion he was some sort of classless rube.

"You'll see. Just promise you won't make any rash judgments, okay? And remember your plans for tomorrow."

As if Ian could forget. Luke dropping the bomb last week that he had a kid had been huge, as had the invitation to have lunch with them Sunday afternoon.

"We're not talking about that right now, remember? I'm on vacation from my love life tonight," Ian said lightly.

Niall smiled and shook his head. "One, you can't take a vacation from your love life. And two, I can't believe Ian Mackay has a love life. My little man is all grown up." He stepped forward and Ian sidestepped, sure Niall was about to pinch his cheeks or something equally creepy.

Niall followed the motion, his raised hand landing on Ian's elbow instead. He cupped it gently, steering Ian closer to the railing. Ethan materialized a moment later and put a hand on Ian's opposite shoulder.

"No vacations," Niall said quietly, nodding toward the dock they were finally tying off at. Ian followed the direction of his nod and saw Leo waving at them exuberantly. He lifted his arm to wave back but faltered a second later when he saw who was standing behind Leo. Luke.

"If you make a scene, I'll never let you live it down, Mack," Ethan muttered in his ear. His tone was more concerned than threatening, and Ian swallowed and nodded. Niall's warnings and the way Niall and Ethan had been hovering on the ride back to the pier suddenly made a lot of sense.

"You know Luke because Leo's his kid," Ian said flatly. Luke hadn't looked away since they'd caught each other's eye, and he looked every bit as grim as Ian felt.

"He didn't know you knew Leo until yesterday. I called him," Niall said. He squeezed Ian's elbow before letting go. "I know you're mad, but he didn't conspire to keep this from you. I mean, yes. He did conceal the fact he had Leo, but he didn't know you already knew Leo. If that makes sense. I talked to him right after you two started dating to let him know I knew you and tell him you were a good guy despite your very poor first impression, but I didn't tell him you worked at Even Keel."

Niall was babbling, which was a sure sign he was anxious. Ian took a breath and tried to clear his racing mind. No matter what Niall thought, he *could* take a vacation from his love life. And he was going to. It was that or have a panic attack, and even Ian wasn't selfish enough to ruin Niall and Ethan's wedding.

"It's fine," Ian said. Ethan's hand tightened on his shoulder, which made Ian laugh. "No, really. It's a surprise. But I'm not going to dive overboard and swim for Tortola. We'll deal. I was going to meet him tomorrow anyway, so I guess that just got moved up."

Ian was doing his best to hide his panic, but from the looks he was getting from Ethan and Niall, he knew he wasn't succeeding. He'd already been freaking out about Luke having a kid, and he'd been psyching himself up for tomorrow's lunch. He liked Luke too much to bail, and that was what had him panicking. Ian didn't mind kids, obviously, or he wouldn't be comfortable volunteering at Even Keel. But he'd never really thought about dating someone who had kids—or having kids of his own. And that's what scared him the most. He could see a future with Luke, which was terrifying in its own right, and now that future included a kid. Of course he was overwhelmed. Anyone would be, Ian reasoned.

The boat jolted as it bumped against the moorings, and Ian shrugged to force his way out of Ethan's grip so he could escape from his spot between them. "I'll be fine. Go get ready to be feted like the glowing newlyweds you are," he said with as much cheer as he could muster. It had the desired effect; Ethan snorted out a laugh and Niall looked exasperated, but the two of them stepped together and closed the gap Ian had left. A moment later they were holding hands and sharing a private smile, and Ian felt a surge of affection for them. He had good friends, and he was going to do his best not to let his drama ruin their wedding day.

Tomorrow, though? He was coming over after lunch with a bottle of Scotch and all bets were off.

HALF THE kids had already thrown their confetti by the time Niall and Ethan made it onto the dock, and the brightly colored flakes littered the ground. Clare had absolutely vetoed traditional confetti, so Ian had compromised with something called ecofetti. It looked like multi-colored snowflakes, but apparently it was completely biodegradable and even better, water soluble, so they'd be able to hose down the dock after the reception to clean everything up. It didn't flutter as nicely as regular paper confetti, but Niall and Ethan didn't seem to mind that as they ran through a storm of it thrown by cheering children.

He hung back to usher the stragglers toward the warehouse, breaking up several confetti fights on the way. The kids were more hyped up than he'd ever seen them, but Ian figured that was probably normal, what with the projectiles and the promise of cake.

Luke was waiting for him outside the door to Even Keel, Leo's hand wrapped tightly in his own. Ian let the last of the group he'd been walking with enter the building before he approached them. The awkward silence dragged on for a few more beats before Luke finally spoke.

"So apparently you already know Leo," he said, and the ridiculousness in his bashful look startled a laugh out of Ian. "Niall gave me a heads-up that he knew you before you two came in for drinks together, but he didn't tell me you were an instructor here until he called last night."

"He's been teaching me knots. I told you about him," Leo said, his chin stuck up in what Ian recognized as stubbornness. He'd seen that particular cant to his head more times than he'd like to admit over the last

155

few weeks. Every time one of the older students teased Leo or told him he wasn't big enough to do something, that look came out.

"You said your new teacher was named Mack."

"He is. This is Mack," Leo said. The words dripped with a level of condescension that Ian thought was pretty impressive for a six-year-old.

"Luke knows me as Ian. Remember? Mack is just a nickname," Ian offered, and Leo's eyes lit up.

"Oh. Well, don't worry. If you get to know him better, you can call him Mack."

Ian stifled a laugh behind his hand. "I think they're cutting the cake, Leo. Why don't you go in and find Josh? He'll make sure you get a piece."

Ian didn't miss the way Leo inclined his head toward Luke for silent permission before trotting inside. Damn. Ian probably should have asked Luke before sending the kid off and offering him cake. Two minutes in, and he was already bombing this dating-a-guy-with-a-kid thing.

"I'm sorry it got sprung on you like this," Luke said after a moment. He shoved his hands into the pockets of his dark wash jeans, which pulled the fabric taut and accentuated his muscular thighs. It was distracting, and Ian tried to pry his eyes away and not let himself get sidetracked. "I thought about not letting him come tonight when Niall called and explained exactly how he knew you and that you were working with Leo, but Leo's been looking forward to this, and I didn't want to disappoint him."

Luke looked like he was about to bolt for the door at the slightest provocation, which helped Ian settle a bit. It was good to know he wasn't the only one who didn't know what he was doing. This was an awkward conversation, but it was easier to have it with Luke's gaze pinned to the ecofetti that covered Ian's shoes than on his face.

"Niall warned me before we docked. I mean, it would have been nice if he'd outright said 'Luke is Leo's dad,' but at least I didn't walk into this completely cold," Ian said. He knew why Niall hadn't told him: he'd have run the other way. Niall knew him well enough to give him just enough advance notice that he wasn't completely blindsided but be vague enough Ian didn't have a chance to avoid the situation. "Is it okay? With you, I mean? That I work with Leo?"

"I'm his uncle," Luke blurted. He swallowed visibly and then raised his head so he was looking at Ian directly. "I have guardianship, but I'm not his dad. He's still legally my sister's kid."

Ian wasn't sure what to say to that, so he kept his mouth shut. There were layers of complications here he didn't even want to try to touch at the moment, though he knew they'd all have to come out at some point. Standing outside his best friend's wedding reception was not the time, though.

Luke seemed to realize that the uncomfortable silence was growing, and he closed his eyes for a moment before speaking again. "That was— sorry." He shook his head. "I don't know how to talk to you about this. I've spent the last few weeks doing everything I could *not* to talk about it. I'm sorry. I'm babbling."

"It's okay," Ian said, and he was surprised to find he meant it. "Better tonight than tomorrow at lunch, right?"

Luke seemed to wilt at the reminder about their lunch date. "You're still coming?"

"Am I still invited?"

Instead of answering, Luke lurched forward and kissed him. Ian was taken off-guard and the force of it caused him to stumble back a step, his hands coming up to brace against Luke's shoulders to keep from sending both of them sprawling. Luke brought his arms around Ian's waist and steadied him without breaking the kiss. Ian returned it with equal urgency and enthusiasm, and he would have let his hands wander down from Luke's shoulders if someone hadn't cleared their throat behind them.

Luke jumped away as if Ian were a live wire, and Ian tried not to be hurt by that as he turned and glared at the person who'd interrupted them. Susannah stood there with a smug look on her face.

"Niall wants you there when they cut the cake. You've got a room full of kids looking at three feet of sugar. It's about to get nasty in there. Might I suggest you continue this later, gentlemen?"

Luke had flushed to the roots of his hair, but Ian refused to let Susannah embarrass him. She'd walked in on a lot worse than kissing when it came to Ian, and the way she quirked her eyebrow at him told him she remembered that as well.

"You are heartless," he told her, but he threaded his arm through Luke's and took him inside anyway.

She waited until they'd started to walk away before following suit, and Ian looked over his shoulder and saw her blatantly checking out Luke's ass.

"Nice," she mouthed.

Ian narrowed his eyes. "Fuck off," he mouthed back.

Luke startled a bit at Susannah's answering peal of laughter, but Ian ignored her and guided him through the door. Things were definitely devolving into chaos inside. Kids were milling around, obviously bored, and the band was playing in the corner. Niall and Ethan were already standing next to the cake. Leo was sitting with Josh at the head table, and Ian had to try hard not to snicker when Luke tensed beside him and made some sort of complicated hand motion that had Leo scrambling to his side.

"I'm going to help the happy couple with the cake. I'll see you in a bit, all right?"

The kids would be leaving after the cake, but Ian wanted to make sure he got to say good-bye to Luke and Leo before they took off. It was silly, especially since he'd be seeing them for lunch tomorrow, but he didn't want them slipping off without a word.

"I KNOW you've been waiting all night for me to say it, so I'll bite the bullet. You were right. The boat was the perfect place for the ceremony," Clare said as she handed Ian a flute of champagne after dinner had been cleared away and the guests had started dancing and mingling. "Go ahead and gloat."

"I would never," Ian answered, offering her a sly smile before taking a sip. He needed the drink. He'd spent an entire dinner sitting next to Mrs. Jim, and with her eagle eyes, she hadn't missed the kiss Luke had given Ian before he and Leo left. Not much got by Niall's old neighbor, and she had a sharp tongue to match her sharp vision. It had been funny when he'd listened in on her giving Niall lectures about his relationship with Ethan back on the island, but now that he was the recipient of her sage advice, it wasn't nearly so funny. He'd been relieved when Ethan's brother had come to save him, since he worked with Mrs. Jim's son and knew her through that. Off the hook or not, though, Ian wasn't wasting any opportunity to drink. He never knew who might corner him next. Weddings were a minefield.

"It's worse than I thought," Clare said ruefully. She put her arm around her brother Frank, who had wandered up. "He's going to be insufferable."

"He just said he *wasn't* going to gloat," Frank said, confusion evident in his expression.

Ian looked at him and gave him a wide-eyed shrug, like he had no idea what Clare's problem was. She was right, of course. He was going to milk this victory for everything he could. The next time she suggested a tofu place for lunch? Totally going to remind her how his plans for Niall's wedding had been better than hers.

"You don't know him as well as I do, Frankie. He's never going to stop bringing it up."

Frank tweaked Clare's nose. "Don't call me Frankie, Clare-bear."

"Well, Clare-bear," Ian said, seizing on the nickname with glee and earning himself a glare from her, "I might get the chance to get to know him better since I'm officially moving here."

Frank and his husband, Warner, lived in Portland, but Ian had met them only once before. It was less than a three-hour drive between the two cities, and from what Niall said, Frank visited Clare pretty often. One of Ian's visits had coincided with Clare's graduation from Bastyr, and Ian had gotten dragged along to the festivities. Warner was a pediatrician, and the debate pitting traditional medicine against homeopathic treatments between Warner and the newly minted homeopath, Dr. Clare Smith, at her graduation party had been hugely entertaining.

"Clare never said," Frank said. He extended a hand and gave Ian's a hearty shake. "Welcome to the Pacific Northwest, even if you did choose the wrong city."

"I didn't say because I didn't know he'd made a decision," Clare said with a dirty look in her brother's direction. She closed in on Ian and wrapped him in a warm hug. "So I take it your date with the mystery bartender went well last week? How did you plug that in to your spreadsheet?"

"Claws in, darling. Not everyone can have a gut as intuitive as yours. Some of us have to work out major life decisions with tangible factors."

"Ian," she said, sounding both fond and annoyed.

He pressed a kiss against her cheek and drew back, careful not to spill his champagne on either of them. Clare gave it a guilty look when she stepped back, like she hadn't remembered he was holding it before she'd thrown herself at him.

"It was a lot more than just one date," Susannah said as she joined them. "And if mystery bartender was the guy—" She broke off at the desperate look Ian shot her. He didn't want anyone to know Luke was here. Bringing attention to that would make it obvious he had a kid, and Ian wasn't ready to have that up for discussion, not until he'd had a chance to process everything.

She gave him a shrewd look and took the glass out of his hand and tipped it back, draining it before sliding it into his open hand again.

"Boundaries," Ian said with a scowl, but she waved off his concern. This was what he was getting himself into moving to Seattle, and part of Ian couldn't be happier. The other part was annoyed she'd finished his drink, even though he was grateful she hadn't told Clare about the kiss. "And no, Clare. I mean, yes. Things are going well with Luke, but no, he's not the reason I'm moving. It's just time for a change."

"And if that change happens to have an ass you could bounce a quarter off, so much the better, eh?" Susannah teased. Frank snorted into his champagne.

"Ian judges people on more than just their looks," Clare said hotly, jumping to his defense. "He—I mean," she floundered and thought for a moment. "I'm sure there are other attributes that attract him to Luke."

"Thanks, but I think your defense made me sound even shallower," Ian said with a smirk. He grabbed a fresh flute of champagne off a passing tray, snagging one for Susannah as well lest she steal his new drink. Clare was clearly mortified, and Ian enjoyed the way Clare flushed at his accusation. She really was too easy. He was well aware he was extremely shallow, though Luke wasn't fully the reason behind his decision to make the move. He'd been on the fence about it for weeks, but tonight he'd realized that most of the people he cared about were in Seattle. Luke wasn't in that group yet, but he was fast approaching it, especially now that he knew Luke was Leo's guardian. That was still a twist Ian couldn't quite wrap his mind around, but in a good sense. Not that Ian was completely comfortable with dating someone who had a child, but at least he already knew and liked Leo, and Leo seemed to like him. He'd been genuinely thrilled to introduce Ian to his uncle, and even more excited when he'd found out Ian was the man who'd be coming to lunch on Sunday.

Even without Luke in the equation, seeing Niall and Ethan tying the knot surrounded by their closest friends had been a wake-up call for Ian. Especially since so many of their close friends were also his, thanks to Niall and his mother hen tendency. There was a lot more pulling Ian to Seattle than there was keeping him on Tortola; the time had come to move on.

"I'm kidding, Clare. You and Susannah are both right. Luke has an amazing ass, but he's also a really funny, interesting guy. We're getting to know each other slowly, which isn't something I've done before. It's nice," he said.

Ian wasn't ready to tell Clare or Susannah about Leo, though he was certain it was only a matter of time before Susannah put two and two together and came up with Ian-is-dating-a-guy-with-a-kid. Ian was sure he'd want to hash over everything with someone soon, but tonight was about celebrating Niall and Ethan's wedding and having fun. He could put off worrying about his increasingly complicated life for the next day.

"You've got a place in the Caribbean, right?" Frank asked when Clare still seemed too embarrassed to speak.

"A house on the beach, yeah. I'll be flying back to get that on the market soon."

Frank whistled. "Beachfront? It'll be hard to find a place here that can match that view, I bet. There's a great harbor here if you want to go the houseboat route. Warner and I love ours."

"Houseboat?" Ian knew Frank and Warner owned a place in Portland, but he hadn't realized it was a boat.

"Sure, it's one of the perks of living in a coastal town." He laughed at Ian's incredulous look. "You should come up and stay with us for a weekend, give it a try. Warner was skeptical at first, too, when I first asked him to move in with me. He loves it now, though."

"I think I'd rather stick to dry land," Ian said. "Besides, I've already rented a loft. I may even go get all the furniture I still have in storage in Los Angeles."

"I didn't know you lived in LA," Clare said, her brows furrowed.

Ian shrugged. "Everyone's got a history."

"Truer words," Frank said as he held his glass out to clink against Ian's.

"You should have told me you found a place. I have a great smudging ritual for empty spaces." Clare didn't seem to catch the exasperated look Frank shot Ian over her head. Ian held back a snicker. He had no idea what smudging was, but Frank obviously knew.

"Not everyone wants the stench of burned sage permeating every room in their house, Clare."

"Alas, the loft is already full of rented furniture, so it's not empty. I moved in a couple days ago to give the newlyweds their privacy, not that it mattered to them," Ian said with mock gravity. Susannah snorted beside him. Ian knew she'd walked in on them in Ethan's office more than once. "Speaking of the happy couple, I'd better go remind them to mingle. Ethan's probably monopolizing Niall somewhere."

Ian kissed Clare and Susannah and offered Frank a hearty handshake before he excused himself to find another drink.

IAN'S MOTHER might have despaired over his playboy ways, but never let it be said she hadn't taught him manners. That's why he was standing in front of a frankly terrifying aisle of toys trying to pick out a gift for Leo before his lunch date at Luke's.

He'd already picked up a gift for Luke: a bottle of reasonably good wine and a newly released murder-mystery paperback by an author he knew Luke liked. He'd also grabbed a bottle of sparkling grape juice for Leo, even though he knew it wasn't likely Luke would open the wine with lunch. He didn't want Leo to feel left out.

Ian shifted the basket in his hands, a frisson of unease running through him when the two bottles clinked together. What was he doing? He had no idea what the proper etiquette was for dating a guy with a kid.

Would it be too much if he showed up with gifts? Would Luke think he was trying to buy his way into Leo's affections?

Then again, he already knew Leo. Hell, he already liked Leo a lot, and Ian was fairly sure Leo liked him as well. He blew out a breath and grabbed a box of building blocks with the picture of a boat on the front of it. It seemed like something Leo would like, and they could build it together after lunch.

If lunch went well enough for there to *be* an after lunch, that was. Ian was a ball of nerves. It was beyond ridiculous. He knew both Luke and Leo. There was no reason to be anxious.

Nodding to himself, Ian put the building set in his basket and set off toward the front of the store to check out before he could talk himself out of it. He was already going to be late because of his indecisiveness. The world would not end if Leo didn't like the Lego set Ian had picked out for him. Ian sighed and doubled back to the toy aisle to look at his choices one final time. He fondly remembered the time in his life—just a few months ago, actually—when hard decisions were whether to take the blond or the brunet home from the bar, not which building set would best bribe a six-year-old into letting Ian date his uncle. Seriously, what was his life?

By the time Ian made it over to Luke's apartment, he'd managed to convince himself that lunch was going to be an utter disaster. It was a surprise when instead of inviting him in when he answered the door, Luke pushed past Ian and stepped out into the hallway, closing the door behind himself.

"So. Slight change of plans," Luke said. "And I am so, so sorry. We usually have lunch with my mom on Sundays, and she showed up a few minutes ago."

Ian hadn't known he could be more nervous, but his anxiety ratcheted up notably at Luke's words. It didn't help that even Luke looked panicked at the prospect of Ian meeting his mother.

"It's fine. I can come back later. I mean, I already know Leo, so the whole 'introduce Ian to Leo' thing was an unnecessary mission anyway."

Luke shook his head. "She's here to see you. I told her we'd see her for dinner instead because you were coming over, and she decided she wanted to meet you."

Ian bit back a curse. He didn't meet parents. Hell, it had never even come up. He wasn't the kind of guy anyone ever wanted to introduce to their family.

"If it's too much, I get it. I can—"

Ian cut Luke off by moving forward and kissing him. The bags in his arms kept him from embracing Luke fully, but Luke had no such encumbrances, and after he recovered from the surprise, Luke wrapped his arms around Ian's waist. Ian kept it brief, mindful of the fact that Luke's mom and Leo were on the other side of the door, but he'd needed some sort of contact with Luke. It had been a long week apart, and Luke offering Ian an out so he didn't have to meet his mother had been so thoughtful, Ian had to do something.

"Right. Anything I need to know before I meet her? I didn't bring her anything, but the wine is kind of a gift for the table anyway, so maybe that counts." Ian leaned in and gave Luke a kiss on the cheek when Luke blinked at him in confusion. "And I brought Leo a Lego set and some grape juice. I didn't want to show up empty-handed."

Luke let out a small laugh. "He hasn't been able to talk about anything other than Mack coming to lunch since we saw you yesterday. He's thrilled; if you brought him a toy, you'll just cement your place as his current favorite person."

Warmth surged through Ian's chest at that. He'd been fixating on making sure he made a good impression with Leo, but he hadn't realized how much he needed Leo to like him. It was obvious Leo was the most important person in Luke's life, and that was how it should be. Even someone as selfish as Ian could understand that. Getting along with Leo was going to be a necessity if he and Luke were going to date, and Ian was unaccountably relieved that Leo seemed open to Ian being involved with his uncle.

"So he's easily bribed? I'll keep that in mind," Ian said, hefting the bag with the Legos and nodding toward the door. "Should we go in?"

Luke gave him a sheepish grin. "I'm sure my mother's been watching at the peephole. She's nosy as hell. That's probably the only thing you need to know before going in there. Nothing is off limits for her." Luke slipped his hand under Ian's shirt and rested his palm against Ian's lower back, guiding him forward as he opened the door. He leaned in to whisper, "And don't talk about Leo's mom, okay? I'm sure you have questions, and I'll answer them all later, but it's not something we talk about in front of him."

Ian hadn't figured it was, but it was nice to have the warning nonetheless. He nodded to let Luke know he'd gotten the message, and a second later Leo was hurtling at him faster than a cannonball. Ian probably would have ended up on the floor if not for Luke's steady presence at his back, keeping him upright when fifty-some pounds of six-year-old wrapped himself around Ian's legs.

"Mack! Do you want to see my room? We're having pot roast for lunch, even though it's a dinner. Do you think we'll have sandwiches for dinner instead, since that's what we always have for lunch? Will you be here for dinner too? Can we tie some knots later?"

Ian heard Luke laughing softly behind him. "Let's let our guest in before talking his ear off, okay, kiddo? Maybe introduce him to Nana?"

Ian would have much preferred dealing with Leo than meeting the imposing figure who was standing on the other side of the small living room. She was tiny, hardly taller than Leo, but she managed to be intimidating all the same.

Leo untangled himself from Ian's legs and stepped back, looking between his grandmother and Ian shyly. Ian could see he was embarrassed, and he didn't want Leo to think that his greeting hadn't been welcome. So Ian dropped to his knees, letting the wine and grape juice bottles clink against the floor as he got on Leo's level so he could look him in the eye. "Hey, bud. I'd love to see your room later. Maybe you could work on this, and we could find a place to display it later?" He took the small Lego kit out of the bag and held it out.

"Oh cool!" Leo grabbed the box and held it up for Luke to see. "It's a boat! Can I open it?"

Ian looked up over his shoulder at Luke, who had a pleased smile on his face. "Sure. Lunch will be ready in a few minutes, though." When Leo ran off down the hall, Luke called him back. "What are you forgetting?"

Leo ran back in, throwing his arms around Ian in a quick hug. "Thank you, Mack!"

When Leo disappeared again, Ian stood up and handed the bottles to Luke. "I wasn't sure what you were making, but I figured a nice bottle of wine was never amiss."

Luke gave the label a cursory examination and shrugged. "I know hops and yeast, not grapes, but I'll never turn down free wine." He leaned in and gave Ian a quick kiss before moving to put it away. The casual intimacy surprised Ian; he'd been expecting Luke to be standoffish around his mother.

"That's my mother, Ian. Mom, this is Ian," he yelled from the open kitchen. Ian smelled the roast when Luke took it out of the oven,

"I'd say I raised him better than this, but I must have gone wrong somewhere," the woman said. She came forward and offered Ian a hand, visibly shocked when Ian brought it to his lips and kissed it instead of shaking it. "You, on the other hand, were obviously brought up with manners. I'm Ruthie. It's nice to meet you."

"Ian Mackay." Ian bowed slightly when he released her hand. "It's nice to meet you, too."

Ruthie snorted inelegantly. "That's not true, but I appreciate the effort. Luke had some very impolite words for me when I showed up to crash your lunch date."

Luke had clearly gotten his honesty from his mother, and it charmed Ian just as much coming from her as it did from Luke. "I admit I was a little worried coming in here, but I think that's mostly passed."

It hadn't, of course. Leo's warm greeting had helped, but Ian was still terrified standing there in Luke's living room alone with his mother. He'd be angry with Luke for abandoning him, but Luke was in the kitchen with half a dozen pots going, so Ian figured a little discomfort was worth it if it hurried lunch along. In the end, it meant less time here.

"Luke doesn't date, so I wasn't going to pass up the opportunity to meet someone who actually caught his attention," Ruthie said, perking Ian's interest. "I don't know how much he's told you about his situation, but he's been doing nothing but work and care for Leo for the last four years. It's good to see him realize he can't put his life on hold forever."

The words were innocuous, but Ian heard the warning in them. Ruthie was telling him Leo was Luke's number one priority. "I don't know much, but I know he's doing a good job with Leo. He's hands down my favorite kid at Even Keel."

The compliment warmed Ruthie up a bit. The stern twist to her features softened at the mention of her grandson. "I offered to take Leo in when Lane left, but Luke insisted he could handle it. And he has. I just hate seeing him sacrificing his own happiness for Leo's. But maybe you can change that."

"I'll do my best," Ian promised. Ruthie looked skeptical, but she didn't call him on it. Which was good, because Ian had hit his limit with parental interaction. "I'm going to see how Leo's doing with the Lego set."

He made his escape down the hallway, following what sounded like Leo voicing several characters who were engaged in some sort of battle. When Ian peeked around the doorframe, he saw that Leo had assembled the boat and was currently using it to wage war against a small army of Lego tanks.

"You might need a bigger navy to take on that fight," Ian said. He settled himself on a patch of uncluttered carpet to watch the battle unfold.

"Can you build me some more boats? Then I could have a boat army," Leo said. Ian dug into the bin of loose Lego parts without hesitation.

"It's called a fleet," he said as he started construction.

"Can we both have one and then we can go to war?"

"Sure," Ian agreed easily. Playing with Leo was preferable to being out in the living room. "You want to be the US?"

"What will you be?"

"Let's see. I used to live in Scotland, but it doesn't have its own navy." Ian hummed thoughtfully. "My grandparents are from Portugal. *Eu vou ser o português.* That means I'll be the Portuguese."

Leo sailed his boat across the carpet to the side of Ian's half-finished ship. "Pow, pow, pow! I sank the Portuguese fleet before it even got in the water!"

Ian let his Lego boat crumble as he wailed dramatically. "*Tudo está perdido!* All is lost!"

He looked up when he heard a chuckle in the doorway. "All is lost, eh?" Luke asked, looking amused.

"He sank the last hope of the Portuguese navy," Ian said with a shrug.

"Come on, Horatio Hornblower, lunch is ready," Luke said, shaking his head. "Nana wants to know what you want to drink."

Leo abandoned his Legos without further prodding and tore down the hallway, shouting for his grandmother. Ian grinned when Luke held out a hand and helped him to his feet. "So you speak Portuguese? That's an interesting development." He pressed a kiss against the side of Ian's throat, giving Ian a good idea of exactly how interesting Luke found it.

"*Meus avós nunca aprendeu Inglês*," Ian said, noting the way Luke melted into his side when he was speaking. "My grandparents never learned English, so my mother made sure I could speak Portuguese fluently. Plus my father doesn't speak it, so any time my mother and I wanted to talk and not have him understand us, *falámos em português*."

That had been Ian's main motivator in learning the language. His mother hadn't cared why he was interested, just that he was and that he had an aptitude for it. He'd been raised bilingual, and his mother made sure he kept up with it, usually peppering their phone conversations with Portuguese to keep him on his toes.

"I'm not going to lie, that's pretty hot," Luke whispered against the shell of Ian's ear before he pulled away. "So, lunch?"

"You say something like that and then you expect me to have lunch with your mother and Leo?"

"Yup," Luke said, eyes twinkling. "What are you going to do about it?"

"*Nada, por enquanto*," Ian muttered, laughing when Luke's eyes widened fractionally at the generic threat.

"Tell me what you said." Luke demanded as they made the short trek down the hallway.

"Nope. If you're not going to play fair then neither am I."

LUNCH WITH Leo, Ruthie, and Luke became a regular thing on Sundays. Ian was surprised at how readily they invited him into their family, as well as how easily he accepted the invitation.

Niall called it the honeymoon phase, which was ironic coming from a newlywed who hadn't taken a honeymoon.

"We're spending Christmas in Tortola, so that counts," Niall said when Ian poked him about it over their weekly lunch. He still saw Niall at Even Keel three times a week, but they didn't get a chance to talk to each other amid all the chaos. Sometimes Ian missed living with Niall and Ethan and having breakfast with them every morning, but having his own space—and the ability to sneak back to the loft for a quickie with Luke after Luke's early yoga class—more than made up for it. But he and Niall made an effort to stay connected, hence the weekly lunches with Niall and the Friday night dinners at The Weathered Mast with Niall and Ethan.

"You go to the island all the time. That doesn't count." Ian pointed his fork at Niall disapprovingly. "You need to go have married sex somewhere exotic."

Niall rolled his eyes. "Most people would consider Tortola exotic."

"Most people didn't live there for years."

"Speaking of, Keandra said you've had a few interested potential buyers on your place," Niall said, and Ian decided to let him change the subject.

"So much for Realtor-client confidentiality, eh?" Niall laughed at Ian's jab. Keandra had been Niall's secretary when he'd owned the real estate firm on Tortola; she'd bought him out when he moved. She wasn't a huge gossip, but her uncle was. Ian was sure that by now most of the locals on the island knew the details of his move. "She hired a decorator to get it all cleaned up to show, but I'm going to have to get back there sooner rather than later to box up anything I want and sign the proxy papers in person."

"You should get a pretty good price for it. Great location," Niall said after he swallowed his bite.

"Yeah, I seem to remember someone saying that exact thing almost five years ago," Ian said drily.

"It was true then, too. You had an excellent Realtor."

"You ever think of taking that up here? You were good at it."

Niall wrinkled his nose. "No. I hated it. Besides, Even Keel is keeping me plenty busy."

Ian had been forced to resign as the charity's accountant when he'd taken the job at Cloud Technologies because it would have been a conflict of interest. Niall hadn't found anyone to replace him, which Ian felt bad about. He still taught classes and took kids out on Saturday sails, though.

"Want me to ask around? I don't know many financial types up here, but if I put the word out with my LA buddies, they might know someone who'd be willing to donate some time to help you manage the books."

Niall shrugged. "I'm letting Josh handle it."

"You're trusting Josh with money?"

"You know he's majoring in finance, right?"

Ian had known that, since he met up with Josh for lunch every few weeks to continue mentoring him on the art of flirtation. But it didn't mean it was a good idea to leave the management of Even Keel's endowment and operating expenses to a college freshman. Before Ian could lay into Niall about how irresponsible that was, Niall burst into laughter.

"Your face," he crowed. "No, of course I'm not letting Josh handle the money. Jesus. I'm using a management firm. Pricey but worth it in the long run, plus they'll take care of doing my taxes."

"Anyone ever tell you you're an asshole, Ahern?"

"It's why we're friends, Mackay," Niall said glibly, still laughing.

THIRTEEN

IAN HAD spent the afternoon with Luke and Leo, and like most Sundays he'd stayed for dinner as well. It had been a struggle getting Leo down for bed after the excitement of ice skating and eating out at a pizzeria. It had been Leo's weekend to pick their date activity, which was why Ian was achy from using muscles he didn't usually need to keep himself upright on the ice.

His reward was waiting for him on the couch, curled up in a blanket and reading yet another of his endless supply of books.

"If he asks for another glass of water, I'm going to make him chug the entire glass while I watch," Ian said darkly as he slid under the blanket.

Luke scooted over to make room for him and let his book drop to the floor. "I think he's probably done. Usually, if he lets you get to the light-turning-off stage, he's done for the night."

"Well, thank God for that," Ian groaned. He let his head fall back against the cushion and closed his eyes. He was exhausted, and he had a fund meeting in the morning he wasn't looking forward to.

"You took us ice skating. Leo's always wanted to go, but I don't know how to skate so I've never taken him."

Ian blinked his eyes open, confused. "Yeah, I was there. He mentioned it last week at lunch when I asked him what he'd like to do when we took him out."

Luke tossed the blanket aside and crawled over to Ian, rising so he could straddle him. "I know," Luke murmured. He nuzzled Ian's neck. "And you listened. And then you took us skating."

Ian knew he was missing something important, but he couldn't think with Luke's mouth doing amazing things to his neck. They'd never taken a make-out session this far at Luke's before, not with Leo down the hall. They usually spent the nights Leo was at Ruthie's over at Ian's, alternating between having sex on every flat surface they could find and lounging around naked, with Luke reading whichever novel he was working through at the moment and Ian catching up on work.

When Luke ground down into Ian's lap, Ian grabbed his hips to still the motion. Ian was definitely on board, but this was a pretty abrupt policy change for Luke. "Is this okay?"

"You mean did your romantic gesture addle my senses so much I've forgotten Leo's here?"

Ian smothered a laugh, because that was exactly what he'd meant, but the look on Luke's face told him agreeing would hurt his chances of getting laid in the next twenty minutes. "No, just checking."

Luke hummed suspiciously but kissed Ian again anyway. "So, my room?" he asked, climbing out of Ian's lap.

"As you wish," Ian said, bowing grandly after he stood up.

"You're no Westley, and I'm certainly no Princess Buttercup," Luke groused, but he grabbed Ian to tow him down the hall all the same.

IAN WOKE with a start, eyes blinking open to a room lit with a predawn glow. It took a moment for him to realize it was the hint of sun on the horizon that had awakened him. Ian was extremely sensitive to light when he was sleeping. He always took care to keep his curtains drawn, and his bed at the loft was positioned so it shielded him from any light that might creep in through them.

He edged up on his elbows when he realized he wasn't at home. What's more, Luke was wrapped around him, his head pillowed on Ian's chest and his arms holding him down. They'd fallen asleep after they'd had sex last night. Shit. He glanced over at the door, grateful it was still closed. Leo must not be up yet. Luke was going to have a coronary if Ian didn't manage to sneak out before Leo woke.

"Luke," he whispered, repeating his name again a bit louder when it had no effect.

Luke turned his head, snuggling tighter against Ian's naked chest. They were both wearing pajama pants, because Luke had some Victorian notions about modesty, and Ian found himself grateful for that at the moment. At least Leo wouldn't find them completely naked if he came in.

"Luke, come on," Ian whispered. He wiggled in Luke's grasp as much as he could, finally running his hand through Luke's hair. He tugged gently until Luke's eyes finally opened. "It's morning. You have to let me up."

Instead of waking up at the proclamation, Luke's eyes slid closed again. He straightened enough to bury his jaw against Ian's neck, and Ian's pulse ratcheted up a bit at the scrape of Luke's stubble against his skin.

Things were spiraling out of control faster than Ian could manage them. He made another attempt at protesting, but Luke continued to ignore him in favor of pressing small, sleep-soft kisses down Ian's neck and over his chest.

Ian's endeavors to stop him ended abruptly when Luke bent enough to nuzzle against Ian's pajama-covered cock, his cheek rubbing against Ian's balls. Ian gasped, his cock filling with blood as Luke sucked him into his mouth, his lips working over Ian's length through the pajamas until he was fully hard.

Ian cupped the back of Luke's neck, forcing him to look up. His eyes were definitely open now, and a sleepy smile curved his lips. He looked gorgeous, but Ian couldn't let him continue. Leo could walk in at any minute.

"It's morning, Luke. I have to go."

Luke glanced over at the clock on the nightstand. It was almost seven. "You'll have time to go home and shower before work," he said quietly before diving back into his previous task, sucking Ian through his pajama pants.

"Luke, Jesus," Ian groaned when he felt a scrape of teeth through the fabric. "Jesus fuck. You have to stop. Leo's home."

Luke pulled back and grinned. "I know. I locked the door last night, remember? He won't be up for an hour or so anyway. We've got time."

Ian gaped at him. "You planned this! You let me fall asleep on purpose!"

173

Luke smirked. "If I'd said 'Ian, I think it's time Leo gets used to the idea of you spending the night,' you'd have panicked."

He palmed Ian's erection and squeezed. Ian's breath hitched, and he pushed up into the pressure, looking for more. "Isn't this a nicer way to do it? We're going to have some nice, slow morning sex, and then you're going to help me make breakfast for all three of us before I have to get Leo to school. Okay?"

Ian made an unintelligible sound as Luke squeezed him again, and Luke must have taken it for the enthusiastic agreement it was, because he wasted no time in rolling Ian's pajama pants down and bending to take him into his mouth.

Luke swirled his tongue over the satiny skin, and Ian felt Luke's erection grinding against his hip, the position awkward since Luke was bent over him. They might have time, but Ian was already too aroused to take things slow. He nudged Luke's hip, tugging a bit on his calf to get his attention. Luke smiled around Ian's cock, receiving the message loud and clear. He let Ian's erection slide free of his mouth and wiggled out of his pajama pants before throwing his leg over Ian and crawling backward until he was straddling Ian's face, his cock rubbing against Ian's lips.

Ian wasted no time, practically swallowing Luke whole as he dove in with gusto, and Luke moaned quietly, wrapping his lips around Ian's cock and mirroring his enthusiastic motions. A few minutes later, Ian was tensing underneath Luke, bucking his hips up as he flooded Luke's mouth with his release. Luke shuddered as Ian moaned around Luke's cock. As soon as Ian's cock stopped spasming, Luke started thrusting his hips down in an impatient motion. Ian took the hint, his slackened lips gripping Luke's length firmly again as he bobbed his head with renewed vigor, and after a few sucks, Luke was coming, groaning against the warm skin of Ian's thigh to muffle the sound.

Luke rested there for a moment until Ian released his cock, then rolled to the side and collapsed bonelessly against the soft mattress. Ian stroked a hand down Luke's calf, the awkward position making it difficult for their usual postcoital cuddle. Luke didn't seem to mind, and Ian was just about to fall back to sleep when the alarm chimed.

"See? I was going to wake you up with plenty of time for you to panic before Leo gets up," Luke said after he'd silenced it. It was still about forty-five minutes 'til Luke would get Leo up for the day.

"You could have just asked me to stay," Ian said petulantly. He snuggled into Luke's embrace when Luke climbed up the bed and wrapped himself around him.

"This was easier."

Ian snorted. Luke was probably right. Ian did have a relatively low startle reflex for any new relationship developments. It was probably best Luke backed him into them instead of having Ian meet them head-on.

"So does Leo know I'm sleeping over?"

"We talked about it yesterday. He's okay with it. He really likes you," Luke said softly. "And it's a nice treat for him, having breakfast with you. Lane's coming into town tonight, and Leo's upset about it."

Ian stiffened. He hadn't met Leo's mother yet, but from what he'd heard about her from Luke and Niall, he wasn't anxious to get to know her. Anyone who could abandon her child in favor of getting high wasn't someone Ian particularly wanted to meet.

"She'll be at Mom's for dinner Sunday. Will you join us?"

Luke had had the promised talk with Ian about Lane and her relationship with Leo shortly after Ian's first lunch with Leo and Ruthie. Lane was still off-limits as a conversation topic, though she'd come up a few more times at Even Keel because she'd been visiting more often. Niall and the psychologist didn't think it was a good idea for Ian to be involved in those conversations, and Ian agreed. If Leo wanted to talk to him as his uncle's boyfriend, Ian was all ears. But Even Keel was a place where Leo should be able to vent and talk without repercussion, which meant he needed an unbiased person to talk with. And since Ian hated Lane a little more after each visit, he was definitely not that person.

Luke said she usually came by for a few days every couple months, but she'd come a handful of times in the last two months. Every one of them had left both Luke and Leo irritable and out of sorts for days, and Ruthie didn't seem to be faring much better.

"Are you sure you want me there?" he asked Luke. There had been two visits since Ian and Luke had gotten serious, and Luke had asked him to steer clear of the apartment both weekends.

"I am," Luke said, and he sounded confident. "If you aren't ready—"

"No, I'll go," Ian said quickly. He wanted to suss Lane out. Leo talked about her occasionally, but it was obvious he didn't like her visits. Ian would like to see one for himself.

Another alarm chimed, and Luke groaned and rolled over to turn it off. "Time to make breakfast," he said as he sat up and eased out of bed.

Ian inched over and slapped him on his ass. "You're going to need pants first."

Luke gave him an unimpressed look but bent to grab his pajama pants and put them on. "Just for that I'm putting you in charge of the pancakes."

Ian perked up. "There will be pancakes? You should have led with that."

LANE WAS nothing like Ian had imagined. He'd pictured a stereotypical addict with pasty skin, stringy hair, and dull eyes. There weren't any pictures of her at Luke's apartment, which Ian had found odd until Luke had explained that Leo refused to have pictures of his mother around because he didn't want to think about her when she wasn't there.

Lane was gorgeous. She'd also been vivacious and talkative at dinner, if a little self-absorbed in her choice of conversation topics. Leo refused to address her directly, so the few questions she had about how he was doing were aimed at Luke, who'd been withdrawn and quiet through the meal.

Most of Lane's questions were aimed at Ian, which he'd expected. When Ian mentioned he'd be traveling to Tortola to put his house on the market, she'd perked right up. After that, Lane had focused all of her attention on Ian, baldly asking questions about his career and finances.

"Enough," Ruthie finally said when Lane asked Ian if he'd ever considered sleeping with a set of twins.

"Hey, it's a legitimate question. More than a few people have asked if I'd be into that once they find out I have a twin," Lane answered, completely unconcerned with her mother's growing horror or the way Luke was folding in on himself. Leo had left the table before dessert—a small mercy, and something very uncharacteristic for him. Ian supposed his normal habits probably didn't apply when his mother was visiting. She turned her slightly manic gaze on Ian. "Did you realize, by the way? That Luke and I are twins? He's older. Five whole minutes, but apparently that makes him the responsible, upstanding one."

Ian hadn't realized Luke and Lane were twins. It underscored how little Luke talked about his sister.

"Lane." Ruthie's tone was ice cold.

"Well he is, isn't he? Luke, the one who has his own apartment instead of couch surfing. Luke, the one who has a job," Lane said, spitting out the last word scornfully. She looked Ian up and down. "Luke, the one who scores a hot, rich boyfriend. Figures, doesn't it?"

Luke pushed back from the table, his napkin falling to the floor. "Mom, I'm taking Leo home. I'll call you tomorrow, okay?"

Ian scrambled to follow him. He heard Lane raise her voice as she and Ruthie started fighting at the table.

"Fuck," Luke muttered as soon as they'd turned the corner. He rested his head against the wall, his hands clenched into tight fists. "She's not usually this bad. Mom is really strict about her using at home, and Lane knows I won't let her see Leo if she's high. I didn't realize she was when we got here."

Ian wondered what Lane was like when she wasn't using. Was it similar enough to tonight's behavior Luke really wouldn't have noticed? Ian was no stranger to cocaine addicts. There were plenty of them in the clubs he used to frequent. Lane's erratic behavior and bright eyes had been noticeable from the get-go. Had Luke been so distracted with making sure Ian was comfortable with the family dinner he hadn't been watching for the signs?

Ian wasn't sure if he should try to comfort Luke or not. His body language was screaming stay away, so Ian didn't touch him. "Should I go get Leo?"

Luke blew out a breath but didn't lean away from the wall. "Yeah. Do you mind? I just need a minute."

Ian brought a hand up and cupped it around the back of Luke's neck, squeezing gently. Luke relaxed a fraction but didn't move, so Ian walked down the hallway until he saw a cracked-open door. Leo was sitting on the floor with army men scattered around him. The room itself was nondescript, with faded blue curtains and a clean but much-mended Star

Wars blanket on the bed. White letters spelling out Luke's name hung over the dresser.

"She ruins everything," Leo said softly when Ian crouched next to him. "Are you going to go away?"

Tears pricked the back of Ian's throat, but he swallowed hard to clear them. "No, bud. Why would I go away?"

Leo swept his hand over the men he'd lined up, sending them sprawling to the ground. "Because."

Luke had been in a serious relationship when Lane abandoned Leo and Luke had taken him in, but Ian didn't know many of the details. He did know the guy had dropped Luke the moment it became clear Luke was going to keep his nephew. From Leo's behavior and Luke's reluctance to introduce Ian to him until they'd been dating for weeks, Ian figured that must have happened a few other times as well. His heart ached for both of them.

"She's your mom, Leo. I'm glad I met her because she's the one who brought you into this world. But it doesn't matter if I like her. It matters that I like you and Luke, and I do. And she's not going to change that, okay?"

Leo nodded, but he didn't look convinced. "She's only here because she wants money."

Ian had deduced as much, but he didn't know how Leo had come to that conclusion. "Did she say something to you?"

"No, but that's all she ever wants."

Ian sighed. "How about we get you home? Where do these guys go?"

He helped Leo pile the army men back into the bin they'd come from. They looked old enough to probably have been Luke's. "Is this where you sleep when you stay with your nana?"

Leo's lips quirked into a small smile. "Yeah. Nana let me choose, and I wanted this room because it was Uncle Luke's." His eyes flicked to the doorway. The door across the hall was closed, but Ian could see the outline where the letters from Lane's name had been affixed. It was clear he'd avoided the other room because he didn't want anything to do with his mother.

"It's a good room. You like *Star Wars*?"

"I like *Clone Wars* better."

"Would you believe I haven't seen that? I haven't seen any of the new movies. Maybe you and Luke could watch them with me. I might need someone to explain things because it's been so long since I saw the originals."

Leo's eyes were still shadowed, but he was smiling by the time Ian herded him down the hall to join Luke. Ruthie hovered by the front door, but Lane was nowhere in sight. Luke caught Ian looking for her and shook his head, holding a finger up to the side of his nose and nodding toward the street. Lane must have disappeared to find another fix.

"I don't know how many more times I can do this," Ruthie whispered to Luke when she gave him a hug.

Luke's response was lost as a car drove by with blaring speakers, but from the drawn look on his face, Ian figured it was something similar.

Leo gave his grandmother a tight hug before taking Luke's hand and letting himself be led out to the car. It wasn't often that Leo allowed that kind of contact, since boys his age usually didn't want to be seen holding their guardian's hand. It spoke a lot to how upset Leo was about his mother's behavior at dinner.

Ian endured the stony silence as they drove for a while, but he reached his breaking point when he heard Leo sigh heavily in the backseat. He couldn't stand Leo and Luke being so miserable.

"I know it's late and it's a school night, but how about we stop for ice cream on the way back?"

Leo usually went wild at the prospect of ice cream, but he shook his head. Luke shot Ian a grateful look for trying but kept quiet.

"No? Rain check then. Maybe I'll bring some when we have our movie marathon this weekend," Ian said. That jollied another smile out of Leo. "We decided we're going to stay in our pajamas and watch all the *Star Wars* movies Saturday, Luke. Probably Sunday, too. Better stock up on snacks. Except I'm in charge of ice cream. Chunky Monkey all around."

Leo made a gagging noise from the backseat, just like Ian had hoped he would. Both Luke and Leo hated that flavor.

"Oh, now you have an opinion?" Ian teased, turning around in the passenger seat to look at Leo.

"Ew, bananas," Leo said with an exaggerated shudder.

"Yeah, *you're* bananas," Ian said, and Leo dissolved into giggles. Luke's hand made its way into Ian's lap. Ian twined their fingers together, holding on as Luke drove.

FOURTEEN

LANE NEVER returned to Ruthie's after she'd stormed out after dinner, and Ruthie was a mess. Luke had even missed his morning Hatha class the next day to drive around and look for her at all her old haunts, and Ian had manned the phones, calling hospitals and police stations.

She finally called from Utah Tuesday afternoon. Ruthie had talked to her, and Lane told her she'd met an interesting guy who was heading to Park City, so she'd caught a ride. From the way Luke had spit out the words when he'd relayed the story to Ian, Ian figured "interesting" was code for someone who had an ample supply of coke and was willing to share.

With Lane accounted for, if not safe, life returned to normal. Luke refused to talk about her, Leo didn't mention her, and Ruthie had replaced open worry with tight-lipped smiles. She seemed tired when Ian dropped Leo off at her house after his lesson at Even Keel. Ian had seen a similar look on his mother's face before she'd left his drunk of a father for good and moved the two of them halfway across the world. Lane was about to hit rock bottom with her family, and Ian doubted she knew. He wondered if she'd care if she did.

Ian did what he could to help take Luke's mind off his sister. They'd run harder than Ian ever had in his life these last few days during their workouts, and Ian had fed him every bit of gossip he could dig up that might interest Luke in the slightest. They'd had a good laugh over Clare's latest Internet dating disaster, and even though Luke didn't know Ian's assistant, Carl, he was well-versed in Carl's all-out war with the parking attendant who'd had Carl's car towed on three separate occasions in the last month.

Yoga always seemed to help get Luke out of his head a bit, regardless of whether he was teaching the class or taking it. After Ian dropped Leo off, he'd come by for Luke's Ashtanga class. In all honesty he probably *still* wasn't quite ready for a class that challenging, but being told he couldn't do something was the surest way to convince Ian he absolutely had to do it, and he'd finally worn Luke down enough to let him in about a month ago.

It was the last class of the day, and they'd lingered long enough cleaning up the room that the locker room was mostly deserted by the time they made it in. Ian was drenched in sweat, both from the rigorous workout and the heat of the room.

"God, I need a shower," he groaned as he leaned against his locker.

"So go take a shower," Luke said, amused.

"Can't."

"And why is that?"

Ian lifted his arms a few inches and let them fall with a smack. "Some sadistic bastard made me hold plank for twenty minutes."

Luke laughed. "It was two minutes, tops."

Ian ignored him and closed his eyes, letting the locker support most of his weight. Plank had been hard, but the shoulder stand they'd done and some intense ab workout that involved a lot of words Ian didn't understand were the final nails in his coffin. Maybe he could beg Luke to drive him home. The thought of walking even a few blocks made him want to cry.

"Come on, you big baby. Drink this and then I'll get you into the shower." He handed Ian a full bottle of water.

Ian was exhausted and sore, but it would take more than that to keep him from responding to something so provocative coming from Luke. "If you wanted an excuse to get me naked, you didn't have to attempt to kill me in yoga, you know. I'd drop trou for you any time."

Luke pursed his lips as he tried unsuccessfully to hold back a laugh. "You're incorrigible."

"It's one of the things that attracted you to me."

"God help me, it really is," Luke said ruefully. "Get your clothes off. They'll be closing in a few minutes, and I don't want to make Chandra stay late to lock up because my boyfriend was too lazy to get in the shower."

"I am not lazy, I am mortally wounded."

Luke laughed. "Fine. Work on getting your mortally wounded self undressed, and I'll ask Chandra if we can have some extra time. Maybe the steam room would help loosen your muscles up a bit."

Ian grimaced but pushed himself off the lockers and started peeling his clothes off. The sweat-damp fabric had cooled as soon as they'd left the hot studio. His skin felt clammy and disgusting, so he braved the tweak in his muscles and pulled his shirt off. He'd moved on to gingerly stepping out of his shorts by the time Luke came back in.

"We're the last ones, apparently. She's leaving, but I told her we'd shut down the steam room and make sure the door was locked behind us when we go."

"Steam first?"

"I think it'll ease a lot of the soreness, especially if it's paired with a massage."

Ian wrapped a towel around his waist after he shucked his underwear. He'd seen more than a few guys in the steam room naked, and putting his ass on a bench other naked asses had been on didn't seem very sanitary to him. That's not to say he wasn't planning on taking advantage of being alone in the steam room with Luke to get naked—he'd just make sure they had something to sit on first.

"And you're volunteering to give me this massage?" he asked skeptically. Luke wasn't the type for casual touches. He wasn't much of a cuddler in bed, and Ian highly doubted massages were a part of his normal repertoire.

"I took a few classes as part of my yoga certification. My instructor thought it was important we know all the major muscle groups and how they connect and work together. Massage was a part of that."

Ian hummed in acknowledgment as they entered the steam room. It wasn't that large—barely big enough to fit half a dozen men at once—but they had it completely to themselves. Luke fiddled with the controls before stepping in, and within a few seconds fresh billows of steam clouded the cubicle.

It did feel nice, Ian had to admit. Especially when Luke unknotted and removed the towel he'd slung around his waist. Luke spread it over the bench and added his own to it.

"Lie down."

Ian complied, gritting his teeth when his muscles protested. Even covered with the towels, the hard bench was far from cozy, especially when Luke climbed on top of him, straddling his ass. Luke supported most of his weight on his knees, but it still wasn't the most comfortable position.

He forgot his discomfort the moment Luke's hands touched his back. They were slick with some sort of oil Ian hadn't noticed him pick up, and Ian couldn't help but moan as Luke dug his thumbs into his lower back and swept them up his spine. Ian shivered at the sensation and his cock twitched against the rough towel underneath him.

"You're building up your core strength, which is good, but you've got to relax into your poses. When you're tense it magnifies the stress on your muscles," Luke chided. His thumbs kneaded the tight spots on either side of Ian's neck. "This is from holding your shoulders too rigidly in your warrior poses. You should feel those between your shoulder blades and in your thighs, not your neck."

Ian tried not to let his head loll back and forth as Luke systematically worked out all the tension in his neck and shoulders. It felt amazing. Even though there was nothing sexual at all about the way Luke was touching him, Ian's cock was fully hard. It throbbed uncomfortably, stuck between him and the hard bench below.

Luke's talented thumbs ran up and down his spine again, and Ian couldn't help but pump his hips a few times as his back arched into the massage. It sent his ass into Luke's crotch. Luke placed a hand against his lower back, forcing him back down.

Ian muttered an oath as his erection ground against the bench. His arousal was reaching a point that it was more pressing than the ache in his muscles. Luke was definitely hard as well, which only made Ian more turned on.

"Ready for a shower?" Luke asked. He ran his hands down Ian's sides and gave his ass a good kneading before tapping it playfully with his palm.

Ian grunted into his arms, which he had pillowed under his head. Luke climbed off the bench. The drag of his hard cock against Ian's ass was a horrible tease, especially since he backed away when Ian raised his hips seeking more contact.

"You've been in here long enough. Let's shower and I'll drive you home."

Ian knew that wasn't a euphemism for anything. Such was the peril of dating a man with a kid. Leo spent the evenings Luke worked at his grandmother's, but she only kept him overnight on Fridays. Ian loved Fridays. It meant he and Luke could have sex as often and as loudly as they wanted without worrying about waking Leo up or getting home in time to get him to bed. Alas, tonight was not a Friday. It was probably already pushing things for Luke to stay late with him at the gym.

"Up and at 'em, tiger," Luke teased from the doorway. He disappeared, and a moment later the steam clicked off. It would take quite a while for all the clouds to dissipate, but the cloying humidity eased a bit. Ian could happily stay there for a lot longer now that it was easier to breathe, but he heard Luke start a shower.

Ian braced himself for protesting muscles and eased himself off the bench. Surprisingly, he felt a lot better. Ian flexed his arms, happy they no longer felt like they were made of lead.

He tossed the towels in the bin on his way to the shower, mindful of the fact that they were the last ones in the locker room so they'd have to make sure it was reasonably tidied. All thoughts of that fled when he made it to the entrance to the showers, though.

Luke hadn't bothered to pull the curtain on the cubicle he was in, giving Ian an unhindered view of him standing under the water stroking himself. Luke's head was tipped back, his eyes closed against the flow of water that cascaded down over his face and body. Ian's cock jumped at the sight of Luke biting his lip to keep his groans quiet as his fist flew over his length at a brutal pace.

Ian made a beeline for Luke, joining him under the hot spray.

"About time," Luke gasped when Ian tugged at his hand and replaced it with his. Luke was rock hard under his grip, his cock already a deep red. "Wasn't sure you'd make it before the show was over."

"If you'd have told me there would be a show, I'd have been here sooner," Ian muttered.

He twisted his wrist on the next upstroke, smirking when Luke's knees gave out and he stumbled, saved only by shooting a hand out to steady himself against the wall.

Ian's cock jumped against his belly, but he could tell Luke was close to getting off, so he ignored it in favor of running a hand up Luke's side and carding it through his wet hair. He urged Luke's head down so he could kiss him, and a moment later Luke was jerking against him, spilling into his fist and groaning into his mouth.

He slowed his strokes, steering clear of the head of Luke's cock as he eased him through his orgasm. Ian wrapped his thumb and forefinger around the base as he cupped Luke's balls with his palm, lightly massaging the tightened skin. Luke shuddered against him and broke the kiss in favor of resting his head against Ian and panting into his neck as he twitched through the aftershocks of his orgasm.

Ian let him have a moment before pressing his still-hard cock against Luke's hip suggestively. Luke raised his head and kissed him again before pulling away.

"Want me to wash your hair?" he asked.

Ian snorted. "I want you to wash my *dick*."

"Romance is lost on you," Luke said despairingly. Ian would have felt guilty, except he knew Luke well enough to know there wasn't a romantic bone in his body. In their relationship, Ian was the romantic one, and that was pretty damning for Luke.

"Just get your hands on me," Ian said. He wasn't above begging.

He almost cursed when Luke grabbed the shampoo, but instead of washing Ian's hair as he'd suggested, he wrapped his hand around Ian's cock. The slick slide of the suds was almost immediately too much, and the soles of his feet started to burn after just a few strokes, a telltale sign he was about to come. Luke shifted his grip and slid behind Ian, letting Ian sag against him as he jacked him. Between the sensation from the soap, the feel of the water still beating down on his oversensitive skin, and the fact that he'd been hard through Luke's massage, it didn't take long before Ian's orgasm overtook him. He slumped fully against Luke as he came, whimpering when the soap that had felt so delicious a moment earlier was suddenly unbearable. Luke seemed to understand, since he backed off his strokes and squeezed Ian's cock lightly instead until he'd worked through the aftershocks.

He startled a bit when Luke started washing his hair, but it felt a lot like the massage earlier. He relaxed into it, wondering how it was he'd never had someone do this for him before. It was weirdly intimate, especially considering that just minutes before Luke had stroked him off. Still, a hand job didn't feel as personal as someone washing his hair. It was odd and domestic, but Ian went with it.

"Rinse," Luke said. He pressed a kiss against Ian's neck and pushed him toward the spray.

As soon as they were both rinsed, Luke turned off the water. There were no towels on the rack, but Luke opened a cabinet tucked off to the side and produced two fresh ones for them. After having Luke wash his hair, Ian was a bit worried he'd want them to towel each other off, but he didn't. That would just have been awkward.

They dressed in companionable silence, and Ian helped Luke pick up all the stray towels and odds and ends around the locker room. An outside cleaning crew would come through before the gym opened in the morning, but employees were responsible for things like gathering up the laundry for the service that took it every day. Ian had gotten into the habit of helping Luke with the menial tasks, since it would be ridiculous for him to wait for Luke to finish if helping got them out sooner.

It was already past Leo's usual bedtime, and Ian felt a wave of guilt at keeping Luke out. He knew Leo wouldn't necessarily mind—the kid was always trying to work whatever angle he could to stay up later on the few nights Ian had been there at bedtime—but it felt like he was stealing Luke's time and attention away from him. It was a learning experience, trying to balance their relationship with Luke and Leo's relationship—and even Ian and Leo's relationship. He was lucky Leo was such an awesome kid. There were plenty of brats out there who would pitch a fit if their guardian took time away from them to spend with someone else, but Leo seemed genuinely thrilled his uncle was dating Ian. The private sailing lessons that came as a perk probably helped.

"I'll walk," Ian said when they were standing outside the gym locking up.

Luke looked at him curiously. "I can drop you."

"You're already running late. I'll see you tomorrow when you pick Leo up from Even Keel. Niall has me teaching his class this week."

He hadn't been on the afternoon schedule since he started his new job, but his hours were flexible and there wasn't any reason Ian couldn't take off an afternoon a week to spend at Even Keel. The two evening classes he taught were fun, but he preferred working with the younger kids who came by after school. Besides, he tended to work late on Fridays anyway so he and Ethan could meet Niall at The Weathered Mast for dinner. It wasn't like it mattered if he was in the office for the typical nine to five business hours, anyway. So much of what he did was after hours, and he had a staff that was always in the office anyway to field phone calls and take the occasional meeting that couldn't be rescheduled.

"I'll tell Leo. He'll be psyched. He said Josh doesn't know his knots as well as you."

Ian chuckled. "Pretty soon he'll know more than me. I told him I'd give him two bucks for every knot he masters, and the kid has been turning out new ones every week."

"Is that why he's constantly got his head buried in that book Niall gave him?" Luke laughed. "How much has he bilked out of you so far?"

"About twenty."

Luke whistled. "That's the first I've heard of it. I wonder what he's squirreling the money away for? Usually he begs to go spend any windfall he comes across."

Ian knew, but Leo had sworn him to secrecy. Leo was saving because he wanted to buy a Kindle for Luke's birthday in a few weeks. Ian told him he'd kick in whatever Leo didn't have, but Leo was determined to save as much as he could for it. It was the perfect gift; Ian also planned to stock it with the classics Luke loved so much.

Ian paused at Luke's car when Luke opened the passenger side door for him. "Seriously, I can walk. Especially if you're going to start treating me like a girl."

Luke cuffed him across the top of his head and pushed him toward the open door. "It's called common courtesy. If Clare heard you say that she'd have your balls."

"She's a vegetarian."

Luke looked up at the sky for a moment. "I question my sanity daily."

"You love it," Ian teased. He climbed in and buckled his seat belt. If Luke wasn't worried about being ten minutes late to pick up Leo, he supposed he shouldn't be either.

Luke closed his door and circled the car to get in on his own side. "I do, you know," he said as he turned the ignition.

"Do what?"

"Love it. Your sense of humor. And the way you're concerned about Leo. How you dropped everything to help me look for Lane. I just, I love you."

Ian was stunned. He'd never had a lover say that to him before. Not even the people he'd lived with. The few relationships he'd been in were about convenience; things were so different with Luke.

"I'm not telling you to freak you out or because I expect you to say it back," Luke said, and he was using his Zen-like yoga instructor voice, which made Ian's neck prickle. He didn't need to be soothed; he was just surprised. "But I realized I do, and I thought you should know. I mean, you know I'm serious about you. I wouldn't have introduced you to Leo otherwise."

"I already knew Leo."

"You know what I mean."

Ian did. Leo was the center of Luke's world. There was so much uncertainty in Leo's life, and Luke was the only thing he could count on. At some point, that had widened to include Ian, which was more than a little terrifying.

"I care about you and Leo," Ian offered. He almost cringed at how stupid that sounded.

"I know you do." Luke reached over and squeezed Ian's knee. "Really, Ian. I'm not drowning in silent man pain over here because you can't say I love you. It'll come in time, or it won't. It doesn't matter, as long as you're there for me and you keep worrying about Leo's bedtime. That's love, even if you aren't comfortable saying it."

Luke stopped at the curb outside Ian's building. "Go call Niall and freak out."

Ian snorted. "I am not going to call Niall and 'freak out' like some sort of teenager."

Luke leaned over and kissed him. "Of course you're not. I'll see you tomorrow. You guys want me to have Chrissy save your usual table for dinner?"

It would take more than Luke blindsiding him with an unexpected I love you to keep the three of them from their Friday night dinner at The Weathered Mast. "Yup."

"Tell Niall hi and I've got a new beer for him to try," Luke said, and Ian flipped him off after he slammed the car door.

He wasn't going to call Niall. That would be ridiculous. Especially since Niall wasn't a huge fan of talking on the phone, and Ethan stocked really good Scotch. Obviously, he was going to invite himself over instead.

Ian didn't bother going up to his loft. Instead, he hitched his gym bag up on his shoulder and opened the app on his phone to hail a cab.

FIFTEEN

IAN WAS in the middle of a phone interview with a grant applicant when Carl knocked on his doorframe and stuck his head in. "Hey, sorry to interrupt, but there's someone here to see you. She says it's a family emergency."

Ian glanced at his cell phone, which was sitting on his desk. No one had called or texted, which meant whoever was downstairs probably didn't have his personal number. He had a sinking suspicion who that might be.

He held the receiver away from his mouth. "Have the front desk tell her I'll be down in a minute," he said quietly.

"You don't want me to have them send her up?"

"No." If it really was Lane, the last place Ian wanted her was anywhere inside Cloud Technologies. There was expensive equipment everywhere, and he didn't doubt for a moment she'd pocket anything valuable she saw.

Carl shrugged and popped back out of his office, leaving Ian to interrupt the interview and make his apologies. They'd only just gotten started, and it was horribly unprofessional, but there was no way Ian was going to leave Lane down there unsupervised longer than necessary.

She was standing in the atrium with a gruff-looking guy in an ill-fitting leather jacket that had several suspicious bulges when Ian made it downstairs. She didn't look nearly as put together as she had when he'd met her a few weeks ago.

JUST AS Ian had suspected, Lane was after money. She'd already tapped out all of Ruthie's resources, and Ian knew from talking with Luke that Luke had cut her off years ago. As the new guy on the scene, it made sense Lane would come to him, especially since she knew money wasn't a problem for him.

That didn't mean Ian welcomed the visit. He'd taken one look at Lane and her mysterious companion and ushered them out of Cloud Technologies. That's how he'd ended up in a diner a few blocks away with a ravenous Lane, who was on her second plate of pancakes. The menacing guy who'd been with her disappeared after giving Ian a hard look and warning him he'd be back for her in a few hours. The threat had been implied, though Ian would have gladly challenged it if he'd thought Lane would stay. He knew she wouldn't. She wasn't at rock bottom yet, and there was no way to get through to her before she reached it. Even then it wasn't a sure thing; it hadn't been for Ian's father. People had to want help, and there wasn't any way to force that. God knows his mother had tried, and Ian was sure Ruthie and Luke had done the same for Lane.

"I just need enough cash to get me square with the guy who took me to Utah. It was a bad scene, and I owe him a couple grand. A friend has jobs lined up for us if we can make it to Sacramento. It's where we're going tonight, if I can get the money to pay Jimmy."

Ian hadn't been on the receiving end of one of Lane's sob stories before, but he'd heard enough from his father to be able to spot the desperation. He wasn't sure if Lane actually believed there would be a job waiting for her in Sacramento, or if she just thought her next fix was there, but either way she was dead set that getting there would be the answer to her problems.

And it probably would be, at least until the money ran out and she hitched her way back to Seattle and showed up at Ruthie's door to start the process all over again.

"How much?"

Lane tensed and wrapped her thin fingers around her fourth cup of black coffee. She'd calmed noticeably since she'd started drinking it, though Ian was sure the food had helped, too. There was no way the caffeine in it could ease her itch for a high-level stimulant like cocaine, but it was clearly helping bridge the gap at least a little bit.

"Fifteen grand."

"I can't just give you money," Ian said.

She crumpled in on herself and moaned softly. There was no sign of the light in her eyes he'd seen at dinner at Ruthie's; they were dull and listless like countless other junkies'. Luke's beautiful sister actually looked like a drug addict now.

"Yes, you can. I know you have it."

Ian sighed. "I never said I didn't. But I can't just give you money, Lane."

"You have to. That guy Jimmy? I owe it to his boss. I thought we were just hanging out and having fun, but he had me on a tab. There's no way I can pay it, and these guys aren't messing around. They want their money. They only let me come back here because I told them I could get it from you. Jimmy's not going to let me walk away if he doesn't have the money."

God, what a disaster. "Lane—"

"Look, Luke and Mom do it all the time. If you were really part of this family, you would too."

"Lane, they care about you. They want you to get the help you need. I can't just give you money that you'll turn around and blow on more drugs."

She straightened, her eyes lighting with the first sign of any fire he'd seen in her since she showed up in the lobby. "This isn't about more drugs. This is about paying for the drugs *I already took*. It's a blur, but we had a couple wild days in Utah. Gambling, lots of drugs. They're not going to accept no for an answer. I need that money."

"So what? I give you the money to pay off this dealer, and then what? You move to Sacramento and get clean?" Ian shook his head. "I don't think so."

She looked down. "I'm not good at getting clean. I've tried before and it never works. And I'm not going to bullshit you and say I will just to get the money."

"I could send you to a rehab center, Lane. Not just a detox program, but a real center where you'd get the help you need." Ian knew the words were falling on deaf ears, but he had to try. "Think about what Leo goes through. Don't you want to get clean for him?"

"Do you think it does Leo any good for me to get killed because I made some stupid choices? I thought you wanted what's best for him," she snarled.

"I do want what's best for him. And what's best for Luke and even you. That's not me paying off this debt for you and letting you go off into the sunset until the next time you need money or a place to sleep and you end up back here high as a kite."

Lane swallowed. "So I won't come back. Give me the money and I won't come back."

"I don't think that would help Leo, either. He needs you. You're his mother."

Lane recoiled. "What? No. I mean, I'll always be his mother. I love him, but I'm not mother material, you know? He's Luke's kid, not mine. I signed papers."

Ian swallowed. He'd asked Luke about it once, and Luke had told him Lane had made him Leo's official guardian. She still retained parental rights, though, and Luke lived in fear of her deciding to retract his guardianship and disappearing with Leo. The social worker who was on their case had helped Luke draw up formal adoption papers, but he'd never worked up the courage to give them to Lane. He'd been too afraid it would send her over the edge, Luke had said.

"You signed papers letting Luke make decisions for Leo, but those didn't give Luke permanent custody," he said carefully.

Lane looked completely shocked. "No. No, I wanted Luke to have custody. I even had Leo's father give up his rights because that's what the social worker said I needed to do so Luke could have him."

Somewhere along the line someone had botched things spectacularly in Leo's case. Ian had never been in the system here in the United States, but he was familiar with the child welfare system in Scotland; if the US system was anywhere near as complicated as the one he'd been in, it was easy to imagine how this relatively minor part of Leo's case had slipped through the cracks. Social workers worked overtime dealing with kids who had no one; the details of Leo's case after he'd already been placed with a loving, responsible family member would have been low priority.

Ian knew he was playing with something he had no business being in, but he couldn't help himself. "Luke has the adoption paperwork at his apartment, but he didn't know if you'd want to sign it."

Ian had noticed them in Luke's desk drawer when he'd been looking for a notepad. He and Luke had talked about it afterward, and Ian understood why Luke hadn't tried to get Lane to sign them. There was a finality to it that Luke just wasn't ready for. Not that he wasn't willing and eager to take full custody of Leo, because he was. But Luke held out hope that Lane would get clean and come back to be part of Leo's life, and he thought the adoption would prevent that from ever happening. He kept hoping that Lane would wake up someday and realize she was missing out on her son's life and come back, but Ian wasn't so sure that was going to happen.

"He—what?" Lane blinked. "Look, I have to go. Jimmy will be back soon, and if I can't pay him, I have to try to run. I have a ride lined up to Sacramento, and they'll leave without me if I'm not there on time."

"Just give me a couple minutes, okay?" Ian pulled his phone out and texted Luke.

Need to talk to you ASAP.

Luke never kept his phone on him at the brewery. He'd dropped one in a vat of beer once, which had resulted in the loss of both the phone and the entire batch of beer. After that he'd kept his phone in the office while he was on the floor.

Lane was looking around the diner like she expected Jimmy to materialize at any moment. "Can we—you said Luke had the paperwork, right? So can I just sign it?"

Ian's mouth went dry. "You want to sign it?"

"Yes, did I not already tell you I thought I *had*?"

Ian wondered how long it would be before she got desperate for another fix. Hopefully, he could get in touch with Luke before she got too far down that road.

"Look, I know I'm a shit mother. And things are about to get worse, so the least I can do for Leo is to make sure he can always stay with my brother."

Lane crossed her arms and started tapping her foot and fidgeting in the booth. "Can you take me to Luke's place? Do you know where the paperwork is? I just want to get this done so I can get out of here."

"I—" Ian floundered, unsure of what to do. "Are you sure?"

Lane gave him a flat look.

"Okay." Ian's keys were up in his office, but he knew where Luke kept a spare. If they were going to make Jimmy's deadline they had to hurry, and he didn't want to waste time going upstairs.

"Let's get to Luke's, then." Lane blew out a breath and straightened her shoulders. It did wonders for her, making her look more like the bright woman he'd first met at the disastrous dinner.

Ian couldn't help but reach out to squeeze her shoulder lightly. He dropped his hand quickly and dropped a few bills on the table to cover their meal. "One stop first."

Lane's expression closed off as she made her way out onto the sidewalk. Her jaw was set in the same determined way Luke clenched his; the resemblance was striking, and for the first time Ian could picture her as Luke's twin instead of just his absent sister. "I told you, I don't have time," she muttered lowly.

"We have time for the bank. We can get you settled with Jimmy before we head to file the paperwork. The courthouse doesn't close for a couple hours."

Lane's surprise was evident. It made her look younger and vulnerable. Ian's chest ached a bit at the sight. She'd obviously expected him to let her go without it. "But you said—"

"You're Luke's family. I'm not going to let you get hurt if I can help it. I'm doing this as much for him and Leo as I am for you."

Lane stared at him for a few moments before nodding. Whatever she'd seen on his face hadn't erased the crease between her brows, but it had eased the tension in her posture a bit. "Okay, then."

It felt like she was agreeing to more than just stopping at the bank. The words had weight to them, just like her appraisal had. Ian wasn't sure, but he suspected he'd just passed some sort of important test.

Lane let Ian take her elbow gently and steer her down the sidewalk, neither of them breaking the silence with small talk. There wasn't much else to say, anyway. Ian wished he'd been able to talk her into a rehab program, but at least he was able to make sure she was safe for today.

IAN TEXTED Luke three more times after Lane left, but he still hadn't heard anything back. He thought about going back to Luke's to wait for him, but he was too keyed up to sit still. Instead, he went back to the office and tried to focus on paperwork.

That lasted all of an hour before he gave up and caught a cab over to Luke's.

Ian had been sure he was doing the right thing in the moment, but after he and Lane had gone to the notary and filed the paperwork at the courthouse, doubt had started to set in. Ian knew this was ultimately what Luke wanted, but what if the hesitation had been about more than just waiting for Lane to be ready for it? He'd never sat down and really talked with Luke about how he felt about having full custody of Leo, aside from Luke mentioning he'd had the paperwork drawn up. Ian had assumed it was what he wanted, going by the things Luke had said over the last few months.

Luke's car was parked in his usual spot downstairs, which had been a surprise. He usually finished late on days he spent at the brewery. Ian's stomach twisted nervously as he made his way up the stairs to Luke's door.

It was yanked open halfway through Ian's first knock. Luke had a thunderous expression on his face, but he stepped aside and let Ian come in.

"Lane was here a little bit ago," Luke said as soon as he'd closed the door. "She said she'd gotten into some trouble in Utah but you'd smoothed it out for her." Luke was seething, his words clipped and his hand clenched around a familiar sheaf of papers. Ian waited for him to continue, sure the other shoe was about to drop. "She also wanted to make sure I had a copy of this before she skipped town. She said you went with her to file the official paperwork at the courthouse."

He tossed the notarized copy of Leo's adoption papers at Ian, and Ian caught them before they could scatter. "Luke—"

"What the fuck do you think you're doing? We aren't playing house, Ian. You can't just fucking do something like this on your own!"

"Calm down, Leo's—"

"Leo is at my mother's because I don't want him anywhere near you right now!"

Ian flinched as if Luke had struck him. Everything Ian had done was to protect Leo. "Just—I'm sorry. She said she was leaving right away, and I didn't want to pass up the chance to straighten things out."

"Straighten things out?" Luke roared, his expression both irate and incredulous. "Straighten things out? Leo's custody arrangement isn't yours to 'straighten out!'"

"I tried to get in touch with you, but she was leaving!"

Luke's face turned an even darker shade of pink at that. "You texted me. You didn't call my cell. You didn't call the brewery. You didn't call my *mother*, who was definitely at home. You decided to do this on your own."

"I didn't decide anything. It was Lane's decision!"

"My sister comes to you for money and leaves with her money and without her parental rights," Luke said flatly. "Do you see why I might be upset here? You forced—"

Ian couldn't let him finish that sentence. "I didn't force her to do anything, she—"

Luke wasn't stopping for anything, the words tumbling out of his mouth so fast Ian could barely understand them. "Are you out of your mind? Do you know what Lane's going to do with that money? It's all going to go to drugs, Ian. She's going to end up dead."

Ian swallowed. At least he could set Luke's mind at ease about this. God, no wonder he was so angry. Had he thought Ian handed over a bundle of cash? Ian was lucky he was speaking to him at all if Luke thought he'd signed his sister's death warrant. "That money had already gone to drugs, Luke. I paid it directly to the guy she was in debt to. I don't know exactly what he was threatening to do to her if she didn't pay, but it was bad enough that she was desperate."

Luke visibly sagged. "Thank God," he muttered. "Fifteen thousand dollars. Jesus Christ. Do you know how quickly she could overdose on that?"

"She could still overdose without it," Ian said baldly. "You can't change who she is, Luke. You're doing everything you can for her by taking Leo in and caring for him. I know you give her money when you can, even though you're sure it's going for drugs. I get it. And I'm sorry I went behind your back and you were so worried, I am. But I'm not sorry you have legal custody of Leo now."

"It wasn't—" Luke trailed off and took a deep breath, like what he was about to say was too hard to get out. "It wasn't a trade, was it? You didn't tell her you wouldn't give her the money if she didn't sign the papers, right?"

Luke's voice was small and scared, and Ian's stomach turned violently. "Did I get her to sell Leo to you? No. Jesus." Ian rubbed his hand over his face roughly. Had Luke really thought he'd do something like that? Ian wouldn't have said a word to Lane about the papers if he hadn't already known she wanted Luke to have official custody of Leo. "I'd already given the guy his money before she signed the papers. One had nothing to do with the other. I just—I know it's what you wanted. It's for goddamn sure what Leo would have wanted if he'd known it was possible. You said you weren't giving the papers to her 'til you were sure she was a danger to Leo, and she was, Luke. Who do you think she'd have gone to if I hadn't given her the money? She'd have brought that guy *here*, Luke. To your doorstep. To Leo's doorstep."

"I'm her brother, Ian. I could have dealt with it. It was my *job* to deal with it. Not yours."

"You have no idea, do you? She may not be at rock bottom yet, but it's a local call from where she is. I know you don't want to look at your sister and see an addict, but that's what she is. She'll go with anyone who offers her a fix, and she'll do whatever she needs to, to get it. That's how she ended up owing that loan shark fifteen grand."

Luke looked shattered, but Ian couldn't stop. Not until he made sure Luke understood. He'd gone about it in the wrong way, but Ian didn't regret what he'd done. "She's too far gone for you to help, Luke. She's not going to miraculously recover just because you want her to. She has to want it, and she doesn't. She won't, maybe not ever, but definitely not until she bottoms out. You want her here when that happens so Leo sees that? I can tell you what rock bottom looks like to a kid. It's tripping over your dad on the living room floor in the morning on your way out the door because he came home the night before but was too blind drunk to make it past the entryway before he passed out. It's getting collection calls because he's taken out a second mortgage your mom knew nothing about to pay for gambling and booze. It's seeing your mom worried to death over what she's going to do one moment and faking a smile for you the next because she doesn't want you to know."

Ian swallowed. "You think Leo doesn't know exactly what's going on? He does, Luke. You can't protect him from this. He sees everything. He worries the next time she leaves, she'll take him with her, did you know that? And now she *can't*, because she signed over her rights to you. She knew it was the best thing for him. Hell, she thought you already had custody, Luke. She thought she'd given that to you with the guardianship papers."

Luke slumped against the wall. "She what?"

Ian lowered his voice and fought to keep his emotions in check. "She thought you already had sole custody. I didn't coerce her into signing the papers. I didn't bribe her by paying off her debt to that sleazeball. She loves Leo, whatever that means for her right now. She wants what's best for him. That's why she left him with you, Luke. He's been yours since the day you took him in. You know that, Leo knows that. Now it's official."

Ian trembled with barely contained anger. He hated conflict. Raised voices, aggression—he'd had enough of that to serve him several lifetimes. But this wasn't a situation he could joke his way out of, and Ian was at a loss. How could Luke think those things? That Ian would give Lane money knowing she'd turn around and buy cocaine with it? That he'd offer to pay her to give up Leo? No matter how much contempt he felt for her, he'd never do that to her.

"I'm sorry, Luke. She showed up at my office with that guy in tow demanding money, or they'd be coming to see you and Leo next, and I panicked. I didn't want him anywhere near either of you, and Lane looked desperate. So I paid him."

"And you didn't mention the adoption papers?" Luke asked flatly.

"No. Like I said, that was Lane's idea," Ian said, clenching his jaw when Luke snorted and shook his head in disbelief. "No, really. She wanted to sign the papers."

Luke blew out a breath and laced his hands in front of his face, pressing his thumbs against the sides of his nose. Ian had seen him do it before when he had a headache. "I think I need to talk to Lane again."

"That's probably a good idea," Ian answered. "And just so you know, I offered to pay for rehab. When she decides she's ready, we'll get her in a good residential program."

He left off his opinion that she might never be ready. God knew his father wasn't. His liver would likely give out long before his stubbornness. Ian had made him the same offer a decade ago.

Luke dropped his hands to his sides. His eyes were glassy with unshed tears and exhaustion. Ian hated that he'd had any part in putting that expression on Luke's face, but the end result was worth it.

"I need you to go." The words were soft, without any of the burning anger Luke had been full of a few minutes ago. The quiet resignation was worse.

Ian's heart broke a little. "Luke—"

"Not for good. Just for now," Luke said, and the constriction that made Ian feel like he was suffocating lifted a bit. "You're important to me and Leo, Ian, and if you're as serious about our relationship as I think you are, then you're going to become even *more* important. But you can't just go off and do whatever you think is best for us without consulting me."

"I know. I'm sorry," Ian said quietly. "I'm not used to relying on anyone else or being accountable to anyone else. I didn't think."

"I know you're sorry. It's not enough right now. I need some time. Just looking at you is too much, okay? Give me some time. Go. I'll text you."

CLARE SAT forward in the squishy loveseat she always claimed in Ethan's library, her hands steepled together. "So basically, you majorly overstepped your bounds and he threw you out?"

Niall elbowed Clare roughly from his perch beside her, but she shrugged. Ian couldn't find any fault in her summation; he'd spent the last twenty minutes running through the entire saga with them, but she'd captured the crux of it.

"I'm sure he's just taking time to process," Niall said diplomatically. "Have you heard from him at all?"

"He texted." Ian took his phone out of his pocket and tossed it to Niall. Clare pushed her way in to see it too, not that it was worth the effort, in Ian's opinion. Luke had only sent one, and it had come before Ian had gotten home after their fight.

I need time.

That had been three days ago, and Ian hadn't heard anything else from him. He'd opted to stay in instead of going to The Weathered Mast for their usual Friday night dinner; Luke would definitely be working, and Ian didn't want to force him to talk to him.

Ethan was gone for the weekend with his rock-climbing buddies, so Ian hadn't hesitated to invite himself over to keep Niall company. Niall always picked him up on Saturday mornings before they headed in to Even Keel anyway, so why not just pack a bag and spend the weekend at his house to save him the trip?

It was easier to justify it that way than for Ian to admit he didn't want to spend the weekend alone.

Niall had apparently been expecting him, if the freezer stocked with Chunky Monkey and his favorite Scotch ready in the library was any indication. Clare had shown up, pizza in hand, forty minutes after Ian had gotten there. There hadn't been a single vegan or soy topping on it; Ian was pretty sure that was a sign of the apocalypse, or at least that his friends knew full well how much he was wallowing.

"Nothing else?" Niall asked, tossing the phone back to Ian.

"Radio silence," Ian answered sullenly.

It wasn't that he didn't deserve Luke's anger—Ian knew full well he did. Luke would be justified in breaking up with him and never letting him see Leo again after the stunt Ian had pulled. But it had felt like the right decision in the moment, and Ian still couldn't bring himself to be unhappy with the end result.

He was regretting the fight. He'd never felt so miserable before. Knowing Luke was hurt and he'd been the one to hurt him was gut wrenching. Guilt was a horrible feeling, he was discovering. The slow burn of it was much worse than anything he'd ever felt before.

"He'll reach out when he's ready," Clare said. "I brought you some chamomile and lemon balm tea to help you sleep."

Ian snorted. "Why would you think I was having trouble sleeping?"

Niall gave him an unimpressed look that had Ian squirming in his chair. "I'll make sure he has a cup before bed tonight," he said to Clare.

It probably couldn't hurt. Ian had spent the night of their fight blind drunk at a bar around the corner from Luke's apartment, alternating between flirting with the people who hit on him and picking fights, according to Niall, who'd shown up with Ethan about ten drinks in and dragged him back to the loft. Ian didn't remember much after his sixth drink, but Niall said he'd been texting him a running commentary about everyone who propositioned him. There had been more than a few; apparently, even dead drunk and depressed as hell, Ian still had game. Oddly, it wasn't as comforting as it should have been.

So the first night hadn't been a problem because he'd been passed out drunk, and the second night he'd still been hungover enough to sleep. But last night he'd barely gotten any sleep; all he could do was replay their argument and see the look of utter betrayal and rage in Luke's eyes when he'd thought Ian had bribed Lane into giving up custody of Leo.

Even the memory of it made Ian sick to his stomach.

"I don't know if he's going to forgive me. He was—I really fucked things up." Ian curled in on himself in his chair, steadfastly ignoring the glass of Scotch Niall had poured for him when they'd settled in the library. The last thing he wanted after Tuesday night was more alcohol.

"He will." Niall sounded so sure, but he hadn't been there. He hadn't seen how disappointed and angry Luke had been.

Hell, Ian was disappointed in himself, and that was probably a first. He'd never felt like this before.

Clare clapped her hands together. "The way I see it, we have three options for tonight. We can sit here and watch Ian pout, which isn't productive at all. We can watch a movie—I brought *Promised Land* and a documentary on school nutrition that looks good. Or we can go dancing."

Ian blinked. "What?"

"I guess it's really two choices because I absolutely cannot sit here and watch you wallow anymore. We've finally found something that doesn't look good on him, Niall."

Niall grinned. "Hard to believe, but I have to agree. Introspective guilt doesn't do anything for your cheekbones."

God, they were ridiculous. Ian couldn't help but smile. "Fine. But I'm not going out, and I refuse to watch anything Clare recommends."

"But *Promised Land* has Matt Damon! And there's a really interesting story behind the anti-fracking—"

"Blanket refusal," Ian interrupted.

"Seconded," Niall chimed in, ignoring the outraged look Clare shot him. He unfolded himself from the loveseat and pulled his tablet off the table. "We will use the magic of streaming Internet to find something as chauvinistic and demeaning as your black heart can handle," he said, opening Netflix and shoving the tablet over to Ian as Clare started in on her conditions.

SIXTEEN

USUALLY, LUKE waited for Leo in the car after his sailing lesson on Saturdays, but today he was standing on the dock. Ian's heart thumped hard in his chest at the sight of him, but from the way Luke had his hands shoved in the pockets of his jeans and the uncomfortable expression on his face, it didn't seem like he was there to sweep Ian into a passionate embrace. Damn Nicholas Sparks and the unrealistic expectations he'd foisted on the world.

It must have been a surprise to Leo, too, from the way he stopped short at the sight of his uncle standing at the edge of the pier.

"Kiddo, I need to talk to Ian for a minute. Can you wait for us inside? I'll come get you in a minute," Luke said.

They didn't keep the building open while they were out on the water, but Ian spotted Niall on the deck of the catamaran. "It's locked up. How about you help Niall finish up on the cat?"

Ian looked at Luke questioningly, and Luke nodded. "Sure. I'll come down in a sec. Don't get in Niall's way."

Leo didn't question them, which was odd for a kid who never stopped talking. He sprinted toward Niall's boat. Ian watched him climb aboard, not looking away until he was sure Niall had seen Leo and knew he was there.

When he turned to Luke, Luke's hard expression had softened a bit. "He'll be fine out there," Ian said. "Niall will keep him busy."

"I know," Luke said. He pulled his hands out of his pockets and left them at his sides. He looked nervous, which was making Ian nervous in turn. They hadn't spoken since Luke had thrown him out of his apartment three days ago. Ian had been a little surprised to see Leo show up that morning; he'd half expected Luke to keep him home. "Listen, this is awkward. But my mom can't watch Leo tonight, and I got called in to cover a shift at the bar. The car needs new brakes, and I could really use the extra cash. Can you watch Leo?"

Ian was stunned by the question. From the moment he'd spotted Luke on the dock, a hundred reasons for him being there had run through his mind. None of them had been a request to babysit.

"Uh, sure," Ian said. It hurt that Luke would trust him with Leo but not trust him enough to ask him to cover the cost of the brakes, but that was classic Luke. Even if they were still together, he likely wouldn't have let Ian pay for a car repair. And that was a big if. Ian hadn't been to the gym since their fight, and Luke hadn't been in touch aside from the terse text he'd sent.

"Great. Thanks. Do you want him at your place? I could pick him up after my shift."

The bar didn't close until 1:30 a.m., and he'd be another hour after that cleaning up. When Luke's mom watched Leo, she usually kept him overnight, but Ian wasn't set up for that and Luke clearly wasn't expecting him to have Leo sleep over. "I can watch him at yours. That way he doesn't have to be woken up and moved," Ian offered.

Luke visibly relaxed. "That would be perfect," he said. He studied Ian for a moment and then looked away. "I didn't want to ask you for that in case you weren't comfortable at my place."

Because he'd thrown him out the last time Ian had been there were the unspoken words in that sentence, but Ian heard them loud and clear. He hadn't envisioned going back to Luke's place without a reconciliation, but he also wasn't going to let their relationship drama affect Leo. He was glad Luke wasn't either. Whatever was happening between them, Luke earned major points for not cutting Ian off from Leo. It was startling just how relieved Ian had been when he'd seen Leo hop on board the boat that morning. A large part of him had been sure Luke would keep him home or have him reassigned to work with someone else.

"He'll be happier at home," was all Ian said in response to that. Because he would be uncomfortable there, and it wasn't ideal, and he wasn't going to pretend otherwise.

Luke must have picked up on the subtext, because he rubbed at his neck in discomfort. "Right. So my shift starts at six," Luke said haltingly.

"I'll be there around five-thirty," Ian said. "Should I pick up something for dinner on my way?"

It was so domestic, except that Luke wouldn't be there for the meal and currently was doing his best to avoid eye contact.

"I have some frozen pizzas if you just want to do that."

Ian did not. "Tell Leo I'll bring Chinese."

Luke nodded. "Sure."

Ian had had enough of the awkward tension. He needed a drink, but it was barely noon and even he had standards. Or at least, he did now. A few months ago he'd have thought nothing of pounding one back at any hour of the morning, usually to help quell a hangover. Life had changed quite a bit, and Ian still wasn't sure he liked his newer, more mature self.

"I imagine Niall's run out of chores to keep him busy. I'll be by in plenty of time for you to get to work," Ian said. He gritted his teeth and forced the next bit out because it was important Luke know how much he appreciated being the one he went to for help. Ian knew Luke's neighbor had watched Leo in a pinch, so him coming to Ian was a big deal. It wasn't as if there were no other options. He was choosing to allow Ian to be involved. "Thank you. For asking me. I know we…." He let the words die off because he didn't really know what they were. "Just, thank you."

Luke was fidgeting uncomfortably again, but Ian was just as discomfited, so he couldn't bring himself to feel bad for him. "Ian, whatever happens between us, you're in Leo's life. I made the decision to bring you into it. Once you're in, you're in. I'm not going to try to keep you from seeing him just because we're fighting."

Ian's shoulders drooped a bit as some of the tension that had been holding him ramrod straight seeped away. This wasn't going to be a one-time offer. That was excellent news, as was the fact that apparently Luke hadn't written their relationship off entirely.

"I really do appreciate that. And for what it's worth, I'm sorry and I miss you," he said quietly. He knew Luke would understand how much it took for him to admit that. Neither one of them was particularly demonstrative, but Ian wanted him to know he was hurting. He missed both of them and was thrilled he wasn't being shut out of Leo's life, but he didn't want to be shut out of Luke's, either.

"I know you are." Luke's tone was soft with a bit of steel to it. He clearly hadn't forgiven Ian for going behind his back and intervening with Lane. It had been a huge fuck-up, and Ian knew it would take time to win Luke's trust back. He hadn't lost all ground if Luke was letting him babysit Leo, though, and that was a major win.

Ian hadn't expected Luke to accept his apology, but the obvious brush-off still stung. "I'll see you later. Go get Leo," he said, nodding toward the catamaran.

"Ian," Luke called when he'd gotten a few feet away. Ian stopped and turned. "We'll talk. Give me a little bit of time, okay? But we'll talk. I want to talk."

Ian felt like a load of bricks had been lifted off his chest. The earlier relief he'd felt was nothing compared to this. "Okay." His lips curved up into one of the first genuine smiles he'd managed since he'd stormed out of Luke's apartment.

IAN THUMBED through a book on Luke's end table restlessly, wishing he'd brought his laptop. He hadn't been thinking about what he'd do after Leo went to bed. Usually when he was at Luke's, the two of them had no problem filling the time after Leo trudged down the hall and reluctantly climbed under his covers.

Tonight Ian had been the one dragging his feet over bedtime. Leo's evening routine was pretty simple, and Ian had no trouble prompting him through changing into pajamas and brushing his teeth. He hadn't argued with Leo when Leo had insisted on three books before bed, nor had he scoffed at the two trips to get a drink in the kitchen.

Leo had been quiet for the past hour, though, so Ian figured he'd finally drifted off to sleep. And now that left Ian with nothing to occupy him for—he checked his watch—another five hours or so.

He'd never gotten into the habit of watching television—at first because he'd been too busy with work and then later because there hadn't been a lot of offerings on the air in Tortola. Luke had a huge collection of movies, but Ian didn't particularly want to delve into them. Too many reminders about movie nights and snuggling on the couch.

There were books piled on just about every flat surface in the apartment, but he and Luke definitely didn't have the same tastes. The book he'd been paging through a minute ago was one he'd read in college—Hemingway's *A Moveable Feast*—but it wasn't something he'd classify as fun to read. Most of the things Luke read fell into that category. There weren't many contemporary thrillers or airport paperbacks on Luke's shelves. Ian's mother would have had a field day with the collection.

Ian had settled in with a game of Tetris on his phone when he heard Leo groan. Ian tossed his phone aside and hopped up, careful to avoid the squeaky floorboards as he made his way to Leo's bedroom, just in case he wasn't already awake.

Ian peeked around the half-open door, expecting to see Leo sitting up. Instead, he saw he was curled into a tight little ball, shivering. His covers had been kicked aside and were puddled on the floor beside the bed, next to the flashlight Luke used to "banish" monsters from the closet. Ian was a little disappointed there hadn't been any for him to vanquish tonight. It was quite the production, and it would have eaten up at least twenty minutes.

He blinked as his eyes adjusted to the dimness of the room. Leo's night-light provided just enough illumination for Ian to avoid the scattering of toys and books all over the floor. They'd played Legos for a good hour before bed, and Ian hadn't had the heart to make Leo clean up the way Luke always did. He greatly regretted that the moment his socked foot came down on a particularly sharp block. Ian bit his tongue to hold back a curse as he limped over to the bed.

Leo felt hot to the touch when Ian tucked the blanket up around his neck, but he was definitely shivering. He was also mumbling quietly and didn't look like he was sleeping peacefully at all. Ian brushed his hand across Leo's temple. Definitely warmer than he should be.

Leo shifted at the touch and burrowed into the blanket but didn't wake. Ian backed his way out carefully and stepped into the hallway. He could call Luke, but he didn't want to worry him. Luke would probably call to check on Leo when he got a break, and Ian could tell him about the fever then. It didn't seem to be bothering Leo too much. He'd been perfectly fine when he'd gone to bed.

Ian sat on the arm of the couch, debating what to do. He didn't know anything about fevers. Hell, he didn't even know where Luke kept a thermometer. He was officially the worst babysitter ever. Ian rubbed a hand down his face and sank down onto the couch cushion. He could call Niall, but Niall probably wouldn't know what to do, either.

Inspiration struck when Ian's gaze roved around the room and settled on the overstuffed bookshelf. He'd call his mom. It wasn't until he'd dialed that Ian remembered the time difference. It was after midnight in Boston. Before he could hang up, his mother answered.

"Ian?"

He blew out a breath, relieved and guilty all at once to hear her voice. "*Mãe*. Sorry to call so late. I guess I'm still not adjusted to the time change. I always think about us being in the same time zone instead of me being three hours behind you."

Her laugh sounded throaty from sleep. "I'm guessing you needed something? You usually call on Sundays."

He hadn't been calling lately, since he spent Sundays with Leo and Luke. He hadn't even told her about the breakup.

"I'm with Leo, and I think he's sick. Luke's at work and I don't know what to do," he said in a rush. He felt like a teenager again, going to her for help solving his problems.

"What kind of sick?"

"A fever. He's asleep but he's hot. He's also shivering and he keeps moving around and kind of groaning."

She was quiet for a moment, and Ian could picture the furrow between her brows as she processed the information. His mother was never one to speak or act before thinking. He'd gotten his impulsivity from his father. In fact, Alban Mackay was just about the only impulsive thing his mother had ever done, and look where that had gotten her. Shackled with a thirty-six-year-old son who woke her in the middle of the night because he didn't know what to do with a sick kid.

"If he's sleeping, leave him be. He'll wake up if he's truly uncomfortable. If he gets up, take his temperature and get him to tell you if anything hurts. He's probably fine."

It wasn't anything Ian hadn't thought of himself, but hearing it from his mother made him feel better. "Okay."

"Just keep an eye on him. If he gets any worse, you should call Luke. Is he at work?"

"Yeah. I don't want to bother him if it's nothing."

"And because you want him to think you can handle things on your own to prove yourself? He won't mind if you call him about Leo, even if he's still angry at you for sticking your nose where it didn't belong. And it didn't, by the way. You had no right to interfere with that."

No one ever said his mother wasn't sharp. He didn't even ask how she knew about that; Niall had probably called her. He was infuriatingly protective like that, and he knew Ian wouldn't tell her himself. Hell, Ian hadn't been the one to tell her he was dating Luke in the first place. Niall had called her up and chatted about it shortly after Ian had texted Niall a photo of Luke's ass, long before Ian found out Niall and Luke knew each other. Niall was a gossipy mother hen, but he was also a loyal friend who cared enough to make sure Ian had the support he needed, even if he had to go behind his back to get it for him.

"I know."

She clucked her tongue. "*Querido*, I wanted to believe it when Niall told me, but I just couldn't wrap my head around it. You're really in love with Luke and his little boy, aren't you?"

Ian's lips curved up into a small smile. "Stupidly, *mãe*."

"Hopefully not so stupid you can't figure out how to fix things," she chided.

"I think he just needs some time. He's letting me see Leo, so that's a good sign," Ian said. He heard the boy in question shifting around restlessly again, and he made his way down the hallway to look in on him. Leo was awake and curled into an even tighter ball than he had been before. His hands were pressed over his ears.

"Leo's up," Ian said to his mother. "I think he might have a headache or something."

"Find a thermometer and take his temperature. Call me back if you don't know what to do," she said.

"I will. Thanks, *mãe*."

"Take care of your *menininho*. I'll talk to you tomorrow?"

"Sure," Ian said. He'd never used the endearment with Leo before, but he liked it. It's what his mother had called him when he'd been his age. Leo was watching him, and Ian could see tears in his eyes. "I have to go. *Te amo.*"

He hung up before she could respond, tucked his phone into his pocket, and crossed the room in three steps, heedless of the killer Legos. "Does something hurt, Leo?"

Leo nodded and reached for Ian. Ian sat down on the bed and wrapped him in a hug, pulling him close so he could rest his cheek against Leo's. He couldn't be sure, but he thought Leo felt even hotter than he had earlier.

"Do you know where Luke keeps the thermometer? I need to take your temperature."

"It hurts," Leo whined. He burrowed his face against Ian's collarbone.

"What hurts, bud?"

"My head," he whined.

Did headaches cause fevers? Ian was woefully undereducated in childhood illnesses. "What does Luke do when your head hurts?"

"He gives me the pink stuff and puts cotton in my ears. I don't like the drops. They're cold." Leo started crying in earnest, and Ian felt helpless.

"Hold on, bud. I'm going to call Luke, okay?"

It was hard to maneuver with Leo crying against his chest, but Ian dug out his phone and dialed Luke's number. It rang and rang before it went to voice mail. Ian's jaw clenched. Luke always kept it on him when he was working, just in case Leo needed him. He had to keep it silenced when he was on shift, though, and the bar might be too busy for him to notice it vibrating. Damn it.

"Hey, Luke. Leo's got a fever, and he's saying his head hurts. I'm going to call around and see if anyone knows what to do, because I have no idea what he needs. Call me, okay?"

He hung up and dialed Niall. It went straight to voice mail. Shit.

Leo was crying even harder now, and Ian rubbed his back as he wracked his brain, trying to figure out who else to call. His mom might be able to offer advice, but she wouldn't be any practical help. He had no idea where Luke kept the thermometer or whether or not it was okay to give Leo whatever pink medicine he said Luke had him take.

A moment later Leo surged up, eyes wide with panic. "Mack, I don't feel good."

"I know, bud. Luke's not answering right now, but he'll get back to us soon." If Luke didn't call in the next five minutes, Ian would call the bar and have the hostess get him.

"No, I mean—" Leo didn't get a chance to finish before he threw up all over Ian and himself.

Ian had no idea what to do. He was so far out of his depth he couldn't even speculate on what the next move should be. This was far from the first time someone had vomited on him, given the wild parties Ian used to attend, so he kept holding Leo through it, stroking his back until Leo finished and started crying again.

"Shh, it's okay," he soothed. He shifted Leo to the bed so he could stand up. "I'm going to get us to the bathroom so we can clean up, and then I'm going to put you on the couch with some Sprite while I change your sheets, all right?"

Leo's sobbing lost a bit of its desperation, and he hiccupped. "You're not mad?"

"I'm not mad, bud. Let's get cleaned up, okay?"

Leo sniffled. "Mom doesn't like it when I throw up. Luke says it's okay, though."

Ian stiffened, and he had to tamp down on the urge to say something unflattering about Lane. "I don't like that you're sick, but it's okay that you threw up, Leo. It's what happens when we get sick. I'm not mad at you."

Leo melted against him. "You're sure? I'm sorry," he said in a small voice.

"I'm sure. Do you feel any better?" He stood and debated how best to get Leo to the bathroom without making an even bigger mess. In the end, he decided to pick him up. Leo went without protest and wrapped himself around Ian as Ian carried him down the hall.

"My head doesn't hurt as much."

"Good," Ian said. He was still worried. Throwing up didn't seem to be something a kid should do when he had a headache. But Leo's face didn't look as pinched with pain as it had before, and he was relieved by that.

It took Ian about ten minutes to get Leo calmed down, dressed in clean pajamas, and settled on the couch with a blanket and a drink. He'd taken off his shirt to toss into the washer with the sheets he stripped off Leo's bed. As worried as he was about Leo, it felt nice to do something so domestic in Luke's apartment. Ian only had to fumble around for a minute before he found clean sheets. He tried Luke on speaker while he was making the bed, but it went to voice mail again. Ian knew business hit a peak around eleven, so Luke might not have a chance to check his phone for a while. The bar phone rang and rang without end. Frustrated, he hung up and tried Niall again.

"I don't think I should come over, babe. Babysitters aren't supposed to have boys over after ten."

Ian sagged in relief. "Leo's sick," he said without preamble. Niall had been snickering at his own greeting but stopped abruptly.

"Did you get in touch with Luke?"

"He's not answering and the bar's line isn't getting picked up." Ian plumped up Leo's pillows and crossed to the door, clearing a path through the toys with a sweep of his foot as he walked so Leo wouldn't stumble on his way back to bed.

Niall was quiet for a moment. "Sick like you need to take him to see someone or sick like he needs some Tylenol?"

"I don't know, Niall!" Ian snapped. "If I knew that, I wouldn't be calling you." He sighed and ran a hand through his hair as he opened the door to Luke's room. He didn't think Luke would mind if he borrowed a fresh shirt, and frankly, he didn't care if Luke *did* mind. "Sorry," he said, instantly contrite. He was frustrated and a little scared, and he knew he was unfairly taking it out on Niall. He pulled a shirt at random out of the dresser. "I don't even know where the Tylenol is, let alone how much to give him."

"Ask Warner," Niall said.

"Frank's husband? Hold on." He dropped the phone and put on the shirt, noting the way it smelled of the organic lavender fabric softener that was one of Luke's few splurges. "Back."

"Yeah, he's a pediatrician. He can at least tell you if Leo needs to be seen by someone tonight or what to do at home."

"You're brilliant, and I love you."

Niall laughed. "I'll text Clare. She can call him and have him call you, okay?"

"Thanks, Niall."

"No problem. Let me know if you need me to come over," he answered.

"I thought I couldn't have a boy over after ten?"

"Exceptions can be made," Niall said, and Ian could hear the smile in his voice.

"Hopefully, we'll be fine. I'll let you know what Warner says."

He slipped the phone into his front pocket after Niall hung up and padded back into the living room to check on Leo. He hadn't moved from the couch, except to slump against the pillows. He was completely out, his hands curled around the cup of Sprite Ian had given him. It was tipping precariously, and Ian gingerly took it and put it on the table. In the light, Ian could tell his cheeks were flushed from the fever. He still felt hot, but he was more relaxed than he had been earlier. Hopefully that meant the headache wasn't back in full force.

Ian jumped when his phone rang. The sound was shrill in the quiet apartment, and he struggled to answer it before it woke Leo. The boy didn't even bat an eye at the noise, though.

"This is Ian," he said.

"Ian? It's Warner. Clare said you've got a sick boy on your hands."

Ian had only spoken to Warner a few times, but he recognized his voice. He sounded more authoritative than he had when Ian had talked to him before, like he'd slipped into his doctor voice. It was oddly reassuring.

"I'm babysitting for Luke's nephew, Leo. He was complaining of a headache, and he threw up. He's got a fever, but he's back to sleep now."

Warner made a noncommittal sound. "How old is Leo?"

"Six."

"Was he complaining of a headache before he went to bed?"

"No, he seemed fine a few hours ago. This seemed to come on suddenly. He did say he felt better after he vomited, but he's still hot."

"Are you able to take his temperature?"

"I don't know where Luke keeps the first aid stuff, but I'll look. Do you think he's okay?"

"When he said his head hurt, was he able to explain how it hurt?"

"I didn't ask. He had his hands up against his ears when I went in," Ian said. He rifled through the medicine cabinet and found a thermometer and a few bottles of kids' medicine.

"That could be an ear infection. Is he sleeping now?"

"Yeah, he's out."

Ian took the thermometer and every bottle that was marked children's back to the living room and put them on the table. "How do I take his temperature?"

"He's six?" Warner asked.

"Yeah."

"If he's still asleep, you can put the thermometer in his armpit and get a fairly accurate reading without waking him up. If he was awake, I'd say take it orally."

It was awkward, but Ian managed to get the thermometer up under Leo's pajama shirt and tucked into the crease of his armpit without waking him. When the thermometer beeped, it said 101.9.

"Is that high?" he asked Warner when he relayed it to him.

"Not terribly for a kid that age. Trust me, he doesn't feel nearly as bad as you would with that temperature. Has he complained of any neck pain? Is he having difficulty swallowing?"

"Not that I know of," Ian answered. God, he felt useless.

"That's good. You're doing fine, Ian," Warner said. He must have been able to hear the frustration in his voice, Ian figured. That, or he was used to dealing with parents in the middle of the night. And clueless babysitters. "Luke will probably want to take Leo in to see his pediatrician in the morning if he's still complaining of the headache, but I think it's probably an ear infection."

"Those can make a kid puke?" Ian asked incredulously.

"It's not a super common symptom, but yes. Did you see any children's Motrin or Tylenol when you found the thermometer?"

Ian scanned the bottles on the coffee table. "I have both."

"Okay, good. Start him out with a dose of the Motrin. Is it a liquid?"

"Yeah."

"All right. There should be a dosing chart on the bottle. I don't suppose you know how much Leo weighs?"

Ian had absolutely no idea. He couldn't even guess. He made a helpless noise, and Warner laughed.

"I didn't think so. Ask him when you wake him to take the medicine; he may know. Kids that age are pretty observant, so he'll probably at least know what he weighed at his last check-up. Find the dose that's listed for his weight and give him that much of the Motrin. If he's really uncomfortable in three hours you can give him a dose of the Tylenol."

God, he hoped Luke was home in three hours.

"What should I do if he throws up again?"

"He may do that a few more times. By itself it's not something to worry about. Just make sure he has a bucket or something nearby and keep giving him water. If his fever rises above 103, or he gets a stiff neck or has trouble swallowing, you need to take him to the ER. Otherwise, he can see his doctor in the morning if he's still sick. Okay?"

Ian blew out a breath. He should probably be writing this down. How did Luke keep track of things like this and make it look so easy? Ian had been alone with Luke for less than four hours and all hell had broken loose.

"Yes," he said when it became apparent that Warner was waiting for an answer.

"Ian, he's going to be fine. Kids get sick fast, and they get better just as quickly. You didn't do anything wrong, and you couldn't have seen this coming." Warner's voice was calm and gentle, and even though Ian was still tense, he responded to the soothing tone. He wondered if it was something they taught in medical school, or if Warner was naturally good at it. "Do you want me to text you the instructions?"

Oh God, did he. "Fuck, yes," Ian said in a rush.

Warner chuckled. "It's overwhelming. Go ahead and give Leo the Motrin and get him back to bed. I'll text you with everything we just talked about so you can forward it on to Luke if you like. And if anything changes, or you have more questions, you can call me at this number. It's my cell, and I'm on call tonight so I'll be keeping an ear out for phone calls anyway."

"I really appreciate it." Ian would have to send him a bottle of Scotch or something. God, what did people who didn't know pediatricians do when their kids got sick in the middle of the night? Ian probably would have bundled Leo off to the hospital if he hadn't had Warner to talk him down.

"It's all part of the job," Warner said. "I'll check in with you tomorrow morning."

"Thank you."

Ian waited until Warner texted over the instructions before waking Leo. Just as Warner had predicted, Leo proudly recited his weight as of his last checkup, which had been almost a year ago, but Ian figured it was close enough. He measured out the orange liquid carefully and gave it to Leo before shuffling him back to bed. He'd barely gotten him to sleep before his phone rang. He sagged in relief to see Luke's name flash across his screen.

"Hey. Is he doing okay?" Luke sounded worried but not panicked, which put him several levels below where Ian had been before he'd talked to Warner. It made Ian even more embarrassed about his freak-out over the fever.

"I think he might have an ear infection," Ian told him, relaying what had happened. He brushed aside Luke's apologies when he got to the part about Leo puking. "It's fine. He's all cleaned up and back in bed, and I gave him a dose of Motrin because that's what the pediatrician said to do."

"Shit, I didn't think to leave his pediatrician's number. I'm not used to anyone other than my mom watching him overnight, and she already has all that. Who did you call?"

"It's a complicated chain, but Niall's friend Clare's brother's husband is a pediatrician, so I talked to him. He gave me a bunch of instructions. I'll text them to you. But he seemed to think it was his ears and he'd be okay."

"He's had ear infections before, and they usually start out like this. I'm sorry that got dumped on you. Do you need me to come home? It's slowing down, so I can probably duck out."

Ian heard the noise of the customers in the background, so he very much doubted that it was slow. Luke was due home in a few hours anyway, and he hated to ask him to cut his shift short, especially now that Leo was back to sleep and things seemed to be handled.

"Nah, I've got it. I'll call you if he gets any worse, but Warner said he'll probably be okay 'til morning."

"Listen to you. You sound like a pro," Luke teased. Ian was sure Luke wished he was the one home with Leo; hell, *Ian* wished Luke was the one home with Leo.

"I sound marginally better than I did when I completely lost my shit and called everyone I could think of," Ian joked weakly. It wasn't far from the truth. He'd probably be living down that panicked call to his mother for a very long time.

"I'm sorry I didn't see that you'd called. I accidentally put it on silent instead of vibrate," Luke said apologetically.

"You're at work. I was talking about waking my mom up when I called her to ask her what to do," he admitted.

Luke laughed. "You called your mom?"

"What else was I supposed to do? I don't know anyone else with kids," Ian said defensively.

Luke's laugh trailed off. "No, you did great. I'm sorry you had to wake up your mom."

"I think she got a kick out of it," Ian admitted. "I don't think it's a call she ever expected to get from me. She was thrilled."

Luke was quiet, and Ian wondered if he'd pushed a little too far before Luke finally spoke again. "I'm off break in a minute. You're good 'til I get off? Otherwise I'll come home. Really, Ian."

"I'm good. I'll call you if he wakes up, but I think he's down for the count."

"It's not just Leo I'm worried about. Are *you* okay?"

Ian's heart sped up at the concern in Luke's voice. "I wasn't, but I am after talking to Warner. I just didn't want to break your kid."

The attempt at humor fell a bit flat because Ian's voice shook a bit as he said it, but Luke laughed anyway. "I'm sure you didn't break him. They're pretty resilient."

"Get back to work. I'll see you in a bit."

Ian blew out a breath as he hung up. He felt wrung out now that the adrenaline that had fueled his panic had worn off. It was barely midnight, and all Ian wanted to do was sleep.

The couch was hardly an ideal place for a nap, but he didn't think Luke would appreciate finding Ian in his bed when he got home. Though Ian did hope he'd be able to apologize his way back into it sometime soon. He just wanted it to be by express invitation.

Besides, he wasn't sure if he'd be able to sleep. Even with Warner's assurances ringing in his ears, Ian was still worried Leo might have more than an ear infection. What if he fell asleep and then couldn't hear him if he got sicker?

He rolled his shoulders and pushed up off the couch to wander into the kitchen. He'd make a pot of coffee and find something to watch on television that would keep him awake, he decided.

A quick look through the cabinets confirmed that Luke hadn't thrown out Ian's coffee, which Ian took as a good sign. If Luke was planning to break things off with him completely, surely he'd have tossed everything of Ian's, wouldn't he?

Ian put the kettle on to boil and busied himself setting up the French press. Luke had jokingly complained that it probably cost more than the rest of his kitchenware combined, and Ian had privately agreed. He didn't pretend he wasn't a coffee snob, and Ian hadn't seen a reason he should have to settle for a subpar coffee maker because the rest of Luke's kitchen looked like it had been salvaged from a thrift store.

He'd slowly been replacing things with higher quality appliances over the last few weeks, and even though Ian was sure Luke had noticed, Luke hadn't said anything about it. The toaster that sparked when the toast popped had been the first to go, followed by the ancient stove-top kettle that was so warped it took eons to boil that Ian had surreptitiously replaced with an electric model.

When the kettle whistled, he pulled it off the base quickly to keep it from waking Leo. The kid usually slept deeply, but Ian wasn't sure if being sick might change that. He didn't want to take any chances. Ian listened for a moment but couldn't hear any stirrings from Leo's room, so he poured the steaming water into the shiny, stainless steel Williams-Sonoma press he'd taken such a ribbing over. He didn't care what Luke said; coffee from it tasted better than from a cheaper French press.

The sound of a key in the lock had him turning in alarm, but a moment later Luke walked in and offered Ian a sheepish grin. "It's not that

I didn't trust you'd be able to handle it, but you sounded so worried, I figured I'd better come home to make sure you were both okay."

Ian bit his lip to hold back a smile as he finished making his coffee. Luke sounded as concerned about him as he had about Leo, which was sweet. "I haven't checked on his fever since he went back to sleep, but he's been a lot less restless."

Luke disappeared down the hall, and Ian put more water in the kettle and set out Luke's favorite mug. He poured himself a cup of coffee and leaned against the counter. He wasn't sure if they were going to have their talk tonight or not, but he wasn't going to leave until he had an idea of where things stood between them.

"You're wearing my shirt," Luke said with a quizzical tilt to his head when he came back. He smiled faintly when he noticed the mug and the kettle and took down a box of tea from the cabinet. Ian had left the part about being thrown up *on* out of his rehashing of Leo's evening when they'd talked on the phone, but things must have clicked in his mind, because when he faced Ian again, he looked horrified. "Oh God. I'm so sorry."

"It happens," Ian said with a wave of his hand. He took another sip of coffee to keep from smiling at Luke's obvious distress.

"I don't think Leo puked on me until he'd lived here for at least six months. You barely got two."

Leo had been almost four when he'd come to live with Luke permanently, but Ian knew Luke had kept him on and off from much younger than that. He doubted Luke had escaped Leo's baby years unscathed, but he didn't say anything. He knew Luke didn't like to talk about the time before Leo moved in with him. Neither did Leo.

"He must like me," Ian said with a negligent shrug that didn't belie how much he hoped that was true.

"He loves you," Luke said bluntly. The kettle whistled, and he kept his back to Ian as he poured the boiling water over the tea bag in his mug. "So do I."

Ian's breath caught. Both he and Luke had very carefully avoided those words after Luke had said them in the car. He didn't know if Luke's reticence on the subject was a response to Ian's reluctance to say them or if he had his own baggage, but whatever the reason, they hadn't been uttered again until now. Ian had assumed he'd panic when he heard them, like he had last time, but they sounded right falling from Luke's lips so easily.

"I do too." Ian's voice was rough, which would have been embarrassing if he hadn't been so overwhelmed. He was glad he was able to speak at all. He hadn't told anyone he loved them other than his mother—ever. He didn't even tell her all that often. He wanted to say the words to Luke, but he couldn't actually bring himself to choke them out. How many times had he heard his father say it to his mother as a way to manipulate her? The word love didn't have much meaning to Ian, but he was finally understanding the sentiment behind it. He did love Leo and Luke; he just couldn't say it.

"I know, Ian. And I know what you did with Lane was because you love Leo and you thought you were helping him, but I can't quite forgive you for it yet."

Luke turned around but kept to his side of the kitchen. If he'd even taken one step in Ian's direction, Ian would have been on him in a second. The distance was probably good, he reasoned. Otherwise Ian wouldn't be able to stop himself from wrapping his arms around him, and Luke very clearly didn't want that right now.

"I'm sorry. I shouldn't have gone behind your back like that. She's your sister and Leo's mom, and I don't have a right to be involved in your relationship with her."

Luke's jaw clenched. "It's not just that—"

They flinched when there was a loud thump from Leo's room, followed by a thin wail.

"He fell out of bed," Luke said as they moved down the hall.

Leo was tangled in his blankets in a heap on the floor, sobbing. Luke scooped him up and sat with him in his lap on the bed, stroking his hair. "You're okay. You just fell out of bed. You feeling better?"

Leo mustn't have truly been awake, because at the sound of his uncle's voice, his crying eased to hiccups and his eyes blinked open. "Luke?"

"I'm back. Ian says you aren't feeling so great, kiddo."

Ian had hung back in the doorway, but he came in a few steps when Leo looked up to find him. "He gave me the orange stuff," Leo said, his eyes still on Ian.

"Did it help?" Luke asked, nestling his chin against Leo's head as he tucked him in closer to his body.

"A little," Leo said, his voice small. "It still hurts."

"You're still hot. We'll go see Dr. Gary in the morning."

"He'll give me the drops."

"Probably," Luke said easily. "Better that than having your ears hurt, huh?"

Leo seemed to consider it before burrowing deeper into Luke's arms. His face was mostly obscured by Luke's uniform vest, but Ian saw his eyes close. He didn't answer, and a minute later Luke was easing Leo back into bed and tucking him in.

"He really hates the ear drops, but they're just about the only thing that makes his ear infections manageable," Luke said after he and Ian had eased their way out of Leo's room. "Dr. Gary said if he has many more this winter he'll probably need tubes."

Ian had no idea what that meant, but he was relieved Luke seemed unconcerned about Leo's tearfulness and continued fever.

"I'm going to try to get some sleep. He'll be up early because of his ears," Luke said. "Thanks for staying with him."

Ian wanted to continue their conversation, but Luke radiated exhaustion, and Ian was practically dead on his feet. It wouldn't do any good to push things tonight. They'd just end up fighting again.

"Can you text me in the morning so I know how he's doing?" Ian felt silly asking, since he had absolutely no right to it, nor did he have any idea what he'd do if Luke texted that Leo *wasn't* better. What could he do? Offer to go with them to the pediatrician? That would be ridiculous.

Luke didn't seem to find anything amiss with the request, though. "I will."

There was a pregnant pause where Luke held his gaze and Ian thought Luke might close the distance between them and kiss him, but the moment passed and Luke edged past him toward his bedroom. Ian allowed him past without comment and let himself out of the apartment, careful to lock the door behind him.

SEVENTEEN

PACKING UP his house in Tortola was easier than Ian anticipated. He made it through in record time, which was more a testament to how little he'd accumulated during his years on the island than to any great packing prowess. The only big thing he had at the house was his bed, and Ian had already purchased a new one for the loft, so he was leaving that.

Aside from a few boxes of books and his wardrobe, there wasn't much he needed to take with him. What few pots and pans and other household items he had were going over to Niall's bungalow, since he didn't have a huge collection of those things either. Niall was keeping his house on the island as well as the yacht moored at the marina, and Ian was already planning to make good use of both of them for future vacations.

He'd signed all the official paperwork to put his house on the market when he'd arrived in Tortola two days ago, and Keandra already had two interested buyers. He'd get a nice chunk of change out of it to invest or put toward buying the loft if he decided to stay in it when his lease ran out.

He'd even made arrangements to sell his car and *Romeo's Rowboat*, though he was sorry to see both go. He couldn't justify the expense of having them shipped back to the States, though. Besides, there was no reason for both him and Luke to have cars; Ian took the train to work and Luke liked driving, so whenever they went out they took Luke's.

Assuming he and Luke had a future, that was. Ian had hated leaving town before they'd fully reconciled, but he was almost positive they were getting back on track. The texts he'd gotten from Luke over the last few days had been significantly less frosty, at any rate.

Ian's cell phone lit up with Luke's picture just as Ian was leaving the dive shop. Seattle wasn't exactly a scuba hotbed, but he was sure having his wetsuit would come in handy at some point. There would be visits to Tortola, after all. Maybe he'd stash his dive gear at Niall's bungalow so he didn't have to haul it back and forth.

He rested the box against his hip as he answered the phone, nodding to Craig as he went by. After the incident with the tourist, and Ian disappearing for a few months only to return and quit, there was no love lost between them. Ian was mildly surprised Craig bothered to wave at him as he let himself out.

"Luke, hey," Ian said, cursing softly when he almost dropped the box trying to open the trunk of his car.

"What the hell, Ian? You're gone?" Luke sounded angrier than Ian had ever heard him, which was quite a feat, given how livid he'd been when Ian told him about Lane.

"Uh, I'm in Tortola, yes," Ian said slowly, unsure how to proceed. He had plenty of experience with angry lovers, but virtually none with angry lovers whom he actually wanted to continue things with. Ian had talked to Luke the day before he'd left to pack up the house in Tortola, and it hadn't gone badly. Luke had let him know Leo had seen his pediatrician and was on the mend. They hadn't had a deep philosophical conversation, but it had been civil, unlike this one. Ian had no idea what had changed in the five days in between.

"Unbelievable. If this is how you deal with conflict, I'm glad I found out before Leo and I got too invested with you."

Ian blinked, struggling to process Luke's words. "I don't understand."

That had obviously been the wrong thing to say, because Luke seemed to get even angrier. "You left, Ian," he shouted.

"I wasn't going to change my ticket just because we had a fight, Luke," he retorted, starting to get a bit angry. He'd been giving Luke the space Luke had asked for. It wasn't like Ian was hiding from him. He'd made it clear he was always just a phone call away.

"So you've been planning to go back all this time? And what, just stringing me along? Fuck you."

Before Ian could answer, Luke hung up. Ian stared at the phone a moment before slamming his trunk and dialing him back. Surprisingly, Luke picked up.

"I am back in Tortola to put my house on the market," he said in a rush, afraid Luke might have answered just to hang up on him again.

That took the wind out of Luke's sails, because when he spoke, his voice held none of the acidity from before. "What?"

"I told you about the trip a few weeks ago. As soon as it looked like I was going to make the move permanent, I started making arrangements to put my place on the island on the market. I'm packing things up and signing the paperwork to put it up for sale."

"You're coming back," Luke said faintly.

"Thursday." Ian couldn't help the smug smile that crept onto his face. Luke had been angry because he'd thought Ian had left Seattle. That was encouraging.

"Leo came back from Even Keel in tears this afternoon because you weren't there. Josh told him you were at your house in Tortola."

Ian winced, his amusement at the situation vanishing now that he knew Leo was upset. "I didn't think to warn him I'd be gone. I'm sorry. Shit. Is he okay? Do you want me to talk to him?"

Ian could hear Luke blow out a breath. "No, it's my fault. I overreacted and I think I scared him. God, Ian. I thought you'd left."

"I wouldn't, not without telling you. And I did tell you I'd be here for a few days, but it was a while ago. A few things have happened since then." Ian kept his tone joking and light, but he tensed up waiting for Luke's response. He'd told him about the trip the day before they'd had the huge blow-up about Lane.

"Now that you say that, it rings a bell." The phone picked up another deep breath from Luke. "Can I see you when you get back?"

Ian's grin returned in full force. "Definitely. It'll be late for Leo, though. My flight doesn't get in until nine."

"I don't care. You've got a ride?"

How had they gone from screaming to something this domestic in the span of ten minutes? Then again, maybe screaming *was* domestic. This was probably a cycle they'd be going through again, and Ian thought it was a bit perverse that he was looking forward to fighting with Luke again. It would mean they'd made up and moved on, which was looking more and more likely.

"Yeah, Clare."

"Is it—do you mind coming over after?" Luke sounded tentative, and Ian didn't like that at all.

"I don't mind at all."

"We can talk, and I need help getting stuff ready for Leo's party."

"Leo's having a party?" It was the first Ian had heard of it. Then again, he and Luke weren't exactly on speaking terms, so why would he have heard of it?

"His birthday's next week, and I told him he could have some kids over."

How had that escaped Ian's notice? He should know things like that, shouldn't he? He was so bad at this. "I didn't realize. What does he want? I can't believe I didn't—"

Luke laughed, cutting Ian off. "You didn't know because I haven't mentioned it. We're obviously nailing this communication thing."

Ian chuckled. "Quite."

"He wants you there. That's actually what he asked for. The party is his present from me, and he wants you to be there as his gift from you."

That made Ian's heart ache a bit, but in a good way. "I'll be there."

"It's not until next weekend, but I have a new batch that's ready to start bottling at the brewery, so I'll be putting in a lot of evening hours and I don't know when I'll have a chance to get everything done if I don't do it tomorrow." Luke was babbling, which was adorable.

"I'm at your service," Ian said teasingly, but it was true. He was so far gone over both Luke and Leo. He'd only known them for a few months at most, but there wasn't much he wouldn't do for them. It was both terrifying and exhilarating, and Ian couldn't wait to get back to Seattle so he and Luke could finally start to move forward again.

"LOOK, CAN we just get this done without arguing? It's important to Leo." Luke ran a hand through his hair, and Ian had to clench his fist to stop from reaching out to smooth the spikes down when he went back to his task.

It was hard to be near Luke and not able to casually touch him. Ian had never thought of himself as an overly tactile person before, but he was realizing he *was* with Luke. He'd had to stop himself from touching him at least six times in the forty minutes he'd been at Luke's apartment. It had been a long day of flights and airports, and now it was nearly eleven at night and he was in Luke's kitchen, still not sure where the two of them stood.

"I'm not arguing," Ian protested. "I'm just not sure what we're doing here."

It was true on multiple levels. Had Luke asked Ian over to help with Leo's birthday party because he'd forgiven him or simply because Leo had asked to have him involved? Were they still together? Luke had told him he wanted to talk, but Ian had no idea how to broach the conversation and apparently, Luke didn't either.

He also had no fucking clue what Pinterest was or why Luke was muttering about it as he lined up jars on the counter, but it sounded ominous. Especially as it appeared to involve glitter.

"We're making party favors for Leo's friends."

"I thought Leo's party was space-themed?" Ian squinted at the supplies spread all over the counter. Glitter, something in neon-colored tubes, jars—none of it screamed space to him.

"Galaxies in a jar," Luke said shortly. He turned the tablet around to show Ian what he was looking at. "Pinterest says it's easy."

"What the fuck is a Pinterest?"

"It's a website with craft ideas on it. One of the moms in Leo's class said she used it to plan the class parties. I'm told we have to have games and favors. I didn't even know kids this age *had* parties, so…."

Luke blew out a breath and turned to the project in front of him. Ian wanted to offer some sort of comfort because he could tell Luke was beating himself up about not having birthday parties for Leo before, but that was ridiculous. Anyone with eyes could see how much Luke loved Leo, and Leo was just as devoted to his uncle. He doubted that would be welcome, though, and it wasn't like Ian knew anything about kids or how to raise them. Maybe Luke *had* done Leo some sort of psychological trauma by not inviting a dozen screaming children into his home to beat on a piñata and eat cake. Doubtful, but possible. He'd have to ask Dr. Green.

What he could do was help Luke with the ridiculous Pinterest project, so he rolled up his sleeves and stepped up to the counter. "So, galaxies?"

Luke offered him a tired smile. "According to the instructions, all we have to do is empty glow sticks into the jars, add glitter and water, and they'll light up. I figured we could do it with the kids before we have cake, and then they could take them home with them in their goody bag. I wanted to try it out tonight to be sure, though."

"Sounds easy enough," Ian said. He unscrewed the top of a small clear jar that looked like it had probably held pickles in a former life.

Luke picked up one of the neon tubes and cracked it. It instantly lit up a pale green, and Ian realized they were glow sticks. He picked another one up and followed suit. This one was a faint blue even though it had looked clear. "How many?"

"Two should do it. We cut the tip off and pour the stuff in."

It was easier said than done. Ian had expected the faintly glowing liquid to be viscous, but it was actually more like a solid. A very clingy, stubborn solid. Despite their best efforts, it took six glow sticks and about ten minutes to get a small puddle of glowing substance into the jar.

"Now glitter," Luke said. He was still scowling at the mess on the countertops. Ian hoped whatever the hell it was that made glow sticks glow didn't stain.

He let Luke take the lead, pouring half a small canister of silver glitter into the pickle jar. "And water," Luke said, letting Ian pour from the jug. "Up to the top."

"So this is a galaxy?" Ian asked. It didn't look like much. The glow stick liquid was still at the bottom and the glitter was in clumps.

Luke screwed the lid on the jar and picked it up. "Now we shake it. The glitter's supposed to stay suspended in the water and the glow stick stuff lights it up."

He shook it, but nothing seemed to happen. The glitter swirled around and settled back down to the bottom.

"Well, that was anticlimactic," Ian drawled, unimpressed.

Luke frowned and shook it again with the same results. The glitter sank almost immediately, and the glow stick liquid seemed to have burnt itself out completely.

"Maybe in the dark?" Ian suggested hesitantly.

Luke shook the jar vigorously and then flipped off the light in the kitchen. Practically everything around them lit up—except the jar. Ian couldn't help himself; he started laughing hard.

"Goddamn it," Luke growled, but a moment later he seemed to realize the ridiculousness of the situation and joined in.

The glow sticks they'd opened and tried to empty into the jar had held more liquid than they'd realized, but most of it had ended up splashed across the cabinets, the countertop, the floor, and themselves than in the jar. It hadn't been visible when the lights were on, but now that the kitchen was plunged into darkness, the liquid lit up like Christmas. Or Luminol.

"It's just—it looks like a fucking crime scene in here," Ian gasped when he could finally take a breath. "Like an episode of *CSI* or something."

He turned to Luke, laughter catching in his throat when he noticed a smear of glowing green across Luke's cheekbone.

"You've got a bit here," he said quietly as he reached up to wipe at it. It wouldn't budge, and Ian's fingers came away glowing faintly.

Luke stared at him for a moment before leaning closer. "I hope this stuff's nontoxic," he murmured. "It's on your lips." Luke closed the distance between them and kissed him. Ian tensed at the unexpected contact, but when Luke deepened the kiss, he relaxed, letting the counter behind him support their combined weight as Luke sagged against him.

It had only been two weeks, but Ian had missed sharing this kind of intimacy with Luke. It wasn't especially intense—Leo was asleep down the hall, so Ian knew they wouldn't be having sex, no matter how much he wanted to—but the feeling of Luke's body pressed against his was comforting. Ian ran his hands down Luke's sides and over the curve of his ass, pulling him closer. It was such a relief to be able to touch him again.

After a minute, Luke broke the kiss and tucked his head in the crook of Ian's neck. His breath was warm against Ian's skin, but it made him shiver. He'd never shared this kind of closeness with someone before. Cuddling just for the sake of being close had been outside his realm of experience before Luke, and Ian found he'd missed that more than the sex.

"I'm still mad at you," Luke said softly, but his tone held fondness, so Ian wasn't worried.

"You probably should be. I fucked up." Ian kneaded the tight muscles in the small of Luke's back. Luke groaned softly and burrowed deeper into Ian's neck.

"Yeah."

Ian nudged the fabric of Luke's T-shirt up so he could massage his bare skin. He hesitated a moment but forged on, knowing he might not get another opportunity for the kind of frankness they seemed to be sharing. It helped that they weren't face-to-face. "I get it now, why you were so angry. And I'll be better about communication, I will. But I need you to know I'll do it again. Fuck up, that is. I'm not good at relationships. Or kids. I have no idea what I'm doing, and I'm scared of flying blind."

Luke was quiet for a few beats, long enough for Ian to worry he'd been too honest. He wanted Luke to know he was in over his head, though. There would be more screwups, more fights.

Just when he started to panic, Luke pressed a kiss against his neck and straightened. He remained in Ian's loose embrace, their bodies flush from shoulders to thighs.

"I will too, you know. You're not the only one who's in over his head. Not with the relationship thing or the kid thing. I'm not going to apologize for being angry at you for what you did with Lane, but I do owe you an apology for how I reacted. I shouldn't have shut you out."

Ian rested his forehead against Luke's and breathed him in. "You and Leo matter to me, Luke. So much that it's terrifying. I know I overstepped with Lane, but I saw how she was tearing both of you apart, and I wanted to do something to help." Luke tensed, but he didn't interrupt. "My father is an alcoholic. My mother left him when I was a teenager, and I've only seen him a few times since. It's not the same, but—"

Luke cut him off with a gentle, searching kiss. Ian leaned into it eagerly, soaking up all the affection and intimacy he could from the contact. He didn't talk about his father, and he liked to pretend he didn't think about him, but that was a lie. Everything Ian had done up until this point was colored by his childhood with an alcoholic father and parents trapped in an unhappy marriage, and he was only just realizing it. His avoidance of serious relationships, his unwillingness to let anyone get too close. Niall had been one of the first to break through that, and it seemed like he'd opened the floodgates. For the first time in his life, Ian had friends. Actual friends who cared about him. And now he had Luke and

Leo. It was overwhelming, but luckily Luke seemed to understand without him explaining it.

"I love you," Luke said when he finally pulled back.

Unlike the last two times, Ian was ready to say it back. "I love you, too."

He saw Luke's throat work as he swallowed hard, and Ian felt a surge of pride. He'd done that. He'd put that adorably wondrous smile on Luke's face.

The kitchen was still luminous, neon color lighting up almost everything but the tiny glass jars, which had stayed resolutely dark. It was ridiculous, but it set the perfect atmosphere.

"You're still glowing," Ian said, cupping Luke's cheek with his palm.

"So are you." Luke brushed a finger lightly across Ian's lips, and Ian shivered.

He was disappointed when Luke dropped his hand and stepped away, looking around the kitchen in despair. "I'll have to find a new craft for Leo's party. This one's a bust."

Ian laughed. "I think he'll survive without a craft."

Luke turned the lights on and started gathering the supplies from the failed attempt. "We should probably get this stuff off before it stains the cabinets."

"Can't see it in the light," Luke said with a shrug. "It's probably fine."

Ian wondered how long the glowing would last. Probably another hour or two. It was a shame it wasn't permanent. Then again, if it was, he'd have permanently glowing lips. "Well, we should definitely get it off ourselves at the very least."

"A shower might be in order," Luke said agreeably.

Ian blew out a breath. He hadn't been expecting Luke to fall into his arms and forgive everything, but Ian had hoped the road to forgiveness would have been a little less bumpy than this. Still, he'd fucked up. If Luke wanted to make him beg for weeks, he would.

That said, he was going to make sure he was in Luke's space as much as possible to help speed that along. "You want me to come by tomorrow?

You said you had other things that needed to be done before the party, and we're running out of time. It'll be Saturday before you know it."

Luke looked at him for a moment before flipping the lights off again. "No. Mom's probably going to take over soon anyway. I think we'll be good."

Ian's breath left him in a whoosh, his disappointment palpable. "Okay."

"I'll see you at the bar tomorrow night?" Luke sounded tentative and unsure, and the ache in Ian's chest eased even more.

"Of course."

EIGHTEEN

THE SOFA cushions jiggled as Luke threw himself down next to Ian, but Ian didn't move. "There's cake in your hair," Luke told him.

"You've had half the piñata stuck to your foot for two hours," Ian informed him without opening his eyes.

Luke must have checked, because a second later Ian heard paper ripping. "Son of a—you knew I was trailing this for two hours and didn't tell me?"

Ian cracked an eye open and looked at the blue streamers Luke was waving indignantly. "It was festive. You were like a comet. Very appropriate for the space theme."

The party had been a success. It had kept Leo and the thirteen tiny hellions who'd been in attendance happy. Luke's apartment looked like a bomb had gone off in it, if bombs were filled with candy wrappers, cake crumbs, and glitter.

"I told you we should have shelved the galaxy idea," Ian muttered as he brushed the sparkles out of one of Luke's eyebrows.

"They liked it," Luke said with a shrug. And they had. Luke had made the executive decision to shelve the idea of filling the jars with glow sticks, and instead they'd given the boys blue glitter and silver star confetti to mix with water and oil. They looked pretty when they were shaken and the glitter and stars rained down inside the jars—which had lasted for all of five minutes before the first boy unscrewed the cap and shook it. Within seconds Luke's entire living room had been wet and shiny.

Ian tried to wipe away the glitter that had transferred to the pads of his fingers, rubbing at it ineffectually until it spread. "Glitter. Someone called it the herpes of the craft world, and now I understand why," he muttered, giving up and wiping his hands on the sofa cushion.

Luke snorted with laughter and snuggled in beside him. Ian had come over early to help set up for the party, and he and Luke had had a good conversation. Luke was still a little angry, and Ian was still a little wary, but for most of the day, it had felt like old times. Ian's only hairy moment of the day—that wasn't child-inflicted, at least—had come when Ruthie cornered him to talk about Lane.

"She's my daughter, and I love her unconditionally," Ruthie had told him, "but she's too caught up in her own head to be any sort of mother to Leo. Thank you for what you did. You give Luke some time, and he'll see that, too."

That was the only time she mentioned Lane or his fight with Luke until she'd taken a sugared-up Leo home with her for the night. "I'm giving you a night to yourselves. Enjoy it," she'd said breezily as she'd whisked Leo off.

That had left Luke and Ian alone for cleanup duty, but Ian didn't mind. Especially when it became clear Luke was content to relax his usual anal-retentive neatness for the night and let the mess sit for a bit while they soaked up the silent, kid-free atmosphere.

"It was a good party. He loved it," Ian said.

"It was three hours of utter hell. But thank you for saying so." Luke twined their fingers together loosely.

"Hell for us, a good time for him. A fair trade, considering it was his birthday."

Luke laughed. "Thank God he only has one a year."

"I wouldn't survive more than one," Ian said with complete honesty.

"The apartment wouldn't survive more than one either," Luke said regretfully, and Ian took that as his cue to start cleaning. He struggled up off the couch and headed into the kitchen to grab trash bags.

"What are you doing?"

"Cleaning," Ian said, holding the empty bag aloft. There were paper plates and plastic cups littering every flat surface.

"We can clean it up tomorrow," Luke said, tugging the bag out of Ian's hand and letting it swirl to the ground.

"Can we really? Are you feeling all right?"

Luke smacked Ian's hand away when he held it against Luke's forehead. "Shut up. I can stand the mess for a few more hours. I'm busy."

Ian's throat went dry at the heated look in Luke's eyes. "Busy doing what?"

"You," Luke said, his lips twitching into a grin when Ian groaned at the bad pun.

"I'm rubbing off on you," Ian said disapprovingly.

"You could be, but I think I'd rather have sex."

Ian couldn't hold back a laugh at that. "I'm starting to see why Niall gets so exasperated when I do this to him."

Luke quirked a brow. "Rub off on him?"

"Watch your mouth, you're talking about a married man," Ian teased. "No, torture him with my bad puns."

"I like your puns," Luke said softly. He cupped Ian's cheek, running his thumb over Ian's cheekbone lightly. "I like everything about you, even your stubborn foolhardiness."

"I also have great hair," Ian said, preening. It drew a laugh out of Luke, just as he'd hoped it would.

"And such modesty."

The tender expression on Luke's face left Ian breathless. "I love you."

"I love you, too." Luke leaned in for an easy, lingering kiss. "Now let's go to bed so I can show you how much I missed you."

NINETEEN

Four months later

"YOU SURE? We can turn back. I'm fine with hiring movers," Ian said when Luke looked at his phone for the fourth time in as many minutes, checking for incoming texts.

That had been Ian's plan all along, after all. He certainly wasn't qualified to drive a truck around the block, let alone the seventeen hours from Los Angeles to Seattle. But Luke had been horrified at the thought that Ian would shell out thousands to move his things up from LA when the two of them could fly down and drive it back themselves for the cost of a few plane tickets, a U-Haul, and a night or two in a hotel.

The thought of spending three days alone with Luke was compelling, and Ian had let himself be talked into the endeavor pretty easily, especially when Luke told him he had a commercial driver's license because he'd worked as a UPS delivery driver before the brewery had grown and started to eat up more of his time. He said he didn't still have the uniform, but Ian didn't believe him. Luke had blushed a gorgeous cherry red when Ian had asked about it; that probably meant he had one tucked away somewhere, and Ian desperately wanted to do a little package delivery role-play.

Everything had been fine until Lane had returned to town two days earlier. She'd successfully completed the ninety-day residential rehab program Ian had gotten her into, and the next step was transitioning to a halfway house, where she'd continue therapy but start integrating into the community again. She'd come back for a long weekend and was staying with Luke's mom, as was Leo.

Luke was obviously distracted and worried about Leo, and to be honest, so was Ian. Lane had seemed bright-eyed and soft-spoken, a complete change from the brash, strung-out woman Ian had met a few months ago. She'd even brought a note from her psychologist clearing her to spend time with family, and Leo was specifically mentioned. They'd taken Leo over for dinner the night she'd arrived, and he'd been cold and distant at first. But as they worked through dinner, and Lane remained sober and attentive, Leo had thawed. By the end of the second day, he'd asked her to be the one to read to him before bed.

Ian knew Luke was cautiously optimistic, but he also knew Lane had flirted with recovery before. It was a dangerous road; if Leo got too invested and she relapsed again, it would be devastating for him. Which was why Ian was in favor of staying and letting someone else worry about moving his stuff up from LA.

"It's fine," Luke answered after a long moment, but even he didn't sound convinced.

"Honestly, I don't mind. Leo's more important than a couch I haven't seen in five years."

Luke flashed him the first real smile Ian had seen out of him since Lane showed up. "I know," he said. "But it's going to be fine. For this to work I have to trust her, and I'm taking a leap of faith. Besides, Mom is there, and she won't let anything happen to Leo. If Lane relapses, she'll throw her out."

The "it's happened before" was left unsaid, but Ian could read it in the tight clench of Luke's shoulders.

"You know you don't have to let her see him," Ian said quietly. No one had brought it up, but the fact that Leo's adoption papers had been finalized last week hung over all their interactions with Lane. Even though he hadn't voiced it, Ian could tell Luke was worried she'd challenge it now that she was sober. There wasn't much recourse for her since she'd signed off on the adoption, but Ian knew Luke would let custody revert to her if she asked for it. Keeping Leo from his mother wasn't something Luke would do, especially if she was serious about her recovery. It broke Ian's heart to see him so anxious.

"I'm not going to cut her off from him," Luke said, the words quiet but underlain with a bit of steel. "And she's been good with him since she came back. He's having a lot of fun getting to know her, and I won't do anything to jeopardize that."

The PA blared, announcing their flight to Los Angeles was boarding. Ian shuffled his ticket. "Are you sure you want to go?"

"Positive," Luke said as he stood up. "Leo is safe and happy, and I've been looking forward to this."

Ian grinned. "Me too."

"Besides, he's been texting me every five minutes, so I know he's fine. I can't believe you gave him a phone," Luke said with a censorious look. "He's six."

"He's a seven-year-old whose primary caregiver is going away for three days. He needed a way to get in touch with you," Ian said defensively.

"My mom has a phone."

"Look at it this way: now he's always reachable. Don't you worry about him when he's at Even Keel after school? What if lessons ended early and he needed a ride?"

Luke pulled Ian in and pressed a kiss against his lips. "I imagine he'd ask *you*, since you're the one who teaches his class and brings him home afterward."

"But if I wasn't there—"

"And where would you be, in this hypothetical situation?"

Ian huffed. "Fine. It was ridiculous, but it was a gift, and I can give him a gift if I want to."

Luke smiled. "Thanks for admitting it." They were in line to board, and Luke gave Ian another quick kiss. "And thanks for looking out for him, even if the way you go about it is wholly inappropriate for his age."

Ian rolled his eyes. "Niall bought one for his niece Camille for her birthday."

"Camille is almost eleven, and she walks home from school by herself three days a week," Luke said. Ian couldn't believe he knew that. Hell, *Ian* didn't know that. Luke shrugged. "Niall tried to make the same argument when I was ranting to him about you buying one for Leo."

Ian let the gate agent scan his ticket and paused, waiting for Luke to catch up as they walked down the jet bridge. "At least Niall talked me out of getting him a data package."

Luke huffed out a laugh. "Small favors."

Ian led Luke toward the plane. It felt like the last year had been full of small favors—little things that added up to a new life and new future for Ian. When he'd taken off for Miami looking to change things up, he'd never imagined he'd end up in Seattle with a boyfriend and a kid who meant the world to him. He'd set out looking for a good time and ended up finding a home instead.

Luke was still antsy when they settled in their seats, and Ian pulled out his phone. The next time Luke looked down at his screen, he started laughing.

Just call him, Ian had texted.

"Do it now before they make you turn it off," Ian said.

"I don't need to call him. I'm just being a worrywart." Luke turned his phone off and tucked it into his pocket. "I'm yours for the next three days."

"Shame we're starting them in such a public place." Ian waggled his eyebrows suggestively, and Luke laughed, just as he'd hoped he would.

"Plenty of privacy at the hotel," Luke said as he primly took Ian's hand, which had worked its way into his lap, and deposited it back on the armrest.

Ian pouted when Luke dug into the backpack at his feet and brought out the Kindle he and Leo had given Luke for his birthday. Luke loved it. If it was possible, he was reading *more* than he had before.

"So you're going to read and leave me bored out of my mind for the next two and a half hours?"

"Don't forget the cab ride to the hotel. I'd say you're looking at a good four hours at least," Luke said. He cocked an eyebrow when Ian groaned dramatically. "Maybe more if I get wrapped up in something good."

"I'll wrap you up in something good," Ian muttered, and Luke dropped his stern look and leaned over and kissed him soundly.

"There's more where that came from if you let me read," Luke said when he sat back in his seat. The woman next to him was studying her SkyMall magazine like it was the most interesting thing on the planet. It made Ian snicker.

"Yes, fine. Tease." Ian had anticipated Luke zoning out all flight long, so he'd brought his laptop to get some work done. Luke snorted when he saw it.

"So much for boredom, eh?"

"I've learned to bring backup when books are involved. You're insatiable."

The woman next to Luke choked, and Luke held up his Kindle and waved it at her. "Reading. An insatiable reader," he said before elbowing Ian in the ribs. He leaned in and whispered his next words. "You're an asshole."

"You've known that from the get-go," Ian said with a shrug.

"I WONDER what sex in the back of a U-Haul would be like," Ian said thoughtfully.

Luke rolled his eyes and sighed gustily. "Lonely. Give me the reservation. I'm going to get the truck."

"Spoilsport," Ian said as he handed the paperwork over. They'd listed Luke as the driver since Ian had no idea how to maneuver something as big as the truck.

Luke sauntered up to the counter, and Ian was positive he'd added an extra wiggle to his step to taunt him. A moment later Luke looked over his shoulder and winked, confirming Ian's suspicion.

Ian would be lying if he said he wasn't quietly freaking out at the thought of moving his things from LA to Seattle. The house in Tortola had sold two months ago, and he'd signed all the paperwork and taken out the obligatory mortgage to buy the loft around the same time, and the permanency of it all was catching up with him. He had a job he loved and he was happy with Luke, but so much had changed for him over the last few months. Ian still felt like this was all a particularly odd and involved dream sometimes, but getting his things from LA would definitely put paid to that fancy. He'd intended to store his things for a few months, a year tops. It had ended up being five, and now he was finally settling in somewhere he'd need things like a blender and real furniture. It was scary.

Luckily, he had Luke to help him through it. Luke, who was currently filling out forms and reading insurance and liability waivers. For all that

Luke liked to pretend he was in over his head being an adult as much as Ian was, he was definitely Ian's role model in all things grown up.

"Ready?" Luke asked, tossing the U-Haul keys from hand to hand, then bouncing them off his foot and catching them again like a Hacky Sack. Maybe he wasn't quite as mature as Ian's inner musings made him out to be. That was a good thing; what would he see in Ian otherwise?

"As I'll ever be," Ian said with a gusty sigh. In truth, he was looking forward to loading up the truck and getting on with the trip and the life he'd put on hold when he'd fled to Tortola for his four-year vacation.

Growing up didn't seem so daunting since he'd found a home.

BRU BAKER is a freelance journalist who writes for newspapers and magazines. She knew she was destined to be a writer by the tender age of 4, when she started publishing a weekly newspaper for her family. What they called nosiness she called a nose for news, and no one was surprised when she ended up with degrees in journalism and political science and started a career in journalism.

While reporting the news is her day job, fiction is Bru's true love. Most evenings you can find her curled up with a mug of tea, some fuzzy socks, and a book or her laptop. Whether it's creating her own characters or getting caught up in someone else's, there's no denying that Bru is happiest when she's engrossed in a book. She and her husband live in the Midwest with their two young children, whose antics make finding time to write difficult but never let life get boring.

Visit Bru online at http://www.bru-baker.com or follow her on Twitter at http://www.twitter.com/bru_baker. You can also email her at bru@bru-baker.com.

Dropping Anchor Series from BRU BAKER

ISLAND HOUSE

BRU BAKER

http://www.dreamspinnerpress.com

Also from BRU BAKER

Read more from BRU BAKER in

Dr. Feelgood

A Dreamspinner Press Anthology

http://www.dreamspinnerpress.com

CPSIA information can be obtained at www.ICGtesting.com
Printed in the USA
LVOW04s2023300915

456406LV00014B/110/P